Nora Roberts published her first novel using the pseudonym **J.D. Robb** in 1995, introducing readers to the tough as nails but emotionally damaged homicide cop **Eve Dallas** and billionaire Irish rogue, **Roarke**.

With the **In Death** series, Robb has become one of the biggest thriller writers on earth, with each new novel reaching number one on bestseller charts the world over.

For more information, visit **www.jd-robb.co.uk**

Become a fan on Facebook at **Nora Roberts and J.D. Robb**

The world can't get enough of J.D. Robb

'Anchored by **terrific characters, sudden twists** that spin the whole narrative on a dime, and a **thrills-to-chills ratio** that will raise the neck hairs of even the most jaded reader, the J.D. Robb books are the epitome of **great popular fiction**'
Dennis Lehane

'Truly fine entertainment . . . sure to leave you **hungering for more**'
Publishers Weekly

'**Wonderful** . . . if ever there was a book for all tastes, this is the one'
Affaire de Coeur

'Whether you're a faithful follower or new to the series, you won't be disappointed in the **edge-of-the-seat suspense**'
Amazon.com

'Well written and **keeps you guessing** to the end'
Sun

'I hope Ms Roberts continues to write new stories for this pair for a long time to come . . . **Long live Eve and Roarke!**'
Bella

'This is a series that gets **better and better** as it continues'
Shots Magazine

'Gut-searing **emotional drama**'
David Baldacci

'A **perfect balance** of suspense, futuristic police procedure and steamy romance'
Publishers Weekly

'**Much loved**'
Daily Express

'Definitely **ticks all the boxes** from beginning to end'
Bradford Telegraph & Argus

'Another **absolutely belting page turner** . . . you won't be able to put it down'
Yorkshire Post

'This is **sheer entertainment,** a souped-up version of Agatha Christie for the new millennium'
Guardian

'J.D. Robb's novels are **can't miss pleasures**'
Harlan Coben

'I can't wait to get out and **buy another**'
Coventry Telegraph

'Another **great read,** another bestseller'
Huddersfield Daily Examiner

'**Compelling** characters with a **dramatic** sci-fi twist'
Cambridgeshire Journal

'A **fast-paced, superbly crafted story** that is an amazing – and possibly unique – combination of top-notch suspense, detection, and intensely romantic sensuality'
Library Journal

'Robb serves . . . **classic whodunit** and noir'
Publishers Weekly

'**Great fun**'
Cosmopolitan

'A **consistently entertaining** writer'
USA Today

'Whether she writes as J.D. Robb or under her own name, I love Nora Roberts. She is a woman who **just doesn't know how to tell a bad story** . . . an authentic page turner, with Eve Dallas – tough as nails and still sexy as hell . . . If you haven't read Robb, **this is a great place to start**'
Stephen King

Have you read them all?

Go back to the beginning with the first three In Death novels

For a full list of J.D. Robb titles, turn to the back of this book

Book One
NAKED IN DEATH

Introducing Lieutenant Eve Dallas and billionaire Roarke. When a senator's granddaughter is found shot to death in her own bed, all the evidence points to Roarke – but Eve senses a set-up.

Book Two
GLORY IN DEATH

High-profile women are being murdered by a knife-wielding attacker. Roarke has a connection to all the victims, but Eve needs his help if she's going to track down the real killer.

Book Three
IMMORTAL IN DEATH

With a new 'immortality' drug about to hit the market, Eve and Roarke must track down a vicious and evil drug dealer and killer – before it's too late.

J. D. ROBB

INNOCENT IN DEATH

piatkus

PIATKUS

First published in the United States in 2007 by G.P. Putnam's Sons,
a member of Penguin Group (USA) Inc.
First published in Great Britain in 2007 by Piatkus Books
Paperback published in 2008 by Piatkus Books
Reprinted 2008, 2010, 2011
This reissue published by Piatkus in 2012

3 5 7 9 10 8 6 4

A CIP catalogue record for this book
is available from the British Library.

ISBN 978-0-7499-5748-3

Typeset in Bembo by Palimpsest Book Production Ltd,
Falkirk, Stirlingshire
Printed and bound by CPI Group (UK) Ltd, Croydon, CR0 4YY

Papers used by Piatkus are from well-managed forests
and other responsible sources.

MIX
Paper from
responsible sources
FSC® C104740

Piatkus
An imprint of
Little, Brown Book Group
Carmelite House
50 Victoria Embankment
London EC4Y 0DZ

An Hachette UK Company
www.hachette.co.uk

www.piatkus.co.uk

Eve Dallas – Personnel File

Name: Eve Dallas

Nationality: American

Rank: Homicide Lieutenant, New York Police and Security Department

Born: 2028

Height: 5 foot 9 inches

Weight: 120 lbs

Eyes: Golden brown

Hair: Light brown

ID number: 5347BQ

Service:
Began police officer training at the Academy in 2046, aged 18.

Family:
Between the ages of eight and ten, Eve lived in a communal home while her parents were searched for. Eve was found with no ID, no memory, and was traumatised having been a victim of sexual assault.

Why Eve is a cop:
'It's what I am. It's not just that someone has to look, even though that's just the way it is. It's that I have to look.'

A teacher affects eternity;
he can never tell where his influence stops.

HENRY ADAMS

As innocent as a new-laid egg.

W. S. GILBERT

1

Pop quizzes were killers. Like ambushing assassins they elicited fear and loathing in the prey, and a certain heady power in the hunter.

As Craig Foster prepared to take his lunch break and finish refining the quiz, he knew how his fifth period US History Class would respond. Groans and gasps, winces of misery or panic. He understood completely. At twenty-six, he wasn't so far removed from the student section of the classroom to have forgotten the pain or the anxiety.

He got out his insulated lunch sack. Being a creature of habit, he knew his wife — and wasn't it just mag being married — would have packed him a poultry pocket, an apple, some soy chips, and his favorite hot chocolate.

He never asked her to pack his lunch, or to make sure his socks were washed and folded in pairs and stacked in the right-hand side of his top drawer. But she said she liked doing things for him. The seven months they'd been married had been the best of his life. And it hadn't sucked up 'til then, he decided.

He had a job he loved, and was damn good at, he thought with a quick burst of pride. He and Lissette had a very decent apartment within reasonable walking distance of the school. His students were bright and interesting – and, bonus time, they liked him.

They'd grumble and sweat a bit over the pop quiz, but they'd do fine.

Before he got down to work, he shot his bride an email.

Hey, Lissy! How about I pick up that soup you like, and the big salad on the way home from work tonight?
Miss you. Love every sweet inch of you!
You know who.

It made him smile thinking about how it would make her smile. Then he switched back to the quiz. He studied his comp screen as he poured out the first cup of hot chocolate and lifted the pocket bread filled with soy products masquerading as thinly sliced turkey.

There was so much to teach; so much to learn. The history of the country was rich and diversified and dramatic, full of tragedy, comedy, romance, heroism, cowardice. He wanted to pass all of it onto his students, to make them see how the country, and the world they lived in, had evolved into what it was in the early months of 2060.

He ate, added questions, deleted others. And he drank deep of his favorite chocolate as a soft snow fell outside the classroom window.

As the days of his own short history ticked minute by minute closer to their end.

Schools gave her the willies. It was a humbling thing for a tough-minded, kick-ass cop to admit, even to herself. But there it was. Lieutenant Eve Dallas, arguably New York City's top murder cop, would rather have been stalking through an abandoned tenement in search of a psychotic chemi-head juiced on Zeus then striding down the pristine hallways of staunchly upper-middle class Sarah Child Academy.

Despite the bright, primary colors along walls and floors, the sparkling glass of the windows, it was, for Eve, just another torture chamber.

Most of the doors along the maze were open, and the rooms beyond empty but for the desks, tables, counters, screens, boards.

Eve glanced over at Principal Arnette Mosebly, a sturdy, heading-toward-statuesque woman of about fifty. Her mixed-race heritage had given her skin the color of caramel cream and eyes of misty blue. Her hair was a glossy black worn in a ball of corkscrew curls. She wore a long black skirt with a short red jacket. The heels of her sensible shoes clicked and clacked on the floor as they walked along the second-floor corridor.

'Where are the kids?' Eve asked.

'I had them taken to the auditorium until their parents or guardians can pick them up. Most of the staff is there as well. I thought it best, and most respectful, to cancel afternoon classes.'

She paused a few feet away from where a uniformed cop stood in front of a closed door.

'Lieutenant, this is beyond tragic for us, and the children. Craig . . .' She pressed her lips together, looked away. 'He was young and bright and enthusiastic. His whole life ahead of him, and—' She broke off, held up a hand as she struggled for composure. 'I understand this sort of thing, I mean to say, having the police involved is routine in matters like this. But I hope you'll be as discreet and efficient as it's possible to be. And that it will be possible for us to wait to – to transport the body until after all the students have left the building.'

Now she straightened her shoulders. 'I don't know how that young man could have become so ill. Why would he have come in today if he was feeling unwell? His wife – he's only been married a few months – I haven't contacted her yet. I wasn't sure—'

'You're going to want to leave that to us. If you'll give us a few moments.'

'Yes. Yes, of course.'

'Record on, Peabody,' Eve said to her partner. She nodded to the guard who stepped to the side.

Eve opened the door, stood at the threshold. She was a tall, lanky woman with a choppy cap of brown hair, with brown eyes that were flat and dispassionate now as she scanned the scene. Her movements were easy as she took a can of Seal-It from her field kit, coated her hands, her boots.

In nearly a dozen years on the force, she'd seen a lot worse than the doomed history teacher sprawled on the floor in pools of his own vomit and shit.

Eve noted the time and place for the record. 'MTs responded to the nine-one-one, arriving at fourteen-sixteen. Pronounced victim, identified as Foster, Craig, at fourteen-nineteen.'

'Lucky we drew a couple MTs on the call who knew better than to move the body,' Peabody commented. 'Poor bastard.'

'Having lunch at his desk? Place like this probably runs to a staff lounge, cafeteria, whatever.' Remaining at the threshold, Eve cocked her head. 'Knocked over a jumbo insulated bottle, the chair.'

'Looks more like a seizure than a struggle.' Peabody skirted the edge of the room, her airboots squishing slightly. She checked the windows. 'Locked.' She angled so she could study the desk, the body from that side of the room.

While her body was as sturdy as Arnette Mosebly's, Peabody's build would never be statuesque. Her dark hair had grown past the nape of her neck and curved up at the ends in a flirty little flip Eve had yet to resign herself to.

'Working lunch,' Peabody noted. 'Lesson plans or grading papers. Allergic reaction to something he ate, maybe.'

'Oh, yeah, I'd say.' Eve crossed to the body, hunkered

down. She'd run prints, do the standard gauge for TOD, all the rest, but for a moment she simply studied the dead.

Spider legs of broken vessels ran through the whites of his eyes. There were traces of foam as well as vomit clinging to his lips. 'Tried to crawl after it hit him,' she murmured. 'Tried to crawl for the door. Get the formal ID, Peabody, verify TOD.'

Rising, Eve moved carefully around the puddles of what Craig's body had voided, and picked up the insulated cup she saw, which had his name engraved in silver over black. Sniffed.

'You think somebody poisoned this guy?' Peabody asked.

'Hot chocolate. And something else.' Eve bagged the cup into evidence. 'Color of the vomit, signs indicating seizure, extreme distress. Yeah, I'm thinking poison. ME will verify. We'll need to get clearance to access his medicals from the next of kin. Work the scene. I'm going to talk to Mosebly again, and pull in the witnesses.'

Eve stepped out again. Arnette Mosebly paced the hallway with a PPC in her hand. 'Principal Mosebly? I'm going to have to ask you not to contact anyone, speak with anyone just yet.'

'Oh . . . I – actually, I was just—' She turned the PPC around so Eve could see the miniscreen. 'Word game. Something to occupy my mind for a bit. Lieutenant, I'm worried about Lissette. Craig's wife. She needs to be told.'

'She will be. Right now I'd like to speak with you, in

private. And I need to interview the students who found the body.'

'Rayleen Straffo and Melodie Branch. The officer who responded said they couldn't leave the building, and had to be separated.' Her lips thinned now in obvious disapproval. 'Those girls were traumatized, Lieutenant. They were hysterical, as one would expect under these kinds of circumstances. I have Rayleen with the grief counselor, and Melodie with our nurse practitioner. Their parents should be with them by now.'

'You notified their parents.'

'You have your procedure, Lieutenant. I have mine.' She gave one of those regal nods Eve imagined were required in Principal Training 101. 'My first priority is the health and safety of my students. These girls are ten years old, and they walk into *that*.' She nodded toward the door. 'God knows what damage it's done to them, emotionally.'

'Craig Foster isn't feeling so well himself.'

'I have to do what needs to be done to protect my students. My school—'

'Right now, it's not your school. It's my crime scene.'

'Crime scene?' Color drained from Arnette's face. 'What do you mean? What crime?'

'That's what I'm going to find out. I want the witnesses brought in, one at a time. Your office is probably the best place for the interviews. One parent or guardian per child during the interview.'

'Very well then. Come with me.'

7

'Officer?' Eve looked over her shoulder. 'Tell Detective Peabody I'm going to the principal's office.'

His mouth twitched, very slightly. 'Yes, sir.'

It was a different kettle altogether, Eve discovered, when you were the honcho instead of the one in the hot seat. Not that she'd particularly been a discipline problem in her day, she remembered. Mostly, she'd tried to be invisible, just get by, just get through and get out of the whole educational prison the day it was legal to do so.

But she hadn't always managed it. A smart mouth and a bad attitude had surfaced often enough to earn her a few trips down to that hot seat.

She was supposed to be grateful the state was providing her, a ward thereof, with an education, with a home, with enough food to sustain life. She was supposed to be grateful to have clothes on her back, even if someone else had worn them first. She was supposed to want to better herself, which had been tough when she hadn't remembered, not clearly, where she'd come from in the first place.

What she remembered most were the smug-toned lectures, the disappointed frowns that didn't quite hide the superiority.

And the endless, the terminal, the all-pervasive boredom.

Of course, it hadn't been smart and spiffy private schools for her, with state-of-the-art educational equipment, sparkling clean classrooms, stylish uniforms, and a one-teacher-per-six-student ratio.

She'd be willing to bet her next paycheck that the Sarah Child Academy didn't run to fist fights in the hallways, or homemade boomers in the lockers.

But today, at least, it ran to murder.

While she waited in Mosebly's office with its homey touches of live plants and stylish teapots, she did a quick run on the victim.

Foster, Craig, age twenty-six. No criminal. Both parents still living, she noted, and still married to each other. They lived in New Jersey, where Craig himself had been born and raised. He'd attended Columbia on a partial scholarship, earned his teaching certificate, and was working on a Master's degree in History.

He'd married Bolviar, Lissette in July of the previous year.

He looked fresh and eager in his ID photo, Eve mused. A handsome young man with a clear complexion the color of roasted chestnuts. Deep, dark eyes, and dark hair worn in what Eve thought they were calling a high-top. Shaved close on the sides and back, brushed high on the crown.

His shoes had been trendy, too, she recalled. Black and silver gels, with ankle wraps. Pricey. But his sports jacket had been dirt brown, worn at the cuffs. Decent wrist unit, which had struck her as a knock-off. And a shiny gold band on the third finger of his left hand.

She imagined, when Peabody completed the scene, there would be under fifty credits in Craig's pockets.

She made a few quick notes.

Where did the hot chocolate come from?
Who had access to the insulated cup?
Shared classroom?
Time line. Last to see vic alive, first to find body.
Insurance policies, death benefits? Beneficiaries?

She glanced up as the door opened.

'Lieutenant?' Mosebly stepped in, one hand on the shoulder of a young girl with milky skin dotted with freckles that went with her carrot-red hair. The hair was long and brushed back into a sleek tail.

She looked slight and shaky in her navy blazer and spotless khaki.

'Melodie, this is Lieutenant Dallas, with the police. She needs to speak with you. Lieutenant Dallas, this is Melodie's mother, Angela Miles-Branch.'

The kid had gotten the hair and skin from Mom, Eve noted. And Mom looked just as shaky.

'Lieutenant, I wonder if this could possibly wait until tomorrow. I'd prefer taking Melodie home now.' Angela had Melodie's hand in a death grip. 'My daughter isn't feeling well. Understandably.'

'It'll be easier all around if we do this now. It shouldn't take long. Principal Mosebly, if you'll excuse us.'

'I feel I should stay, as a representative of the school and as Melodie's advocate.'

'A representative isn't required at this time, and the minor child's mother is present as her advocate. You'll need to step out.'

There was an argument in Mosebly's eyes, but she tightened her jaw, stepped out of the room.

'Why don't you take a seat, Melodie?'

Two fat tears, one for each big blue eye, spilled out. 'Yes, ma'am. Mom?'

'I'm going to be right here.' Keeping hands joined, Angela took the seat beside her daughter. 'This has been terrible for her.'

'Understood. Melodie, I'm going to record this.'

With the nod came two more silent tears. At the moment, Eve wondered why the hell she hadn't taken the scene and sicced Peabody on the kids. 'Why don't you just tell me what happened?'

'We went into Mr Foster's class – um, Rayleen and I. We knocked first, because the door was closed. But Mr Foster doesn't mind if you need to talk to him.'

'And you needed to talk to Mr Foster.'

'About the project. Ray and I are project partners. We're doing a multimedia report on the Bill of Rights. It's due in three weeks, and it's our big second-term project. It counts for twenty-five percent of our grade. We wanted him to see the outline. He doesn't mind if you ask him questions before class, or after.'

'Okay. Where were you before you went to Mr Foster's classroom?'

'I had lunch period, and my study group. Ray and I got permission from Ms Hallywell to leave study group a few minutes early to speak with Mr Foster. I have the pass.'

She started to reach into her pocket.

'That's okay. You went inside the classroom.'

'We started to. We were talking, and we opened the door. It smelled awful. That's what I said, I said: "Holy jeez, it really stinks in here." Tears rained again. 'I'm sorry I said that, but—'

'It's okay. What happened then?'

'I saw him. I saw him on the floor, and there was like, oh, gosh, there was all this vomit and everything. And Ray screamed. Or I did. I guess we both did. And we ran out and Mr Dawson came running down the hall and asked us what was the matter. He told us to stay there and he went back. He went inside. I watched him go inside. And he came out really fast, with his hand like this.'

She clamped her free hand over her mouth. 'He used his talkie, I think, to call Principal Mosebly. And then Ms Mosebly came and called the nurse. And then the nurse, Nurse Brennan, came and took us to the infirmary. She stayed with us, until Mr Kolfax came and he took Ray with him. I stayed with Nurse Brennan until my mom came.'

'Did you see anyone else go into Mr Foster's room, or leave it?'

'No, ma'am.'

'When you were walking from your study group to the classroom, did you see anyone?'

'Um. I'm sorry. Um. Mr Bixley was coming out of the boys' restroom, and we passed Mr Dawson on the way. We showed him our pass. I think that was all, but I wasn't paying attention.'

'How did you know Mr Foster would be in his classroom?'

'Oh, he's always in his classroom before fifth period on Mondays. He always has his lunch in there on Mondays. And the last fifteen minutes is when he allows students to come in and talk, if they really need to. Even before that he doesn't mind if it's important. He's so nice. Mom.'

'I know, baby. Lieutenant, please.'

'Nearly done. Melodie, did either you or Rayleen touch Mr Foster, or anything in the classroom?'

'Oh, no, no, ma'am. We just ran away. It was awful, and we ran away.'

'All right. Melodie, if you remember anything else, any little thing at all, I need you to tell me.'

The child rose. 'Lieutenant Dallas? Ma'am?'

'Yeah?'

'Rayleen said, when we were in the infirmary, Rayleen said that they would have to take Mr Foster away in a big bag. Do you? Do you have to?'

'Oh, Melodie.' Angela turned the child into her, held tight.

'We're going to take care of Mr Foster now,' Eve said. 'It's my job to take care of him, and I will. Talking to me helps me do my job, it helps me take care of him.'

'Really?' Melodie sniffled, sighed. 'Thank you. I want to go home now. May I go home now?'

Eve met the girl's drenched eyes, nodded, then shifted her gaze to the mother. 'We'll be in touch. I appreciate your cooperation.'

'This has been very hard on the girls. Very hard. Come on, sweetheart. We're going home.'

Angela draped her arm around Melodie's shoulders and walked her from the room. Eve pushed away from the desk, followed them to the doorway. Mosebly was already heading for the pair.

'Principal Mosebly? Question.'

'I'm just going to escort Mrs Miles-Branch and Melodie out.'

'I'm sure they know the way. In your office.'

Eve didn't bother to sit this time, but simply leaned back on the desk. Mosebly steamed in, fists knotted at her sides.

'Lieutenant Dallas, while I perfectly understand you have a job to do, I'm appalled by your dismissive and arrogant attitude.'

'Yeah, I get that. Was it Mr Foster's habit to bring his own lunch and beverage to work?'

'I . . . I believe it was. At least several days a week. We have a Nutritionist Certified cafeteria, of course. And State-approved Vending. But many members of the staff prefer to bring their own, at least occasionally.'

'He generally eat alone? At his desk?'

Mosebly rubbed her thumb and forefinger over

14

her forehead. 'As far as I know he took his lunch in his classroom two or three days a week. A teacher's work encompasses more than can be done during school hours. There are lesson plans, grading, reading, lecture and lab preparations. Craig, like most of the staff, was also pursuing his own further education, which requires study and writing, and so forth. He'd lunch at his desk so that he could work while he ate. He was dedicated.'

The anger seemed to drain out of her. 'He was young and idealistic. He loved teaching, Lieutenant Dallas, and it showed.'

'Did he have any problems with anyone on staff?'

'I'm really not aware of any. He was a friendly, easygoing young man. I felt, both personally and professionally, that we were fortunate to have him on our faculty.'

'Dismiss anyone lately?'

'No. We have very little turnover here at Sarah Child. Craig was in his second year with us. He filled a hole left by one of our teachers who retired after fifty years of service. Twenty-eight of those years were given right here, at Sarah Child.'

'How about you? How long have you been here?'

'Three, as principal. I have twenty-five years in education, and in administration.'

'When did you last see Mr Foster?'

'I saw him briefly this morning.' As she spoke, Mosebly went to a small cold box, took out a bottle of water. 'He'd come in early to use the fitness facilities, as he did routinely. All staff are permitted to use the machines, programs, the pool, and so on. Craig made use of the privilege nearly every morning.'

She sighed as she poured water into a short glass. 'Would you like some, Lieutenant?'

'I'm good.'

'I had a swim myself this morning, and was just leaving the pool area when he came in. We said good morning. I complained about the traffic, and kept going. I was in a hurry. I heard him dive in,' she murmured, then took a slow sip of water. 'I heard the splash as I opened the locker room door. Oh, God.'

'What time was that?'

'About seven-thirty. I had an eight o'clock phone conference, and I was running behind because I'd spent too long in the pool. I was annoyed with myself, and barely spoke to Craig.'

'Where'd he keep his lunch?'

'Why, in his classroom, I suppose. Possibly the lounge, but I don't recall I've ever seen him put anything in or take anything out of the friggie or cupboard in there.'

'Would the classroom be locked?'

'No. The school is, naturally, secured, but individual classrooms aren't locked. There's no purpose, and the Sarah Child program is based on trust and responsibility.'

'All right. You can send for the second witness. Rayleen Straffo.'

Mosebly nodded, but there was nothing regal about it this time. 'What about the other students? My staff?'

16

'We're going to need to interview the staff before any leave the building. You can dismiss the students, but I'll need your registration list.'

'Very well.'

Alone, Eve pulled out her communicator to tag Peabody. 'Status.'

'The body's just being transported. The ME on the wagon concurs with your poisoning assessment, though he won't commit until the vic's on the slab. The sweepers are on scene. It looks as if the vic was working on his comp at TOD. Putting together a pop quiz for his next class.'

'There's a motive,' Eve said dryly.

'I hated the pop quiz, and question its constitutionality. I did a quick check of the comp, and found the vic sent out an email from that unit to an LFoster@Blackburnpub. com at twelve oh six today. No communication in or out prior to.'

'Wife's name is Lissette. Content?'

'Just a sweetheart note, offering to pick up dinner on the way home from work. Recipient responded in the same tone, in the affirmative at fourteen-forty-eight. Return post was not read.'

'Okay. I'm waiting for the second wit. I'll send the principal back to you, have her set you up somewhere. Get started on interviewing the staff and let's nail the time line in each case. I'll take my share of them in here once I finish with the kid. Meanwhile, verify the wife's residence and place of employment. We'll notify after we leave here.'

'And the fun never ends.'

Eve clicked off as the door re-opened, and again Mosebly entered with her hand on the shoulder of a young girl.

This one was blonde, with a cascade of curls held back from her face with a violet band. The band matched her eyes. They were puffy at the moment, red-rimmed, dominating a face of dewy skin with a slightly tipped-up nose. The mouth, rosy and bottom heavy, quivered.

She wore the same kind of uniform as Melodie, with the addition of a small gold star pinned to the lapel of the blazer.

'Rayleen, this is Lieutenant Dallas. Lieutenant, Rayleen is here with her father, Oliver Straffo. I'll be just outside if I'm needed.'

'Have a seat, Rayleen.'

'Lieutenant.' Oliver kept his daughter's hand in his. His voice resonated in the room, like a good actor's in a theater. He was tall, gilded like his daughter. But his eyes were a cold, steel gray. She'd met them before. In court.

High-powered, high-dollar, high-profile defense attorney, she thought.

Crap.

2

'I'm allowing this interview,' he began, 'in this place, at this time, because I feel it's in the best interest of my daughter's emotional well-being. However, if I don't like the tone or the texture of this interview, I will stop it and take my daughter away. Is that clear?'

'Sure. I was going to dig out the thumbscrews, but I don't remember where I left them. Have a seat. Rayleen, I just need you to tell me what happened.'

Rayleen looked at her father first, got his nod. Then she sat, as he did, with admirable posture. 'I found Mr Foster. Melodie was with me. It was awful.'

'Explain to me how you found him. How you got to his classroom at that time of day.'

'Yes, ma'am.' She took a deep breath as if to prepare herself for an oral report. 'I was in my study group, but I wanted, especially, to talk to Mr Foster about the project I'm working on with Melodie. It's worth a full quarter of our second-term grade in US History, and I wanted to do the best I could. I'm ranked first in my grade, and this is one of the most important projects of this term.'

'Okay, so you left study group for Mr Foster's classroom.'

'Yes, ma'am. Ms Hallywell gave us a pass so we could go to Mr Foster's class early. He always has his lunch there on Mondays, and he lets students come in during the last fifteen minutes to talk to him, if they need to.'

'What time did you leave study group?'

'I have the pass. It's time-stamped.' Again she looked at her father for permission, then drew the pass out. 'Melodie and I each have one. That's the school rule. It says 12:47 P.M.'

Eve made a mental note to walk the route to gauge the time it would take. 'You went directly from study group to the classroom.'

'Oh, yes, ma'am. Loitering in the hallways between classes is an infraction, and three infractions within a thirty-day period results in a loss of privileges.' Her voice went prissy, reminding Eve that Rayleen was just the sort of kid she'd done her best to avoid in the cell block of school. 'I don't have any infractions on my record.'

'Good for you. How long did it take you to get from study group to Mr Foster's classroom?'

'Oh, it couldn't have been more than a couple of minutes. Maybe three? I'm not absolutely certain, but we went right there. We were just talking, about the project, and some ideas for it. The door was closed, so we knocked first, then we opened it. And it smelled bad. It smelled sick, I guess. Melodie said something about the smell, and . . .' She pressed her lips together. 'I laughed. I'm so sorry. I didn't know, Daddy, I didn't know.'

'It's all right, Ray. Of course you didn't know.'

'Then we saw him. He was lying there, and he was . . .' She hiccupped twice, then simply crawled out of her chair and into her father's lap.

'It's all right, baby. It's all right, Ray.' His eyes lasered into Eve's as he stroked Rayleen's hair. 'Lieutenant.'

'You know I need to finish this. You know it's vital to get the details as quickly as possible.'

'I don't know what else.' Her voice was muffled as she pressed her face to her father's chest. 'We ran, we ran away. And Mr Dawson was there, and he said to stay where we were. I sat down, I think. I sat on the floor, and we were crying, and Mr Dawson came back. His hands were shaking when he took out his talkie and called Principal Mosebly.'

'Did you see anybody else go in or out of the classroom?'

'Principal Mosebly went to the door, then she called for the nurse and they took us – Melodie and me – to the infirmary.'

'On the way to the classroom, did you see anyone?'

'I think, yes, I think Mr Bixley came out of the boys' room, the restroom. He had his toolbox because one of the sinks was stopped up. That was before, before we passed Mr Dawson and showed our passes. I went in first, into the classroom first. I was the first to see him.'

She lifted her tear-streaked face. 'I don't see how Mr

Foster could be dead. I don't see how. He was my very favorite teacher.'

Her shoulders shook as she clung to her father.

'You can't need any more from her,' Oliver said quietly. 'I'm taking her home.'

'If she remembers anything else—'

'If she does, I'll contact you.'

He rose, and carrying his daughter, strode from the room.

Eve started with Eric Dawson. He was a science teacher, in his middle fifties, and had been instructing at the academy for fifteen years. He carried a little paunch, and since his shirt buttons strained over it, Eve assumed he was in denial over it. His sandy hair showed a little glint of gray at the temples. Pockets of fatigue dogged his light brown eyes.

'I didn't go in,' he told Eve. 'No more than a step or two. I could see . . . Anyone could see Craig was gone. I'd been annoyed with the girls, all that screaming. I thought they'd seen a spider or something equally foolish.' He paused, passed a hand over his face. 'But as soon as I saw them . . . Even silly girls don't reach that level of hysteria over a spider.'

'Did you see anyone else, other than the two girls?'

'I'd just left Dave Kolfax and Reed Williams in the staff lounge. We'd had lunch together, as we sometimes do. And I passed Leanne Howard going in. I was going to the chem lab to set up for the next class.'

'When did you last see Mr Foster alive?'

'Oh, God. God. In the lounge, before classes this morning. I was having a coffee, and he had a tube of Pepsi from Vending. He didn't drink coffee. I used to tease him about it. We talked a little about a mutual student, Bradley Curtis. His parents are divorcing, and Brad's grades have been sliding. We agreed it was time for a meeting with the parents and a counselor. Then, ah, Reed came in. Yes, to grab a coffee. When I left they were talking about some action vid they'd both seen recently. I didn't see him again until . . .'

'How did you get along?'

'With Craig? I liked him quite a lot. Quite a lot,' he repeated quietly. 'I was, well, unconvinced when he first came on staff last year. He was so young – the youngest member of the teaching staff. But he made up for a certain lack of experience with enthusiasm and dedication. He cared a great deal, a great deal about the students. He must have been ill and not known it. He must have had some sort of condition. To die that way. It's inconceivable.'

The sentiment was echoed by every staff member Eve spoke with. She finished up the session with Reed Williams, English department.

No pouch on this one, Eve noted. He had a strong, lean build that told her he took advantage of the fitness center facilities. His hair was a deep, rich brown tipped with gold to simulate sun streaks. His square jaw was deeply clefted under a firm mouth. His eyes of sharp, bottle green were heavily and darkly lashed.

He was thirty-eight, single, and wearing a suit that she estimated had cost him a stinging slice of his monthly pay.

'I saw him this morning, in the fitness center. He was doing reps when I came in. I don't like to talk when I'm working out, so it was just a, well, a nod of acknowledgment. I'd say we were in there together for about twenty minutes. He headed out, waved. He generally took a swim after a workout. I was in there another ten minutes, I'd guess. Grabbed a shower, dressed. Then I saw Craig again in the lounge, with Eric. Eric Dawson.'

'Did Mr Foster have anything with him?'

'With him? No, just a tube of Pepsi. We talked vids for a few minutes, then headed off to class. I ran into him again in the staff restroom.' Williams smiled slightly and showed a single dimple in his left cheek to go with the cleft. 'Just a kind of "How's it going?" as we used the facilities. I guess that was right about eleven. Just before. The classes start on the hour, and I wasn't late.'

'How did you get along with him?'

'Fine. We got along fine.'

'You both liked action vids. Did you hang out socially?'

'Now and again, sure. I went to his wedding last year – most of the staff did. We had a beer together a couple of times.' He shrugged. 'We weren't best pals, but we got along. Mirri would know him better, socially.'

'Mirri.'

'Hallywell. English department, Drama. They saw each other outside the school.'

'On a social level.'

'Sure.' He smiled a little again, and there was a smirk behind it. 'They have a standing date Wednesday nights. To study.'

With the initial interviews done, Eve tagged Peabody again. 'Bixley.'

'Hernando M., Maintenance. He was dealing with a plumbing problem in the boys' john down the hall from the scene. He passed the two wits and Dawson on his way out.'

'Buzz?'

'No. He's late sixties, worked here for twelve years. His two grandsons attend on his employee tuition rate. Seems like a solid type.'

'Hallywell.'

'Mirri C. Finished her about fifteen minutes ago. English department, runs the Drama Club and directs the school plays. I'm about to interview the last on my list. Is there something about Hallywell? I didn't get a buzz from her either.'

'I want a quick followup. If she's still here, I'll track her down. Find me when you're done.'

'She was pretty broken up – Hallywell. Might check one of the washrooms. I'd say she'd need to compose herself before she left.'

Following Peabody's advice, Eve tried the staff restroom closest to the lounge where Peabody was conducting interviews. The door required a key card; Eve used her master.

And found a woman sitting on the floor in front of the bank of sinks, weeping.

'Mirri Hallywell.'

'Yes. Yes.' She choked back a sob, sniffled, mopped at her face with a tissue. The face was splotchy from the crying jag, the pale blue eyes swollen from it. She had dark hair worn in a brutally short Caesar style and tiny silver hoops in her ears.

'I'm sorry. Are you with the police? I've already talked to a detective.'

'My partner. I'm Lieutenant Dallas. I need to ask you a few more questions.'

'Oh, God, oh, God. I don't know what to do. I don't know what to say.'

Eve crouched. 'It's rough when a colleague's killed, so suddenly.'

'It's horrible. We weren't just colleagues. We were friends. We were good friends. None of this seems possible.'

'How good friends?'

Mirri let her head fall back. 'That's a terrible thing to imply, a terrible thing to think about someone like Craig. Someone who can't speak for himself anymore.'

'I speak for him now. That's what I do.'

'Then if you're going to speak for him you should know he loved his wife. They loved each other. I envy that, what they have together. I'm her friend, too. I'm her friend, and I don't know how to begin to help her through this.'

'You and Craig saw each other every week, outside work.'

'We had a study date on Wednesdays.' Fire came into the ravaged eyes. 'For God's sake, is that what everything whittles down to for people like you?'

'If it was innocent, why get pissed off?' Eve countered.

'Because he's dead. He's dead.'

She drew in a shaky breath. 'We were both working on our Master's degrees. We'd go to the library or a coffee shop, study together for a couple hours. Maybe have a beer afterward. We're going out – I mean, oh, God, I mean we were supposed to go out tomorrow, to the vids. Craig and Lissy and this guy they fixed me up with. I hate being fixed up, but they talked me into this one last month, and it's worked out pretty well so far. So we're doing a double date.'

'Mirri, if you and Craig had anything going, now's the time to tell me.'

'There's nothing to tell. I'm not so desperate I'd poach a friend.' She scrubbed her hands over her face. 'I was going to call Lissy, come in here and call her, even though they said we weren't to contact anyone. I thought, I need to do that for her, she needs to hear about this from a friend. But I couldn't.'

Mirri drew up her knees, pressed her face to them. 'I just couldn't. I didn't know what to say, how to say it, and I didn't have the guts to try.'

'That's for us to do.'

'What can you say?' Mirri demanded. 'What can you say to someone like this? She's expecting he'll be there when she comes home. And he won't be there. Not tonight, not ever. What can you say?'

Then she sighed, pushed herself to her feet. 'It's not your fault. I wish it were. I wish it could be your fault and I could scream and rave at you for it. Would you tell Lissy . . . would you just tell her how sorry I am, and that if I can help, if I can do anything . . . I'll be there.'

Lissette Foster was an editorial assistant for a small publishing house with offices in midtown. The background Peabody accessed listed her as twenty-four, a native of Martinique who had moved to New York to attend Columbia. The only blight on her record was an underage drinking rap when she'd been nineteen. She'd been given probation, and community service.

Her mother remained in Martinique. Her father's whereabouts were unknown.

'So,' Peabody continued, 'speaking of the islands, how was your vacation?'

'It was good.' A week of sun, sand, and sex. What would be better? 'This snow's starting to stick.'

'Yeah, we're supposed to get maybe four inches. Are you looking seriously at the wife?'

'She's first on the list. Spouses tend to be.'

'Yeah, but newlyweds? I know how it's supposed to be tough the first year, adjusting and whatever, but poison? It's sneaky and distant. A spouse gets pissed, it's usually bloodier, and more personal.'

'Usually. If his lunch was poisoned, where did the lunch come from? Consensus is, from home. Wife had the easiest access. Although consensus also is the vic left the bagged lunch in his classroom. Unlocked room. He comes in early, dumps his stuff in the classroom, heads to the fitness center. Again, fairly easy access for anyone.'

'Motive?'

'Other than the pop quiz? Not clear as yet. The wit? Rayleen Straffo is the fruit of Oliver Straffo's loins.'

'Oh, shit? Seriously? Does she have horns and a tail?'

'If so, well hidden.' Eve tapped her fingers on the wheel as she thought of Straffo. 'He could get a lot of screen time with this, playing the Daddy card. Outrage, concern, blah, blah.'

'It'd be just like him. You're going on Nadine's new show this week. You can balance his bullshit.'

'Don't remind me. Stupid damn friendships. They always cost you.'

'You're so soft and sentimental, Dallas.'

'Yeah, I love that about me.' Judging the snow, the insanity of New York drivers in same, Eve swung into a parking lot two blocks from the address. 'I'm not trying for street parking in this snowing crap.'

'I can use the exercise. I, like, ate my way through the holidays, and am expecting McNab to spring for something resembling chocolate for Valentine's Day, so I need to lose in advance. What are you getting for Roarke?'

'For what?'

'For Valentine's Day?'

'I just got his Christmas stuff five minutes ago.' She stepped out of the car, remembered the scarf stuffed in her coat pocket. Pulling it out, Eve swung it around her neck.

'Two months ago. And it's *Valentine's* Day. For sweethearts. You need to get him a gooey card and a sentimental token. I already got McNab's. It's a talking picture frame with our names inscribed on it. I put this shot of the two of us his father took at Christmas? He can keep it in his cube in EDD. Roarke would like something like that.'

'Roarke already knows what we look like.' A minicoupe skidded at the light, fishtailed into the crosswalk, and earned the curses and snarls of pedestrians.

She loved New York.

'Oh, speaking of pictures, I've got a new crop of Belle. Have you seen her since you got back?'

'No. Is she asking for tats and belly rings already?'

'Come on. She is so seriously adorable. She's got Leonardo's eyes and Mavis's mouth, and—'

'God help us if she inherits their fashion sense along with it.'

'She smiles at me, every time I pick her up.' Above her scarf, under her watchcap, Peabody's eyes went to brown goo. 'People say that's gas, but she smiles at me. She's getting so big, and she's . . .'

While Peabody rhapsodized about Mavis's infant daughter, Eve listened to the music of New York. The blasting horns, the arguments, the rumbling ad blimps from overhead.

Through them were the voices, a rat-a-tat of conversations, a litany of complaints.

'So, what are you going to take her?'

'What? Taking what? Where?'

'To Belle, Dallas, when you go to see her. The gift?'

'What gift?' Seriously stymied, Eve stopped in the middle of the sidewalk. 'Why do I have to take a gift?'

'Because.'

'*Why?* Didn't I do the shower thing, with gifts, then the hospital thing?'

'Yes, but when you go to visit the baby at home for the first time, it's traditional to—'

'Who makes this up?' Seriously aggrieved, Eve jabbed a finger into the marshmallow puffiness of Peabody's winter coat. 'I demand to know who makes these rules. It's madness. Tell me who it is, and I'll have them committed for psychiatric evaluation.'

'Aw, Dallas, you just need to bring her a little teddy bear or a pretty rattle. It's fun shopping for baby stuff.'

'My ass. You know what's fun?' Eve hauled open the door of the office building. 'Finding out who poisoned some poor slob of a history teacher. That's my idea of fun. Any more talk about shopping, gifts, babies, gooey cards or Valentine's Day, my boot's going so far up your ass you'll think the toe's your tongue.'

'A week at the beach sure sweetened your mood. Sir,' Peabody muttered when Eve's look fried off the top layers of her skin.

Eve turned on her heel toward the security station, and badged the guard. 'Lissette Foster.'

'Just a minute, please.' He ran the badge number, the ID ploddingly, thoroughly. 'Yes, sir, you're cleared. Lissette Foster . . . Foster, Foster. Here we go. She's with Blackburn Publishing. Editorial. Uh . . . that's on the ninth floor. Bank of elevators to your right. Have a productive day.'

'Yeah, you bet. Native of Martinique,' Eve began as they stepped into an elevator to be assaulted with quiet, mind-melting music. 'Student visa, most like, work visa maybe. She'd get her green card by marrying a US citizen. And keep her status here as his widow.'

'Easier ways to get a green card.'

'Sure. But maybe things weren't working, and divorce within two years cancels out the green. Maybe there was more going on in those Wednesday night sessions with Hallywell than studying. You got a job here, you want a life here. Killing to keep it isn't a stretch.'

They stepped off into a small reception area where a woman sat behind a white counter. She wore a headset and a big, welcoming smile.

'Good afternoon!' she said so enthusiastically Eve's eyes slitted. 'Welcome to Blackburn Publishing. How may I help you today.'

'Lissette Foster.'

'Of course. I can certainly find out if Ms Foster's free. May I say who's here to see her, and the nature of your business?'

Eve simply took out her badge again. 'We'll explain all that to Ms Foster.'

'Oh.' The woman's eyes bugged as she stared at the badge. 'Oh, my. Excuse me.' She swiveled around, spoke into the mouthpiece of her headset in a hissing whisper. 'Lissette Foster.' Clearing her throat, she darted a glance back at Eve. 'Lissette, there's someone here in Reception to see you. It's a *police* officer. I don't know. I really don't. Okay.'

With her smile strained at the edges, the woman turned back to Eve. 'She'll be right here. If you'd like to sit—'

'We're fine.'

By the time Eve had unwrapped her scarf, a woman was striding out on ice-pick heels. Those alone indicated some level of insanity to Eve. The heels were cherry red, the pencil-slim suit stone gray. Inside it was an excellent body.

Lissette Foster had luminous skin, heavy-lidded, and currently annoyed, nut brown eyes. Her hair was nearly the same shade and worn ruler-straight to brush her shoulders.

She moved with purpose, Eve thought. Like a woman with a fire in her belly. It might have sparked from anger, from ambition, or passion, but it was hot.

'You're police?' Lissette demanded in a brisk tone made exotic by the French accent.

'Lieutenant Dallas, Detective Peabody. We—'

'Oh, for Christ's sake! I told him we'd keep the music down. Arrest me then.' Drama quivering, she held out her arms, wrists together. 'Arrest me for playing music after the ungodly hour of nine P.M. on a Saturday night. I should be dragged away in chains! Just because some retired cop has *issues* is no reason to have police coming to where I work. Does he want me to get fired?'

'Mrs Foster, we're not here about your music. We'd like to speak with your privately. Your office would be best.'

'Office?' Lissette let out a very lusty laugh. 'I'm an editorial assistant. I'm lucky I've got a cube. What's this about?'

Eve turned now to the woman at reception. 'I need a private room. Office, conference room, lounge, whatever. I want it now.'

'Certainly, certainly. The conference room isn't booked right now. You can—'

'Fine.' Eve looked back at Lissette. 'Let's go.'

'What's this about? I have a meeting with the boss in . . . oh, God, ten minutes. She hates anyone to be late. If you think you can pitch a story idea to someone at my level, I can promise you, you're wasting your time.'

She wound her way through a maze of cubes and narrow hallways, past offices with tiny windows, corner offices with views to kill.

'Look, I shouldn't have talked that way about Sergeant Kowoski. Maybe the music was too loud. My husband and I were playing around, pretending we were at some hot club. We were probably a little drunk, and a little loud. I don't want any trouble.'

She stepped into a room with a dozen chairs around a wide table, long counters along each side wall and screens front and back.

'Can we do this quickly? I really don't want to be late for my meeting.'

'We'd like you to sit down.'

'This is ridiculous.' Blowing out a breath, she yanked out a chair, sat. Then came straight back to her feet again, with alarm in her eyes. 'Oh, God. Has something happened to my mother? Was there an accident? *Maman?*'

'No.'

How did you tell someone the person she expected to be waiting for her at home wouldn't be there tonight? Or any other night? Eve remembered. You told them fast, without flourishes.

'It's regarding your husband, Mrs Foster.'

'Craig? He's still at school.'

'I'm sorry to tell you, your husband's dead.'

'That's a terrible thing to say to someone. That's a vicious terrible thing to say. I want you to leave, right now. I'm going to call the police. The *real* police and have you arrested.'

'Mrs Foster, my partner and I are the real police, and we're the investigators on your husband's death. He died today at approximately twelve-thirty.'

'Of course he didn't. He didn't. He was at school. That's his lunch break, and he sent me an email just after noon. I packed his lunch this morning. He's at school, at the Monday faculty meeting right now. And he's fine.'

Her breath began to come quick, choppy. Her color was fading even as she fumbled a hand behind to brace the table as her legs went out.

'You should sit down, Mrs Foster,' Peabody said gently. 'We're very sorry for your loss.'

'No. No. Was there a bomb? Was there a bomb at school? Oh, my God. Is he hurt? Is Craig hurt?'

'He died,' Eve said flatly. 'I'm very sorry.'

'But he . . . But he . . . You could make a mistake. You must have. I should call him. You'll see. I should call him. But he's in his Monday meeting. He's not allowed to have the 'link on when he's in his Monday meeting. We'll go there.' She pushed away from the brace of the table, swayed. 'We'll go to the school and to Craig. I need my coat. I'll just get my coat.'

She looked around, dazed. 'Silly, so silly. I couldn't remember where I was for a minute. I need . . . what is it?'

'Sit down, Mrs Foster.'

'No, we have to go. To the school. We have to—' She jumped at the sound of a knock. A blonde in power red stepped in.

'I'd like to know what's going on here. Lissette?'

'Elizabeth.' Lissette wore the dull look of sleepwalkers, and survivors. 'Am I late for the meeting?'

'Peabody.' Eve nodded toward Lissette, then moved to the blonde. 'Who are you?'

'I'm Elizabeth Blackburn, and who the hell are you?'

'Dallas, Lieutenant, NYPSD. I've just informed Mrs Foster that her husband's dead.'

'He's . . . what? Craig. Oh, sweet Jesus. Lissy.'

Perhaps it was the pet name, or the tone of grief in it, but as Elizabeth started across the room, Lissette simply slid to the floor. Elizabeth went down on her knees, gathered Lissette up.

'Craig. My Craig.'

'I'm sorry. Lissy, Lissy, I'm so sorry. Was there an accident?' she demanded of Eve.

'We'll need to speak with Mrs Foster about the circumstances.'

'All right, all right. My office is to the right, end of the corridor. I'll bring her there to you as soon as she's able. She needs a few minutes, for God's sake. Just wait in my office.'

They left Lissette in the arms of her boss. There were a number of curious looks from offices and cubes, but no comment until they reached the corner office at the end of the hall. At that point a little brunette popped out like a jack-in-the-box.

'Excuse me! That's Ms Blackburn's office.'

'Where she just asked us to wait.' Eve yanked out her badge. 'Go back to work.'

Inside was a glossy workstation, a cushy sofa, and two pretty chairs. A fairly stunning flower arrangement stood on the table under the south-facing window.

'If she faked that reaction,' Peabody began, 'she's got major talent.'

'Not so hard to fake if you practice. But yeah, it seemed genuine. Go on out before they get here, have someone show you her cube. I want to know what she has in there.'

'On that one.'

Eve wandered to the windows, pausing long enough to note what Lissette's boss kept on her desk. A framed photograph of a girl somewhere in her blossoming teens, a loaded disc file, a pile of memo cubes arranged in a pyramid, and a file that revealed artwork for what was likely a disc cover when Eve flipped it open.

Outside the windows, snow continued to fall on the city in thin, slick flakes. An airtram chugged through it holding a clutch of miserable passengers.

Personally, she thought, she'd stick with the vicious traffic on the slick streets below.

She turned as Peabody stepped back in.

'Nothing much, and not a lot of room for it. Files, memos, notes on current work. She's got a wedding picture of her and the vic in a really nice frame. I'm betting wedding present. Some snaps of him, or them, pinned to the cube walls. Oh, and a little file of ads and pictures from decorating magazines. That's about it.'

'All right. We'll give her another minute, then we'll take this back in the conference room. We'll swing by the morgue next. I want to know exactly what killed Craig Foster.'

It didn't take a minute. Seconds later Lissette came in, leaning heavily on Elizabeth Blackburn.

'You're just going to sit,' Elizabeth told her. 'And I'm

going to sit with you. I gave her a soother,' she said to Eve, then jutted her chin pugnaciously before Eve could speak. 'And don't even think about starting on me about it. She needed something. It's mild, and won't keep her from talking to you.'

'You her boss or her legal rep?'

'I'm whatever she needs me to be right now.'

'Are you sure?' Lissette's voice was cracked and raw, and carried the awful pain of fading hope. 'Are you absolutely sure there's no mistake? That it's Craig?'

Knowing her strengths, Peabody took point. She moved to the couch where Lissette sat with Elizabeth. 'I'm very sorry. There's no mistake.'

'But . . . He wasn't sick. We had full medicals before we got married. He was healthy. People don't just . . . Did someone hurt him? Was there an accident at the school?'

'We need to find out why and how this happened. We have to ask you questions. You can help us find out.'

'I want to help. I want to know. I love him.'

'Let's start with this morning. You said you packed his lunch.'

'I did. I always do.' Her eyes fluttered, widened as she shot a hand out to grip Peabody's arm. 'Was something wrong with the sandwich? He liked that awful processed poultry substitute. Did it make him sick? Oh, my God.'

'We don't know that, Mrs Foster. Did anyone come to your apartment today, before your husband left for work?'

'No. He leaves so early. He liked to use the fitness center at the school. He takes good care of himself. He does. We do. Elizabeth.'

'You're doing fine. How much more of this?' Elizabeth demanded.

'Was your husband having problems with anyone at the school?' Eve asked.

'Craig? No. He loved it there.'

'How about prior relationships? Did either one of you have trouble with a former relationship?'

'We were together two years before we got married. You know how you meet someone, and it's just it? Your whole life is there, that minute. That's what it was like for us.'

Eve stepped forward, then sat so her eyes were level with Lissette's. 'If you want to help, you need to be straight with me. Absolutely straight. Did he gamble?'

'He wouldn't even buy a lottery ticket. He was careful with money.'

'Did he use illegals?'

She bit her lip. 'Um, we did a little zoner in college.' Her gaze slid toward Elizabeth's.

'Who didn't?' Elizabeth patted her arm.

'Recently?'

'No.' Lissette shook her head at Eve's question. 'Absolutely not. He could be dismissed for any illegals use. Plus, he really feels strongly about setting examples for his students.'

'Were you having financial problems?'

'Nothing serious. I mean, we had to juggle a little sometimes, especially since Craig wants to save. Sometimes I spend more than I should, but he's so careful it balances out. He saves for things. Important things. He . . . he took tutoring work last year for extra money. Then he used it to bring my mother to New York for Christmas. He knew how much it would mean to me, so he worked extra and he bought my mother a shuttle ticket, and paid for her hotel because we don't have room. He did that for me. No one's ever going to love me like that again. No one could. Not ever in my life.'

Because the tears started again, Eve rose. 'I'm sorry for your loss, and appreciate your cooperation at this difficult time.' Crappy words, she thought. And the only words. 'Is there anyone you'd like us to contact for you?'

'No. No. Oh, God, Craig's parents. I have to tell them. How do I tell them?'

'We can take care of that for you.'

'No, I have to. I'm Craig's wife. I have to do this.' She got shakily to her feet. 'I have to see him. I don't know where he is.'

'He's with the medical examiner now. I'll contact you as soon as you're cleared for that. Do you have someone who can go with you?'

'I'll go with her. No, Lissy, I'll go with you,' Elizabeth insisted when Lissette teared up again and shook her head. 'You just sit for a minute while I walk Lieutenant Dallas and Detective Peabody out. Sit right here, I'll just be a minute.'

She moved quickly, and purposefully, not stopping until they'd reached an intersection in the maze. 'How was Craig murdered?'

'I didn't say he was.'

Elizabeth turned, looked dead into Eve's eyes. 'I know who you are. I keep up with who's who in New York. Lieutenant Eve Dallas, Homicide.'

'I don't have any information to give you at this time. Mr Foster's death is under investigation.'

'That's bullshit. Just bullshit. That girl just lost the love of her life. Like that!' Elizabeth snapped her fingers. 'She needs answers.'

'She'll have them, as soon as I do. How well did you know him?'

'I met him a number of times. He'd come in every now and then, and Lissy would bring him to company parties and events. Sweet boy. Dopey in love. Bright. He struck me as bright, like Lissy is. Two bright young people getting started with their life, their careers. You're bright, too, from everything I've read, heard or seen of you. You get those answers for Lissy. You get her that much to hold on to.'

'That's the idea.'

3

Eve looked to find the first of those answers at the morgue. The air always smelled just a little too sweet there, like a careless whore who'd used perfume instead of soap to disguise some unpleasant, personal odor. Tiles – floor and walls – were an unrelieved white, pristine and sterile.

There was a vending alcove where staff or visitors could order their choice of refreshment, though Eve imagined many who passed by would prefer something stronger than the muddy soy coffee or sparkling soft drinks.

She strode down the white-tiled corridor where, behind thick doors, death lay in sealed drawers or on slabs waiting for the right questions to be asked.

She pushed through the doors of an autopsy room to see Chief Medical Examiner Morris already at work to the wicked rhythm of what she thought might be Dixieland jazz. His sealed hands were bloody to the wrists as he lifted Craig Foster's liver from his body to the scale.

'Ah, why don't I go score you a Pepsi.' Peabody was already taking a step back. 'Thirsty work. Be right back.'

Ignoring her, Eve continued into the room. Morris

glanced up, his eyes behind his microgoggles canny and faintly amused. 'She still queezes when I'm cutting.'

'Some never get past it.' When had she? Eve wondered. Too long ago to remember. 'You're getting to him quickly. Appreciate it.'

'I always enjoy working on your dead, and feel you enjoy me having my hands in them. What's wrong with us?'

'It's a sick old world. How about the tox?'

'Music off,' he ordered. 'I assumed you'd want that straight away, and put a red flag on it. Still snowing?'

'Yeah, it's crap out there.'

'Personally, I enjoy the snow.' He worked smoothly, weighing the liver, taking a small sample of it. He wore a sleek black suit under his protective smock, with a silver shirt that shimmered as he moved. His dark hair was in one tightly coiled braid, looped at the neck and twined with silver cord.

Eve had often wondered how he managed it.

'Want a look?' He put the sample on a slide under his scope, gestured to the screen. 'The tox confirms poisoning. Ricin, very concentrated, very lethal. Very quick in this case.'

'Ricin? That's from beans or something, right?'

'And you win the trip for two to Puerto Vallarta. Castor beans, to be precise. Ricin's made from the mash after processing. It was used as a laxative once upon a time.'

She thought of the state of the body, the crime scene. 'It sure as hell worked.'

'Superbly. His liver and kidneys failed, and there was internal bleeding. He'd have had severe cramping, rapid heartbeat, nausea, very likely seizures.' Morris studied the screen as Eve did. 'Ricin dust was used – and is still used on occasion – in bioterrorism. Injection of ricin was a favored assassination method before we discovered handier ways.'

'Your all-purpose poison.'

'Very versatile. The lab will process, but I can tell you it appears he drank it – in his hot chocolate.'

'His wife made the chocolate.'

'Ah. I love domestically inclined females.'

'I don't see her for it. Married a handful of months, no obvious motive. And she copped to making it without a blink.'

'Marriages, even new ones, can be a terrorist camp.'

'Damn right, but she's not popping for me. Yet anyway.'

'Good-looking young man,' Morris commented. 'Athletic build, and I'd say, a harmonic homogeny of races.'

'Harmonic homogeny.' Eve shook her head. 'You kill me. He was a teacher – history, private school Upper West Side. Left his lunch in his classroom, habitually. Ate at his desk Mondays, habitually. No security cameras in the classrooms or corridors. Private schools aren't required to have them. Wouldn't have been hard for anybody to doctor his drink. What we're missing at this point is why anyone would. Guy's coming off as a nice, harmless mensch.'

'Someone, I'd say, didn't like your mensch. This kind of

poisoning isn't just lethal, it's extremely painful.' Hands deft as a violinist's, Morris removed the heart. 'He didn't live long after he ingested it, but while he did, he suffered a great deal.'

She looked back at the body. What did you do, Craig, to piss somebody off this much? 'His wife wants to see him. She's notifying his parents, and I assume they will, too.'

'After nine this evening. I'll have him prepared for viewing.'

'I'll let them know.' She frowned back at Morris. 'Where the hell do you get castor beans?'

He only smiled. 'I'm sure you'll find out.'

Peabody, slightly shame-faced, loitered by Vending. 'Before you say anything, here's a nice cold tube of Pepsi. And I put my time to good use. I've started runs on the staff members at Sarah Child, *and* verified life insurance policies on both the vic and his wife. Vic gets his through work bennies. Fifty thousand, with the wife as beneficiary.'

'Pretty piddly motive.' Eve took the tube, pleased it was, indeed, nice and cold. 'We'll hit their financials, see if she had any major debts. Maybe she's the gambler, or the one with an illegals habit.'

'But you don't think so.'

'No, I don't think so.' Eve cracked the tube, swigged as they walked. 'Unless there's more money somewhere, the fifty doesn't do it for me. And if there was marital discord, let's say, a spouse generally goes for contact, for the personal. This was nasty, but remote. He pissed somebody off.'

Peabody rewound her scarf, replaced her gloves as they hit the doors and the cold exploded like an ice boomer. 'Rejected lover, colleagues in competition.'

'We'll want to look closer at Mirri Hallywell.'

'Parents of a student who he disciplined, or who wasn't doing well in his class.'

'Jesus.' Eve jammed her hands in her pockets, and discovered she'd lost yet another pair of gloves. 'Who kills because their kid gets a big doughnut in a history class?'

'Parents are weird and dangerous creatures. And I worked up another theory. Maybe it was a mistake.'

'It was ricin poisoning, and Morris's take is that the dose was intense and quickly lethal.'

'See, what I mean is, maybe one of his students was upset with him.' Peabody mimed a sulky face. 'I'll fix that meanie Mr Foster. Doctors his drink thinking he'll maybe get sick. Oops.'

'Not entirely stupid.' They climbed into the vehicle where they hissed out the breath the blustery cold had them holding.

'Jesus, Jesus, why is there February?' Eve demanded. 'February should be eliminated altogether for the good of mankind.'

'It is the shortest month, so that's something.' Peabody actually moaned as the heat came on. 'I think my corneas are frozen. Can that happen?'

'They can in fucking February. Let's stick with Foster's nearest and dearest first. We'll go by their building, talk to a few neighbors. Most particularly the retired cop.'

'Once a cop,' Peabody nodded, and began to blink cautiously to help her potentially frozen corneas thaw out. 'If there was anything off going on, he'd probably have noticed.'

Henry Kowoski lived on the second level of a four-story walkup. He opened the door only after scanning Eve's badge through his security peep, then stood taking her measure.

He was a stocky five-eight, a man who'd let his hair thin and gray. He wore baggy trousers with a flannel shirt and brown, scuffed slippers. In the background, the entertainment screen was tuned to the *Law and Order* channel.

'Seen your picture on screen a few times. In my day, cops didn't angle for face time.'

'In my day,' Eve countered, 'the world's lousy with reporters. Going to let us in, Sergeant?'

It might have been the use of his rank that had him stepping back with a shrug. 'Sound off,' he ordered the screen. 'What's the beef?'

The place smelled like it had been just a little too long since laundry day, and not long enough since takeout Chinese night. The space was what realtors liked to call Urban Efficient, which meant it was one room, with a stingy bump for a kitchen, a short, narrow cell for a bath.

'How long were you on the job?'

'Thirty years. Last dozen of them out of the Two-Eight.'

Eve searched her mind, pulled out a single name. 'Peterson the LT when you were there?'

'Last couple years, yeah. He was a good boss. Heard he transferred out a while back, moved clear out to Detroit or some such where.'

'That so? I lost track. You've had some complaints about the tenants up above here? Fosters.'

'That's damn right.' He folded his arms. 'Playing music – if you can call it that – all hours of the day and night. Stomping around up there. I pay my rent, and I expect my neighbors to show some respect.'

'Anything else going on up there but loud music and stomping?'

'Newlyweds.' His mouth twisted. 'Deduce. What the hell do you care?'

'I care since Craig Foster's in the morgue.'

'That kid's dead?' Kowoski took a step back, sat on a ratty arm chair. 'Fucked-up world. It was fucked up when I picked up my shield, and it was fucked up when I turned it in. How'd he buy it?'

'That's under investigation. Any trouble between them? Upstairs?'

'With dove and coo?' He snorted. 'Not likely. Sooner lock lips than eat, from what I've seen. If there was yelling, it wasn't a fight – if you get me. The girl's a noisy lay.' Then he puffed out his cheeks, blew out air. 'I'm sorry about this. They pissed me off, I won't say different, with the noise up there. But I hate hearing he's dead. Young guy. Teacher. Had a smile on his face every time I saw him. Course if you've got yourself a woman looks like her who's ready to bang you every five minutes, you've got a lot to smile about.'

'How about visitors?'

'Her mother was here a couple days 'round Christmas. Got some other young people who came in and out now and then. And a couple of loud parties. Both of them came home stumbling drunk New Year's Eve, giggling like a couple of kids, shushing each other.'

He shook his head slowly. 'Fucked-up world. You're wondering about criminal activity? You got yourself a couple of straight arrows with these two, you want my take. Up every morning, off to work, back every evening. Socializing now and again, sure, but these were homebodies. Shoulda stayed home more, I guess, and out of that fucked-up world.'

They spoke with the handful of neighbors who were home, and the rhythm remained stable. The Fosters were a happy and newly married couple, young urban professionals who enjoyed each other.

'We work three angles,' Eve decided as they headed back downtown. 'The vic, the school, the poison. They're going to intersect somewhere.'

'Maybe through the science department. We can find out if they were studying poisons, or ricin in particular.'

'Dawson's a science teacher,' Eve considered. 'Let's do a deeper run on him. You tag him meanwhile, ask about what gets mixed up in their lab.'

'Got it. And if we're leaning toward somebody in the

school, or affiliated with it, we should check the students' records. See if Foster had any go-round with one of them, or the parents of same.'

Eve nodded. 'Good. Let's look at the staff members we've verified were in the building before classes started. If I were going to slip something in somebody's go-cup, I'd want to get it in before the place got crowded. We'll write this up, then start digging.'

'Hate to dig on an empty stomach. Not to be a whiner, but we haven't had a dinner break, and it's nearly eight. Maybe we could—'

'Eight? Dinner?'

'Jeez, Dallas, just a hoagie.'

'Shit, shit. *Shit!* Dinner. Eight. French place. Fuck, fuck. Why is it nearly eight?'

'Well, because the Earth rotates on its axis while it orbits around the sun. You're supposed to be somewhere.'

'Roarke. Corporate wife duty.' Eve wanted to pull at her hair. 'I missed the last two, and I can't do the no-show again. La Printemps. That's it.'

'La Printemps? Oh la la! That's megachic. Totally. And it's Upper East Side. Hate to point this out, but we're low on the lower West Side.'

'I know where the hell we are.' She batted her fist on the wheel as she spun into the garage at Cop Central. 'I have to go. I have to do this. I'm already late. Goddamn it.'

'The case is going to hold for the night,' Peabody pointed out. 'We've got nothing but paperwork now anyway. I can write the report, and we'll do the runs and the digging in the morning.'

'Copy the report, my home and office units. Anything else in your notes that strikes you. Get out, get out! I gotta get to this stupid French place.'

'Aren't you going to go home and change first?'

'Into what? I don't have time.' Then she grabbed Peabody by a fistful of puffy coat. 'Do this one thing for me. Tag Roarke, tell him I'm on my way. Caught a case, running late, but I'm heading there now.'

'Okay.'

'I can't do it. He'll see I'm in regular clothes, and he told me I should take a change into work, but I nixed it. Like I want to go prancing out of Central in some fancy dress.' Aggravation all but streamed out of Eve's pores. 'Do you know the grief that causes me?'

'Honestly? I don't know how you suffer through it. I'd crack like an egg in your place.'

'Oh, bite me and tag Roarke.'

She all but shoved Peabody from the vehicle, and was whipping the wheel and speeding out.

She couldn't remember what she'd tossed on that morning, and since she was driving like a maniac, couldn't afford the time to check herself out. The traffic, the *stupid* snow, the need to weave and dodge made switching to autopilot an impossibility.

She probably smelled of death.

Well, it was his own fault, she decided. He'd married her,

hadn't he? It wasn't as if she hadn't made full disclosure on what a crappy wife she'd make for a man like him.

She'd had to go and fall for a man who owned the lion's share of the known universe, and had to – on occasion – trot out his wife for that odd and awkward mix of social business.

He wouldn't complain that she was late. In fact, he wouldn't even be annoyed with her. If a cop had to get married – and God knew they were better solo – she couldn't do better than hooking up with a man who understood that the job messed with personal plans. Constantly.

And because he wouldn't complain or be annoyed, she felt even more guilty for forgetting the dinner, and more determined to beat the hellacious traffic.

She broke one of her own rules, hit the sirens, and used the cop for personal gain.

After barely avoiding clipping bumpers with a Rapid Cab, she went vertical, then hung a screaming right on Fiftieth, zigging, zagging her way over to Third before heading uptown again.

She should've told Peabody to tell Roarke to have everyone order without her. Not to wait. Why hadn't she thought of that? Now they'd probably be sitting there, starving, while she killed herself and many innocent bystanders trying to get to a restaurant where she wouldn't even be able to read the damn menu.

'Guidance System on!' she ordered. 'Where the hell is this place. Restaurant, New York City, *La Printemps*.'

One moment please while your request is programmed. La Printemps is located at 212 East Ninety-third, between Second and Third Avenues. Would you care to make a reservation?

'I've got a damn reservation. Guidance off.'

Even with the kamikaze driving tactics, she was thirty minutes late. And by the time she managed to double park, which would bring the wrath of thousands and possibly cause an intercity riot, she was later still.

She flipped on her On Duty light, then sprinted the last half-block.

She paused outside to scoop her fingers through her hair a couple of times, then looked down at her dark brown trousers. She saw no overt signs of blood or other bodily fluid staining them or the navy V-neck, and considered the lack a big plus in her favor.

Horns were already blasting in protest of her parking arrangement as she stepped out of the blowing snow, and into the fragrant and muted music of five-star French.

The maître d' swooped down on her like a vulture on road kill. 'Mademoiselle. I regret, we cannot seat walk-ins.'

'How do you seat anyone if they don't walk in?' She shrugged out of her coat. Peabody had the megachic right, Eve noted. Every woman in the place sparkled and gleamed. 'Check the coat, Pierre. And it's your ass if it's not here when I leave.'

'Mademoiselle, I must ask you to leave quietly.'

'I'll be sure to do that, after I eat.' She smoothed down the brown jacket, to be sure her weapon was concealed. Though she was tempted to flash it, just to watch the tight-assed maître d' crack his head on the floor as he passed out.

'Now we can go a round right here,' she suggested, 'and give your diners a show along with dinner, or you can tell me where my party is. Reservation Roarke.'

He lost color, shade by shade until he'd gone from robust to pasty. Apparently the name of Roarke carried as much power and threat as a police issue. 'I beg your pardon, Madame Roarke.'

'Dallas, Lieutenant. Where's the table?'

'If you would please follow me.'

'My coat. I like that coat.'

'Of course. It's a beautiful garment.' He snapped his fingers. 'See to Madame . . . to the lieutenant's coat. If you will? Your party is already seated. It would be my pleasure to bring you a cocktail.'

'Whatever they've got's fine.' She scanned the room with all its gilt and glory, then followed the chastened maître d'.

He saw her coming. Knowing she'd be late, he'd chosen the table with that in mind. He loved watching her walk into a room, carelessly long strides, those cop's eyes seeing every detail.

And in the simple jacket and pants she, in his eyes, outshone every woman in the room. When their eyes met, he got to his feet.

'Good evening, Lieutenant.'

'Sorry I'm late.'

'Champagne for my wife,' he said without taking his eyes off her. He drew her chair back himself. 'Let me introduce you to Natalie and Sam Derrick.'

'So this is Eve! I'm just thrilled to meet you.' Natalie flashed a mile-wide grin, even as her gaze tracked over Eve's clothes.

'Glad you could join us.' Sam held out a hand the size of a rump roast, pumped Eve's twice. 'Roarke's told us it's hard for you to get away from work.'

'I just can't think how you investigate *murders*.'

Eve glanced back at Natalie. 'First I need a body.' She felt Roarke's hand pat her thigh twice. 'It's a lot of details,' she continued. 'And not nearly as interesting as it comes across in a vid or on screen.'

'I'm sure that's not true. But I don't suppose we want to talk of unpleasant things.' Natalie beamed again. 'Sam was just about to tell the story of how he caught the biggest bass in Jasper County.'

'Wow.' It was all Eve could think to say, and she was grateful for the glass of champagne now in her hand. And the fact that Roarke had given her free one a squeeze under the table.

Just look at him, she thought, sitting there as though he couldn't be more interested or enthralled to hear about some stupid fish. And, of course, he'd know that every eye in the place would be turned on him at some point during the evening.

She couldn't blame them. He sat, at ease, the half-smile on his gorgeous face, the light of interest in those laser blue eyes. Candle- and lamplight gleamed in his hair, that thick mane of black.

When his lips curved more fully, her heart actually bumped her ribs. He could still do that to her, chase her heart to a gallop, stop her breath, melt her bones. And do all of that just with a look.

At some point she was given a menu, and on a quick scan saw that it was, indeed, the sort of fare that caused mild fear in her rather than hunger.

Sam and Natalie weren't as terminally boring as she'd imagined they would be. Though there was a lot of talk about the sort of outdoorsy activities that caused more discomfort in her than fancy French food.

Hunting, fishing, hiking, riding in boats on rivers, sleeping in tents.

Maybe it was a kind of cult Roarke wanted to infiltrate.

But there was some humor in them, and an obvious enjoyment of the moment.

'This is just wonderful. Sam, this lobster puts your big bass to shame. You have to have a taste. We don't spruce up very often,' she continued as she held her fork up for her husband. 'We're country people, and that's how we like it. But it sure is fun to do the big city in a big way. I guess you're used to it,' she said to Eve.

'I don't spruce up very often either. Obviously.'

This time when Natalie smiled, there was more warmth to it. 'Honey, if I looked like you in pants and a sweater, I wouldn't wear anything else. Next time, you'll have to come out and see us, and we'll throw you a real Montana feed. Roarke, you're just going to have to bring Eve out to see us.'

'I'll have to do that.' He lifted his glass, smiled over the rim at Eve. And when someone said his name, and he glanced toward them, Eve saw something come into his eyes, just a flash of it. A something she'd only seen when he looked at her.

It was gone, shuttered down into polite pleasure. But it had been there. Very slowly, Eve tracked her gaze over, and saw her.

She was stunning, in a bold red dress that managed to be both elegant and sexy. Long legs ended in the glitter of paper-thin silver heels. Her hair was a long, waving stream of delicate blonde, clipped at the sides with something small and sparkling. Her eyes were brilliantly green, full of life and excitement that translated to sexual power. Her lips were full, very red and lush against luminous skin.

'Roarke.'

She said it again in a kind of throaty purr that brought up the hackles on Eve's back. And she glided as such women do, to the table, holding out her hands for his.

'"Of all the gin joints in all the towns in all the world,"' she murmured as he rose, and lifted her face for a kiss.

'Magdelana,' he said with the Irish in his voice cruising

through the name, and he brushed her lips very lightly with his. 'What a surprise.'

'I can't believe it's you!' Magdelana laid her hands on his cheeks, stroked. 'And as handsome as ever. More. The years agreed with you, lover.'

'And with you. Eve, this is an old friend of mine, Magdelana Percell. Magdelana, my wife, Eve Dallas, and our friends, Sam and Natalie Derrick.'

'Wife? Oh, of course, of course. I heard. One does. I'm delighted to meet you. And you,' she said to the Derricks. 'You'll have to excuse me for breaking into your meal. All I saw was Roarke.' She smiled down at Eve, that glitter in her eyes. 'You understand.'

'Oh, yeah.'

With another full-wattage smile, Magdelana dismissed Eve, then all but melted into Roarke. 'I've only been in town a few days. I was going to contact you, see if we could make a date to catch up. It's been, my goodness, ten years?'

'Nearer to twelve, I'd think.'

'Twelve!' She rolled her exquisite eyes. 'Oh, Franklin, forgive me! My escort, Franklin James. This is Roarke, his wife, and the Derricks.'

'We know each other.' Roarke held out a hand. 'Hello, Frank.'

He was thirty years her senior, by Eve's gauge, looked prosperous and hale. And, she thought, slightly besotted.

'We'll let you get back to your dinner.' Magdelana ran

a hand down Roarke's arm – a light, somehow intimate gesture. 'I'm just thrilled to see you again.' And this time she brushed her lips against Roarke's cheek. 'We'll have lunch, won't we, and talk a walk down Memory Lane. You won't mind, will you, Eve?'

'The lunch or the walk?'

Magdelana laughed, a frothy gurgle. 'We'll have to have lunch ourselves, us girls. And tell secrets about Roarke. I'll be in touch. So nice to meet you.'

Conversation picked up again, over food, and fishing. Though Roarke's face betrayed nothing but interest in his companions, Eve knew him. So she knew while he ate, he drank, he spoke, his mind was across the elegant room where the stunning Magdelana sipped wine in her bold red dress.

When the evening was done, they put the Derricks in one of Roarke's limos for the drive back to their hotel, then got into Eve's vehicle.

'There have probably been a dozen murders committed due to the way you parked this thing.'

'Who is she?'

'I told you, she and Sam own not only a very large portion of Montana, but one of the most successful resorts in the state.'

'Don't play me that way. Lover.'

'An old friend.' He shifted, his eyes meeting Eve's. 'And yes, we were lovers. It was a long time ago.'

'That much I already know.'

He sighed. 'She was in the game. We . . . competed for a while, then we worked together on a couple of jobs. Then we parted ways.'

'She's a thief.'

'She was.' He said it with a shrug. 'I wouldn't know if she continues in that profession.' He reached out, and since Eve had gotten behind the wheel, flicked at her hair as she drove. 'What does it matter to you?'

I saw something in your eyes, she wanted to say. 'Curiosity,' she said instead. 'She's a looker.'

'She certainly is. Do you know what I thought when you walked into the restaurant?'

'Thank God she doesn't have blood all over her shoes?'

'No, but good point. I thought, there is the most compelling woman in the room. And she belongs to me.' He laid a hand briefly over hers. 'Thanks for tonight.'

'I was late.'

'I noticed. New case?'

'Yeah. Caught it this afternoon.'

'Tell me about it.'

She ordered herself to put old lovers out of her head, and gave him the basics.

4

She grabbed a shower to wash away the long day, and tried not to obsess when Roarke didn't make his usual play to join her under the hot jets. A woman who got herself twisted up because her man – who'd led a very full and . . . adventurous life before they'd met – ran into a former lover was just asking for stomach spasms.

And she didn't get herself twisted up, Eve reminded herself as she stepped out of the shower and into the drying tube. Or she never had before this.

She was making too much of a . . . of a glint, she decided. Of a fraction of a second. Whoever Roarke had bounced on more than a freaking decade before had nothing to do with now.

Nothing at all.

He wasn't in the bedroom when she went back in. But that meant nothing either. She dragged on some sweats, hunted up some socks that turned out to be cashmere, then headed toward her home office.

Roarke's adjoined hers. The door was open, the lights on. No reason not to step over and see what was going on.

He was at his desk, the suit jacket and shirt replaced

by a black sweater. The furry pudge that was their cat was curled on the corner of the workstation. Galahad blinked his dual-colored eyes, then lowered them to lazy slits.

'Working?' Eve said, and felt stupid, awkward.

'A bit. You?'

'Yeah.' She couldn't quite figure out what to do with her hands, so she hooked her thumbs in her front pockets. 'I figured I'd put some time in.'

He gave her his attention. He had a way of doing that even when he had a zillion things going on. 'Want some help?'

'No. No, I got it. It's just routine stuff.'

And his attention shifted away from her, back to his comp screen. 'All right then. Let me know if you change your mind.'

'Yeah, okay.'

'Lieutenant,' he said as she turned away. 'Try not to drink more than a gallon of coffee.'

For some reason it made her feel better that he'd poked at her. She moved into the kitchen of her work space, and programmed her AutoChef for a half pot instead of the full one she'd have ordered up otherwise.

It was good he had some work to do, she thought. They'd both just do what they did for a few hours. She carried her coffee to her desk, and started to call up Peabody's report on Craig Foster.

Cursed.

'Might as well just do it,' she muttered. 'Get it off my brain.' She started the run on Percell, Magdelana, manually, ordering text only on her comp screen. It took some time to find her particular quarry, but she narrowed the search by approximate age, physical description – and unless she'd been way off on the accent – nationality. And scored.

Percell, Magdelana. DOB: March 12, 2029. Born: St Paul, Minnesota. Parents: Percell, James and Karen. Hair: blonde. Eyes: green. Weight: 115 pounds. Height: five feet five inches.

Eve skimmed over her education, but noted that Magdelana had graduated high school early – at fifteen. Had attended Princeton and graduated in just under three years on an accelerated program. Cum laude.

'So she's smart.'

Married: Dupont, Andre, June 22, 2048. No offspring. Divorced: March 2051. Married: Fayette, Georges, April 5, 2055. No offspring. Divorced: October 2059.

Approximate net worth: thirteen point five million U.S. dollars.

Residences: Paris, France; Cannes, France. No criminal.

Eve sat back.

The official data was slim, and the no criminal doubtful as Roarke had said they'd worked together. Even if she hadn't been convicted, even if she hadn't been arrested, there should have been some note in her file about being questioned at some point or other.

He'd cleared it for her, Eve thought, and felt something tighten in her belly. He'd hacked in and tidied up her data, the same way he'd taken care of his own once upon a time.

He'd protected her.

Because it was harder to accept than she'd imagined, Eve ended the search. She already knew more than she wanted to know.

She dove into work, reading Peabody's report, the case notes. She started runs on staff members as she set up a murder board. And was foolishly pleased when Galahad padded in to leap up and stretch out on her sleep chair.

'What we have here,' she told him and picked up her coffee, 'is your Average Joe. No big highs, no deep lows. Cruising along with his average life without, apparently, getting in anyone's way. Then one day he gulps down his homemade hot chocolate during his working lunch and dies a very nasty death.

'So who was that pissed off at Average Joe? What was there to gain by his death? Look at his financials. Living within his means, such as they were. Death insurance, sure, but not major. No holdings, no real estate, no fancy artwork. Financial gain is way down on our list here.'

She eased a hip on the edge of her desk, studied the data on her wall screen as she drank her coffee. 'And here's Mirri Hallywell. You could call her an Average Jane. Worked with the vic, hung out with him, had little study sessions with him, and so on. Just friends though. Now, in your opinion: can two attractive people of the opposite sex, in the same age group, with the same interests who enjoy each other's company, spend time together and remain only friends? Or will sex, as sex is prone to do, rear its ugly head?'

She glanced toward the adjoining office, annoyed that her line of thinking had circled back around to Roarke and his former playmate.

'It's possible, sure it's possible. No sexual spark, maybe. Or the platonic thing is just the level the relationship reaches. Hallywell, however, did have opportunity. As did, naturally, the vic's wife. Could be the ugly end of an ugly triangle. Just that simple.'

But it didn't *feel* like that.

'Want the guy, kill the wife. That's what I'd do. There's the old "If I can't have you no one will" gambit, but why now?'

She went back to her notes, to the interviews. No one she'd spoken with had mentioned any sort of upset, argument, controversy or scandal involving the victim.

'Average Joe,' she repeated, looking back at the now snoring cat. 'Mr Clean Machine.'

'If you're talking to Galahad, you're wasting your time,' Roarke pointed out.

'He's taking it into his subconscious.'

'The only thing in his subconscious is a yearning for salmon. How's it going for you?'

'Circles and dies on me. No motive, no suspects. He's just not the type to buy it this way. In a mugging, sure. Some random act, absolutely. Everybody's the type for that. But someone he knew planned this out, set this up, executed it. And no one who knew him has a reason, that I can find, to want him dead.'

Roarke wandered in to take a look at the ID picture of the victim she had on her wall screen. 'He wouldn't be the first to have some secret life tucked under the average.'

'No, and I'm going to keep digging at the surface. Could've been banging that one.' Eve lifted her chin toward the wall screen as she brought Mirri Hallywell up.

'Pretty.'

'Yeah, the wife's prettier. And according to the retired cop who lives below their apartment, the newlyweds were nailing each other every five minutes, so affair seems superfluous. Still, guys never get tired of sex.'

Roarke patted her ass. 'Indeed we don't.'

She split-screen Mirri and Lissette. Opposite types, physic- ally, she thought. 'For some, sex is ice cream, and they want a nice variety.'

Roarke only smiled. 'I've settled on my single flavor.'

'Yeah, but you worked your way through the menu a few times first. Foster was young,' she continued when Roarke laughed. 'Hadn't had a lot of time to experiment.

It doesn't play all the notes for me,' she murmured. 'But it's the only tune I've got at the moment.'

He turned now to study her murder board. 'Money is, I assume, not in the equation.'

'Not enough of it.'

'Rage?'

'Have to be cold, dead cold. This wasn't a crime of passion. Poison's . . . aloof. Especially if you're not around to see it do its work. Not discounting rage,' she added. 'I just can't find any. Everybody liked him.'

'That's what they said about the Icoves,' he reminded her.

She shook her head. 'This guy's nothing like them. The Icoves were lofty, smug, crazy, sure, but rich and privileged and in the spotlight. This guy was happy in the wings. Going to take a look at his apartment tomorrow,' she said. 'Go through his files at school. Maybe he wasn't the one with a secret. If he knew something, suspected something worth being poisoned for . . .' She shrugged. 'I'll find it.'

'No doubt.' Roarke stepped over, touched his lips to her brow. 'And you can start the hunt in the morning. You've had a long day of cop work and wifely duties.'

'Guess I have.' She let him take her hand to lead her out. 'The Derricks were okay. But I still don't want to go to Montana.'

'That's your cow fear talking. We could go out for a couple of days and stay at the resort. Maybe do a little horseback riding.'

'Oh, there's a lifelong dream. Getting up on some animal that weighs ten times what I do and saying, "Giddyup."'

'It's surprisingly exhilarating.'

'I'll stick with chasing down psychopaths for my thrills, thanks.'

She wondered if he'd gone horseback riding with Magdelana. She wondered how many times *he'd* ridden Magdelana.

Goddamn it.

She turned in the bedroom doorway, pushed him back against the jamb and pressed her lips to his in an avid, energetic kiss. 'Or that's good,' she said, and took a quick bite of his lower lip, 'as second place on the thrill-o-meter.'

'Second place, is it?'

'Well, psychos are pretty damn thrilling.'

'I'll just have to try harder, won't I?' He reversed their positions quickly, had his mouth on hers, his hands under her sweatshirt. 'Wouldn't want my wife seeking out homicidal maniacs just for a bit of a rush, would I?'

'All in a day's work. But . . .' She boosted herself up, wrapped her legs around his waist. 'I've clocked out.'

Their mouths met again, hot and seeking. Then she took hers on a crazed journey of his face, his throat. The taste, *his* taste – it was everything she craved. He was everything.

She kept her legs locked around him when he lowered her to the bed, wound her arms around his neck. 'Tell me you want me.'

'Always. Endlessly.'

'Show me.'

Desire. She could feel it in him. In his hands, in the way they moved over her, in what they took, in what they gave. She could taste it on his lips, that heat.

And still it wasn't enough. She knew only that she needed more.

For the first time since they'd come together, she wasn't sure what that more was. She only knew there was a small, cold place inside her that hadn't been there before. She needed it warmed, she needed it filled.

Desperate, she rolled with him, dragging at his sweater, digging her fingers into flesh and muscle. 'Touch me,' she demanded. 'Touch me. Touch me.'

Her urgency surprised him. Aroused him. So he feasted on her skin, used his hands to take her over. She moaned his name, a sound of both pleasure and plea. And still she quaked, quivered with needs not yet met.

'Eve.' He lay a hand on her cheek, wanting to see her eyes, to see into them. 'Look at me.'

She did what he asked, struggling to let herself fall away. Just fall away. 'Inside me. I want you inside me.'

She rose up, not in offer but demand, and guided him to her.

Linked, as only they could be, she told herself. Their rhythm, their heat, their scent. She watched him watch her until her vision blurred. Until there was only speed and movement, the building − frantic and wild − toward that final, sharp-edged release.

When she lay curled against him, her skin dewed from passion, there was still that small, cold place inside her where the heat hadn't quite reached.

In the morning, he was up and out of bed before she was. But he wasn't in the sitting area, drinking coffee while he watched the financial reports on screen.

She readied for the day, keenly missing the routine – the conversation, sharing breakfast. Why wasn't he there, telling her she was wearing the wrong jacket with the wrong pants?

And the night before? Why hadn't he pushed himself into her work? Why wasn't he here, right now, nagging her to eat something?

She strapped on her weapon harness with an irritated jerk. It was just fine. He was busy, so was she. She didn't need or want the man in her pocket every hour of the day.

She strode to her office to retrieve files, though she'd already copied them to her unit at Central. She turned casually toward his office door, had taken only one step when she heard his voice.

'No, I was up. Yes, old habits die hard.'

On the 'link, Eve realized, and since there was only his voice, he had it on privacy mode.

'It was, yes, quite a surprise. I would, of course. I'm sure we do. Why don't we say one o'clock then, at Sisters Three. I think you'll like it. Shall I send a car for you? No, Maggie, it's no trouble. I'll see you then.'

Maggie, Eve thought as her stomach sank. Not Magdelana, who was glamorous and just a little distant. But Maggie, who was warm and affectionate.

She stepped into the doorway and saw she'd done the nearly impossible and caught him off guard. Still, she couldn't read him in that instant when he stared off into some thought or memory that wasn't hers to share. Then his attention, along with a distracted smile, was on her.

'There you are.'

'Yeah, here I am. At your desk early.'

'I had a 'link conference with London at six our time.' Behind him the laser fax signalled an incoming he ignored. 'I was about to head back and talk you into breakfast.'

'Full of meal plans today. Lunch?'

'Sorry? Oh, yes. Apparently Magdelana remembered I'm an early riser.' He slipped the date book he had on his desk into his pocket as he got to his feet. 'We'll have lunch.'

'So I heard. You're going to want to be careful there, pal.'

'Of what?'

'It wouldn't be the first old friend you've had come around hoping you'd dip back into the game for old times' sake. You might want to remind her you're sleeping with a cop these days.'

Irritation, faint as a whisper, passed over his face. 'I've no intention of dabbling in old habits.'

'Old habits die hard, didn't you say?'

Now a hint of ice came into his eyes, into his voice. 'Eavesdropping now, Lieutenant?'

'I was standing in my office. Your door was open. I have ears.'

'Then use them to hear this. I've having lunch, nothing more or less.' His head angled slightly while those wild blue eyes narrowed speculatively on her face. 'Or don't you trust me?'

'I'd trust you a hell of a lot more if you didn't refer to her as an old *friend* when we both know she was a hell of a lot more.'

'What she was is nearly a dozen years in the past. Years before I ever set eyes on you.' Now simple bafflement joined the irritation and the ice. 'Christ Jesus, are you jealous of a woman I haven't spoken to, seen or thought of in years?'

Eve only looked at him for one long moment. 'You're thinking of her now,' she said and walked away.

She jogged down the steps, and there was Summerset, Roarke's majordomo, his guardian, his man of all work. And the chronic pain in her ass. He stood, tall and thin in unrelieved black, his pewter hair swept back into wings, and cool disdain in his dark eyes.

She only grabbed the coat, which was draped over the newel post. 'If you say a word to me, just one fucking word, I'll yank that stick out of your ass and beat you bloody with it.'

She strode toward the door, then spun around. 'And tell your *keeper* if I were the jealous type I'd have beaten *him* bloody two years ago. Goddamn it.'

Summerset arched his brows, speculated, then glanced up as Roarke came to the top of the stairs.

'The lieutenant seems more abrasive than usual this morning,' Summerset commented.

'She's having a mood.' Hands in his pockets, Roarke frowned at the front door. A damned uncharacteristic mood, he thought. 'Magdelana's in town. We're having lunch today. Apparently, Eve doesn't like it.'

He met Summerset's eyes and the expression in them had the temper he'd barely gotten back under control straining again. 'Don't start on me. I've had enough drama for one day, and it's not even eight in the bloody morning.'

'Why would you complicate your life?'

'I'm not. I'm having fucking lunch. Leave it be,' Roarke warned before walking away.

The snow at the curbs had gone to dirty gray, and slick patches of ice were booby traps on the sidewalks and people glides. Half-frozen commuters stood bundled to the eyes waiting at maxibus stations. On the corners, glide-card vendors had their grills smoking as much for personal warmth as business.

Her vehicle gauge listed the ambient temperature as a hideous four degrees.

She hoped Roarke froze his Irish ass off.

Sitting in snarled traffic, she let her head drop down to the wheel. She'd handled it the wrong way. She didn't know how the hell she should've handled it, but she knew she'd bungled it. Now he was going to be pissed at her when he met that . . . slut. That couldn't be good strategy.

And why the hell should she need any strategy anyway?

'Forget it, forget it,' she told herself. 'Barely a bump in the road.'

Still she steamed about it all the way downtown, brooded over it as she crammed herself in the crowded elevator up to Homicide.

She went straight to her office with barely a snarl for the bull pen. Closed the door, programmed coffee.

Work space, she reminded herself. No personal business allowed. That was it, that was all. She decided to drink her coffee and stare out her tiny window until her mind was clear enough to work.

She was still drinking, still staring when, after a quick knock, Peabody walked in.

'Morning. How was the dinner thing?'

'I ate. Get your coat. We're going to the vic's apartment.'

'Now? Should I contact Lissette Foster to make sure she's—'

'I said get your coat.'

'Yes, sir.'

Peabody didn't speak again until they were in the car. 'Did I miss something? Are we looking at Lissette as prime suspect?'

'When did you think we'd cleared her?'

'I didn't, but I thought we felt she was an unlikely for this.'

'She had the opportunity. As for motive, spouses can always find one. Sometimes it's just because you married an asshole. This is where we start.' She drove for a time in silence. 'I want to see where he lived,' she said more calmly. 'How he lived. How they lived. His body tells us he was a healthy man in his middle twenties who died from ingesting a lethal dose of ricin. That's about all it tells us. That doesn't mean that's all the vic has to say.'

'Okay, I get that. Is everything all right?'

'No, it's really not. But I'm not going to talk about it. Let's do the job.' But the silence that dropped back was worse. Eve dragged a hand through her hair. 'Talk about something else. You never shut the hell up most of the time. Talk about something else, for Christ's sake.'

'Ummmm. I can't think of anything. It's too much pressure. Oh, oh! I know. Are you all set for tomorrow night?'

'Set for what?'

'Now.'

'If it's now, it's not tomorrow night. What did you smoke for breakfast?'

'All I had was rehydrated grapefruit. The holiday weight just won't get the hell off me. It's all cookies.' Peabody gave a mournful sigh. 'My ass is entirely made up of cookies.'

'What kind? I like cookies.'

'Every kind,' Peabody said. 'I have no strength against the mighty variety tin of Christmas cookies. My grandmother still makes them from scratch.'

'I thought cookies were made of sugar.'

'Scratch *is* from sugar – and flour and eggs and carob chips and butter. Mmmm, butter.' Peabody closed her eyes and dreamed of it. 'Like from cows.'

'Cows are a milk thing.' Eve waited while a herd of pedestrians tromped across the crosswalk. 'And I don't understand why anyone wants to drink something that comes out of a cow like, well, piss.'

'You make butter from milk. If you're talking real deal. Damn it, now I'm hungry. I can't talk about cookies, my ass is expanding just from the conversation. I was talking about something. Oh, *Now*.'

'It was now, it became then. It's now all over again.'

Brow knit, Peabody turned her head to look at Eve. 'You're trying to confuse me, and hey – nice job. You know I mean Nadine's new show. You're first up tomorrow for the premiere.'

'And I'm trying not to think about it.'

'It's going to be mag. What are you wearing?'

'I thought, just for a kick, I'd try clothes.'

'Come on, Dallas, the show's national and satellite and it's getting megahype. Let Roarke pick out your outfit.'

Eve's eyes narrowed into sharp slits; she felt a snarl rising in her throat. 'I know how to dress. I've been wearing clothes for years now.' She thought of Magdelana again, and the bold red dress with silver shoes. 'I'm a cop, not some fashion whore. If he wanted someone who struts around on stilts wearing fancy dresses, he shouldn't have married me.'

'I don't think your wardrobe was a big factor.' Cautiously,

Peabody dipped a toe in dangerous waters. 'Did you guys have a fight?'

'Not exactly. But I think we're due.' Eve punched it to swing around a sedan, then zipped onto a second-level street spot. 'This is close enough.'

'I'll say.' Peabody got her wind back, then jogged down to the sidewalk behind Eve.

The bitter cold drilled straight to the bone, and a whipping wind raced down the urban canyons. Eve shoved her ungloved hands into her pockets, and pushed her mind back to the job at hand.

'She's got nothing to hide, she won't have a problem with us looking around her place. Otherwise, we can get a warrant quick enough. We look for any sign of the poison, that includes the beans themselves, or any byproduct. I want to go through his data and communications, any discs, and paperwork. I want to know what he kept in his top dresser drawer, hidden in his coat pockets. The works.'

Peabody sighed with relief when they entered the building and shut out February's blast. 'If their place is like Kowoski's, it won't take long.'

After the hike up the stairs, Eve knocked on the door. It was opened by a woman with tired eyes and glossy dreadlocks. 'Can I help you?'

'Lieutenant Dallas and Detective Peabody to see Lissette Foster.'

'You're the police investigating Craig's death. I'm Cicely Bolviar, Lissy's mother. Please come in. She's in the bathroom.'

Cicely sent a worried glance toward the closed bathroom door. 'She's taking a shower. She didn't sleep last night. I'm going to make breakfast. She needs to eat something. I'm sorry.' She turned back to Eve and Peabody. 'Please sit. Would you like coffee?'

'Don't trouble.'

'It's no trouble. I want to make her something. We're meeting Craig's family this afternoon to talk about . . .' Her lips quivered. 'To talk about arrangements. I want to make her something to eat.'

'When did you get to New York, Ms Bolviar?'

'Late last night. I came as soon as . . . when Lissy called to tell me, I came. She needs her *maman* now. He called me that, too. *Maman*.' She moved into the kitchen bump, then stood as if she didn't know what to do next.

'It was here she wanted to live, my Lissy, and because she had Craig, I didn't worry. In a few years, he told me – they were so young – in a few years, they'd start a family, and I'd be *Grandmaman*. That's what he said. Do you know what this person killed? They killed that sweet boy, and that family he and Lissy would have made. They killed that joy. Do you know how this happened?'

'We'll need to speak with your daughter.'

'*Bien sur*. Please sit. I'll make coffee. They have egg substitute. At home, I have eggs from the chickens my neighbor keeps, but here . . . He was a sweet boy.' Her tired eyes gleamed with tears. 'Such a sweet boy. This should never have happened. Please sit.'

There was a bright blue couch with bright green pillows and two chairs covered in the same vivid colors done in wide stripes. A streamlined workstation took up one corner of the room while a small table with two chairs stood in the other. The arrangement, the order, the flashing colors gave the stingy space style and function.

Cicely walked to the bathroom door, rapped lightly. '*Mignon*, the police are here. The lieutenant and detective. She'll only be a moment,' she told Eve. 'I'll make the coffee now.'

Lissette came out in loose pants and a sweatshirt with thick socks on her feet. She looked like a woman who was suffering from a long illness. Her color had gone pasty, her eyes were dull and swollen. She moved as if her bones hurt.

'You know something more?' Her voice was like rusted metal. 'Something about Craig?'

Eve got to her feet. 'Have a seat, Ms Foster.'

'I went to see him. We went to see him. His parents and I went to that place. It wasn't a mistake. You said it wasn't. It broke them to pieces. His mom and dad, it broke them to pieces. What will I do now?' As if suddenly aware of her surroundings, she looked around the little apartment. 'What will I do? *Maman*.'

'There, my baby. Sit now.' Cicely came back, eased Lissette into a chair. 'Please, can't you tell us something? Anything? It's so hard not knowing why, or how.'

Eve looked into Lissette's eyes. 'Your husband was killed when he ingested a lethal amount of ricin.'

'Ingested? Ate? Ricin? What is it?'

'It's poison,' Cicely murmured and her eyes were huge now, horrified now. 'I know this. This is poison.'

'Poison? But why would he . . . how did he . . .'

'It was in the hot chocolate,' Eve told Lissette and watched the woman go gray.

'No. No. No. That's not right. I made it for him. I made it myself. Every morning once the weather gets cold. And when it warms again, I make him sweet cold tea. Every day. You think I hurt Craig? You think I—'

'No, I don't.' After more than eleven years on the job, Eve knew when to trust her gut. 'But in order to clear you so that we can pursue other avenues, we'd like to look around the apartment. We'd like your permission to search it, to go through your husband's computer, his work, his personal items.'

'Wait. Please.' Lissette gripped her mother's hand. 'You said poison. You said Craig was poisoned. How could he have taken poison by mistake?'

'They don't think it was a mistake,' Cicely said. 'Do you?'

'No.'

'But then . . .' Color came back into Lissette's face, dull and red as she slowly rose to her feet. 'Deliberately? Someone did this to him? For what? He hurt no one, ever. Not ever.'

'Ms Foster, we believe ricin was added to your husband's drink at some point on the morning he died.'

'But *I* made the drink. I made it.' She rushed over to the little kitchen area. 'Here, right here. Every morning I make his lunch because it pleases him so much. It takes only a few minutes, and it pleases him so much, I . . .'

Cicely murmured in French as she went to her daughter.

'No, no, no. I made it just like every morning. The sandwich, the fruit, the chips he likes. And I made the chocolate like you taught me, *Maman*. He loves it. Right here, right here.' She spread her hands. 'I made the chocolate.'

'Lissy.' Cicely laid her hands on her daughter's damp cheeks. 'Don't do this.'

'Lissette, did you make the drink in a black insulated thermos?'

'Yes, yes.' Lissette leaned against her mother. 'The jumbo sized go-cup. With his name on it. I gave it to him when he started at the school, a little gift, and the black lunch bag.'

'This is what he'd normally carry to school?'

'Every day, yes. Every day. What difference does it make?'

'It's just details,' Eve said easily. 'We're investigating both how and why this was done, so details matter. We'd like to look through your apartment.'

'Why?' Lissette stared down at her hands. 'Why would anyone hurt Craig?'

'I don't have answers for you at this time.'

'You want to look through our things because it will help you find the answers?'

'Yes.'

'Look at anything, at everything. He has more at the school. On his computer there, in his desk there. Do whatever you need to do. I don't want to watch. I don't want to watch while you go through our things. Can we go out?'

'Yes, of course.'

'Maman, we'll go out, and let them . . . Maman, someone killed Craig. Maman.'

Eve stood back as the mother comforted the daughter, as she helped the grieving widow into boots, coat, scarf.

'I'll take her to breakfast,' Cicely told Eve. 'There's a place down the street. We'll be there if you need us.'

'Thank you.' Eve waited until the door shut behind them. 'Took the same cup every day.'

'Fits his MO.' Peabody said. 'Routine.'

'Yeah, so he not only habitually drank the same thing every day, but out of the same thermos. Used that same thermos for over a year. Maybe, for efficiency's sake, the killer bought a dupe, just switched the cups.'

'We can run the make and model, retail outlets.'

'Yeah, we can. Let's do the room first. Let's go to work, Peabody.'

5

There was nothing in the apartment that spoke of murder. No poisons hidden away in secret compartments, no threatening correspondence or incriminating photographs.

There was, as far as Eve could see – as far as she could *feel* – only the lives of two everyday people whose marriage had still been shiny and new.

The shared work area held his professional debris, and hers, as well as silly, sexy emails they sent to each other. Signs, Eve thought, of that first rush of love and belonging where nothing was more important or immediate as the two of you. There were 'link transmissions to and from Lissy and her mother, one from Mirri Hallywell who'd talked to both the Fosters – confirming a study date with Craig and chatting with Lissy about a date with someone called Ben.

The night before he died, Craig Foster had outlined the pop quiz he would never spring on his students, and had put nearly an hour into a paper on the economic and social developments of post–Urban Wars.

The screen saver on the comp unit was a wedding portrait – Lissette in flowing white, Craig in formal black, sharing what Eve assumed was their first kiss as husband and wife.

'It's a tough one,' Peabody commented when they were back in their vehicle. 'Looking around that place, everything's new. Everything was just getting started. Now it's done. The good wine glasses – had to be a wedding gift – barely used. Matching towels and shower curtain, dried flowers from her wedding bouquet, the disc of the ceremony and party. It's tough.'

'It's tougher because nothing in there pointed to motive. They don't have money, they don't use illegals, the probability of either of them having an affair at this stage is next to zip. So what was his secret?'

'His secret?'

'People have them. Little pockets they keep to themselves. Things a man wouldn't share with his wife.'

Frowning, Peabody shook her head. 'At their stage, and from the vibe, I don't see them keeping secrets.'

'That's what makes them secret,' Eve muttered, and hunted up parking near the school.

Inside they passed through security, waited to be cleared. She saw a couple of staff members crossing the main hall. Each wore a black armband. 'Let's go over the timing and movements. If the ricin didn't come from home, it came from here.'

Peabody pulled out her memo book. 'Vic signed in at six forty-two. His wife's statement has him leaving the apartment about six-thirty.'

'He walked. Find an apartment close to work so you can walk and save transpo costs. It would take seven, eight minutes to walk it, so it's unlikely he made any stops on the way. Nothing open at that hour on the route. Closest twenty-four/seven is three blocks west.'

Peabody nodded. 'There's a deli a block over, but it doesn't open until seven.'

'Okay. So he puts on his coat, gets his briefcase, his packed lunch, kisses his wife good-bye, and walks to work. Comes in the main, like we did. Goes through security, gets signed in. He's going to work out, so he'd go to his classroom, store his stuff for the day. Coat, gloves, hat, scarf. Briefcase, which contains his last meal.'

She headed that way now, taking the most logical route. 'No one interviewed mentioned seeing or speaking to him before he made it to the fitness area. He goes upstairs first.'

She stopped at the classroom door, uncoded the police seal, entered. 'Puts the briefcase on the desk, stows the lunch in the drawer, hangs up his coat. Efficient guy, orderly guy,' she murmured. 'Wears the workout gear in. Takes his duffle with his school clothes with him down to the fitness area.'

'Affirmative.' Peabody read her notes. 'We've got the duffle with his workout gear in it.'

'Goes down to the main level,' Eve continued as they backtracked. 'Goes down to work out, leaving his classroom – including his go-cup – unattended.'

'Yeah.'

They walked back out, and toward the fitness area.

'According to wit statements, he's already in the gym, on the machines when he's first seen.'

'Reed Williams, approximately seven-ten.'

'What time did Williams sign in?'

'Six forty-five.'

'So what was Williams doing between six forty-five and seven-ten? We'll have another chat with him. Mosebly stated she saw the vic in the pool area as she was leaving it at approximately seven-thirty.'

'Signed in at six-fifty.'

'Bunch of early birds. We'll follow up with her, too. And sooner than later,' Eve added when Mosebly strode toward them.

'Lieutenant, Detective. I was alerted by Security that you were here.' She wore unrelieved black today – skirt, jacket, boots. 'I'd appreciate it if you'd check in with my office when you come to the academy.'

'Thought you might have shut down for the day,' Eve countered. 'Considering.'

'After meeting with our mental health counselors, I decided against it. It's felt the students will benefit more from routine, and being with each other, able to talk openly about their fears and feelings. We had a moment of silence this morning, and are planning a memorial for later this week. Has there been progress?'

'The investigation is ongoing. What did you do before you took a swim yesterday?'

'I'm sorry?'

'You signed in at six-fifty. What did you do?'

'Let me think. So much has happened since . . . I went to my office to check my day planner, and organize for the day. I had an eight o'clock. Why?'

'It's in the details. Did you see anyone? Talk with anyone prior to the swim?'

'Yes, actually. I spoke briefly with Bixley as I came in. He was clearing the steps – the snow? I asked him to be sure to check them periodically during the day. And I saw Laina Sanchez, our chief nutritionist, as she came in right behind me. I made some comment about the weather, I believe. Then I went to my office, spent some time reviewing my day. Took my swim.'

'Did you go through the fitness area?'

'No, I used the staff locker room to change into my suit, then went straight into the pool. What happened to Craig, Lieutenant? Rumors are flying, and it's only more upsetting for all of us not to know.'

'He was poisoned. Can anyone access the fitness area?'

'*Poisoned?*' She took a step back. 'Dear God. Did he eat anything out of Vending? Out of the lounge, the cafeteria? I need to speak with Laina right away.'

'He didn't get it from the school's supplies.'

Relief, instant and full, flashed on Mosebly's face. 'Thank God. It's terrible,' she said quickly. 'Of course, it's terrible that something he brought from home was responsible. But I have to think of the students, the rest of the staff.'

'Sure.'

'So, it was an accident, then. An allergic reaction of some kind.'

'It's homicide,' Eve said flatly, and saw the relief drain away. 'Principal Mosebly, I need to know the whereabouts of everyone who was here that morning before class. And up to the time Foster had his lunch. Can anyone – staff, students – access this area?'

Eve nodded toward the doors for the staff fitness center.

Mosebly's hand fluttered at her heart. 'I have to know what happened. If this was a deliberate act, the students could be at risk—'

'I have no reason to think they are. It was specific. Answer the questions.'

Mosebly pressed her fingers to her temples. 'It's staff only from this side. Key cards are required. The students have their area, which is accessed from the other side of the pool. The staff may use the aquatic area before and after classes when there is no scheduled practice for meets. Swim meets. Oh, my God. Poison.'

'Key card,' Eve said, and gestured to the door.

Mosebly drew one from her pocket, swiped it.

Eve entered. It was a small, efficient area not currently in use. Cross-trainers, weights, mats. Her gym at home was larger and had juicier equipment, but she thought it was a well-designed space. And a nice perk for the staff.

'Foster made regular use of the machines?'

'Nearly every day. The staff is encouraged to use the

facility. Most do, once or twice a week. Some, like Craig, made better use of it.'

Eve nodded, wound her way through the room, out a second set of doors. The locker room was clean and again, efficient. Counters, toilet stalls, three showers on each side, separated by opaque glass. Men's, women's.

'Which of these lockers was his?'

'We're not assigned specific lockers,' Mosebly explained, in the hurried tones of someone who, obviously, wanted to be elsewhere. 'If the light on the keypad is red, it's in use. When green, one simply uses it, locks it with any six number code.'

'I see three here on red.'

'Some use a locker routinely, keep their gear in there for convenience.'

'I'm going to want to see the contents.'

'You can't just open a locker that someone's using.'

'Yes, I can. Peabody?'

'Locker and storage facilities in educational complexes, offices, and public buildings aren't protected under the Privacy Laws,' Peabody stated as Eve drew out her master. 'In the course of a police investigation, a duly authorized member of the NYPSD may access such storage.'

'This is invasive and unnecessary. It's obvious to me that whatever substance caused his death was in something he brought from home.'

Eve leaned on the lockers. 'See, it's not obvious to me. And in matters like this, you can say *I'm* the principal.'

'You can't possibly believe any member of this staff would wish or cause Craig harm.'

'Sure I can.'

The first locker held a pair of women's air sneaks, a cosmetic kit including lip dye, deodorant, hair gel, lash enhancer, several sample-sized tubes of skin-care creams, some fragrance.

'I may be a layperson in this arena,' Mosebly said tightly, 'but it's very clear Craig suffered some tragic allergic reaction to something he ate or drank. And, again, to something he brought from home.'

'Yeah, I'd say that's clear to you because anything else would be really crappy publicity for the school.'

The next locker had the men's version of the first. Shoes, a toiletry case that included a comb, some hair product, skin cream. There was a pair of swim goggles and an underwater headset.

'It's my responsibility to protect the reputation of this academy. I'm going to contact our lawyers immediately.'

'You do that.' Eve moved to the next locker as Mosebly strode out. 'Unlikely candidate for this.'

'I don't know.' Unable to resist, Peabody made a rude and childish face at Mosebly's back. 'She's got a pissy attitude if you ask me.'

'Sure. But if she was going to do Foster, big odds she'd have done it off school property. We'll take a closer look, in case the school loyalty's a facade, but I can't see her wanting to bring scandal to her hallowed halls or a smear to her standing as the principal. Well, well, lookie here.'

The next locker had the requisite shoes, and a very slick faux leather toiletry case. The products inside were more high-end than the others had been. Among them was a generous supply of condoms.

'Funny place to keep those raincoats,' Peabody commented. 'Unless you're planning on getting action in the school locker room.'

'Which I'm just betting is against the rules.' Eve took out a little pill case. 'Looks like Stay-Up to me. Naughty boy. RW,' she added, reading the initials etched on the case. 'Reed Williams is my guess.'

While Peabody went to pull Williams out of class for questioning, Eve continued to follow the course of Craig's morning and walked to the staff lounge.

She passed a couple of young boys who gave her long stares. Silently, they held up passes.

'Do I *look* like a hall monitor?' she demanded.

'We're required to show our passes to adults. Staff and parents,' one told her.

'Do I look like a parent?'

'I dunno.'

'You go wandering around here a lot?'

'We have passes.'

'Yeah, yeah. Answer the question.'

'We're going to the library for research material for our science project.'

'Uh-huh. Were you out of class any time yesterday before noon?'

They slid sideways glances toward each other before the first boy spoke. 'Maybe we were going to the library for research material yesterday, too.'

'We showed Ms Hallywell our passes.'

'When?'

The second one gave a careless shrug. 'Sometime. Are we in trouble?'

'You're going to be if you don't answer the question. In case you're wondering, I don't give a rat's ass if you were sneaking off to drink beer and gamble.' She ignored the delighted snort from the first boy. 'I want to know what time you saw Ms Hallywell, and where you saw her.'

'It was second period, the last half. Um. Ten-thirty or like that. She was coming down Staircase B. Over there. How come you want to know?'

'Because I'm nosy. Where was she going?'

'I dunno. Teachers don't have to tell you. Teachers don't have to tell you, but you have to tell them.'

'Yeah, it's always been like that.'

'If you're not a teacher or staff, and you're not a parent, you're supposed to have a pass.' The first boy gave her a narrow stare.

'Report me. Now get lost.'

They took off at a darting run, shooting glances back over their shoulders. 'Probably building a homemade boomer for their science project,' she muttered, and took out her notes. From ten to eleven, Foster taught his advanced class, utilizing the third-floor media room. 'Interesting.'

She used her master on the lounge door. With classes in session it was unoccupied. In her mind, Eve saw Craig zipping in, grabbing his reward soft drink, post workout, preclass. Chatting vids.

Most, if not all of the staff would have been in the building by then, and certainly the majority of the students. And Foster's thermos sat easily accessed by anyone in his second-floor classroom.

Just as it had while he'd worked out, while he'd taught his advanced class.

What would it have taken? she wondered. A minute? Two? Step in, open the drawer, pour in the poison. Or just switch go-cups. Close it up, walk out again.

A smart killer would have had a backup plan in case anyone had come in. Just leaving a note for Craig. Just needed to check a paper. Easily done if you kept your head.

She turned as Peabody came in with Williams. 'Can't this wait?' he demanded. 'It's a difficult enough day without me having to leave my class with a supervisor droid.'

'Then let's not waste time. Did you leave your classroom at any time between ten and eleven yesterday?'

'Second period, Monday. That's a group study session. Yes, I stepped out for a few minutes.'

'To do what?'

'I used the restroom. I drink a lot of coffee.' To prove it, he moved to the AutoChef, programmed a cup. 'I always step out for a short time during that class.'

'That classroom is on the same level, the same section as Foster's. You see anyone? Anyone see you?'

'Not that I recall.'

'You keep a locker in the fitness center.'

'Some of us do. It's easier than bringing a change of shoes every day.'

'You don't just have shoes in your locker, Reed. In my experience, when a man keeps that many shields close to hand, he has plans for them.'

There was a brief hesitation, then Williams took a slow sip of coffee. 'The last I checked, condoms weren't illegal.'

'But I ask myself, what might Principal Mosebly have to say about such a generous supply of them in your locker? Or the board of directors, the board of – what is it? – education.'

'Again. Condoms aren't illegal.'

'Still. What might they think about one of the staff here scoring booty in the locker room, so close to all those innocent young minds and bodies?'

'Carrying protection is just that – carrying protection.' In a nonchalant move, he leaned back as he drank his coffee. 'You have a weapon strapped on, but as far as I know, you haven't stunned anyone in the building.'

'Early days yet,' Eve said lightly. 'What else I was thinking was how about those innocent minds. Those innocent bodies. Pretty little girls, so easily lured.'

'Well, for Christ's sake.' At this, he set down his coffee quickly, shoved out of his slouch against the counter. 'That's despicable and it's disgusting. I'm not a pedophile. I've been a teacher for fourteen years, and have never touched a student in any way that could be considered inappropriate.'

'By whose scale?' Eve wondered.

'Listen. I don't like girls. I like women. I like women a great deal.'

Eve was more than willing to buy that claim. 'Enough to bang them on school property?'

'I don't have to answer questions like this. Not without a lawyer.'

'Fine, you can call one when we get downtown.'

Shock replaced temper. 'You're *arresting* me?'

'Do you want me to?'

'Listen, listen. Jesus.' He raked his fingers through his hair. 'So I've had a few encounters. It's not a crime, but it is questionable behavior as far as my job is concerned. But those encounters were with consenting adults.'

'Names.'

He tried a little charm with a smile that asked for understanding. 'Lieutenant, this can't possibly have any bearing on why you're here. And a couple of them are married.'

'A couple of them.'

'I like women.' That smile widened. 'I like sex. It doesn't hurt anyone.'

'Craig ever notice you liking sex in the locker room?'

'No.'

He said it too quickly, and Eve saw the lie. 'He was a straight arrow, wasn't he? He comes across you having an encounter, he's going to be shocked. Maybe pissed. He threaten to go to the principal?'

'I had no problem with Craig; he had no problem with me. Ask anyone.'

'I will. We'll talk again.'

'Kind of slimey,' Peabody commented when he'd left.

'Kind of a motive. He was lying about Craig knowing about his locker-room games.'

She wandered as she spoke and brought the layout of the locker room back into her head. Lots and lots of places for nooky, she decided, if you wanted it that way.

'Maybe he can't talk Craig out of reporting it, or just fears he will at some point. Protects himself, his job, his lifestyle. He was out of his classroom while Craig was out of his. Opportunity. Puts him, at the moment, top of my list. Let's take Hallywell.'

'Do you want me to bring her in here?'

'No, let's try this one in her element.'

Bells chimed as they stepped out of the lounge. Immediately kids poured out of classrooms to swarm the corridors, to send the noise level soaring. They looked and sounded, to Eve's mind, the way she imagined locusts did when they swarmed over . . . whatever locusts swarmed over.

'Or like ants,' Eve thought, 'scrambling out of their hill.'

Out of self-preservation, Eve would have ducked back in the lounge until the deluge passed, but one of the kids aimed straight for her.

'Lieutenant Dallas. Excuse me, please.'

Little blonde, Eve thought, sharp eyes. 'Rayleen.'

'Yes, ma'am. Was Mr Foster murdered?'

'Why do you say that?'

'Because I looked you up on the computer, and that's what you do. You investigate murders. You've done a lot of them. My father said you would have been here yesterday because it was a suspicious death. But that can mean accident, natural causes or self-termination, too. Is that right?'

'Yeah, that'd be right.'

'But you're here again today, and asking questions again today, and everyone's talking about what maybe happened.'

Rayleen pushed at her long curls, held back today with a pair of white barrettes in the shape of unicorns. 'A lot of people are asking me because I was the one who found him. I don't want to tell them what isn't true. So was Mr Foster murdered?'

'We're looking into it.'

'I don't see how he could have been because he was too nice, and because this is a very safe school. Did you know it's considered one of the top schools not only in the city, but in the state of New York?'

'Imagine that.'

'I'm the top of my class here.' With another of those prissy smiles that made Eve want to twist the pert little nose out of joint, Rayleen tapped a finger on the gold star she wore on her lapel.

'Whoopee.' Eve started to skirt around Rayleen, but the girl danced backward.

'But if Mr Foster *was* murdered, my mother's going to be even more upset. I'm her only child, you see, and she worries about me. She didn't want me to come to school today.'

'But you're here.'

'We had a discussion. My parents and I. I have perfect attendance, and that's factored into my overall rating. I didn't want to miss class. Melodie didn't come though. My mother talked to hers, and Melodie had bad dreams last night. I didn't, or I don't remember. I liked Mr Foster, and I wrote how much I'm going to miss him in my diary. I wish he didn't have to die.'

'It's rough.'

Rayleen gave a wise and soulful nod. 'Maybe I could help. Maybe I'll remember something that will help. Or I'll hear something or see something. I'm very smart, and very observant.'

'I bet. You leave it to us.'

'I don't know what's going to happen now.' Her violet eyes glimmered with tears. 'No one tells us. I worked hard on the project for Mr Foster, and now I don't know if I should finish it. I have to go to class now.'

'Tough being a kid,' Peabody observed as Rayleen walked off with her head down. 'Tough when you have something like this spoil the innocence you only have for a handful of years anyway. She's never going to forget walking into that classroom and finding him.'

'Murder doesn't leave anyone innocent. It shouldn't. Let's track down Hallywell. Hit Dawson, too.'

They learned Ms Hallywell hadn't come in for classes, but found Dawson in the chem lab, instructing the students on a project. When he spotted Eve at the doorway, he told his students to begin, then stepped out.

'Do you need me? I can only take a few minutes.' He angled himself so he could see through the half-opened doorway, to what his students were up to. 'They're doing a simple test to identify an unknown substance, but I'll need to keep my eye on them.'

'Unknowns such as what?'

'Oh, sugar, salt, cornstarch, baking powder.'

'Why not just taste it?'

'Well. Ha-ha. That would be cheating.' He sobered, eased the door closed a little farther. 'Is it true about Craig? He was poisoned?'

'Word travels.'

'At light speed. Arnette's admin overheard her talking on the 'link to the school's legal counsel. Then saw Dave, told him, who ran into me, and so on. I can't believe it.'

'Do you know what ricin is?'

'Ricin?' His eyes widened. 'Yes, yes, of course. But . . . but Craig, how could he have been poisoned by ricin?'

100

'That's what we're going to find out. Do you know how to make it? Ricin?'

'I . . . not precisely,' he said after a moment. 'But I can look it up if you'd like me to. It should only take me a minute.'

'That's okay.' She peered around him, studied the equipment. 'Could you make it in there?'

'Ah . . .' He pursed his lips. 'I could probably manage it, between the equipment here and what I could requisition or jury-rig. You want me to make ricin, Lieutenant? I'd have to get permission,' he said with apology. 'No toxics are permitted in the labs, or anywhere on school property for that matter. But if it would help, I'm sure—'

'No, but thanks. So . . . how often does one of the kids sneak in and manage to build a stink or smoke bomb?'

He smiled, and he reminded Eve of an amused monk. 'Oh, at least once a term. I'd be a little disappointed if they didn't. If children don't push the edges now and again, what's the point of being a child?'

For now, Eve checked Dawson off the list and drove to Mirri Hallywell's apartment. It was a few blocks from the Fosters', and she didn't answer the door.

'We'll try her 'link numbers,' Eve said as they started back down again. 'I think we'll take this out of the school, at least for now. Further interviews at the subjects' residences. We'll take it home to them. We're going to go through the female staff's data, cull out the more attractive. Odds are we'll find one or more who'll admit to dancing in the gym with Williams.'

Even as she reached the outside door, it opened, letting in a blast of cold air, Mirri Hallywell, and a thin reed of a man.

'Excuse me. Oh. Oh. Lieutenant Dallas. Were you looking for me?'

'That's right.'

'I was . . . we were . . . We went to see Lissy. This is Ben. Ben Vinnemere. We went to see Lissy, and she told us you said Craig had been murdered.'

'Mirri, why don't we go upstairs? We can talk upstairs. You should sit down.' Ben turned his brown eyes on Eve. 'We're all a little shaky. Is it all right if you talk to us upstairs?'

'That's fine.'

'We couldn't stay.' Leaning against Ben, Mirri started up the first flight of stairs. 'It seemed intrusive. She has her mother there, and that's best. I don't know what to do for her. Do you think we should go back?'

'Not today,' Ben replied. 'We'll do whatever we can to help her tomorrow. She needs today. So do you.'

When they reached her door, he took Mirri's key, opened it himself. 'I'm going to make some tea. You sit, and I'll make some tea. Lieutenant?'

'I'll pass.'

When he gave Peabody an inquiring look she nodded. 'Tea would be great. It's Peabody. Detective Peabody.'

'I feel numb,' Mirri stated. 'In my chest, and the back of my skull. She said he'd been poisoned. Ricin. Ben knew what that was.'

'I'm a copy editor for *The Times*,' he explained as he got out cups from a cupboard in the kitchen alcove. 'I know all sorts of things.'

'He explained, but I don't see how . . . I can't see why.'

'Where were you yesterday morning between ten and eleven?'

'Me?' Still wearing her coat, Mirri dropped into a chair. 'Ten? Drama Club meeting. We're working on the spring play.'

'The entire hour.'

'Yes. Well, I had to go down, check with Home Science. They're designing some of the costumes as part of their grade this term. I'd forgotten to take the disc of designs when I'd been in there the day before.'

'You signed in just after eight yesterday. Your first class isn't until nine.'

'I tutor some students on Mondays and Thursdays. Eight to eight forty-five. I was late, actually. I don't understand why . . .' Suddenly realization and shock rippled over her face. 'Oh, yes, I do. Ben.'

'They have to ask, Mirri.' His voice was calming as he came back with her tea, pressed the cup into her hands. 'They have to ask questions, gather information. You want to help, don't you?'

'Yes. Of course. Yes. I've never been questioned by the

police before. Now twice in two days, and knowing what happened to Craig . . .'

'Did you see anyone outside the classroom during that period?'

'Let me think a minute, the whole day's turned into a messy jumble in my head.' She closed her eyes, took a slow sip of the tea. 'Yes. I remember seeing two of the boys going to the library. Preston Jupe and T. J. Horn. They use the "research" ploy a few times every week if they can manage it.'

She opened her eyes again. 'If there was anyone else, it just didn't register. I was thinking about the play, and annoyed with myself for forgetting the disc.'

After giving Peabody her tea, Ben sat on the arm of Mirri's chair, laid a hand gently on her shoulder.

'Are you aware of any friction between Craig and any member of the staff?'

'I'm not. I wasn't. Honestly, I don't think there was any to be aware of.'

'Did you have sexual relations with Reed Williams?'

'No! Oh, God. Absolutely not.' She blushed crimson, right up to her hairline. 'Ben, I never—'

'It's all right. Is that the one Craig called Casanova?'

Mirri winced. 'Yes. He asked me out a couple of times, but I wasn't interested. He's too slick and studied. And besides, it's complicated when you work with someone, so I didn't want to get started down that road.'

'Do you work out, use the school facilities?'

'Not as often as I should.' She blushed again, just a little this time. 'Hardly ever, actually.'

'Did Craig ever discuss Reed William's sexual activities with you?'

'This is very uncomfortable. I guess I mentioned to Lissy, a few months ago, that I was thinking about going out with Reed. I was having a really long dry spell. She said something to Craig about it, because he told me that Reed was involved with someone he shouldn't be involved with, and he thought I should steer clear. I did.'

'Did you always do what Craig advised?'

'It wasn't like that. I trusted his instincts, and they matched my own in this case. To be embarrassingly honest, I was just feeling lonely. I'm not the sort men chase after.'

'Excuse me?' Ben said, and she managed a smile.

'You didn't have to run very fast.'

'Who was Williams involved with?' Eve asked.

'I don't know. I couldn't pry it out of Craig and I gave it a damn good shot. Who doesn't like some gossip? But he was tight-lipped about it. I don't think he even told Lissy, because I asked her. Or if he did, he swore her to secrecy. Reed has a reputation. I think he enjoys having one. Ladies' man. It wasn't what I was looking for.'

'Excuse me?' Ben said again, and this time got a watery laugh out of her.

'Ben.' She sighed it, leaned her head into him. 'Reed's a good teacher, and he's very insightful with the students. But he's not the sort of man I'd trust my heart with.'

Eve wanted thinking time, so closed herself in her office when she got back to Central. She generated a diagram of the school, of the movements of various members of the faculty.

She entertained the notion that perhaps Williams hadn't limited his games to coworkers. While she believed he'd steered clear of the kiddie pool, maybe he'd dipped into the parental area.

Checking the security log, she noted seven parents had signed in the morning in question. She began runs on all of them, and struggled not to think about what Roarke was doing as she worked.

Tried very hard not to think about him sitting down to lunch with an ex-lover.

6

She would be late. In business, Roarke remembered, Maggie had been as timely as a German train. When it was personal, when it was pleasure, she enjoyed keeping a man waiting.

It had been a ploy he'd found amusing once, even foolishly charming. She would, always, come dashing into a restaurant, a club, a party, a half an hour after the appointed time, her face alight with laughter and apology. And her eyes full of the knowledge that they both knew what she was up to.

So he'd told her noon, and made the reservation for 12:30.

He arrived a few minutes early, slid into the corner booth waiting for him. Ordered mineral water. He waved away the wine list. He had no intention of drinking toasts to times gone by.

He scanned the restaurant, thinking it was the sort of place Magdelana had loved – and Eve tolerated. Plush, polished, crowded with people who were willing to pay the tab to see and be seen nibbling on overpriced salads.

His temper was still raw-edged from the argument – if that's what it had been – with Eve that morning. And from the cool disapproval on Summerset's face. He disliked, intensely, being questioned and doubted by the two people he believed knew and understood him best.

Where had that lack of trust come from? That uncharacteristic flash of jealousy in Eve? Be careful, she'd warned him, he thought – and found himself insulted all over again.

So he couldn't be trusted to share a meal in a public place with a woman he hadn't seen in years? It *was* bloody insulting, and the insinuation was intolerable.

And it was damn well something they'd come to terms with in very short order.

Best to put it out of his mind, he told himself. He'd have lunch with the woman who had, he supposed, influenced a portion of his life at one time. And later, he'd deal with the woman who had changed his life.

Magdelana came in as he remembered – in a rush – hair and hips and legs swinging. And with a laugh, she slid into the booth and pecked his cheek. 'I'm criminally late.'

'I only just arrived myself.'

'Oh.' There was a pout, just for an instant, then another laugh. 'You know me too well.' She brushed her hair behind her shoulders before sending him her quick and wicked smile. 'Well enough to remember what I like to drink?'

'Stoli martini, straight up,' he said to the waiter. 'Very dry. Twist of lemon.'

'I'm flattered.'

'I have a good memory.'

'And for you, sir?' the waiter asked.

'I'm fine.'

'I'll be right back with your drink madam.'

When he left, Magdelana lifted Roarke's glass, took a small sip. 'Water?'

'I've afternoon meetings.'

After setting his glass down again, she rubbed her hand over the back of his. 'You always did take work so seriously. But then, it looks good on you. In fact, it looks amazing on you. You were rising fast back in our day, but now?'

She sat back, jeweled eyes sparkling. 'How does it feel, lover, to be Roarke – a man of insane wealth, power, and position?'

'I have what I want, and having that is always satisfying. And you?'

'Between, and restless and unsure. Just out of my second marriage, which is lowering as I gave it a hell of a good try.' She gave him a quick, under the lashes glance. 'I divorced Andre, or he divorced me years ago. We, in the end, divorced each other. It was revoltingly civilized.'

Casually, Roarke sipped water. 'He was a civilized man, as I recall, when we chose him for a mark.'

'You're angry with me? Still?'

'Why would I be?'

'Oh, well, I'd hoped to get some alcohol into my system before I did this. But we'll do it dry.'

She shifted so they were face to face, and her emerald eyes were direct and steady. 'I'm so very sorry for how I ended things, the way I just left you without a word.'

'With the mark.'

'With the mark,' she agreed with a long sigh. 'It seemed more entertaining, and more profitable at the time, to marry him rather than steal from him.'

Watching her, Roarke inclined his head. 'Playing me instead of him.'

'I didn't mean it that way, but yes, that's the way it was at the bottom of it. And I'm sorry.'

'It was a long time ago.'

'All the same.' Again, she laid her hand over his. 'I could use youth and foolishness as excuses, but I won't. It was a terrible thing to do. Selfish and headstrong.' She paused when the waiter brought her drink, poured it from the silver shaker with some ceremony.

'Would you like to hear the specials of the day?'

Another ceremony, Roarke thought. A kind of theater where the dialogue was peppered with sauces and reductions and scents.

She wore the same scent she'd used years before. A signature, perhaps, or a deliberate choice to tease his memory.

She had been young, he thought – not yet twenty. How many selfish and headstrong acts had he committed before the age of twenty? Too many, he could admit, to count.

They'd enjoyed each other once, and he'd cared once. So, he'd take the apology, and let it go.

When they'd ordered, Magdelana sipped her martini, eyes smiling at Roarke over the rim. 'Am I to be forgiven?'

'Let's call it bygones, Maggie. We've put a lot of time and distance between then and now.'

'Nearly twelve years,' she agreed. 'Now here we sit, and you're the married one.'

'I am.'

'And to a cop!' Her laugh bubbled out. 'You always were full of surprises. Does she know about your . . . hobbies?'

'She knows what I was, what I did.' Remembering that, he felt the leading edge of his irritation with Eve dull. A little. 'I no longer indulge in old habits, and haven't for some time.'

'Really?' She started to laugh again, then blinked. 'You're serious? You're out of the game? Completely?'

'That's right.'

'I always thought it was in your blood. I gave it up because it was fun to have Andre's money to spend as I liked, without having to do anything for it other than look good and be charming and witty. I never expected you to retire for any reason, at any time. But I suppose your wife insisted.'

'I was nearly all the way out before I met her. It was a simple matter, and a simple choice to close the door on the rest after we became involved. She never asked.'

'No?' Watching him, Magdelana traced a scarlet nail around the rim of her glass. 'She must be quite a woman.'

'She is, yes. A remarkable woman.'

'She'd have to be. Would I like her?'

For the first time he laughed. 'No. Not a bit.'

'What a thing to say.' She slapped playfully at his arm. 'I'm sure I would. We have you in common to start.'

'You don't.' His gaze was cool and clear. 'I'm not who I was.'

Sipping again, she sat back to study him. 'I suppose none of us are who we were. I liked who you were then. I . . . Well.' She shook her head, set down her drink. 'That was then.'

'And now? What is it you want?'

'To have lunch with an old friend, and make amends. That's a good start, isn't it?' she asked as their salads were served.

'To what, exactly?'

'Well, that hasn't changed at any rate.' Lifting her fork, she shook it at him. 'Your suspicious nature.' When he said nothing, she toyed with her salad. 'I've missed you, and I admit with the changes in my life recently, I've been feeling a bit nostalgic. I had a good run with Georges – my second husband – and I was fond of him – am fond of him, really. Our relationship afforded me quite a bit of the style and freedom I'd gotten used to having with Andre. More, actually. For a while.'

'Style you always had.'

Her lips curved. 'Yes, but I liked not having to work for it. I never enjoyed that end as much as you.'

'Divorce hasn't left you destitute.'

'Hardly. I outlasted the terms of the prenup both times and I'm solid.' She shrugged. 'And at loose ends. I'd planned to contact you, when I worked up the courage. Running into you last night that way . . . I nearly turned around and left again. But you saw me, so I braved it out. How'd I do?'

He gave her an easy smile. 'Smooth as ever.'

'I was hoping to surprise you, but wanted to prepare for it, set the stage. Tell me, does your relationship with your wife afford you any freedom?'

He understood the question and the very open invitation under it. Nor could he misunderstand the hand she'd laid lightly on his thigh.

'I don't equate marriage with prison, but see it as a promise. A maze of them. I take promises very seriously.'

'Still . . .' She touched the tip of her tongue to her top lip. 'If promises aren't flexible, they're more easy to break.'

There was a challenge in her eyes, and the come-on-let's-play laughter along with it. He'd found the combination all but irresistible once. 'Bending them only changes them into something they weren't meant to be in the first place. You should know, Maggie, before you say or do anything that would embarrass you that I'm completely in love with my wife.'

She stared at him for a moment, intensely, as if trying to see the con. Slowly, deliberately, she lifted her hand from his thigh, set it back on the table. 'I assumed you had some angle for aligning yourself with a cop.'

'If you knew her, you'd understand Eve is no one's mark. Regardless, I wouldn't betray her for anything. Or anyone.'

'Well . . .' Then she gave that pretty shrug again, that quick and wicked smile. 'No harm in trying.'

It was best, he decided, to table that area of conversation. 'How long do you plan to be in New York?'

'It depends. You might help me with that.' When he raised a brow, she laughed. 'That's not a proposition, lover. I'd hoped to ask for your advice. Investment advice.'

'I'd think you'd have your own people for that.'

113

'Georges's people – and however civil we are, it's delicate. I have a very nice cushion of disposable income. Unreported assets. I'd as soon not involve Georges's very efficient and by-the-book advisors in my investments. But an old, trusted friend who's considerably skilled in this sort of thing. You're the one who taught me, long ago, the value of . . . cushions. I was thinking real estate, tucking it under a few layers to avoid the tax dogs.'

'Are you looking for additional income, turning a profit or sheltering your cushion?'

'All, if I can manage it.'

'How soft is this cushion?'

She caught her bottom lip between her teeth as her eyes danced. 'About fifteen that's tucked – deeply – away. I was fond of Andre and of Georges, as I said, and enjoyed the lifestyles we shared. But I never expected it to last forever in either case. I juggled a bit here and there along the way. And I have some jewelry that doesn't really suit me. I'd like to turn that liquid. Discreetly.'

'You'd want property in New York?'

'That would be my first choice, unless you've a better suggestion.'

'I'll think about it. I'll be able to give you some options, Maggie, but you'll have to create those layers yourself. I can point you in the right direction, and to the right people. That's all I can do.'

'That would be more than enough.' Her hand touched his arm again, rubbed up and down. 'I appreciate it. I'm staying at Franklin's pied-à-terre for the time being. I'll give you the address, and my contact numbers.'

'Enjoying the benefits of companionship with a wealthy, older man?'

She forked up salad, flashed a grin. 'Wouldn't be the first time.'

Eve located a single plant in New Jersey that processed castor oil. It was worth the trip, she decided, particularly since she felt cooped up in her office.

Along the way, Peabody caught her up with her own investigative results. 'I ran the names of parents or child care providers who signed in yesterday. Shuffled down the list those who had confirmed appointments with faculty members, and those who signed in and out during the times the vic was known to be in his classroom. Leaves us four potentials.'

'Do any of them connect to Foster?'

'Two had kids in his classes this term. I wanted to check, see if either kid had trouble there, academically, or discipline problems. But Principal Mosebly's being pissy about sharing the records.'

'Is she really?' The idea gave Eve something like a warm glow. 'It'll be a pleasure to take her down on that. I'll get a warrant.'

'That's what I like to hear.'

'Of the other two, one got a knock for assault a couple years ago. She went after some guy with a baseball bat at a Little League game. Broke his shoulder.'

'There's team spirit.'

'She got off with community service and anger management, paying his medical bills. The guy sued her,' Peabody added, 'settling out of court for an undisclosed amount. Want me to get more details on that?'

'We'll ask her personally.'

'Hallie Wentz, single, one female child, age eight, Emily. Hallie's a party planner.'

'They pay people to plan parties. I don't get it. If you're bound and determined to have a party, how much of a deal is it to have one?'

'Three words: Mavis's baby shower.'

Eve tried not to squirm. 'That went okay.'

'That went uptown because you had somebody, that would be me, handling the details.'

'And did I pay you?'

Peabody frowned, scratched her jaw. 'I am forced to say: Touché.'

'Nobody should be forced to say *touché*.'

'Feeling better?'

'Than what?' Eve countered as she slipped off the turnpike.

'Than you were this morning.'

'I was just having a thing, mostly in my head.' That's what she'd decided. 'Finished with it now.'

It had been stupid, and embarrassingly *female* to get worked up over some blonde in a red dress. They'd have had lunch by now, she calculated, and he'd be back in his office taking his next meeting to plan global financial domination.

Back to normal. And that was that.

It barely took any effort to put it out of her mind, again, as they badged plant security and waited for clearance. And the manager.

She was a peppy little thing, all of four feet ten in her work boots. She had a wide smile and sparkling eyes that made Eve wonder what she'd consumed during her last break.

'Stella Burgess, nice to meetcha. Something I can help you with?'

New Jersey was as deep as the Hudson in her voice as she beamed welcome and cooperation.

'You process castor beans at this facility.'

'Sure do. We process a variety of agricultural products for nonconsumptive use. Your castor oil's used in some industries as a lubricant. Not so much in the U.S. of A., but we export. It's also used in the preparation of leather goods. We export that, too, and ship directly to certified clients nationally. You want to see the processing operation?'

'Probably not. Do you have accounts for the oil in New York?'

'I sure can check on that for you, Lieutenant. That'd likely be for artisans, craftsman, and like that there, ones who like to use natural products only. You want I should get you a list?'

'Yeah, I want you should. As soon as you tell me why you're handing all that over with a smile.'

''Scuze?'

'You don't ask questions, Stella. You don't do any dance about privacy of accounts. Just sure, here are the names.'

Stella flashed her teeth again. 'Yeah, sure. I got the memo.'

'What memo would that be?'

'From the top dog. It got sent out first of the year. Full cooperation from all managers, department heads, supervisors, and yadda-yadda is expected to be given to Lieutenant Eve Dallas if and when she has occasion to request information or services. Right?'

'Right. I'll need an employee roster, too. Current, and back the last six months.'

'You got it.' Stella pointed her index finger, thumb cocked. 'Give me five, okay?'

'Sure.'

As they waited, Peabody cast her eyes to the ceiling and whistled a tune.

'Shut up, Peabody.'

'I'm just wondering what it's like to be married to a guy who owns so many things you don't know the half of them.' Then she gave Eve an elbow nudge. 'He sent out a memo.'

'It takes the fun out of it. He cut out my intimidation perk.'

'Saves time, though. And it's really considerate. He's always thinking about you.'

'Weird.'

But it was nice to hear it, even though it made her feel only more stupid about how she'd behaved that morning.

She would run cross-references and searches on the lists provided. That she could do back at Central, or at home. For the moment, they'd knock on a few doors. Starting with Hallie Wentz.

Hallie lived in a two-story townhouse, running her business on the street level. Eve would have tagged her as the exact opposite of Stella Burgess. Hallie was tall, slim, wearing fashionable ankle-breakers. Her eyes were cool and suspicious as she studied Eve's badge.

Obviously, she hadn't gotten the memo.

'What's this about? I've got a client coming by in ten minutes. Cops aren't good for business.'

'Craig Foster.'

'Oh.' Hallie blew out a breath, glanced toward a doorway. 'Listen, my kid's in the next room. She's pretty upset about what happened. I really don't want her to have to talk to the cops about this. Not until she feels better.'

'Actually, we're here to talk to you.'

'Me? About Mr Foster? Why?'

'We're talking to everyone who was on school grounds yesterday.'

'Right. Right. Wait a minute.' She walked to the doorway, peeked in, then eased the door nearly closed. 'Studying,' she said to Eve and Peabody. 'Kid's a gem. What do you need to know?'

'We'll start with why you were there.'

'Show and Share Day. Em wanted to take Butch in for it. Our African Grey. Parrot?' she explained. 'He's a big guy. She couldn't handle his cage herself, so I carried it to class for her.'

'You signed in at eight-twenty, didn't sign out until ten forty-two. How far did you have to carry Butch?'

'It's a big school,' Hallie said, coolly again. 'Are you interrogating all the parents?'

'It's not so big it took you better than two hours to deliver a parrot. Did you see or speak with Mr Foster yesterday?'

'No, I didn't.'

'But you've had occasion to see and speak with him in the past.'

'Sure. Em had him last term. He seemed like a good one. She did really well in his class, and he showed a lot of interest in her.'

'Did you have any interest in him?'

Hallie drew a breath. 'I don't hit on Em's teachers, and if I did, I'd go more for the little blonde who runs the Drama department. I'm gay, for God's sake.'

'You have an assault on your record, Ms Wentz.'

'Fuck that.' Temper sparked like flying embers. 'That idiot son of a bitch deserved the broken shoulder, and a hell of a lot more. You know what he called my Em? Lesbo spawn.'

She sucked in another breath, held up a hand until she got herself under control. 'He said that to me, so all I did was warn him to knock it off. But he kept it up, and started calling out things during the game. He called her a dyke. As in you can't hit for crap, you little dyke. It wasn't the first time he'd tossed out ignorant homophobe comments at a

120

game, but they were tossed at me, not shouted out so she could hear. Nobody talks to my kid that way. I'd had enough.'

If the rundown were true, Eve was surprised the woman hadn't aimed for the asshole's skull rather than his shoulder. 'Did Mr Foster have anything inappropriate to say to your daughter?'

'Hell no. He was a decent guy, as far as I know. A good teacher, made his class fun for the kids. Emily liked him, a lot. She's upset and confused over this. I don't want her to be any more upset and confused than she has to be.'

'Then tell us why you were on school grounds for two hours and twenty-two minutes.'

'Jesus. I hung around in the class awhile, talking to some of the kids and Janine – Mrs Linkletter – about Butch. Getting him to talk for them. Then . . . Listen, does this have to go on the record?'

'It depends on what "this" is,' Eve told her.

'It doesn't apply to what happened, so I just want you to say – if you agree it doesn't – it doesn't have to get around.'

'All right.'

'I slipped down into the kitchen. Laina Sanchez, the head nutritionist, moonlights for me. She's not supposed to take outside jobs. I don't want her to get in any trouble.'

'She won't, not over that.'

'We just talked about an event we have coming up next week. A change in menu the client wanted. I had a cup of coffee while I was there. I didn't have a meeting until eleven, and it was only a couple blocks away, so I hung. That's it.'

'Okay. She'll verify that?'

'She will, but listen, don't ask her about it at the school, okay? Mosebly gets wind, she'll come down on Laina.'

'Are you and Laina involved?'

Hallie relaxed enough to grin. 'Not like that. I used to date her sister, a half a million years back. I helped her get the position at Sarah Child when they needed a new nutritionist. She's got a two-year-old kid to feed, and another well on the way. She and her husband need the money I can toss her.'

'We're not looking to jam her up.' Something more here, just a little more, Eve thought. 'Did you see anything or anyone out of the ordinary?'

'I didn't. Classes were just starting when I went down to the kitchen. Second period would have been going on when I left. I'd help if I could. Something bad like this happens around my kid, I want to know who, what, and why. I can't protect her otherwise.'

Maybe protection was an angle, Eve mused, as they traveled the block and a half to the next name on the list.

'She goes after a guy with a bat because he calls her kid names.'

'You'd have done the same,' Peabody pointed out.

'Hard to say as I'm not a lesbian and don't have a kid, but, yeah, the guy sounds like he earned his knocks. What might a parent do to protect? Maybe it wasn't a parent or a teacher Foster had something on, if indeed he had something on anyone. Maybe it was a kid.'

'What can you have on a six- to twelve-year-old?'

'Naive Free-Ager. Kids do all sorts of sticky things. Maybe he caught one of them stealing, cheating on an exam, giving out bj's in the bathroom, dealing illegals.'

'Jeez.'

Eve worked it through. 'Calls the parent in for a little chat, warns that this will have to be reported. The kid will require disciplinary action, counseling, maybe expulsion. One of the top schools in the state, according to Straffo's annoying kid. You don't want your kid kicked out or something dicey going on the record. It can't be reported if Foster's dead.'

'Talk about involved parenting. I've been checking on any parent conferences the vic had on his schedule for the week before the murder.'

'Let's look for repeat conferences. And when we get the warrant, we'll see if any student name recurs with other instructors.'

None of the others on the list were currently at home. They got a sullen teenage girl at one residence who reported that her parents and the little creep – who Eve assumed was her younger brother – were at a basketball game. At another the droid housekeeper informed them that the mother had taken *young miss* to karate practice, and that the father was tied up at a late meeting.

Back at Central, Eve campaigned for her warrant, and did a mental victory dance when she copped it without breaking a sweat. Her only disappointment was that it was too late in the day to catch anyone at school to access the records she wanted.

She started to run her cross-references, stopped. She was already at the end of shift. She could work at home and lure Roarke into it. It would be a kind of peace offering for that morning, she supposed.

They'd have some dinner, and she'd bring him up to date. Since they were his employee and client lists she'd be running, it seemed only fair he had a part of it.

And she missed him, she admitted as she shut down for the day. She missed *them*.

Just as she pushed back from her desk, Peabody poked her head in. 'There's a Magdelana Percell out here, wants to see you.'

The center of Eve's belly sank, then tightened like a fist. 'Did she give you the nature of her business?'

'She said it was personal. I don't remember her from any of the lists we're working on, but—'

'No, she's not on any. Send her back, then go home.'

'Home? But it's only twenty minutes past end of shift. Whatever will I do with this unexpected largess?'

'Report to my home office, oh-eight hundred. We'll catch some of those names before they go wherever the hell they go all day. Then we're at the school. Warrant came through.'

'Score for our team. Dallas? I can hang if you'd rather.'

'No, I don't rather. Send her back.'

It was no big, it was no deal, Eve reminded herself. She'd just see what Percell wanted, then go home. Forget about her.

It wouldn't be the first time she had some ridiculous conversation with one of Roarke's formers. It was unlikely to be the last.

She heard the telltale click of girl shoes on the aging floor, and made herself feel ridiculous by pretending to flip through a hard copy of a report.

When she glanced up, Magdelana was all sultry smiles in a sleek black suit with a silky fur collar.

'Thanks for seeing me,' she began. 'I'm not sure you remember, but we met briefly last night. I'm—'

Eve wasn't going for the smile, and she sure as hell wasn't going for sultry. Her tone was flat. 'I know who you are.'

'Oh, well then,' Magdelana said after a beat. 'What a maze this place is! The hub, I suppose, of New York's law enforcement. And this is your office?' She glanced around, scanning the dented file cabinet, the skinny window, the battered desk. Her perfect eyebrows winged up. 'Not what I expected, really. It is Lieutenant, isn't it?'

'That's right.'

'Hmmm. I hope I'm not interrupting some vital sort of police work.'

'As a matter of fact . . .'

Magdelana blinked those emerald eyes once. 'This is awkward. I was hoping it wouldn't be. I wanted to come here, to see you, to ask if I could buy you a drink when you've finished your work.'

'Why?'

'I suppose I wanted to make it clear I didn't want to cause any trouble.'

Eve leaned back in her chair, swiveled idly. 'Have you killed anyone since entering my jurisdiction?'

'No.' There was a quick, sharp smile. 'Not since then.'

'In that case, we're clear.'

'Eve.' Her voice was smooth, as was her move as she eased a hip onto Eve's desk. 'I only wanted to reassure you that what was between me and Roarke was over long ago. We were practically children when we were involved. You don't have a thing to worry about.'

Eve cocked her head. 'Do I look worried?'

'I don't know you, so how can I say? Roarke did mention I wouldn't like you, and I suppose I'm just contrary enough that I wanted to prove him wrong. So I hoped we could have a drink, and diffuse any potential problems. Especially since he's going to be helping me with some of my affairs.'

'Funny.' And the fist in her belly went slippery and sick. 'You look like the type who can handle her own affairs just fine.'

'Business affairs. We'd both know Roarke has no equal when it comes to financial affairs. Or, let's be honest, *any* sort of affair.' She gave a light laugh. 'But this is strictly business, I promise. After we had lunch today and he agreed to work with me, it suddenly occurred that you might think it was something other than business. After all, he's a gorgeous and alluring man, and he and I were . . .'

'*Were* would be the operative verb.'

'Yes. Absolutely. You see, I caused him pain a long time ago, I don't want to be responsible for that again. If things work out as I hope, I'll have business in New York for some time. I'm hoping we can all be friends.'

She knew bullshit when it was being tossed at her by the shovelful. 'You know, Ms Purcell, I'm at absolute capacity in the friend department. You'll have to apply elsewhere. As for Roarke and his business, that's his deal. As for you, let's get this straight: You don't look stupid, so I don't believe you think you're the first of Roarke's discarded skirts to swing back this way. You don't worry me. In fact, you don't much interest me. So if that's all?'

Slowly, Magdelana slid off the desk. 'The man is just never wrong is he? I don't like you.'

'Aw.'

She moved to the door, then stopped, leaned on the jamb as she looked over at Eve again. 'Just one thing? He didn't discard me. I discarded him. And since you don't look stupid either, you know that makes all the difference.'

Eve listened to the click of those heels. When they'd receded, she leaned back in her chair, closed her eyes as her stomach churned.

Because no, neither she nor Percell were stupid.

7

Fatigue dragged at her when she turned through the gates. Out of the unrelenting noise, the crowds, the quick temper, and vicious pace of the city, she thought, and into Roarke's world.

Exclusive, private, perfect. The long sweeping drive, which curved through the snow-covered grounds where no tromping feet, no impatient traffic had marred that pristine white carpet, led the way to the big stone house with its many windows.

They gleamed with light, warm, and gold.

She'd grown used to it, she thought, to sliding through those iron gates, to seeing the stunning home spread and jut with its towers and turrets, like a fantasy in the dark.

Room after room ranged behind that glass and stone, some practical, some elegant, some fun. All beautiful, all reflecting his vision. What he'd needed to build, to have, to hold.

Not just for the status, the elegance, the privilege – though with Roarke those would play a part – but because he'd needed, very much needed, to make a home.

What had she added to that? she wondered. Some clutter,

an orphaned cat, an office that was undoubtedly plain and lacking in style by his standards.

Hell, by most anyone's.

But she'd learned to fit there, had made a home there with him. Hadn't she? Despite the odds, they had a life there that mattered to both of them.

She wouldn't let some ghost from the past put a blight on that.

She left the car in front, climbed the steps to the grand front doors. Roarke may have built it, but this was her territory now, too, her turf. No one was going to invade it without getting bloody.

She walked in, and Summerset slid out into the foyer, the cat a fat shadow at his heels.

'Let me just say kiss my ass and avoid the rest of the conversation,' she began. 'I've got work.'

'He isn't home yet.'

Her stomach squeezed, just a little as she shrugged out of her coat. 'Thanks for the report.'

'He had to reschedule some meetings in order to take a personal lunch.'

Eve tossed her coat over the newel post and whirled. At least now she had a handy target for the rage that churned with the sickness in her belly. 'Couldn't wait to rub my face in that one. I bet you're just dancing a jig that Maggie's in town. Well, you can—'

'On the contrary,' he interrupted with absolute calm. 'I couldn't be less pleased. I'd like a moment of your time.'

'For what?'

His jaw tightened, and she saw she'd been wrong. There were ripples under the calm.

'I dislike discussing Roarke this way, and you're only making it more difficult. However, my concerns leave me, I feel, little choice in the matter.'

Her mouth was dry now. 'What kind of concerns?'

'Come into the parlor for a moment. There's a fire.'

'Fine, fine.' She stalked in. The fire simmered, red and gold. All the rich fabrics gleamed while the antique wood, so lovingly tended, glowed. And standing in the room, she felt chilled to the bone.

'Will you sit?'

She only shook her head, walked to the window to stare out. 'What do you need to say to me?'

'I'll pour you some wine.'

'No.' She couldn't handle wine with her head beginning to throb. 'Just spill it.'

'She's a dangerous woman, Lieutenant.'

'In what way?'

'She manipulates, she maneuvers. She enjoys the adventure of conflict. And she has power, as truly beautiful women usually do. In her case, it was well honed even a dozen years ago, and I don't imagine it's lost its edge.'

'No,' Eve murmured. 'She's got a punch.'

'And added to it, she has a strong intellect.'

'How long were they together?' When he said nothing, she looked back at him. 'Don't tap dance around this. How long?'

130

'A number of months. Nearly a year.'

She had to turn back to the window because there was a pain now, just under her heart. 'Long time. Why did it end?'

'They had planned a job – weeks of planning.' She may not have wanted wine, but he did. He wanted something to get him through this. 'The mark was a wealthy man with a superb collection of art.'

Summerset moved to a painted cabinet, and taking a decanter poured himself a short whiskey. 'Magdelana's part was to intrigue him, to develop a relationship. He was much older than she, and had a penchant for young, vibrant women. She would access information from the inside, the security, the routine, the placement of the artwork. They decided on a pair of Renoirs. Just the two. Roarke was, even then, not the sort to dip too deeply into one well. The day they were to complete the job – with her and the mark on his yacht – she eloped with the mark.'

'Bird in the hand.'

'Precisely. He had to scrap the job, of course, not being sure the information he had was valid, or that he wasn't being set up. It cost him quite a bit, on several levels.'

'But he didn't go after her, make her pay?' She turned back again. 'He didn't do that because he was more hurt than he was angry. Did he love her?'

'He was infatuated.'

Something twisted in her. 'Worse. That's worse.'

'Agreed.' He sipped. 'He tolerated a great deal from her

during the time they were together. She enjoyed risks, both personal and professional. You've seen her, she has a light. He was attracted to it.'

'She's smart,' Eve managed. 'Educated and smart. I did a run on her.'

'Naturally. Yes, she was a very intelligent young woman.'

'He'd admire that. He'd like that, even over the physical, that would count.'

He hesitated a moment. Summerset had seen her take a hit, on full, right in this very room. But the words he had to say would do more damage. 'She knew art and music, and literature. He'd always been thirsty to know, to experience the things that had been denied to him as a young boy. She had a head for figures, and an appetite for, well, glamour, you could say.'

'And she liked to steal. That would have appealed to him.'

'She enjoyed taking. If he bought her a gift, she'd bubble over it for a time, but much preferred if he'd lifted it. And always, she wanted more, and got more without directly asking. She has a way. She'll want more now.'

'She came by my office before I left.'

'Ah.' He looked down into his glass again, drank more. 'She would, sprinkle a few dark seeds under the guise of smoothing the water.'

'Something like that. She wanted to twist me up, and I knew it. But she got the dig in, she got it done. She said he'd agreed to work with her on some business stuff. If she talked him into doing another job, or even just setting up the groundwork for her – Christ.'

'You can't allow it.'

'I don't *allow* Roarke. No one does.'

'You have influence, use it. She's a blind spot for him, and always was.'

'All I can do is ask him straight out. I can't fight with innuendoes and wiles.' The headache was grinding in her skull, and pain was twisting her gut. 'The first are insulting to both parties, and I don't have any of the second. Not on her level, that's for fucking sure. In the end, it's his choice. It always was. I've got work.'

She started out, stepped, and made herself turn around, meet Summerset's eyes. 'She's a manipulator. I get that. She's also beautiful, polished, sophisticated, smart. Smart enough, I'd bet your skinny ass, to settle happily with what Roarke's got at his fingertips now. Basically, she's just the type I'd think you'd do a happy dance if he flipped me for.'

She had to take a breath so her voice would stay steady. 'She wouldn't track blood into the house, she'd know just what dress to wear to the next dinner party. And she wouldn't forget there *was* a goddamn dinner party because she was standing over a dead body. So, why tell me all this?'

'She would be a sparkling accent on his arm. She speaks flawless French and Italian, and has a limitless supply of charm when she wishes to dispense it. And she'll use him. She'll take, take more. If it was necessary, or if she simply had the whim, she'd toss him to the wolves to see who'd win.'

He finished the whiskey. 'You, Lieutenant, are often crude, you are certainly rude, and have very little sense of how to be the wife – in public – of a man in Roarke's position. And you would do anything, no matter what the personal risk, to keep him from harm. She will never love him. You will never do anything but.'

No, she thought as she walked away, she'd never do anything but. And wasn't it strange she'd forgotten just how much fear and misery love could carry with it?

She'd never felt any of this before she'd met him. Never felt this twisting, this aching, the shaky fear of losing.

And never felt the thrill or the comfort, the stunning happiness that laid so thickly over everything else.

She went straight to her office, programmed a full pot of coffee. Before Roarke, she'd often – most often – bury herself in work. No reason she couldn't do the same now.

More, she had a duty to honor.

A man was dead. A man, by all current evidence, who'd been a nice guy, an ordinary sort of guy who had actually had something to give to society.

She had no evidence, no reason to believe he'd hurt anyone, had wished harm on anyone. Hadn't performed salacious acts, used or trafficked in illegal substances.

Hadn't stolen anything, extorted anyone. Hadn't cheated on his wife.

Having lunch wasn't cheating, she thought as she carted her coffee to her desk. Banging another woman like a steel drum a dozen years before marriage wasn't cheating.

Roarke wouldn't cheat on her. She could rest easy on that point.

But would he want to? That was the sticker.

And that had nothing to do with Craig Foster.

She sat, braced her elbows on the table, and rested her head in her hands. She just had to clear her mind, that was all. Clear it out. Should probably take a blocker for the goddamn stupid headache pounding inside her skull.

Annoyed, she yanked open the top drawer, knowing Roarke had left a case in there with the little blue pills inside. She hated taking pills, but she'd never be able to think unless she popped one.

She swallowed the blocker, chased it with coffee as Galahad jogged in to get a running start for the leap to her desk. He plopped his ass down and stared at her.

'I've got to work.' But it was an odd comfort to run her hand over his head and have him stretch under the stroke. 'I've got to be able to work or I'll go crazy.'

Shifting, she inserted the data discs she wanted to run first.

'Computer, cross-reference both employee and client list, disc A with student guardians, administration, faculty, and support staff lists, disc B. Report any matches.'

Acknowledged. Working . . .

'Secondary task, standard data run on all names on disc C, include criminal, financial, employment, marital, education.'

Acknowledged. Working . . .

Maybe something would pop on one of the parents or child care providers who'd been in the building that morning.

'Subsequent task, display data on faculty, administration, and support staff of Sarah Child Academy, in alpha order, on wall screen one.'

Acknowledged. Data displayed on wall screen one . . . Primary task complete. No matches . . .

'Yeah, that would've been too easy. Using the same lists, cross-reference search for family relations, former spouses or cohabs.'

Acknowledged. Working . . . Secondary task is now complete. Choice of display?

'Display on comp screen.' Sitting back with her coffee, she studied the data.

There was nothing hot. A couple of hand slaps here and there – the ever-popular illegals possession for personal use, a four-year-old shoplifting charge. No violent crimes, no cage time for any.

Before she began on the data on her wall screen, she closed her eyes and let her mind wind back through what she knew, what she wanted to know.

Poison in the hot chocolate. Thermos unattended and accessible at several points during the morning. Habitual.

'Wait.'

She sat up, eyes narrowed, then tried another angle. She contacted Lissette Foster. 'Lieutenant Dallas,' she said. 'I'm sorry to disturb you. I have a couple of questions. You made the hot chocolate yourself, every morning.'

'Yes, I told you. I made it for him.'

'You ever drink it?'

'No. Too many calories,' she said wearily. 'I used some real chocolate along with the soy milk and the powdered mix. He didn't know.'

'Sorry?'

'Chocolate's so expensive. He didn't know I bought it, added it in like my mother always did. He liked it so much, said no one made it like I did. It was the half ounce of real chocolate I mixed in every morning.'

'Anyone else know about that addition?'

'My mother. She taught me how to make it. I mentioned it at work, I'm sure. Sort of bragging about it. I think I might have told Mirri. It was just a little secret from Craig. He wouldn't have wanted me to spend the money on him.'

'I noticed the mix in your kitchen, and the stash of liquid chocolate inside a box of Vital Fem.'

Now Lissette smiled, just a little. 'He'd never poke around in my vitamins, so I kept the chocolate there.'

'We sent the mix and the liquid to the lab. Anyone else know where you kept them?'

'The mix, maybe. Not the chocolate. You think . . .'

'The lab will determine if any of the ingredients were tampered with. Was anyone in your apartment the weekend before your husband's death?'

'No.' She rubbed her eyes wearily. 'I don't think so. I was out for a while on Saturday, shopping. But Craig was home. He didn't mention it.'

'Does anyone have a key, a spare? Your code.'

'Mirri does, for emergencies. But—'

'Okay. Your building doesn't have security cameras or a doorman.'

'We couldn't afford one that ran to those. It's a nice neighborhood. We never had any trouble.'

'All right, Mrs Foster. I appreciate the time.'

So here's a what if, Eve mused. What if person or persons unknown accessed the Foster apartment, knowing the habits. Poisoned the powder. Maybe Craig had a visitor he hadn't told his wife about.

Or . . . Maybe it didn't have to be the day before, she thought. Maybe he'd lucked out a few times, hadn't gotten any of – or not enough of the poison.

She pulled up her lab report, read off the contents of the go-cup. There was no real chocolate listed.

So the killer hadn't known about Lissette's secret recipe.

Considering, she rose and walked to her murder board. She studied her victim, the shots of the scene. Tapped her fingers on her thigh as she studied the thermos.

Nothing special about it, she decided. Just your average

go-cup, jumbo size. About fifty bucks. Solid black, with the vic's first name scripted in silver across the body. Looked new.

Used it every day, every working day for over a year. Why did it look brand-new?

Maybe it was new. She'd already speculated on that one, and now she was stepping over her own feet. Damn it.

'Faster,' she murmured. 'Simpler. For fifty bucks, you could switch the good stuff with the bad in three seconds. You don't have to pour out the original chocolate, pour in the killing drink. You just take the whole damn thing, shove the good in your briefcase or pack, leave the bad.'

Smarter, she thought. Not as messy.

She pulled out the sweeper's report, already knowing she wouldn't have missed such a vital listing if a second engraved thermos had been found in the building.

'Computer, run probabilities on the following options as pertains to case number HP-33091-D. Poison was added to vic's go-cup on the morning of his death. Option next, vic's go-cup was switched with an identical one containing the poison, again on the morning of his death. Which option has the highest probability?'

Acknowledged. Working . . .

Eve added more coffee to her mug, paced around the board. Sat back at her desk.

```
Probabilities on both options have no viable
difference with current data . . .
```

'Big help.' And it would matter, she decided. It would matter just how.

With the absence of the real chocolate in the poisoned drink, the theory of the mix being tampered with inside the Foster apartment was out of the running.

Adding it on the spot was easier, more efficient. Still a risk factor involved.

But just replacing the whole shot, now that was smart, most efficient, most foolproof.

They'd do a more thorough search of the school the next day. But if she were to bet, she'd lay her money on the killer taking Craig's cup as a souvenir. Or certainly disposing of it well off school grounds.

She called up the physical description of the cup, started a search for retailers in the city and online who sold that specific brand and model, with personalization option.

There were more than twenty retail stores in Manhattan alone offering that specific item, and three times that through online vendors.

But it was a break, she thought. Whether or not the cup itself played, she knew the drink had been made by the killer. Someone who didn't know Lissette's secret ingredient.

She was reaching for her coffee again when she saw Roarke in the doorway.

'Lieutenant.'

'Hey.'

They watched each other, warily, as he came into the room. 'I'd hoped not to be this late.'

'Happens.'

```
Cross-referencing task complete. No matches
found.
```

'Sometimes the world's not as small as you want it to be,' she commented and picked up her coffee.

'Long day for you.'

'Back at you.'

He sat on the corner of her desk, his gaze level with hers. 'Are we at odds here, Eve?'

She hated, *hated,* that she just wanted to lay her head down on the desk and weep. 'I don't know what we are.'

He reached out, skimmed his fingertips over her hair. 'You pushed some button on me this morning. Irritated the hell right out of me. Don't you trust me then?'

'Do you think I'd be sitting here if I didn't?'

'That being the case, there should be no problem between us.'

'Nothing's that simple.'

'I love you, absolutely. Nothing's simple about it, but it's complete. You never kissed me good-bye this morning.' He leaned down, brushed his lips over hers.

141

She couldn't help it, the love simply welled up. 'Bye,' she murmured, and made him smile.

He brushed her lips again, warm and sweet. 'Hello. I'll wager you haven't had any dinner.'

'I'm spinning my wheels on this investigation. Haven't thought much about food.'

'Think about it now.' He took her hand, linked their fingers, and used the other to scratch the cat when Galahad bumped his head against Roarke's arm. 'You're looking tired, Lieutenant, and hollow-eyed the way you do when you haven't eaten or gotten enough sleep. I'll punch in burgers, that usually tempts you. And you can tell me about the case.'

He didn't want to discuss the morning, she thought, or his meeting with Magdelana. He was nudging it all aside, very smoothly. But it had to be discussed. Had to be front and center.

'She came to my office.'

Nothing changed on his face, not by the smallest flicker. It was hardly a wonder he was lethal in business negotiations.

'Magdelana?'

'No, the Queen of the May.'

'A bit early for her. Does she work anything like the February groundhog?'

'Gee, that's funny. But to get back to the topic. She came to see me at the end of shift. Thought we could have a nice, chatty drink, be pals. Guess what my answer was?'

He pushed off the desk. 'I'm sorry if it upset you,' he said as he moved to a wall panel, opened it to take out a bottle of brandy. 'She's outgoing, impulsive. I imagine she was curious about you.'

'Is that what you imagine?' She felt the anger warring with something inside her, something she recognized as acute distress. 'Even after you told her she wouldn't like me.'

He glanced at Eve, poured the brandy, replaced the bottle. 'No more than you would her. Very likely she intended to make the gesture and prove me wrong.'

Blind spot, Summerset had told her. 'I think that was pretty low on her list of intentions. You're going to work with her?'

This time irritation escaped control just long enough to show. 'I'm not, no.'

'Then she's a liar?'

'If she said I was, she misspoke, or you misconstrued.'

'*I* misconstrued?'

'Christ Jesus.' He knocked back some brandy. 'You're trying to box me into a corner here, and there's none to be had. We had a perfectly innocent lunch, at which time she asked for my help with some investments she wants to make. I agreed to give her some direction, and some names of people she might work with. It's nothing I haven't done for other people countless times before.'

'She's not other people.'

'Bollocks to this.' And there was the temper, rich and ripe.

'Did you expect I would say, "Sorry, can't give you the names of a few money people as my wife doesn't like the fact we shagged a dozen bloody years ago?" This isn't like you, Eve.'

'I can't say, as I haven't been in this position before.'

'What position, exactly?'

'Having a woman you have feelings for thrown in my face. Knowing she meant for me to feel exactly that.'

'As I'm not a bleeding droid I've had feelings for other women before I met you, and you've run into a few of them. As for Magdelana, why would she want to antagonize you?' he demanded. 'She'd have nothing to gain. You're over-reacting, and making a situation out of something that happened years before I knew you existed. Do you need reassurance from me? Promises, pledges? After all we've come to be to each other?'

'How it is she's made all the moves, and I'm in the wrong here? You don't see her.'

'I see you. I see my wife twisting herself into a jealous knot over something long past.'

He set the brandy aside again, ordered himself to be calm. 'Eve, I can't go back and change what I was, what was done all those years ago. I wouldn't if I could. Why would I? If I took a step then, it somehow brought me here. To you.'

That wasn't the point, she thought. Or was it? But every-thing that wanted to come out of her mouth sounded, even in her head, like the whining of a needy woman. 'Can you tell me she doesn't want to pick up where you left off?'

'If she did, or does for that matter, she'll be disappointed. Eve, you and I didn't come to each other as children, or as innocents. If either of us wind ourselves up over relationships that came and went before our own, we'll forever be in knots.'

'Excuse me?' She pushed to her feet. 'You beat the hell out of Webster right in this room.'

'He had his hands on you, in our *home*. That's bloody different.' The words lashed out, hot-tipped and razor sharp. 'And never did I think you invited it, encouraged it, or would have tolerated it. You and I went round, Lieutenant, because you threatened to stun me. What in fucking hell do you want?'

'I guess to know what in fucking hell she wants. Is she planning a job? Does she want you—'

'If she is, it wasn't mentioned to me. In fact, quite the opposite. And if she is, it would be no business of mine. Is that how you see me? So spineless that I'd slip back not only over the line, but into another woman's bed?'

'No.'

'Whatever she might want, Eve, she'll get no more from me than what I agreed to give. Some basic investment options. Should I have my admin write that up in the form of a contract for you?'

Her throat burned, the headache was back, and she'd accomplished nothing but pissing him off while putting Magdelana squarely between them. 'I hate this. I hate feeling this way, acting this way. I hate that we're standing here arguing about her. Putting her in the center of it.'

'Then stop.' He moved to her then. He laid his hands on her shoulders, ran them up and down her arms before drawing her against him. 'If we're to argue, at least let's argue about something real. Not this. You're not just the center of my world, Eve.' He kissed her brow, her temples, her lips. 'You're the whole of it.'

She flung her arms around him, held hard. He'd answered, she told herself. Put it away, put it aside. 'It's your fault I love you like this.' For a moment, she pressed her face to his shoulder. 'That I'm stupid with it.'

'Of course it is.' He brushed a hand over her hair, laid his cheek against it. And felt his own insides relax again. 'We'll feel stupid together. Better now?'

Better, she thought. But it wasn't over. She was afraid enough of what might happen next that she told herself, again, to let it go. Just let it go. 'Good enough.'

Telling herself to change the tone, she eased back. 'Burgess in New Jersey was very cooperative.'

'I'm delighted to hear it.' He traced a fingertip down the slight dent in her chin. 'Who is Burgess and why is he being cooperative in New Jersey?'

'She. She manages your plant there, and got your memo.'

'My . . . ah. I sent one out to various holdings right after the first of the year. Came in handy today, did it?'

'Cut through the crap. Just fyi, I don't really mind cutting through the crap myself, but thanks. You process castor beans.'

'I'm sure I do.'

'Ricin, the poison that killed Foster, comes from the mash after the beans are processed into oil.'

His eyes narrowed. 'Is the plant connected?'

'So far, I can't find a connection between anyone on my suspect list and the plant. Would've been nice and tidy. I don't have a motive either, or not a clear one. It's possible Foster saw, at some time, one of the other teachers diddling someone inappropriate during school hours. Murder's a pretty harsh reaction to being caught with your pants down.'

'Perhaps Foster was blackmailing the diddler, or the diddlee.'

'No evidence of it, and it veers out of his characteristic orbit. I haven't found a single person he wasn't on good terms with, including the infamous diddler. Waiting for lab reports, and I'm taking a look at every member of the faculty, support staff, and administration. Along with parents of students. I got no buzz on this one, nothing that feels hot.'

'Why don't I take a look at some of it. Fresh eyes, new view.'

'Couldn't hurt.'

He'd forgotten to nag her to eat some dinner, she thought as he sat to look over her data. Slipped his mind, she decided. Probably for the best. She didn't have much of an appetite.

When she slept, she slept in patches, and the patches were full of dreams. The dreams were conversations, mixed and jumbled from her arguments with Roarke, her interviews, her interlude with Percell. With the voices tangling inside her head, she awoke exhausted.

But he was there where he was in the mornings, drinking coffee in the sitting area of the bedroom, financials scrolling on the screen, the sound muted.

Eve dragged herself to the shower and tried to flood out the fatigue with the jets on full and hot.

When she came back into the bedroom, he'd switched to the morning news. She headed straight for the coffee.

'You didn't rest well,' he said with a long look at her face.

'Case is bugging me.'

'Wish I could've been more help.'

She shrugged, carried the coffee to the closet. 'Maybe something will loosen up today.'

'There's a change of clothes in the bag there, for your spot tonight with Nadine.'

She frowned at the hanging bag. 'Why do I need to change?'

'Consider it a precaution in the event you have a normal day and end up with blood on you, or tear your pants while tackling a suspect after a mad foot chase.'

'The way things are going, I'll spend most of today buried in paperwork and getting nowhere.'

'In that unhappy event – no, not that jacket.'

'What's wrong with it?' Though she scowled in irritation, a part of her was so happy with his comment – the normalcy of it – she wanted to grin like an idiot.

'It's not particularly screen-friendly.'

'Neither am I.'

'True enough. However . . .' He rose, wandered to her closet.

'I don't need you to pick out my clothes.'

'Oh, darling Eve, you so absolutely do.' He pulled out a jacket in bronze tones she swore she'd never seen before, paired it with deep brown trousers, a cream-colored turtleneck.

'Be wild and crazy,' he added as he draped the pieces over the back of the sofa. 'Wear some earrings. Small gold hoops, perhaps.'

When she started to snarl, he caught her face in his hands and kissed her – long, slow, and deep. 'I love that mouth,' he murmured, 'especially when it's about to be sarcastic. How do you feel about bacon and eggs.'

'More enthusiastic than I feel about small gold hoops hanging from my earlobes.'

But she found a pair, dressed, pleased that he'd poked at her about her clothes.

And just as she was about to sit down with him, as the cat leaped on the arm of the sofa to eye the bacon, Roarke's pocket 'link beeped.

She knew the minute he pulled it out to check the display. 'Take it,' Eve said even as he started to slide the 'link back in his pocket. 'I guess she's an early riser.'

'I switched her to voicemail. Let's eat before this gets cold.'

149

'Take it,' Eve repeated. 'Peabody'll be here any minute anyway. I'll see you later.'

'Damn it, Eve.'

'Later,' she said again, and kept walking.

8

'Nice threads,' Peabody commented, coming in as Eve was coming down. 'Roarke, right?'

'Who else? Since obviously if left to my own devices I'd commit such fashion felonies as would frighten small children and embarrass multitudes.'

'Misdemeanors, anyway. We're not going up to your office? Your AutoChef?'

'No.' Eve yanked on her coat as Summerset stood silently by. 'Everybody's getting a goddamn early start today. My vehicle better be where I left it,' she snapped at him. 'Or I'm getting it myself, dragging you out, and running you over with it.'

'What you call a vehicle is outside, currently embarrassing the house.'

'Peabody.' Eve gestured for the door. Eve waited until Peabody went outside. 'I want to know if she comes here. I want to know if she comes into this house. You got that?'

'Yes.'

She marched out into the cold, hatless, gloveless, then slid behind the wheel. 'First address.'

Peabody gave it to her, then cleared her throat. 'Rough night?'

'Life's full of rough nights.'

'Look, if you want to talk about it or just spew, that's what partners are for.'

'There's a woman.'

'No possible way.'

It was said so quickly, and with such easy confidence Eve would have been comforted under any other circumstances. 'There's a woman,' she repeated. 'One he used to be involved with a long time ago. Seriously involved. She's back, and she's making moves. He doesn't see them as moves. He doesn't see what she is under the gloss. We've got a problem.'

'You're sure—' It only took one look from Eve for Peabody to blow out a breath. 'Okay, you're sure. First I'm going to say he wouldn't twist on you, not with anyone. But having some bitch put moves on him is a steamer. You want to go have a talk with her, put a little muscle into it. We can tune her up, put her ass on a shuttle for Siberia.'

'Sounds good.' She stopped at a light, scrubbed her hands over her face. 'Can't do it, can't touch her, can't beat her to death with a hammer and bury her in White Plains.'

'Bloomfield would be better than White Plains anyway.'

It got a weak laugh. 'I don't know how to do this, how hard to push him, how far to stand back. I don't know the steps and strategy. I think I've already screwed up.'

'Dallas? I think you should tell him this hurts you.'

'I've never had to tell him something like that before. He sees stuff in me before I have to.' She shook her head. 'It's fucking me up. It's fucking us up. And I've got to put it away and do my job.'

She ran down her conversation with Lissette Foster, and the deletion of the key ingredient in the contents of the go-cup.

'So it indicates that the poison was added to the drink prior to coming into the school, and most likely in a dupe vessel.'

'Well . . .' Peabody juggled it in her head. 'Poison's a method females opt for more often than males.'

'Statistically, yeah.'

'According to Lissette, Mirri Hallywell knew about the key ingredient. What if, knowing we'd cop to the recipe, she deliberately left it out. Lissette would end up being her alibi.'

'Convoluted,' Eve mused. 'But not impossible.'

'Or Lissette could have left it out deliberately, same reason. And yeah,' Peabody said before Eve could comment, 'it doesn't bounce very well.'

'If you don't toss the ball, it never bounces. We'll keep the possibilities in the mix.'

Eve angled toward the curb, and when she got out it did her spirits good to see the disdain in the doorman's eagle eyes.

'Can't leave that heap there, lady.'

'Hey, you know how many sexual favors my partner here had to promise to score that ride?'

'You were supposed to perform them,' Peabody reminded her.

'Maybe I'll get around to that. Meanwhile . . .' She pulled out her badge. 'You're going to watch over that heap like it was an XR-5000, fresh off the showroom floor. And you're going to buzz up and tell – who are we seeing here, Peabody?'

'The Fergusons.'

'You're going to tell the Fergusons that we've come to chat.'

'Mr Ferguson's already left the building this morning. Breakfast meeting. Mrs Ferguson's still inside.'

'Then get hopping.'

He looked none too pleased, but rang the apartment and cleared them inside.

Into chaos.

Eileen Ferguson had a child of indeterminate age on her hip. He had some sort of pink goo circling his mouth and was wearing footed pajamas decorated with grinning dinosaurs.

Eve figured if dinosaurs grinned it was because dinner was about to be served. So why did adults decorate their offspring with carnivores? She'd never get it.

In the background came screams and barks and whoops that may have been glee or terror. Eileen herself wore a rust-colored sweater, loose black pants, and fuzzy slippers the color of cotton candy. Her brown hair was slicked back in a long tail and her eyes, a quiet hazel, seemed eerily calm given the noise level.

Eve wondered if she'd toked before answering the door.

'This must be about Craig Foster. Come in at your own risk.' She stepped back. 'Martin Edward Ferguson, Dillon Wyatt Hadley.' She didn't shout, but her voice, perfectly pleasant, carried. 'Settle down right now, or I'll dismantle that dog and shove the parts into the recycler. Sorry, coffee?' she said to Eve and Peabody.

'Ah, no.'

'Dog's a droid-terrier mix. I had a moment of complete insanity and bought it for Martin for his birthday. And now, we pay the price.'

But Eve noted that the noise level had dropped. Perhaps, at one time or another, other items had found their way into Eileen's recycler.

'Have a seat. I'll just put Annie in her chair.'

The chair was a round and colorful deal with dozens of bright buttons and rolling things to entertain curious fingers. It beeped and it buzzed and let out what Eve thought was a fairly creepy chuckle. But Annie was immediately engaged.

'Word is that Mr Foster was poisoned.' Eileen dropped into a black scoop chair. 'Is that true?'

'We've determined Mr Foster ingested a poisonous substance, yes.'

'Just tell me, is it safe for me to take these kids to school?'

155

'We have no reason to believe the students are in any danger.'

'Thank God – on so many levels. I don't want anything to happen to Martin – or any of them. But, sweet Jesus, I don't want to be saddled with four kids all day.'

'Four?' Eve repeated, and felt an immediate flood of fear and sympathy. 'Only Martin Ferguson is listed as your child on school records.'

'I've got kid duty this week.'

'Which is?'

'I take the group – that's Martin, and Dillon from upstairs, Callie Yost, she'll be here in a minute, and Macy Pink. We pick her up on the way; she lives a block down. Haul them to school, pick them up at the end of the day. In case of school cancellation or the enormous number of school holidays, I deal with them. We cycle – every week one of the parents has kid duty.'

'You signed in the day Mr Foster died at shortly after eight and were there for forty minutes.'

'Yeah, got them in early, dumped them in Early Care, then I had to take the dozen cupcakes to the nutrition center for clearance.'

'Do parents or students routinely bring in outside food?'

'Not without much to-do. It was Martin's birthday, hence the cupcakes. I had preclearance for them. You can't take in outside food for student groups without preclearance. You have to fill out a form,' Eileen explained, 'note down the type of food and all the ingredients in case any of the kids have allergies or conditions, or cultural restrictions – parental restrictions.'

Eileen paused and began to take tiny clothes out of a basket and fold them into tinier shapes. 'Pain in the butt from my view, but the rules are fairly strict. The principal and the nutritionist have to sign off on it. It's like national security. I got them cleared, paid the fee for the juice I forgot to bring to go with the cupcakes. Then I realized I'd picked up Callie's school bag instead of Annie's diaper bag, and had to go back to Early Care, make the switch. At which time I realized, clued in by *eau de Annie,* that she desperately needed the diaper bag. I dealt with that. I guess it could've taken forty minutes.'

'During that time, who did you see or speak to?'

'Well, Liana – the nutritionist – Lida Krump, early care provider, and her assistant, Mitchell. I saw Principal Mosebly briefly. We passed in the hall as I was leaving and spoke for a minute. How are you, happy birthday to Martin, and so on. I actually saw Craig Foster going into the staff lounge. I didn't even stop to talk to him, just sent him a wave and kept going. I wish I'd taken a minute, but you always think you're going to have a minute more, some other time.'

'Did you know him well?'

'As well as any of the staff, I suppose. I'd run into him now and again in the neighborhood, and we had the usual conferences. Twice each term there are parent teacher meetings, more if needed. They're routinely needed for Martin,' she added with a wry smile.

'Martin had trouble with Mr Foster?' Eve asked.

'Actually, Martin responded really well to Craig. Craig loved what he did, you could tell.'

'But you were called in for meetings.'

'Oh, yeah.' She laughed now. 'They term Martin "exuberant," which is teacher-speak for a wild child. We're going the private school route because there's more one-on-one time, more discipline. It's working.'

There was a crash, hysterical laughter, and mad barking. Eileen smiled wryly. 'Mostly.'

'What about other staff? Reed Williams, for example.'

'Sure I know him.' Though she said it casually, her gaze shifted away, for just a moment.

'Did you see him outside of the school, Mrs Ferguson?'

'No. Not me.'

'Meaning others did.'

'Maybe. I don't see what that has to do with Craig.'

'Details are important. We understand Mr Williams had or pursued a number of sexual relationships.'

'Oh, boy.' She blew out a breath. 'He made what you could call a play – very subtle, very slick. Nothing I could call him on if I'd been inclined to. But you know when a man's feeling you out. And most men know when a woman's not interested. He backed right off. I've never had any trouble with him, or from him.'

'But others did?'

'Look, I know he hit on Jude Hadley. She told me, and she told me she met him for drinks. She's divorced, and she was tempted. Then she decided no, it wasn't something she wanted to get tangled up with. Especially since I saw Williams and Allika Straffo.'

'You saw them?' Eve prompted.

'At the holiday party at the school? It was just a . . .' She shifted, obviously uncomfortable. 'I saw how they looked at each other. And at one point, he touched her, just brushed his hand down her arm. But she pinked up. He wandered out, and a few seconds later, so did she. They came back separately, ten, fifteen minutes later. She had that look – you know, soft and loose. If they hadn't had a quickie I'll eat that damn droid pup.'

'Interesting,' Eve said as they stepped back into the chill of winter. 'Allika Straffo, mother of one of the kids who finds the vic, is reputedly having quickies with Williams, who had the opportunity to kill Foster.'

'And Foster threatened to report Williams, which would involve Allika Straffo? Okay, but I tell you, I can't see Williams getting worked up enough to poison Foster over the threat of being reported for having an affair with a student's mother.'

'Straffo, on the other hand, is married, and married to a powerful man. She might've gotten worked up enough.'

'No record of her in the building on the day of.'

'Her kid was.'

'Her . . . Come *on*, Dallas. You think she set her kid up as a hit man. Hit girl. Hit kid.'

'Maybe the kid was protecting Mommy.'

'Okay, wait.' Peabody climbed into the car. 'First, let's remember we're talking about a ten-year-old girl.'

'Kids have been known to kill.' She'd only been eight when she'd killed her father. When she'd stabbed him over and over and over.

'Yeah, generally out of panic, fear, rage, impulse. But generally a nice, upper-class ten-year-old girl doesn't spike the teacher's go-cup with ricin. It's a little extreme.'

'Yeah, it is. Maybe she didn't know she was poisoning him. Mom says, "Hey, let's play a game. Let's trick Mr Foster today."'

'It's pretty hard for me to swallow that a mother gets her kid to off a teacher because she's been having private lessons from another.'

No, Eve decided, it didn't bounce very well. Still. 'It's worth dropping by and chatting with her.'

The Straffos's penthouse topped a sleek silver bullet of a building that afforded river views from its shimmering glass windows or wide terraces.

Both the doorman and building security were appropriately snooty, but also efficient enough to verify the police identification and clear them within moments.

The door of the penthouse was opened by a young woman with freckles dusting a wholesome face that was topped by carrot-red hair. Her brogue was as thick as a slice of brown bread.

It gave Eve a quick hitch in the belly to hear it, to think of Roarke.

'The missus will be right with you. She and Rayleen are just finishing breakfast. What would you like me to bring you then? Coffee, tea?'

'We're good, thanks. What part of Ireland are you from?'

'I'm from Mayo. Do you know it?'

'Not really.'

'It's lovely, so you'll see if you have the chance to visit. I'll take your coats, shall I?'

'That's all right.' Eve followed her down the wide foyer – a sweep of steps to the right, open archways leading to open rooms with tall, tall windows. 'How long have you worked for the Straffos?'

'That'd be six months now. Please make yourself at home.' She gestured toward the sleek twin sofas plumped with gel pillows. There was a fireplace, flush and white against the wall, the flames turned on in an eerie blue that matched the fabrics. Tables were clear cubes with lush flowers spiking and trailing inside them.

'Are you sure I can't bring you something hot to drink? It's a cold one out there today. Ah, here comes the missus now. And there's our princess.'

Allika was blonde like her daughter, but with highlights expertly streaked through the short swing of hair. She had eyes the color of ripe blueberries and skin as white and soft as milk. She wore a trim sweater set to match her eyes, and stone-gray pants that showed off long legs.

She held her daughter's hand.

Rayleen's face was bright and eager. 'Mom, these are the

161

police who came to school. This is Lieutenant Dallas and Detective Peabody. Did you come to tell us you found out what happened to Mr Foster?'

'We're still working on that.'

'Rayleen, you need to go with Cora now and get your coat. You don't want to be late for school.'

'Couldn't I stay and talk, too? It would be an excused absence, like a doctor's appointment, and wouldn't count against my attendance.'

'Not today.'

'But I'm the one who found him. I'm a witness.' Even as Rayleen pouted, Allika took her daughter's face in her hands, kissed both her cheeks.

'Be my good girl now and go with Cora. I'll see you when you get home from school.'

Rayleen let out a heavy sigh. 'I wish I could stay and talk,' she said to Eve, but went obediently with Cora.

'She's handling this horrible thing so well, really. Still, she had nightmares last night. It's terrible of me, I suppose, but all I keep wishing is that it had been another child to find him with Melodie. Is there anything more? Something you didn't want to say in front of Rayleen?'

'Can you tell us if you, your daughter or your husband had any trouble with Mr Foster?'

'Trouble? No. He was Rayleen's favorite teacher, really. Top marks, across the board in his class. Rayleen's an exceptional student. Craig made her class leader. She's also class leader in her Literature class and in Computer Sciences. She loves school.'

'When was the last time you saw Mr Foster?'

'At the last parent teacher conference in, hmmm, November. No, no, I'm sorry, that's wrong. It would've been at the holiday party in December. The school suspends the last two classes of the day, and the parents or guardians are invited. The school orchestra and choral group play and that can be interesting,' she added with a quick laugh. 'There're refreshments after the program. I saw him there, spoke with him. Rayleen gave him a little gift. A coffee mug she'd made in pottery class. This is all so tragic. I wish I could keep her home.'

She kneaded her fingers on her thighs. 'Ray's determined not to miss school, and my husband's very firm about her continuing classes, the normalcy. I'm out-voted,' she said with a quick smile. 'I suppose they're both right, but it's hard to send her there after this.'

'Did Mr Foster ever speak to you about Mr Williams?'

'Mr Williams?' There it was — that flicker over the face that was shock and guilt and a little bit of fear. 'Not that I can recall. Why would he?'

'You and Mr Williams are friendly.'

'I try to be friendly with all the staff at Sarah Child.'

'More friendly with some than others.'

'I don't like your implication, and I don't understand it.' She got to her feet, but the gesture was one of panic rather than authority. 'I think you should go now.'

'Sure, we can do that. We'll just go by your husband's office, discuss this with him.'

'Wait.' Allika held up a hand as Eve started to rise. 'Wait. I don't know what you've heard or what you believe, but . . .' She glanced toward the foyer, took a quiet breath as she heard Rayleen chattering with Cora as they left for school. 'It's not your concern, it's not your business.'

'Anything that touches on Craig Foster is our business.'

'My personal life . . . You have no reason to talk to Oliver about . . . about gossip.'

'Did Foster know about you and Reed Williams? Did he tell you, tell Williams he would report your affair?'

'It wasn't an affair! It was . . . it was a lapse, a momentary lapse. I broke it off weeks ago.'

'Why?'

'Because I came to my senses.' She pushed at her hair. 'I have . . . with the holidays coming, I have trouble with depression. Our son, our Trev, died three years ago, Christmas morning.'

'I'm so sorry, Mrs Straffo,' Peabody put in. 'How did he die?'

'He . . .' Allika sank down again. 'We were spending the holiday at our home . . . We had a home in Connecticut. He, he wasn't quite two. Trev. And he was so excited about Santa. He got out of bed early. It was still dark when . . . He fell, he fell down the stairs. Such a long way, such a little boy. He must have been running, they said, running down to see what Santa had brought, and he fell and his neck . . .'

'I'm very sorry,' Peabody repeated. 'I don't think anything can be more difficult for a parent.'

'I broke to pieces. It took months of treatment to put me back together. I don't think I'll ever be completely back, or that I should be back. But we had Rayleen. We had another child, and she needed us. We don't have the house in Connecticut, but we have Ray, and she deserves a normal life.'

'You became involved with Reed Williams,' Eve prompted, 'because you were depressed.'

'I know it's not an excuse; I knew it as it was happening. As Christmas gets close, I hurt, and when I hurt, I shut down some part of me. Reed – it helped block it out, that's all. It was exciting, and it was foolish. My husband and I, we aren't the same people we were before Trevor died. But we're trying, we keep trying. I was stupid and selfish, and if he finds out, it will hurt him. I don't want that.'

'And if Foster had reported it?'

'He didn't know.' She laid a hand on her throat, rubbing, rubbing as if at an ache. 'I don't see how he could have. He never said anything to me, and we talked – I told you – at the holiday party. It was a mistake, yes, but it was just sex. Only twice. Only twice. It didn't mean anything more than that to me or to Reed.'

'Did Williams say anything to you about Foster?'

'We didn't do a lot of talking. It was physical, it was shallow, then it was over.'

'Was he upset that you ended it?'

'Not at all, which – I admit – only made me feel more stupid.' She closed her eyes, straightened her shoulders, opened them again. 'If for some reason you need to tell Oliver about this, I'd like to speak with him first. I'd like to try to explain before he hears it from the police.'

'I don't, at this time, see any reason to discuss it with him. If that changes, I'll let you know.'

'Thank you.'

They managed to pigeonhole the others who'd signed in on the day of Foster's death, but had nothing solid after the interviews. Eve headed back downtown.

'How many times do you think Allika Straffo's been stupid during her marriage?'

'I think this is the first. She seemed too nervous, too guilty, too remorseful for it to be a habit. You ask me? Williams scented vulnerability and moved in. And I don't think Foster knew.'

Eve glanced over. 'Why?'

'Because from everything we know about him, he comes over as a really straight shooter. I can't see him having a casual, normal party conversation with Allika if he'd seen her doing the deed with Williams. And she'd have sensed his knowledge. High sexual levels increase instinct, I think. She'd have been excited, and guilty, and she'd have known if he knew. I think she just made a mistake.'

'Is that what adultery is?' Eve asked.

Peabody squirmed a little. 'Okay, it's a betrayal, and it's

an insult. She betrayed and insulted her husband with Williams. Now she has to live with it. And Roarke isn't about to betray or insult you in that way.'

'This isn't about me.'

'No, but there's some overlap in your mind. There shouldn't be.'

Should or shouldn't, it was there, and she didn't like it. But she did her job. The lab found no trace of ricin in the mix or liquid Eve had taken from the Foster apartment. That confirmed the poison was introduced on scene.

She went back to her time line, adding details from the morning interviews. In and out, she thought. People in and out, lingering, wandering, passing each other.

She needed a link to the poison.

She wandered around her board, sat back at her desk. Closed her eyes. Leaned up again and reread her own notes and reports. Got up, paced.

But her mind just wouldn't stick. Thinking to give it a boost, she opened the back of her computer, reached in to where she'd taped a candy bar to the inside of the case.

And it was gone.

'This is fucked up.' She could see a trace of the tape where it had stuck when the candy had been yanked out. The insidious candy thief had struck again.

Not for the first time she considered putting eyes and ears in her office. A little surveillance, a little chocolate, and she'd bust the thieving bastard.

But that wasn't the way she wanted to win. This, she thought, was a battle of wills and intellect, not technology.

Her disgust with having her chocolate fix nipped out from under her nose kept her occupied for the next few minutes. Then she gave up, contacted Dr Mira's office, and browbeat Mira's admin into an appointment.

She shot down copies of the files, shot another set to her commander, with a memo to Whitney that she was consulting the profiler.

She closed her eyes again, thought about coffee. And fell asleep.

She was in the room in Dallas. Icy cold, with the dirty red light from the sex club across the street blinking. The knife was in her hands, and her hands were drenched in blood. He lay there, the man who'd given her life. The man who'd raped her, beat her, tormented her.

Done now, she thought, a grown woman holding the knife instead of a child. Done now, what had to be done. A grown woman whose arm screamed with pain from the child's broken bone.

She could smell the blood, smell the death.

Cradling her broken arm, she stepped back from the scene, turned to escape.

The bedroom door was open, and inside two figures moved fluidly, somehow beautifully on the bed. The light flashed over them, off them, over. His hair was dark and gleaming, his eyes brilliant. She knew the curve of his face, his shoulders, the line of his back, the ripple of muscle in it.

The woman he was inside moaned out her pleasure, and her gilded hair shone in the ugly light.

The pain was worse than the broken bone, worse than the rape. It vibrated through her every cell, every muscle, every pore.

Behind her, Eve's dead father chuckled. 'You didn't really expect him to stay with you? Look at him, look at her. You don't even come close. Everybody cheats, little girl.'

And she was a little girl again, trembling with sickness, with pain, with helplessness.

'Go ahead, pay them back. You know how.'

When she looked down, the knife was in her hand, its blade wet and red.

9

If looks could kill, the stare Mira's overprotective admin aimed would have dropped Eve on the spot. She managed to survive it, and went in to find Mira at her desk.

As always, Mira looked calm and collected. Her sable hair had grown longer, and was sassily waved today in a style Eve hadn't seen on her before. It always gave Eve a jolt when people changed that sort of thing. Put them out of context, she decided.

It was a younger, sportier style and rippled back from Mira's lovely face. She wore one of her pretty suits in a color Eve supposed was gray but looked to her like shimmering fog, and somehow made Mira's eyes, a soft blue, look deeper.

She wore it with silver; spirals at her ears, a braided chain with a pendant that had a clear stone centered in an etched setting around her neck.

Eve wondered if Roarke would have considered it screen friendly, and decided what it was, was somehow perfect.

'Eve.' Mira smiled. 'I'm sorry, I haven't had a chance to read the file.'

'Squeezed in your schedule.'

'There's always a little wiggle room. You'll give me the gist,' she continued as she rose to go to her office AutoChef. 'Tough case?'

'Mostly they are.'

'You look especially tired.'

'Getting nowhere. The vic was a teacher. History, Private school,' she began and filled in the blanks while Mira programmed the flower tea she liked.

Mira gestured to a chair as Eve spoke, then took one herself as she handed Eve one of the tea cups.

'Poisoning is remote,' Mira commented as she sipped. 'Keeps the hands clean. No physical contact necessary. Passionless, most usually. Often a female mode. Not exclusively, of course, but often a choice.'

'I can't pin down a motive. Highest on the list is murder to silence him. He was, allegedly, aware that one of his fellow teachers liked to rack up affairs with faculty members, mothers of students.'

'Which, potentially, would be grounds for disciplinary action, even dismissal. Ricin poisoning,' Mira mused. 'A little old-fashioned, even exotic. And not as efficient as other options, but easier to come by if you've any knowledge of the science.'

'Worked pretty damn well.'

'Yes, it certainly can. So the murder was planned, timed, executed. Not impulse, not in the heat of the moment. Calculated.'

Balancing the saucer on her knee in a way Eve found

both baffling and admirable, Mira continued. 'It's possible, of course, that the poison was already in the killer's milieu, and that easy access made it the method chosen. From what you've told me, the victim was unaware he was in any danger, was under any threat, had incurred anyone's anger.'

'He was going about his routine,' Eve confirmed. 'No one close to him reports any hitch in his stride.'

'I would say that the killer harbored this resentment, this anger or this motive while continuing to go about his business. Planned the details, accessed the method. The killing was simply something that needed to be done. He didn't need to watch the victim die, or touch him, speak to him. He wasn't concerned that, in all likelihood, it would be a child or children who discovered the body.'

Mira considered it another minute. 'If it was a parent, I would have to say it's one who puts his own needs and desires above that of his child. A teacher? One who sees the children as a job, as units rather than children. This was a means to an end. Efficiently done, with a bare minimum of involvement.'

'He's not looking for attention or for glory. He's not crazy.'

'I would say not. But someone who can follow a time-table, and works in an orderly fashion.'

'I'm going to look at the faculty again, the support staff. Timetables are the bedrock of school systems, the way I remember it. And someone inside the system would have a better, and clearer, knowledge of the vic's schedule.'

She pushed up and paced a little. 'Besides, they're supposed to be there. Required. Nothing suspicious about showing up for work, doing your job. Some of the parents, the guardians come in with a kid here and there, deliver something, hold a meeting, but the killer had to know if his name was on the sign-in list when it generally wasn't, we'd take a good look.'

'Would it be possible for someone to have accessed the building without signing in?'

'There's always a way, and it's going to be checked out. But I don't like it.' Eve sat again, pushed up again in a restless way that had Mira watching her. 'It keeps the name out of the loop – potentially – but it's not as efficient as just signing in as usual. Riskier than needed. The murder was risky, but like you said, calculated. Times. I bet the son of a bitch practiced.'

She stuffed her hands in her pockets, absently toyed with loose credits. 'Anyway, thanks for the time.'

'I'll read the file, give you a more formal profile and opinion.'

'Appreciate it.'

'Now, tell me what's wrong.'

'I just did. Dead guy. No solid leads.'

'Don't you trust me, Eve?'

It was what Roarke had asked her the night before, in nearly the same patient tone. And it broke her. Her breath hitched in and out once before she controlled it. 'There's a woman,' she managed.

Mira knew Eve's heart and mind well enough to understand it was very personal, and nothing to do with murder. 'Sit down.'

'I can't. I can't. There's a woman he used to know, used to be with. He might've loved her. I think he did. God. She's back, and he's . . . I don't know what to do. I'm messing it up. I can't stop messing it up.'

'Do you think he's been unfaithful?'

'No.' Undone, she pressed her fingers to her eyes. 'See, part of me wants to say, "Not yet." And the rest of me says, "That's bullshit." It's not his way. But she's here, and she's – she's not like the others.'

'Let me say first that in my personal, and my professional opinion, Roarke loves you to the point where there isn't room for anyone else. And I agree, being unfaithful to you isn't his way. Not only because of that love, but he respects you – and himself – far too much. Now. Tell me about the woman.'

'She's beautiful. Seriously beautiful. She's younger, prettier, and classier than me. She has bigger tits. I know that sounds ridiculous.'

'It certainly doesn't. I dislike her intensely.'

Eve laughed even as a tear escaped and was dashed away. 'Yeah. Thanks. Her name's Magdelana. He calls her Maggie sometimes.' She pressed a hand to her belly. 'I feel sick. I can't really eat, can't really sleep.'

'Eve, you need to talk to him about this.'

'I did. We did, and all we did was circle and piss each

other off. I don't know how to work this way.' Torn between frustration and fear, Eve dragged her hands through her hair. 'I just don't know the ropes. Summerset told me she's dangerous.'

'Summerset?'

'Yeah.' There was − almost − amusement at the surprise in Mira's tone. 'Kick in the head, right? He actually prefers me over her, for Roarke. Right now, anyway.'

'That doesn't surprise me in the least. Why does he say she's dangerous.'

'She's a user, he says. Left Roarke flat about a dozen years ago.'

'A long time. He'd have been very young.'

'Yeah.' She nodded, seeing Mira understood. 'It cuts deeper when you're young, before you really build up the skin for being hurt that way. See, she left him. That's worse. It's worse because it's unfinished business to him, because it didn't just come to its natural conclusion or whatever. She walked out on him. And then, she walked back in.'

She sat now, on the edge of the chair. 'We were in this fancy restaurant. Business dinner, and I was late. Caught this case, and I didn't change, so I was, you know. And then she said his name. He looked over, and she was an eyeful. Red dress, blonde. It was there, just for an instant, it was there in his eyes. He doesn't look at anyone but me like that, but he looked at her. Just for a second. Not even a second, half a heartbeat. But it was there. I saw it.'

'I don't doubt you.'

'There's heat between them. I can feel it.'

'Memories, Eve, are powerful forces. You know that. But remembering feelings doesn't make them viable.'

'He had lunch with her.'

'Hmm.'

'He was all open about it and everything. No sneaking around behind my back, no sir. And he said she asked him for some business advice. But she said – she came to my office.'

'She came to see you?'

Eve had to stand again, had to move again. 'She said she wanted to buy me a drink, have a chat. All smiles and let's-be-buddies. But what she said wasn't what she was thinking, not what she had in mind. God, that sounds stupid.'

'It doesn't,' Mira disagreed in that same calm tone. 'You're trained to hear what's not said. And even when it's this intensely personal, you'd hear.'

'Okay.' Eve let out a breath. 'Okay. She was scoping me out, dropping little tidbits. She made it sound as if she and Roarke were going to work together. She's playing me, and I can't find the rhythm to kick her the hell off the field.'

'However satisfying that might be, kicking her off the field won't solve this for you. He has to do that. Have you told him this is hurting you?'

'I feel stupid enough. He hasn't done anything. The fact that they have this heat and history between them, well, he can't do anything about that. It is. She knows it, and she'll use it. Then . . . I guess he'll have to make a choice.'

'Do you doubt he loves you?'

'No. But he loved her first.'

'Do want my advice?'

'I guess I must since I dumped all this on you.'

Mira rose, took Eve's arms. 'Go home, get some sleep. Take something if you must, but get a couple of hours of sleep. Then tell Roarke how you feel. Tell him you feel stupid, that you feel hurt, that you know he hasn't done anything. Feelings aren't always rational and reasonable. That's why they're feelings. You're entitled to yours, and he's entitled to know what yours are.'

'Sounds good in theory. Even if I could work up the chops for that, I can't do it. I have that goddamn deal with Nadine tonight.'

'Oh, of course. *Now*'s premiere. Dennis and I will both be watching.' She did something then she rarely did, or Eve would rarely allow. Mira brushed her hand over Eve's hair, then leaned in, kissed her cheek. 'You'll be wonderful, and when it's done, when you've had a decent night's sleep, you'll talk to Roarke. Maybe he does have a choice to make, but everything I feel, everything I know says absolutely that choice will always be you.'

'She speaks French and Italian.'

'That bitch.'

Eve managed a laugh, then did something she'd never done. She simply lowered her brow to Mira's and closed her eyes. 'Okay,' she said quietly. 'Okay.'

★   ★   ★

The churning and airing of all those emotions might have given her a drilling headache, but despite it, she felt better.

When she walked back into her division, she saw Peabody sitting at her desk in the bull pen talking to a small, dark-haired woman. Peabody patted the woman on the arm, rose.

'Here's the lieutenant now. Dallas, this is Laina Sanchez. We've been talking. Maybe we can use the lounge?'

'Sure.' She saw now, as Laina levered to her feet, that the woman was several months into gestation.

'I thought I should come in.' Laina's voice was faintly accented and throaty. 'I talked with Hallie after you interviewed her. Detective Peabody interviewed me at the school the day . . . the day Craig died. So I came in to see her.'

'Fine.' In the lounge she saw Baxter and Trueheart – the slick and the innocent – at a table in a corner with a skinny, jittery guy wearing sunshades.

Funky-junkie, Eve decided. Probably one of Baxter's weasels. She flipped through her mental files to try to pin down what cases the pair was working while Peabody offered Laina a drink.

Underground homicide, she remembered. Dead tourist who, it appeared, had been trying to score in one of the nasty holes under New York's streets.

Baxter's gaze flicked to hers too briefly to measure, but in the look she saw that the junkie had something that was heating up the investigation.

At least somebody had a decent lead.

She went for water because the coffee in the lounge was revolting. And settling down, let Peabody run it.

'We really appreciate you coming in like this, Laina. Lieutenant, Laina came down on the subway. I told her we'd have her driven home. That's all right, isn't it?'

'No problem.'

'Laina, would you like to tell Lieutenant Dallas what you told me?'

'All right. I moonlight for Hallie sometimes. I know she told you, and that I'm not really supposed to. But the money helps, and Hallie's been very good to me. She told me you'd spoken to her, and what was said.'

'Why don't you tell me, Mrs Sanchez?'

'Yes.' Laina nodded. 'First I wanted to tell you that we did meet in the kitchen that morning. We had coffee, talked awhile about some menu changes, and just . . . well, we just talked, as friends do.'

Now she shifted, laying a hand on her bump of belly. 'Hallie told me you'd asked about Mr Williams, and if he'd . . . if there had been anything personal between them. Of course Hallie's not interested in men in that way. But we also talked about what she didn't tell you, because she's my friend.'

'There was something personal between you and Mr Williams?'

'No.' Laina flushed and closed a hand over the little silver cross she wore around her neck. 'No, no, I'm married. This means there are lines that aren't crossed. For me and my

179

husband, this means there are lines. For Mr Williams, the lines are less defined. He flirted with me. It was uncomfortable because of our positions, but, I thought, harmless. Then he touched me. He put his hand on my breast.'

Eve waited a beat. 'And?'

'I hit his hand with a spoon,' Laina snapped out, full of indignation. 'Very hard. He thought it was funny. I didn't tell my husband. He wouldn't have thought it was funny. I didn't tell anyone because I didn't want to lose my job.'

'Did he continue to harass you?'

'Mr Williams asked me to dinner, and asked me for drinks, and asked me to bed. He touched me again, and that time I slapped his face. He wasn't discouraged. I should've reported him, I know, but when I said if he didn't stop, I would, he just shrugged. He'd been there a lot longer than I had, and he'd be believed before I would. He'd say that I approached him, and I'd be fired.'

'What did you do?'

'Nothing. I'm ashamed to say I did nothing. He left, and I kept working. I cried. I couldn't help it. And Craig came in, and found me crying. He asked me what was wrong. I didn't tell him, but I think he knew. He would have passed Mr Williams going out, so I think he knew. And Mr Williams never bothered me again after that. I think Craig told him to leave me alone.'

She let out a sigh, drank some water. 'I should have told you, Detective Peabody, all of this when you talked to me that day. But I didn't think of it. I was only thinking that

Craig was dead. He was such a sweet man, and he was dead. I never thought of that day.'

'When did this happen? The day Craig found you crying?'

'It was before the holiday break. Weeks and weeks ago. So I don't see that it means anything. But Hallie said I should tell you. That you should know everything. I wish you wouldn't have to tell my husband. He'd be angry with me for not telling him, and angry with Mr Williams. He'd cause trouble at the school.'

'There's no reason we need to tell your husband, Mrs Sanchez, but let me tell you something. If you were sexually harassed by Williams, you should report it. If he did this to you, he's done it to others. He shouldn't hold the position he does, and he shouldn't get away with it. You could get yourself a lawyer and sue his ass on top of it.'

'Who'd believe me?'

'I believe you.'

Eve sat where she was another moment while Peabody took Laina out to arrange for her transportation home. Williams, she thought. Despite no evidence of violence in his MO, he was a sexual predator. Not such a big leap from that to murder.

Either way, the son of a bitch deserved to have the shit kicked out of him.

She stood just as Baxter headed in her direction. 'Dallas,' he began, then studied her with a cocked head. 'Sister, you look like something the cat wouldn't bother to drag in.'

'That's Lieutenant Sister, and bite me.'

'One good chomp would probably do it the way you're looking. Anyway. We got hot on the Barrister case.'

'Tourist from Ohio, right?'

'Omaha. Same difference. The concerned citizen Trueheart's escorting out has come forward as a wit.'

'That mope one of your weasels?'

'Yeah, he's on my roll.' Baxter got comfortable, planting his ass on the table. 'Thing is, he saw it go down, scratched his butt over it for a day or so, then tagged me. Vic went down the underground, under Broadway and Thirty-eighth. Hell's Fire. You know the joint?'

'Yeah. S and M theme, lots of party favors. Mock human sacrifices nightly. I like to drop in to relax after a long shift.'

Baxter grinned. 'Just your style. So the vic strolls in, flashy wrist unit, shiny shoes, big attitude. Rents a slave, pays for the deluxe bondage package.'

'Deluxe?'

'That would be your chains, whips, ball gag in your choice of colors, minitazer, leash, and collar. Three-hour rental.'

'What, no costumes?'

'Costumes are the Super Deluxe pack. But he sprang for one of the display cubes so he could put on a show for the crowd.'

'Nice.'

'He wants to score before he gets his rocks off, so he zeros in on Sykes.' Baxter, not as fussy about coffee as Eve, walked over and keyed in his code on the machine. 'You want?'

'No. I can live without drinking mud made from dirt and horse piss.'

'He wants a free sample – can you beat it – wants a freebie before he pays. Sykes tells him to fuck off, but the guy hounds him. He's got plenty to spend, but he wants a taste first. Pokes at Sykes, flashes a wad. "Gimme a taste and if I like it, I'll buy a full bag." So Sykes, who'd had a free sample or two himself, says, "I'll give you a taste, fuck face, see how you like this." And proceeds to stick him a couple dozens times with his buck knife.'

Eve waited until Baxter planted his ass again. 'He got the point across.'

'Har. After said point is made, Sykes hauls Barrister's dead body up, carries him out of the club, and dumps him at the bottom of the stairs on the passage down on Broadway. Where he was subsequently tripped over by a couple of idiot college kids who thought they'd like an underground adventure.'

'An urban fable. You know where to find Sykes?'

'Got a couple of haunts in addition to his last known. I figure on trying the last known first. Try to keep my kid above the sidewalk. It's a jungle down there.'

'Either way, close it up.'

'I thought I'd let Trueheart take the lead on the interview once we have Sykes in the box. Give him some play.'

Eve thought of the baby-faced Trueheart. It would

probably be good for him, and Baxter wouldn't let it go south. 'Your call. Notify Illegals after you close it up. They can tag on whatever charges they want to pick from the menu. But sew up the Murder Two first.'

'That's the plan. Oh, and break a leg.'

'What?'

'That's what you say to somebody before a performance, which seems pretty damn stupid to me. *Now.* Nadine.'

'Christ,' was all she said, and stalked out.

She found Peabody at Vending just down from the bull pen. Peabody's face was a study in concentration as she scanned the offerings. 'Energy Bar or Goo-Goo bar. The Energy Bar is, of course, nutritionally balanced, but the Goo-Goo is delicious and will provide me with great joy until the guilt sets in. Which should it be?'

'You're going to go for the fake chocolate and sugar. Why torture yourself over it?'

'Please, Lieutenant, this is a process. The torture is part of the process. Goo-Goo it is. You want?'

What she wanted was the candy bar she'd hidden in her office, but that was not to be. 'Yeah, what the hell.'

While the machine chirped out the Goo-Goo jingle and the nutritional data until Eve wanted to smash it with a hammer, she and Peabody stood munching on candy. 'I want Williams picked up, brought down for questioning. We'll send a couple of big, stone-faced, intimidating uniforms to the school.'

'Nice touch. Scary, but it's like you're saying you don't have time to go get him yourself.'

'We'll book Interview Room B. Baxter and Trueheart are bringing in a suspect. We'll leave A for them.'

'I know a couple of uniforms who'd be perfect for the pick-up.'

'Get it done.' Eve frowned down at the candy. 'These things make you feel a little nauseous?'

'Oh, yeah, that's part of the thrill.'

Eve handed the last half of her Goo-Goo to Peabody. 'Go wild. Meanwhile, I'm going to try to broker us another warrant to go through Williams's residence, all his e-toys.'

Eve contacted APA Cher Reo, and learned the pretty blonde was already in the building. They met in Eve's office where the coffee, at least, was prime.

'You know,' Reo began, 'you'd think things would slow down in this kind of weather. But despite the cold, the ice, the wind, people are still raping and robbing and ripping at each other.' Reo took an appreciative sip of coffee. 'Kind of makes me proud to be a New Yorker.'

'We don't let winter get in the way of our mayhem. So, about my dead teacher.' Eve brought her up to date, made the pitch for a search warrant.

'Will Sanchez file a complaint?'

'Can't say. Right now she's worried if her husband clues in he'll perform mayhem on Williams. But she came in, and she told it straight. This guy's hunting on school grounds.'

'Do you suspect he's hunting students?'

'I've got nothing that points that way, but it's not out of the question. It looks to me like the vic had a come-to-Jesus talk with him. No reason for Williams to back off on Sanchez otherwise. Other statements indicate Craig saw him in a compromising position with someone he shouldn't have been compromising with. The school's not only a good gig – pays well, nice bennies, clean and shiny, but it's an all-you-can-screw buffet for someone like Williams.'

'Gee.' Reo downed coffee. 'Why can't I ever get a nice guy like that?'

'Maybe you'll prosecute and convict him, then you could be penpals.'

'Oh, if only.'

'So. If the vic threatened Williams's standing, he may have decided to eliminate the threat.'

'No history of violence, no criminal record, no civil suits?'

'No, but you've got to start somewhere. It's enough for a warrant, Reo.'

'Maybe. I can work it,' she decided. 'But the fact that the guy's a pig doesn't make him a murdering pig. Find me something that says he is.'

As Reo headed out, she glanced back. 'By the way, looking forward to seeing you and Nadine tonight.'

Eve only sighed and rested her head in her hands. Then she shook it, and contacted Feeney, her friend and the captain of the Electronic Detectives Division.

His face came on screen – comfortably lived in, baggy

at the eyes, topped with wiry ginger and gray hair that went in any direction it chose.

'Yo,' he said.

'Need a man in the field. Since Peabody hasn't irritated me today, I'd like McNab if you can spare him. On scene e-work. Warrant's coming through.'

'Who's dead? Anybody I know?'

'Teacher. Private school. Ricin poisoning.'

'Yeah, yeah, got wind of that. Education's a risky business. You can have my boy.'

'Thanks. An . . . Hey, Feeney, did your wife ever give you any grief about . . . other women.'

'What other women?'

'Yeah, there's that. But like, when you were training me, and we partnered up, we worked pretty tight.'

'Wait a minute. You're a woman?'

It made her laugh and call herself a fool. 'Turns out. McNab can meet us in fifteen, in the garage. Appreciate it.'

McNab was a fashion plate from the tips of his long, shiny hair to the stacked soles of his purple airboots. His calf-length parka was in eye-watering orange, and his watch cap had zigzags of both colors. His earlobes were studded with a multitude of tiny silver balls.

Despite what Eve considered his questionable wardrobe choices, he was a solid EDD man. His fingers were nimble, his green eyes sharp.

He stretched out on the backseat on the drive, and from the movements Eve caught in the rearview, and Peabody's muffled giggles, he was snaking his hand between the front seat and the passenger door to tickle his cohab.

'You want to retain use of that hand, Detective, you'll keep it off my partner until your personal time.'

'Sorry. Your partner shatters the power of my will.'

'Keep it up, and I'll shatter all your fingers.' She swung to the curb.

Williams's building couldn't boast a doorman, but she noted there was solid security. All three badges had to be scanned and cleared before the outside doors clicked open to the small lobby. She spotted security cams in the lobby along with a couple of chairs and a fake palm tree.

'Five-E,' Peabody told her.

They stepped into one of the two elevators where Eve asked for the fifth floor. 'A couple of steps up from the vic's living space.'

'Williams has been certified and teaching for nearly fifteen years. He also has his Master's. He'd make easily four times what the vic did. Not counting any private tutoring he might pull in on the side and not report.' Peabody linked pinkies with McNab, then unhooked as they reached five.

'Record on,' Eve announced, then drew out her master. 'Dallas, Lieutenant Eve; Peabody, Detective Delia; McNab, Detective Ian, entering the apartment of Williams, Reed, by duly authorized warrant.'

She dealt with the locks. 'McNab, I want you to check out any D and C's, correspondence, conversations, what he's been looking at, what he's been buying. The whole shot.'

She frowned at the apartment. The living area wasn't spacious, but it was as large as the victim's entire place. It boasted no particularly exciting view, but there was a wide gel couch in gleaming black, lots of shiny chrome. She noted a mood screen, a snazzy entertainment system.

The art on the walls was stark and modern. A circle, a line, all in primary colors on white. The windows had privacy screens, and they were engaged. She wandered to the turnout that was the kitchen. Sleek and shiny there, too, she noted. White, black, red. What equipment there was looked glossy to her, and she was willing to bet it was trendy.

'Take the kitchen, Peabody. If he dabbles in poison, he might just be stupid or arrogant enough to keep it in there. I'll take the bedroom.'

It was an eyeful. She imagined Williams thought of it as sexy. She found it just a little creepy. The bed was the focal point, a wide pool draped in a shimmering red spread that looked wet. Flanking it were two thick faux fur rugs in black.

She considered the lighted mirror angling from the ceiling a cliché, and laughable. Art here ran to pencil drawings of stupendously endowed couples copulating in various positions.

She lifted the shimmering red spread, found black sheets, and beneath them a gel mattress that undulated under pressure.

Ick.

The drawers in the table beside the bed held a cornucopia of sex toys and enhancements, including a couple of illegal substances classified as date rape devices. She bagged them into evidence.

'You make this part easy,' she said aloud, and moved to the closet.

She noted his professional wardrobe on one side – a couple of suits, sports jackets, shirts, trousers. His leisure wear on the other was considerably less conservative.

She wondered who would actually enjoy seeing a grown man in a black skin-suit.

'Hey, Dallas, you've gotta see—' McNab stopped, whistled. 'Wow. Sexcapades.' He studied one of the black-framed sketches. 'These two have to be double-jointed.' He scratched his throat, then bent from the waist to study it from a different angle.

'What do I have to see?'

'Huh? Oh, sorry, got sucked in. Sex is this guy's religion. It's kind of admirable in a sick way. He spends a lot of time on his comp: chat rooms, websites – all sex spots. Orders a lot of toys.'

'Yeah, he's got a nice supply. Including a little Whore, a little Rabbit.'

McNab's easy amusement vanished. 'Not admirable, even in a sick way.'

'Any correspondence with the vic?'

'Not on that unit.'

'Research on poisons? Ricin or others?'

'Nothing. May be buried deeper, and I can take it in and look. His school work is on there, too. Lesson plans, grade book, like that. Nothing that looks off on that end.' He cocked his head up. 'Bet there's a camera in there.'

'Camera.' She narrowed her eyes at the mirror. 'Really.'

'Five gets you ten on it. Want me to have a look?'

'You do that.' She moved to search the bath. 'Stay out of the toy drawer.'

'Aw. Lieutenant Spoilsport.'

10

They found no evidence linking Williams to the poison, or Craig Foster's death, but they found plenty to tangle him up. Eve ordered in a team of sweepers, just to tie it off, then prepped for the interview.

'We're going to start with the murder, standard routine questions,' Eve told Peabody. 'He hasn't lawyered up. Feels too cocky.'

'You ask me, this guy thinks with his cock most of the time.'

'You got that right. So we use it. Just a couple of girls. From that quick preview of the discs McNab dug up, this one likes multiples. So we poke at him about the vic, then we jam him with the illegals we found in his place, then we work him on the murder again.'

Juggle it, Eve thought as she went into the interview room. Keep him off balance.

'It's about damn time. Do you know how long I've been waiting?' Williams demanded. 'Do you have any idea what it does to my professional reputation to have a couple of police goons pull me out of class?'

'We'll get to that professional reputation in a minute. I

need to log this interview in, give you your rights and obligations. Formalize it.'

'My rights?' His body twitched, as if he'd experienced a small electric shock. 'Am I under arrest?'

'Absolutely not. But this is a formal interview, and there's procedure designed to protect you. Do you want something to drink besides that water? Coffee – it sucks – a soft drink?'

'I want this done so I can get out of here.'

'We'll try to keep it moving.' She logged in for the recorder, read him the Revised Miranda. 'Do you understand your rights and obligations in this matter, Mr Williams?'

'Of course I do. That doesn't make this any less annoying.'

'I'm sure it doesn't. Now, let's go over your movements on the day Craig Foster was murdered.'

'Christ! I've given you my statement already. I've cooperated.'

'Listen.' Eve sat, stretched out her legs. 'This is a homicide, and one that took place in a school where minors have been involved and affected.'

She turned her hand over, palm up, in a gesture of what-can-I-do. 'We have to dig for every detail. People often forget details, so we routinely repeat interviews.'

'We're sorry for the inconvenience,' Peabody added with an understanding smile. 'We've got to be thorough.'

'Fine, fine. Try to get it right this time?'

Oh, yeah, Eve thought. Very cocky and used to intimidating the girls. 'We'll do our best. From your previous statement, and the statements of others, you saw and or spoke with the victim at least twice on the day of his death. Is this correct?'

'Yeah, yes, yes. In the fitness center, early, then in the lounge just before classes began. I told you.'

'What did you and Mr Foster talk about in the fitness center?'

'We didn't. I told you that.'

Eve flipped through the files. 'Mmm-hmm. But you and the victim did have occasion to have conversations previously.'

'Well, Jesus, of course. We worked together.'

'And were those conversations less than friendly?'

'I don't know what you're talking about.'

Eve folded her hands on top of the file, smiled winningly. 'Then let me be clear. When Mr Foster pinned your ears back about fishing in the work and parental pool for sex, would you consider those conversations of a friendly nature?'

'I consider that question insulting.'

'It seems from the statements we have from women you harassed or seduced, many of them found your advances and behavior insulting.' She closed the file and smiled again. 'Come on, Reed, we know the score, you and me. These women didn't complain. They liked the attention, they liked the excitement. You didn't slap them around and rape them. It was consensual, and Foster – from what I gather – poked his nose in where it didn't belong.'

Williams drew a deep breath. 'Let *me* be clear. I've never denied that I enjoy a certain amount of sexual success with women. It's not illegal for me to enjoy that success with coworkers or with parents of students, for that matter. Unethical, perhaps.'

'Well, it actually is illegal to perform sexual acts in an educational facility when minors are present. So, if you had that success during school hours, on school grounds – where you kept a supply of condoms – you've committed a crime.'

'This is bullshit.'

'It is sort of nitpicky, I grant you, but I have to follow the law. I can talk to the PA about giving you the brush on that, but I need to get the details on record.'

'I never had sex with anyone in an area the students could access.'

'Okay, that's a plus. But you did have sex in areas the victim could access. Correct?'

'Possibly, but we're talking about a grown man. I'd like to know exactly what you meant about some women being insulted, giving statements about their relationship with me.'

'I can't tell you the names, part of the agreement with them. Like I said, it's obvious to me it was consensual. Who knows why they're circling now.'

'I'd say it's the upset about the murder,' Peabody put in. 'These women aren't used to talking to cops, so when they do, especially about something as shocking as murder, things just jump out of their mouths. We've got to follow up, Mr Williams. It's not exactly the kind of work we like doing. Live and let live, in my opinion, when it comes to this area. But we've got to get it taken care of.'

'I had sex, nobody got hurt. End of story.'

'But Craig Foster disapproved,' Eve prompted.

'For a guy with that hot a wife, he was pretty puritanical.'

'You move on her, too?'

'Just felt her out when he first came on staff. At that point, she was too into him, into them. Now, a few months more, the marriage gets routine, and I might have given her another sniff. But there are plenty of others. I'm good at what I do.'

'Yeah. I bet. Craig might've been a little jealous of that. You think?'

Williams lifted his brows. 'I never thought of it that way, but yes, maybe. Probably, in fact. He was a nice enough guy, and a damn good teacher, I'll give him that. For the most part, we got along fine. He did get nosy, and a little pushy, about some of my activities. Personal ones.'

'Did he threaten you?'

'I wouldn't call it a threat.'

'What then?'

'A lecture.' Williams rolled his eyes.

'Did this lecture cause you to cease those activities?'

'I was a little more discreet, you could say. A little more choosy.' He lifted a shoulder. 'No point in stirring things up.'

'But you weren't worried about him going to Mosebly with his disapproval, or even over her head to the board?'

He smiled now, serenely. 'I never figured he'd have the chops for that. He didn't like making waves. Basically, it was a non-issue for me.'

'Well.' Eve tugged on her ear. 'It may not have been one for him, especially if he was aware that you used illegal substances in some of those private activities.'

'What?'

'Street name Whore, street name Rabbit, which we found in your bedroom toy chest. Oh, didn't I mention that with the information gathered and statements taken we were able to secure a warrant to enter and search your residence? Bad boy, Reed. Bad, bad boy.'

'This is outrageous! This is entrapment.'

'This is the warrant.' Eve slid the hard copy from the file. 'We take a very dim view on the use and possession of these particular substances, no live and let live about it. So does the PA. I bet the board of Sarah Child, and the teachers' union also take dim views.

'And here's something else,' she continued, and for the first time, he began to sweat. 'It makes me, with my suspicious mind, wonder if a guy can score those particular items, he might just be able to score enough poison to eliminate a threat. He put the pressure on you, didn't he?'

She rose now to walk around behind him, lean in over his shoulder. 'Interfering little bastard, shoving his puritanical views into your personal life. You have a good thing going. Coworkers, support staff, mothers, guardians, care givers. Like plucking plums off a low branch for a guy like you. He was going to cut you off from that branch, he jeopardized your job. No, your whole career.'

'No, it wasn't like that. No, he didn't.'

'Sure he did. Others might have known, or suspected, but they looked the other way. No skin off theirs. But this one, he takes it on himself to do something about it. Lecture you? Asshole had no right, did he? And there he is, day after day, in your face, keeping his eye on you in case he doesn't like what you're up to. Sitting at his desk every day with his neatly packed lunch from home. Routine. Boring. And a sticky thorn in your side. Where'd you get the ricin, Reed?'

'I never had any ricin. I didn't even know what the hell it was before this. I didn't kill anyone.'

'It must've pissed you off that Mirri Hallywell would rather study with him than roll around on that big red bed with you. It's a fucking insult. You had to take him down. Had to do it. So you slipped out of class while he was away from his, and you took care of it. Quick, easy. Done.'

'That's a lie! That's crazy. You're crazy.'

'There are ways to soften this, Reed. Say he was blackmailing you. Stalking you. A constant threat. It was him or you. You had to protect yourself.'

'I never went near his classroom that day. I didn't kill him, for God's sake. I was with someone when I left my class that morning. I have a witness.'

'Who?'

He opened his mouth, shut it tight. Then he stared hard at the table. 'I want a lawyer. I demand my right to speak to a lawyer. I'm not saying anything else until I have one.'

'Okay, but just FYI? You're under arrest for possession of illegal substances and for dispensing them, we've got that from your naughty camera. You can contact your lawyer before you're booked.'

Eve went through the interview in her mind, and added to her murder board. She had stills of the bottles from his sex drawer, and linked him on that board with Laina Sanchez, Allika Straffo, Eileen Ferguson, Mirri Hallywell. Who else had he approached? she wondered. Who had he succeeded with, failed with?

She needed to review all the discs from his bedroom camera. And wouldn't that be fun? At least she had McNab picking through the building's security discs for the last three days. Though she doubted they'd score in that area.

She got coffee, but it wasn't working for her. She was tired to the bone, and caffeine wasn't going to change that. She put in a request to subpoena Williams's financials. With the illegals charge that would be a dunk.

She checked her messages to find Nadine Furst had called twice to remind her of airtime, to wear something appropriate, to ask if she had any solid leads on the Foster case.

Nag, nag, nag.

And why hadn't Roarke buzzed in to nag her?

Too pissed at her for flipping him off that morning, she thought. Well, she hadn't been the one with a former playmate on her fucking pocket 'link.

She started to sit, started to sulk, and Peabody poked her head in. 'Williams's attorney is here, and guess who it is.'

It took Eve one beat. 'You've got to be shitting me.'

'I don't know whether or not I shit you as I didn't say it was—'

'Oliver Straffo? What kind of sick irony is this?'

Peabody's face moved to sulk at having her scoop dumped. 'Well, he walked in, big as life, and is advising his client to make no further statements, answer no more questions until they consult. Then he wants to talk to us.'

'Hmmm.' Eve glanced at her board where she had Allika Straffo's picture lined up in Williams's shooting gallery. 'This should be interesting.'

Who knew what about who? Eve wondered and thought of Rayleen, the kid. How was she going to find out who knew what about who without blowing the situation up in the faces of the innocent?

Maybe Straffo had a right to know his wife had tossed up her skirts for a slime like Williams. But it wasn't her job to rat out a foolish wife unless it closed her case.

'Eggshells,' Peabody murmured as they stepped toward the interview room.

'What? You want eggs?'

'No, I meant we're going to have to walk on eggshells here. Be really careful,' she explained.

'I thought it was something like "You can't make scrambled eggs without breaking some."'

'No, it's "You can't make an omelette without breaking some eggs." But this is more like the opposite in the food saying spectrum. Eggs have been broken, but we don't want to crush the shells.'

'It's a stupid saying because if the eggs are already broken, who gives a damn about the stupid shells?' Eve wanted to know. 'But I get it. Let's go.'

She saw immediately that Williams had his confidence back. A high-powered defense attorney could do that for a suspect, guilty or innocent. Straffo sat in his conservatively and perfectly cut suit, hands folded on the table.

He said nothing until Eve started the record.

'One of my associates is already drafting a motion to have the warrant you secured invalidated, and the search deemed illegal.'

'You won't get it.'

He smiled a little, gray eyes hard as steel. 'We'll see. In the meantime your attempts to involve my client in the murder of Craig Foster are ludicrous. Sexual indulgence isn't a crime, nor is it a route to murder.'

'Sex and murder walk hand in hand like lovebirds, Straffo. We both know it. The victim was aware of your client's *indulgence* on school property, during school hours. Which is, as you also know, illegal.'

'It's a misdemeanor.'

'And grounds for dismissal from the educational facility. Even, as I've done my research, grounds for the revocation of the license to teach in this stare. Self-protection also walks along with murder.'

'You don't have even a blurry circumstantial case, Dallas. You have suspicion of what may be inappropriate and unwise behavior. You have no evidence that my client and the victim ever argued. In fact, I can and will provide statements from their coworkers that they did not and were, in fact, on friendly terms. You have no link to the murder weapon and my client, no witnesses that saw him enter the victim's classroom on the day in question, because, in fact, he did not so enter.'

'He was unaccounted for during a period of time when the victim was absent from the classroom, and as classes were in session, his entering same would not have been witnessed.'

'He was not alone during that period, and should it become necessary, we will provide you with the name of the individual he was with. As I have not reached this individual and discussed this, I prefer, as does my client, not to divulge the name at this time. We are confident, however, that she'll corroborate Mr Williams's statement.'

'You had plenty of time and plenty of opportunity to get in and out of that classroom,' Eve said to Williams. 'And you had plenty of motive.'

'I—'

'Reed.' All Straffo did was say the name, and Williams stopped speaking. 'All you have, Lieutenant, is a questionable search and seizure, which has netted you nothing that connects my client to this murder.'

'There's nothing questionable about the search and seizure. And your client's abhorrent habits caused the victim to nudge your client into a corner. He has stated, on record, that the victim learned of his habits and called him on it.'

'The situation was discussed between them, after which

they continued their friendly working relationship.' Straffo closed his own file, one he hadn't so much as glanced at during the interview. 'If that's all you've got, I've requested my motion to overturn the warrant be fast-tracked. I'd like my client moved to an appropriate holding area until his release.'

'Your kid goes to that school. Your kid was one of the ones who found Foster. Did you see the crime scene photos? You're going to sit there and defend the man suspected of causing that?'

Straffo's face went harder still, his voice colder. 'Not that I have to rationalize the fact that everyone is entitled to a defense, but I've known Mr Williams for more than three years. I believe him to be innocent.'

'He had Whore and Rabbit in his nightstand. He's known to fuck around in the school, when your daughter is there.'

'Allegedly.'

'Allegedly, my ass. Is that the kind of person you want teaching your child?'

'This is an inappropriate conversation, Lieutenant. This interview is at an end.' He rose, closed his briefcase. 'I'd like my client taken to holding until the motion is ruled on.'

She looked Straffo in the eye. 'Peabody, take this sack of shit to holding. You know, Straffo, sometimes you get just what you deserve.'

The motion was tossed out. Eve went to court and watched Straffo and Reo battle it out. The warrant held, the search and seizure held, and so did the arrest for possession and distribution.

It was Straffo who won the battle of bail or remand.

Outside the courtroom, Reo gave a shrug. 'He wasn't going to get me on that motion, I wasn't going to get him on remand. I figure this was a draw. Get me enough for a murder indictment, Dallas, and I'll have that disgusting hump back in a cell.'

'Working on it.'

'Straffo's going to want to deal on the illegals and my boss is going to agree with him.' Reo shot up a hand, anticipating Eve's argument. 'It works how it works, Dallas, and we both know it. So unless you can prove that he slipped that crap to someone without their knowledge or consent, he's going to get a fine, mandatory counseling, and probation.'

'What about his teaching certificate? Revocation.'

'You really want to shut him down?'

Eve thought about Laina Sanchez crying in the kitchen. 'Yeah, I really want to shut him down.'

Reo nodded. 'I'll look into it. You know, you'd better get moving. You're on air in a couple hours.'

'Shit.'

As Eve headed reluctantly for Channel 75's studio, Roarke was clearing his desk so he could do the same. He hoped his being there would make it better for Eve, not worse.

He didn't know, couldn't tell how it would be, and that stymied him. She wasn't a predictable woman, he thought, but he knew her. Her moods, the rhythm of them, her gestures, her tones.

Now she'd blurred on him.

He wanted it all back in focus. Needed it to be. But he'd be damned if he'd blur his own image to pacify some absurd and imaginary offense she was clinging to.

She's warned him, questioned him − interrogated more like, he thought with a spurt of heat. Doubted him and made him feel guilty when he'd done nothing to feel guilty about.

He thought of Magdelana's hand on his leg, and the invitation she'd offered. Well, he'd shut that straight down, hadn't he? Straight down and straight off.

Under any other circumstances, he might have told Eve about that sort of move, so they could joke about it. But it was perfectly obvious that this was the sort of information he'd best keep to himself.

And bloody hell if *that* didn't make him feel guilty.

Bugger it. He was going to demand trust, he thought as he rose to stand at his wide window. That was non-negotiable. Almost everything else was, he admitted, and slid a hand into his pocket to finger the gray button he carried with him.

Hers. As she'd been his, somehow, from the first time he'd seen her. Nothing and no one had ever struck him as she had, standing in that truly deplorable gray suit with her cop's eyes on him. Nothing and no one had ever held him as she did, and always would.

So anything else was negotiable. He could give and give

more, and always find he had just another well to dip from. Because she continued to fill him, over and over again.

He could bear the anger between them, he realized. Tempers were part of what they were. But he wasn't entirely sure he could bear this rift. So they'd have to find a way to span it.

As he turned, his desk 'link beeped. Interoffice, he noted. 'Yes, Caro.'

'I'm sorry, I know you're due to leave in a few moments. But there's a Ms Percell here to see you. She says it's personal. I'm sorry, but she talked her way up through security. I have her in the waiting area.'

He considered having Caro dismiss her. If anyone could shake Magdelana off, it would be Caro. And that seemed unfair to all involved. Using one woman to shield him from another woman because of yet *another* woman's ridiculously suspicious mind.

Damned if he was going to be led around by the nose that way, even by the woman he loved.

'It's all right. You can send her in. I'll need my transpo in ten minutes.'

'All right then. Oh, tell your wife, we'll be watching her.'

'I think I'll wait until it's done to mention it. She's annoyed by the whole business. Thank you, Caro.'

He scooped a hand through his hair, glanced around his office. A long way from what once had been, he thought. In every possible way.

Time to find a way, he supposed, to make it crystal-clear

to the women currently squeezing him from both sides, that there was no going back to what had been and no desire at all to take the trip.

She came in, a golden fur tossed over her arm, her hair sexy and tumbled, her face glowing with energy. And yes, she reminded him of what once had been. There was no way to avoid it.

'Look at you! Look at this!' After tossing her coat over a chair, Magdelana turned a circle.

Roarke met Caro's eyes, nodded, and she backed quietly out of the room. Closed the doors.

'The den of the global mogul, both sleek and plush, tasteful and absolutely male. Well, it's all you, isn't it?' She moved toward him, both hands extended.

He took them, briefly. There was no way to avoid that either, without making them both look like idiots. 'How are you, Maggie?'

'Right now? How I am is incredibly impressed.' She glanced at the desk. 'What exactly do you do here?'

'Quite a bit of what needs to be done, with a healthy portion of what I choose. What can I do for you?'

'Offer me a drink.' She sat on the arm of one of his chairs, crossed her long legs. Tossed her long hair. 'I've been shopping, and I'm worn to the bone.'

'Sorry. You caught me on my way out.'

'Oh.' Her lips pouted. 'Business, I suppose. You always were one for business. I could never understand that you actually liked to work. Still . . .' She uncrossed her legs to rise, then wandered toward his window where New York spread and speared. 'Lovely benefits.' She looked back at him, over her shoulder. 'I suppose I always pictured you in Europe though, carving your way through the Old World.'

'New York suits me.'

'Apparently, it does. I wanted to thank you. I've had some meetings already with the money people you suggested. It's early to say, but I think this is going to work out very nicely. I'd never have known where to start without your help.'

'I think you'd have found your way well enough. You've been busy,' he added. 'Shopping, taking meetings, visiting my wife at Central.'

Wincing, Magdelana turned around, stood framed by the energy and towers of the city. 'She told you. I was afraid of that. I don't know what I was thinking – well, yes, I do. I was just so curious about her, and wanted to get to know her a little. It didn't go well.'

'Didn't it?'

'I bungled it, no question. She disliked me before I walked in the door, and when I'd calmed down and licked my wounds, I understood that perfectly. Here, I was . . .' Smiling easily, she spread her arms, '. . . a former *amorata* of her husband's, sauntering in, offering to buy her a drink, all smiles and friendly overtures. She must have wanted to slap me.'

'She rarely slaps. A good bare-knuckled punch is more her style.'

'I'm so sorry. I was completely wrong. And she was so . . . harsh, it put my back up. I don't know how to make amends for it. Did I cause you trouble at home?'

'I told you that you wouldn't like her.'

'And you were right, as usual. It's odd, isn't it, when you cared for us both. In any case, I am sorry. I suppose, in a way, I was looking for contacts, connections. Friends. I'd hoped she and I would get along. After all, what we had, you and I, is ancient history.'

The invitation came back into her eyes, and her voice went soft, alluring. 'Isn't it, Roarke?'

'It is.'

'Well. Oh, well. I suppose she might be thinking history repeats, and I admit I was hoping it would. I don't suppose I should apologize to her?'

'It wouldn't be necessary. Or wise. I wish you well, Maggie, of course, but if you're looking for contacts, connections, and friendships through me, I'll have to disappoint you. It annoys my wife.'

'Oh.' Her eyebrows shot up, and her lips trembled into a faint smirk before she controlled it. 'If you were anyone else I'd have to say she's certainly tamed you.'

'Rather than rise to that, or sink to it, I'll just say she makes me happy. I'm on my way out, Maggie.'

'Yes, so you said. I'll just apologize again for causing trouble, thank you again for helping me on a business level.' Her voice trembled, just a little. 'I shouldn't keep you.'

She walked over to pick up her coat. 'If you're really on your way out, maybe I could walk down with you.'

'Of course.' When she held out her coat, he helped her into it, then retrieved his own. 'Do you have a car, or do you need one?'

'I have one, thanks. Roarke . . .' She shook her head. 'I guess I just want to say, again, that I'm sorry. And admit, just here, before we go down and that's the end, that I can't help being sorry it's never going to be me again.'

She squeezed his hand, stepped away.

He used his office 'link, told his admin he was leaving for the day and escorting Ms Percell out of the building. Then he moved to the side of the room, pressed a mechanism concealed in the molding with his thumb. The wall opened into his private elevator.

'Handy.' Magdelana laughed, as a woman does when she's fighting to be careless. 'Gadgets, they were one of your things. I've heard your home here is spectacular.'

'We're very comfortable there. Ground floor,' he ordered, and the elevator slid smoothly down.

'I'm sure you are. Your wife must enjoy the . . . comfort.'

'Actually, it's taken some adjusting for her.' The warmth shifted over his face. 'And sometimes yet, it embarrasses her a little.'

'I've heard of an embarrassment of riches, but can't imagine being embarrassed by them.'

'Money doesn't mean to her what it does to either of us.'

'Really?' She looked up at him, liquid eyes. 'And what does it mean to us?'

'Freedom, of course, and power and that comfort. But under it all.' He looked down at her, smiled a little. 'It's the game, isn't it?'

She smiled back, her face mirroring regret. 'We always understood each other.'

'That we didn't, no.' He stepped out, automatically taking her arm to lead her across the marble expanse of the lobby with its moving maps, its busy shops, its banks of live flowers.

Outside his limo, then hers, slid smoothly to the curb. When he walked her to her car, she turned. The dampness in her eyes shone now in the sunlight. 'Maybe we didn't understand each other. Maybe that's true. But there were good times for us, weren't there? There were good times.'

'There were.'

She lifted her hands to his cheeks. He curled his fingers gently around her wrists so they stood a moment in the cold and the wind. 'Good-bye, Maggie.'

'Good-bye, Roarke.' Tears glimmered on her lashes as she slipped into the warmth of the limo.

He watched it pull away, a sleek white whip through the ocean of traffic.

Then he got into his own car to go to his wife.

11

Eve was dragged through the station by a peppy little assistant named Mercy. Eve decided she had none as she bounced along the corridors, whipping Eve through checkpoints and keeping up a rapid-fire monologue as she all but skipped along in zippy black skids.

'Everyone's positively juiced to extreme about tonight's premiere. Nadine's about the biggest thing in media right now, and the station's totally gone that she opted to stay with us and do this show. And having you as the first guest is beyond mag. I mean, the two of you are, like, so extremely scorching.'

Mercy had pink hair tailed up in little butterfly pins, with what seemed to be their tiny progeny flying out of the arch of her left eyebrow.

It was disconcerting.

'You need to meet the producer and the director and the exec tech, then we're going to head straight to makeup and wardrobe. I can get you anything you want. I'm totally yours for the show – coffee, tea, water – we got flat and fizzy – soft drinks. Nadine says you go for coffee. We're going to pop in on the director, real quick.'

'I don't want to—'

But she was almost shoved into an office, had her hand pumped, before she was corralled into another office, with another hand pump.

The air was vibrating so fast it made her head ache.

Then, with Mercy still yapping like a Pomeranian on Zeus, Eve was dragged into makeup where the brightly lit mirrors gleamed over the long, long counter crowded with a dizzying array of pots and tubes and brushes and strange instruments that looked like some wicked tools designed for torture.

Worse – worse than the idea she was pressured by the brass and by friendship to appear on screen, worse than the yapping in her ear, worse than the knowledge that some or all of those instruments and pots and tubes would be used on her – was the woman who stood behind a high-backed black chair grinning a toothy grin.

'Oh, Mother of God.'

'You two know each other, right?' Mercy babbled on. 'Trina, I'm going to leave Lieutenant Dallas in your magic hands, go get her coffee. Nadine stocked some special for her. Anything you want?'

Trina, her hair a black-and-white fountain on top of her head, her eyes an unearthly green, whipped a bright blue cape from a hook. 'Water'd be good. Flat.'

'Be right back!'

'You look like dog shit, Dallas,' Trina commented.

'This is a recurring nightmare. I'm just going to punch myself in the face until I wake up.'

'You've got enough bruising under your eyes, you look like you've already been decked a few times today. I'll fix it.'

'Why are you here? Why is it you?'

'First, because I'm the best and Nadine knows it. She can get the best. Second, because of you. If it wasn't for you, I'd never have worked on Nadine at your place.'

Trina snapped the cape like a matador at a bull. 'Appreciate it.'

'So, somehow, I brought this on myself.'

'You're lucky it's me. Because I'm the best, and because I know you, and I can − thousands couldn't − make you look like yourself.'

'I already look like myself.'

'No, you look like dog shit. But you're under there, and I know how to find you. Plus, I gotta pump it up for the cameras, but I won't make you look like an LC on the prowl.'

In her life there were few who struck an active chord of fear in Eve. Trina was one of them. As if she knew it, Trina smiled again, tapped the back of the chair.

'Sit. It'll be over before you know it.'

'Remember, I'm armed.' But she sat. What choice did she have?

'So how come you don't look like you just got back from vacation? Mavis said you and Roarke took a few days at the beach.' She scooped her fingers through Eve's hair, frowned, let the hair shift through. 'Need a little trim.'

'God. Oh, God.'

Trina simply put the cape over Eve. 'And how come you haven't been over to see Mavis and that sweet baby since you got back?'

One thing about the cape, Eve noted, she could wring her hands if she felt the need. And no one could see. 'I haven't had time.'

'Your best and oldest friend just had a kid.' Trina lowered her head so her face was pressed to Eve's, so those green eyes pinned Eve's in the mirror. 'You know I had to sit on her to keep her from coming tonight. It's too cold to take that baby out. You gotta make time.'

'All right. Okay.'

'Belle's the most beautiful thing that ever drew breath, I swear.' Straightening again, Trina pressed her thumbs on some point at the back of Eve's neck, moved down her shoulders. 'You're a mess of knots, as usual.'

Eve just closed her eyes. She heard Mercy come back in – yap, yap, yap – then go away again. She heard the little snips and buzzes as Trina did whatever the hell she did with hair. She jolted when the chair eased back.

'You gotta relax, okay? You don't look good, I don't look good.'

'I obsess about that all the time.' And Eve closed her eyes again. It was one night, she reminded herself, and she'd get through it. Small change in the big scheme.

Fingers and thumbs pressed gently along her jaw, over her temples, along the sides of her neck, her shoulders. The clever acupressure and draining fatigue combined to pull her into sleep.

She surfaced to a murmur of voices, to light brushing, almost a tickling over her face. And she scented him. Even before her head cleared enough for her to recognize the rhythm and tone of his voice, she scented Roarke.

'Just about done,' Trina was saying. 'What she's wearing's fine – so I guess you picked it – but I'll take a look at the other deal you brought in, in case it's better. Wardrobe's going to want to have a look anyway.'

'I'm not changing,' Eve muttered.

'And she's back.' Trina eased the chair back up. Since it was facing away from the mirror now, all Eve saw was Roarke.

'Morning,' he said, and taking her hand, ran his thumb over the back of it. 'You look rested.'

'Miracles performed daily,' Trina claimed. 'Let's just polish off the hair.' Something must have gotten through as Trina put down the tools of her trade. 'You know, we'll hit that right before we go on. I've got to check on a couple things anyway and Nadine's due in for her touch-up. Green Room's just across the hall, to the right. It's nice.'

She took off the protective cape. 'Want a look before you head out?'

Eve rose, glanced toward the mirror. As advertised, she looked like herself. Brighter, she supposed, with her eyes and her lips defined and smudged up with color, but she was recognizable. And the dog shit had been well and truly buried.

'Okay,' she said.

'Okay?' Trina snorted. '*Now* you look like you've been on vacation. Don't spill anything on that jacket because I think they're going to want to go with it.'

'I'll see she behaves.' Taking Eve's hand again, he walked with her across the hall into the Green Room that was actually pale peach.

There was a generous wall screen currently tuned to Channel 75's programming, generous sofas and chairs in a calming sea green, and a generous tray of fruit, cheese, crackers on a wide counter.

'I didn't expect you to come.'

Roarke raised a brow. 'Of course I came. It's a big night.'

'And you brought the other gear in case I messed up what I already had on.'

'Just part of the service.'

'I figured you'd be pissed at me.'

'I imagined you'd be pissed at me.' This time when he took her hands, he brought them both to his lips. 'Why don't we cancel that out? I had a considerable brood on most of the day, and I'm tired of carrying it around.'

'I thought you told me the Irish like to brood.'

'Oh, we love it. We use it to write songs and stories. But I've had enough of that for the time being. And never enough of you.'

Her heart lightened. How had she managed to stand, she wondered, when it had been so heavy? 'I love you.'

He drew her in, touched his lips to her brow, her cheeks,

the shallow dent in her chin, then laid them warmly over hers. She pressed against him, her arms linked around his waist, as together they deepened the kiss.

'I'd offer you my office,' Nadine said as she leaned on the door jamb, 'but Dallas has already been in makeup.'

Eve kept her arms linked for a moment more before she stepped back. 'You sicced Trina on me.'

'I *gave* you Trina,' Nadine corrected. 'She's damn good, which is why I hired her for the show. Plus, for tonight, I figured your point of view would be "better the devil you know."'

'Got a point,' Eve decided.

'You look good, which is essential. Strong, alert, smart, attractive,' Nadine mused, walking a circle around Eve. 'And all cop. We'll leave the glamour for me.'

'You wear it so well,' Roarke commented. 'You look radiant, Nadine, and polished as a jewel.'

'I do, don't I?' Laughing, Nadine shook back her chic bob of streaky blonde hair, did a styling turn in the electric blue suit with its pencil-thin skirt and waist-cinching jacket. The heels were black skyscrapers that set off the wink of a diamond ankle chain.

'I didn't think I'd be nervous, but I am. There's a lot riding on this first show. Dallas, I don't want to prep you. I don't want the interview to be stale or rehearsed, but I do want to go over a few points.'

'I'll get out of your way then,' Roarke began, but Nadine shook her head.

'No. You can run faster than I can in these shoes if she makes a break for it. Let's just sit.'

'Something to drink then.' Roarke gestured to the well-stocked counter. 'Or eat.'

'After.' Nadine pressed a hand to her stomach as she sat on one of the sofas. 'My system's on full alert.'

'I'm good,' Eve said. 'What's to be nervous about? It's what you do.'

'That's what I tell myself, but I've never done exactly this before. And this was the big gold hoop. Now that I've got it in my hot little hand, I can't afford to drop it. So . . .'

Nadine scooted to the edge of her chair as if she might be the one to make a run for it. 'We'll have to touch on the Icove case. That's what got me the gig. But I'm not going to linger on that. I'm going to want to revisit that after the book and the vid hit. The baby market business is still fresh, so we'll discuss that. Speaking of babies, Belle was well named. God, she's beautiful, isn't she?'

Eve squirmed. 'Sure.'

'I've done an interview with Tandy, and with Mavis on that one, and we'll air pieces of those during the spot. We're going to talk about what you do, how you do it. How much will you be able to tell me about the Foster homicide?'

'The investigation's ongoing.'

Nadine didn't miss a beat, or the chance to smirk. 'I'm going to need more than that – leads being pursued, avenues explored, the players, the scene, the victim. It's called *Now* for a reason. But we'll keep that until we're on. It's a hard news show, but I will have to ask about Roarke.'

Nadine put up a hand before Eve could speak. 'I can't interview Roarke's cop in a venue like this without asking about Roarke. Don't worry, it's not boxers or briefs, just an overview, we'll say.'

She aimed an amused, inquiring glance at Roarke, who only laughed and shook his head.

'How you manage to balance the work with your life,' Nadine continued. 'If marriage has changed how you do the work, or how you look at the job. We'll get on and off. So . . .'

She checked her wrist unit. 'I've got to get touched up. Trina will take a last look at you in a few minutes, then Mercy will bring you into the studio. And we'll go from there. Dallas.' Nadine pressed a hand on hers. 'Thanks.'

'You better hold that till after. You may not like my answers.'

'Thanks,' she said again, and rose. Then she turned to Roarke. 'How about one right here, big guy?' She tapped a finger to her lips. 'For luck.'

He stepped to her, kissed her lightly on the mouth. 'Here's to a thirty-percent share.'

'Your lips, God's ears.'

In the end, it went okay, as far as Eve could tell. Though she couldn't understand how anyone could be juiced about sitting in front of an image of the city, under hot lights while robocams slithered around like snakes.

Theme music shimmered out, and she heard Nadine take three quiet breaths while some guy on the floor signalled with his fingers. Then Nadine aimed her eyes toward one of those robots.

'Good evening. I'm Nadine Furst, and this is *Now*.'

They did, as Nadine had said, touch on the Icove case from the previous fall. Yes, Eve believed the laws against human cloning were correct and just. No, she didn't hold the clones themselves responsible for what the Icoves had done.

She watched the clips as the separate interviews with Tandy Applebee, her husband and their infant son, and Mavis, Leonardo, and Belle were run. Both women got teary as they spoke about their friendship, and how Eve had saved Tandy's life, saved the baby – who they'd named Quentin Dallas Applebee – from being sold in the black market, and had broken the ring only hours before their babies had been born.

'How does that make you feel?' Nadine asked.

'Like I did my job.'

'Just that?'

Eve shifted. What the hell. 'Sometimes it gets personal. It's not supposed to, but it does. This was personal. Mavis and I go back, and she and my partner are tight. Mavis is the one who pushed me, pushed us, to look for Tandy. She deserves a lot of credit for that, for standing up for a friend.

You could say, in this case, it was friendship that ultimately connected the cases, and cleared them both. The job's not just about clearing a case, it's about justice. I did my job.'

'A demanding, dangerous, high-powered job. You're married to a man with a lot of demands on his time, who some might term dangerous, and who is certainly high-powered. How do you balance the work with your private life?'

'Maybe by knowing it's not always going to balance, and being married to someone who gets that. A lot of cops . . . There can be friction in the personal area,' she amended, 'because the job means you put in long hours, inconvenient hours that mess up schedules. You miss dinners or dates or whatever.'

'Which may seem minor,' Nadine said, 'but in reality, those dinners, dates, and so on are part of what makes up a personal life.'

'Lapping into personal life is part of it, that's all. It's just the job. It's tough for a civilian to deal, day after day. In my opinion, cops are mostly a bad bet in the personal arena. But some make it work. It works, I guess, when the civilian gets it. When the civilian respects and values the job, or at least understands it. I got lucky there.'

She shifted her gaze to where Roarke stood behind the range of cameras. 'I got lucky.'

They broke for the ads that paid the bills, and Trina marched over with a flurry of brushes.

'Nice,' Nadine told her.

'Is it almost over?'

'Nearly there.' She thought, but didn't say, what a moment it had been when Eve's gaze had shifted away, when the emotion had swarmed into her eyes on her claim that she'd gotten lucky. Thirty-percent share? Nadine thought. Her ass. That single moment was going to blow the ratings out of the stratosphere.

'Your current case,' Nadine began when they were back. 'The shocking murder of Craig Foster, a history teacher. What can you tell us?'

'The investigation is active and ongoing.'

Flat voice, flat eyes, Nadine noted with satisfaction. All cop now, and the contrast was perfect. 'You've said that to know the killer, know the victim. Tell us about Craig Foster. Who was he?'

'He was, by all accounts, a young and dedicated teacher, a loving husband, a good son. A good man, and a creature of habit. He was frugal, responsible and ordinary in the sense he did his work, he lived his life, and enjoyed both.'

'What does that tell you about his killer?'

'I know that his killer knew and understood Craig Foster's habits, and used those habits to take his life, to take a husband, a son, a teacher. That he did so not in heat, not on impulse, but with forethought and calculation.'

'What makes this crime particularly heinous is that it was committed in a school where children from the ages of six to thirteen walk the halls. In fact, the body was discovered by two young girls.'

'Heinous? Murder by definition – by its nature – is a heinous crime. Where it took place, in this case, might make it more callous to some. It was also efficient.'

Nadine leaned forward. 'How so?'

'The victim's habits. The killer had only to observe and note the victim's daily routine, know the schedule, and use those elements. Having students, teachers, support staff in and around the halls, in and around classrooms and other facilities was an advantage. He took it.'

'Your suspects. You've interviewed a number of people thus far. Today you brought in Reed Williams, another teacher at Sarah Child Academy for questioning.'

'We questioned Mr Williams, and have charged him in another matter. He is not charged with Mr Foster's murder.'

'But he is a suspect? Your prime suspect?'

'The investigation is active and ongoing,' Eve repeated. 'Until it's closed, we'll continue to question a number of individuals. I'm unable to tell you more at this time.'

Nadine made a few more forays; Eve blocked her. When the director signalled the time, Nadine leaned forward again. 'Tell me this, if the killer's watching right now, what would you say to him?'

'That my partner and I stand for Craig Foster now. We have a job to do, and we're damn good at it. He should go ahead and watch plenty of screen now because they don't provide one in the cage he'll be living in for the rest of his life.'

'Thank you, Lieutenant Dallas. This is Nadine Furst,' she said to the camera. 'Good night, for *Now*.'

'You were perfect,' Roarke said when they were finally able to get out of the station.

'It must've gone okay, seeing as Nadine jumped up and did a victory dance the minute the stupid cameras went off.'

'Perfect,' he repeated, and turning her to him, laid his mouth on hers. 'Except for the misuse of a pronoun.'

'Huh?'

'You said "I got lucky." The correct statement, darling Eve, is "We got lucky."' He kissed her again, softly. 'We.'

'I guess we did. No vehicle?' she added with a glance around the lot.

'I had it taken back so I could drive home with my wife.'

'In that case, you take the wheel.' She paused. 'I'm glad you hung around.' When she got into the car, she stretched out her legs. Sighed. 'Nadine gets off on that whole circus. Takes all kinds.'

'It does. There are a lot of people who may be wondering how you do what it is you do, day after day. So, is this Reed Williams your man?'

'He's top choice right now. And get this, Oliver Straffo's his lawyer.'

'Straffo's a little high dollar for someone on a teacher's salary.'

'Williams does all right – private sector, tenure. But it

was Straffo's kid who found the body. This guy's looking good for doing Foster, in his kid's school, where his kid can slip on the blood and vomit, and he's representing him. Yeah, takes all kinds.'

'It's possible Straffo believes he's innocent.'

'Yeah, maybe. Straffo doesn't know that his own wife was one of the notches on Williams's belt. Williams likes to hunt and gather among the staff and mothers. Has the morals of a rabbit, and Rabbit's one of the things we've got him on. Had some in his toybox in his bedroom. It's the illegals we charged him with so far, and that's where Straffo answered the call. It bugs me.'

'Lawyers do what they do, Lieutenant.'

'Yeah, but say you had a kid and you find out one of her teachers is playing twist the pretzel in her school.' Because her current position was too comfortable, and she feared she might just drop into sleep, Eve pushed up. 'That he uses illegal substances for his own sexual satisfaction. Do you figure you'd jump to defend him?'

'It's hard to say, but at first thought, unlikely. Then again, maybe Straffo has the morals of a rabbit, too.'

'Bet he wouldn't jump so fast if he knew his client had dipped into his own personal well.'

'Do you intend to tell him?'

Eve thought of Allika, her guilt, her fear. 'Not unless it pertains to the case. If I find and can prove that Williams killed Foster because Foster knew about the affair, yeah, Straffo's going to get some bad news.'

'Are you sure he doesn't already know?'

'No, I'm not sure. And I'd be looking hard at him, too, if I could place him at or near the scene. He was in his office by eight-thirty that morning. That gives him a little squeeze time to have done it, but it's a very tight squeeze. He was in a partners' meeting from eight-thirty to nine, and in his office again, with his paralegal, admin, and several others in and out until he left for a lunch meeting at noon. He's looking clear on this.'

'I'm not quite sure why you would have looked at him. It wasn't Foster doing his wife, after all. Now if Williams had been murdered . . .'

'Reputation.' She shrugged. 'It's not such a stretch that Foster was killed to protect a reputation. Williams – that beeps the loudest. But I don't think Straffo would have cared to have his wife's infidelity made public.' She fought back a yawn. 'Bad for the image.'

'I can promise, Lieutenant, that if I were in Straffo's position, I'd aim for you and your paramour. Not some innocent bystander.'

'Back at you.' But because it made her think of Magdelana again, Eve shut it off. 'Anyway, we'll keep squeezing Williams, see what oozes out. Um . . . I'm getting poked from various directions that we – I use *we* as it's going to be the only pronoun in this case – need to go see Mavis and the kid.'

'All right.'

'That's it? Just all right?'

'It'll be fine. We survived the birth. A baby all wrapped up in a pink blanket should be a welcome relief after that ordeal.'

'I guess. Peabody says we need to take a gift. A teddy bear or something.'

'That should be simple enough.'

'Good. You do that part. I don't get the bear thing. Aren't bears something people generally try to avoid so as not to be mauled?'

When he laughed, she glanced over. And just looking at him, seeing the laugh in his eyes when he looked at her, had everything inside her going warm.

She laid her hand over his as he drove through the gates of home. 'Let's try for that balance Nadine was asking about,' she said. 'And for a while, no case, no work, no obligations. Just you. Just me.'

'My favorite combination.'

She made the move, wrapping her arms around him, rubbing her lips to his when they were out of the car. And the warmth that had bloomed inside her spread like spring. Every doubt, every hurt, every fear, every question drained away in it.

Just you, she thought again as they glided into the house. Just me.

By tacit agreement they made their way to the elevator. The stairs would take too long. Once inside, riding up, he nudged her coat off her shoulders, and she his. But the gestures weren't hurried, weren't frantic. Instead they were smooth and easy, with the knowledge they'd reclaimed something that had slipped, just for a moment, a finger's span out of reach.

In the bedroom there was a glimmer of moonshine, soft and blue through the windows, through the skylight over the bed. They undressed each other, distracted each other with long, lingering kisses, long, lingering strokes.

Her heart felt as if it were back, exactly where it belonged, and beating fast and thickly against his.

'I missed you,' she said, holding tight. 'I missed us.'

'A ghra,' he murmured, and thrilled her.

She was his again, completely his again. His strong, complicated, and endlessly fascinating wife. Close and his, with nothing between them. The taste of her filled him, the long, lean lines of her enticed him.

Here was the balance Nadine had questioned, and that no one who didn't feel it, didn't know it, didn't have could ever fully understand. They simply fit, all the complex and ragged edges of both of them, simply fit. One to the other, to make each whole.

When they lay on the bed she wrapped around him, and she sighed again. A sound he knew meant they were home, at last. Needing to give, he used his lips, his hands, his body, until the sigh became a moan.

No one else, she thought, could ever reach her as he did. And, feeling him quiver at her touch, knew for him it was the same.

As she rolled over that first liquid crest, she cupped his

face in her hands. She brought his lips to hers once more for a kiss of shattering tenderness.

'My love,' he repeated in Irish. *My only. My heart.* She heard his voice as he slipped inside her, saw his eyes as they moved together.

Slow and lovely and real. And every brutal thing that belonged to the world was separate from this. Then fingers twined, mouths meeting, they slipped away together.

Later, curled against him, content and drifting, she murmured, 'Lucky us,' and she heard him chuckle in the dark before she slid into sleep.

12

He was incensed. He couldn't believe she was going to go through with it. Bluffing, he decided. She was bluffing.

Reed Williams cut through the water with hard, angry strokes. He'd tried sweet talk, he'd tried temper, he'd tried threats. But that damn Arnette was being hardnosed about this – the principal standing on principle.

Or professing to be. Hypocritical bitch.

Bluffing, he thought again as he kicked off the wall of the pool and streaked his way to another lap. He'd just do another five laps, let her stew a little.

He'd been sure she'd stand by him, or if she wavered, she'd value her own position enough to secure his.

It was that fucking cop, he decided. Had to be a dyke – she and that brown-eyed partner of hers. Real bitches.

Most women were, you just had to know how to handle them.

And if he knew anything, he knew how to handle women.

Knew how to handle himself. Knew how to handle whatever came along.

He'd handled Craig, hadn't he? Poor bastard.

No way they were going to hang the poor bastard's

murder on him, especially with Oliver Straffo in his corner.

And wasn't that lovely, lovely irony? Not that Straffo's wife had been a particularly exciting lay. But all that guilt and misery had given a certain flavor to the quick bump at the holiday party, and the single nooner at his place.

But God knew, he'd had better.

He wasn't going to resign over a little sex, that was for damn sure. And if Arnette followed through and began termination procedures, well, he'd warned her. He wouldn't go down alone.

Once he reminded her of that – again – she'd settle down.

A little winded, he finished his final lap, gripped the edge of the pool as he began to remove his goggles.

He felt a little prick, a little buzz just below the crown of his head. He lifted a hand to swat at it, as if it were a mosquito. His fingers tingled.

His heart began to thud, his throat to close. As his vision blurred he blinked, saw someone. He tried to call out, but his voice was a croak. He tried to pull his body from the pool, but his hands, his arms were already numb. He lost his grip, hit his jaw on the edge.

He felt no pain.

Gasping, he struggled to keep his head above water. He choked, and flailed, ordered himself to float. Just to float until he could think again.

'I'll help you,' his killer said. And with the long pole of

the pool net reached out. Pressing it lightly on his shoulder, pushed him down, held him down with no real effort at all.

Until his struggles stopped.

Eve stepped out of the shower feeling reborn. She'd been off her stride, she admitted, off her feed, and just plain off for a few days. But that was done.

She was grateful only a few people knew she'd let herself obsess over and get turned inside out about some smug, manipulative blonde. Magdelana Percell, she promised herself as the warm air of the drying tube swirled, was officially history.

She snagged a robe and decided she was hungry enough to eat what Roarke called a full Irish. Once she had that and some coffee under her belt, she was heading straight down to Central.

She was going back to the beginning of the Foster investigation with her mind clear. Maybe the personal blur had caused her to miss something.

She stepped out, and Roarke was there, sipping coffee, scanning the last of the financials while the cat bumped his head against Roarke's arm. As if to say, 'Aren't you going to eat? Where's breakfast?'

'You feed that lardass yet?' she asked.

'I did, yes, though he'll call me a liar. I, however, was waiting for you.'

'I guess I could choke something down. Some eggs and whatever.'

'You need some whatever.' He rose, cutting her off before she reached her closet, and gave her ass a deliberate squeeze. 'You've lost a couple pounds in the last few days.'

'Maybe.'

'My gauge has pinpoint accuracy when it comes to you.' He kissed her between the eyes. 'A full Irish is in order, I'm thinking.'

'That's plenty of whatever.' She went to her closet with a smile on her face. It was good to be back in synch.

'If I'm clear, and you can manage it,' she began as she grabbed clothes, 'maybe we could bop by Mavis and Leonardo's. I can tag her later, see if they're up for it.'

'Suits me.' He switched to the morning news before going to the AutoChef. 'A teddy bear, was it?'

'Peabody said. Or something in that realm.'

'I think we both might leave that one up to Caro. No doubt she'll know just the thing. Just let either her or me know if I should come down to Central or meet you at their place.'

She was strapping on her weapon harness when he turned. 'It's a pity you couldn't have appeared on Nadine's show like that. The shirtsleeves, the weapon at your side. Sexy and dangerous.'

Eve only snorted, then sat to put on her boots.

He crossed over to set down their plates, and after one steely warning look at Galahad, pulled Eve to her feet. 'Sexy,' he repeated, 'dangerous. And mine.'

'Better back off, ace. I'm armed.'

'Just the way I like you. What do you say we do the obvious and clichéd for Valentine's Day? A romantic dinner for two, a great deal of champagne, dancing, and incredible amounts of inventive sex.'

'I might be available for that.' *When the hell was Valentine's Day again?*

He laughed, reading her perfectly. 'The fourteenth, my sentimental fool. Which would be the day after tomorrow. If work interferes, we'll just have a very late dinner for two, and so forth.'

'You're on.' And because it just felt right, she laid her head on his shoulder.

She missed the first sentence or two the chirpy on-air reporter said. Even when Roarke's name was announced – and her own – she might have let it slip.

But he stiffened against her so she focused on the screen. The air inside her body simply evaporated, and left her hollow.

He stood with Magdelana, stood close, looking down at her. Just the barest hint of a smile on his face. A face Magdelana held intimately in her hands.

'. . . identified by our sources as European socialite Magdelana Percell, recently divorced from Georges Fayette, a wealthy French entrepreneur. It appears Ms Percell has an eye for wealthy men as she was seen lunching with Roarke only days ago at the exclusive Three Sisters restaurant here in New York. According to our sources, the pair enjoyed seasonal salads and a great deal of intimate conversation. We wonder if Lieutenant Eve Dallas, one of New York's top cops, and Roarke's wife of the last year and a half, is investigating.'

'Fuck me,' Roarke muttered. 'What bloody bullshit. I'm sorry they—'

He stopped whatever he was going to say as she was pulling very slowly, very deliberately away from him. And he saw her face. It was sheet white, her eyes dark and shocked against the utter pallor.

'Christ Jesus, Eve, you can't—'

'I have to go to work.' The words jumped so in her throat, in her head, she wasn't sure they came out in the right order.

'Bollocks to that. To *all* of this. I did nothing, and you should know it – damn it, you should know without me saying it. I walked her out of the building. She came to see me, and I gave her less than ten minutes before I showed her the door. I felt small doing so, if you must know, but I'd rather hurt her feelings than cause you a moment of unhappiness.'

She spoke as slowly and deliberately as she'd moved. 'I need you to back off.'

'Fuck that! Fuck it, Eve. Am I to be tried and condemned because some moron had a vid-cam at the right moment? A moment when a woman I once cared for said good-bye? Do you think I'd have embarrassed you, or myself come to that, in this way?'

'You did, you did embarrass both of us this way. But that's not important, that's not the point.'

'Damn if I'll apologize for helping a woman into her car on a public street in the middle of the bleeding day.' He dragged his hand through his hair in a gesture she recognized, even now, as absolute frustration. 'You're too smart for this. You know there are people who love nothing more than to spread dirt around people like us. And you would accuse me—'

'I haven't accused you.'

'Oh, aye, you have, of all manner of things.' Frustration turned on a dime to rage and insult. 'And you do it without a word. I'd rather have the words as hard as they might be than that look on your face. It's killing me. Let's have this out then, once and for all, and be bloody well done with it.'

'No. No. I don't want to be here right now.' Carefully, she picked up her jacket. 'I don't want to be with you right now. Because I can't fight right now. I can't think. I've got nothing. So you'll win, if that's what you need, because I've got nothing.'

'This isn't about winning.' The utter misery on her face, in her voice, drowned the temper. 'What I need is to know you believe me. That you trust me. That you know me.'

The tears were coming; she wouldn't be able to hold them back much longer. She put on her jacket. 'We'll get into it later.'

'That one thing, Eve,' he said as she turned away. 'Answer that one thing. Do you believe I'd betray you with her?'

She drew in what little she had and turned to face him.

'No. No, I don't believe you'd betray me with her. I don't believe you'd cheat on me. But I'm afraid, and I'm sick in my heart that you might look at her, then at me. And regret.'

He took a step toward her. 'Eve.'

'If you don't let me go now, this will never be right.'

She made it out of the room, down the stairs. She heard Summerset say her name, and kept moving. Get out, was all she could think. Get away.

'You need your coat.' As she yanked at the door, Summerset draped it over her shoulders. 'It's very cold. Eve.' He spoke her given name quietly, and nearly shattered her last line of defense. 'Will you let her use you both this way?'

'I don't know. I—' Her communicator beeped. 'Oh, God, oh God.' She bore down. 'Block video,' she ordered. 'Dallas.'

Dispatch, Dallas, Lieutenant Eve . . .

She shoved her arms into the sleeves of the coat as she was ordered to Sarah Child. She responded as she strode out to the car.

And she felt Roarke watching her from their bedroom window as she drove away to do the job.

Eve stood over the body of Reed Williams and blocked out everything but the work. She knew Eric Dawson – who'd found Williams floating and had jumped in to try to save him – was currently in the locker room with a uniform.

The med-techs who responded had fought to revive him, even after Dawson's attempts, then Nurse Brennan's, as CPR had failed.

So her crime scene and the body had been severely compromised. And Reed Williams was still very dead.

She crouched down, examined the bruise and shallow laceration along his jaw. Otherwise, from her exam, his body was unmarked. He was wearing black swim trunks, and a pair of blue-lens minigoggles floated in the pool.

As Peabody hadn't yet arrived on scene, she turned the body herself to study the back, the legs, the shoulders.

'No visible trauma other than the jawline, some superficial scratches consistent with being pulled out of the pool on the back. No sign of struggle.' She rose, began to walk around the pool. 'No visible blood. Might've been blood, and it was washed away.' Frowning, she looked around for a weapon that might have caused the wound on the jaw.

'Vic stands near the pool. Somebody strikes out, vic falls back into the water. Lost consciousness and drowns? Maybe, maybe, but the bruise isn't that severe. But maybe.'

She kept walking, and studied the edge of the pool. Walked back, hunkered down again, and used microgoggles and a penlight to get a better look at the wound. 'Flat. More a scrape than a cut. In the water already maybe. Yeah, it's the right angle, isn't it? Vic's taking his swim, gets to the wall, holds onto the edge for a minute. That's what you do. Slips, loses his grip, knocks his chin on the skirting. But why? Just clumsiness? Didn't strike me as a clumsy guy. And does that knock end up drowning him? Or did he have help?'

She went back to the body, shook her head. 'There's no skin under his nails. No sealant, no nothing. Clean as a damn whistle. What do you do if somebody holds your head under? You fight, you scratch. And if I'm standing on the skirt of the pool holding some guy under – for instance, a strong guy, a guy who works out regularly – I'm probably going to give his head a good thump against the wall for insurance. Easy to mistake a head knock for accidental.'

Frowning again, she began to search, to feel the back of Williams's head. No bump, no laceration, no trauma.

Looked simple, looked easy. Looked accidental.

And she thought: *No fucking way.*

'Bag and tag him,' Eve ordered and straightened. 'ME to determine. Priority request for Morris. I want the sweepers to go over the edging. I'm looking for blood or skin.'

She moved off, into the locker room where Dawson sat in a baggy sweatsuit drinking hot coffee. 'Officer.' Eve nodded to the uniform. 'Detective Peabody should be arriving momentarily. Direct her here.'

'Yes, sir.'

'Mr Dawson.'

'He was floating.' Dawson's hands began to shake a little. 'He was floating. I thought at first he was just . . . just floating, the way you do. Then I saw he wasn't.'

'Mr Dawson, I'm going to record this. Do you understand?'

'Yes, yes.'

'Mr Williams was already in the pool when you came in to the area?'

'Yes, he was . . .' He drew a long breath, set the coffee cup aside. 'Actually, I was looking for him. I'd seen Arnette – Principal Mosebly, and she asked if I would take Reed's fourth-period class today – that's my study period. She told me he'd been suspended and she was going to initiate termination proceedings, unless he resigned within the next twenty-four hours. I felt terrible about it.'

'You were friendly with Mr Williams?'

'We all got along here. We were all friendly, there was never any trouble here. Until . . . Oh, God.' He dropped his head again, pinched the bridge of his nose. 'I agreed to monitor the class, but asked if I could speak with him, to get some idea of his lesson plan. I don't know.'

He braced his head, hair still damp, in his hand. 'She said she assumed he was cleaning out his lockers. I glanced in the lounge, but he wasn't there, so I went into the fitness center. His locker was still activated, but he wasn't on the machines. I just stepped into the pool area, to see . . .'

'What did you see?'

'He was floating, facedown. At first, I . . . I thought – I maybe said, "Damn, Reed, this is a damn mess." He kept floating, and I realized . . . I jumped in. You're supposed to grab a flotation, but I didn't think. I just jumped, and I turned him over, towed him to the side. I got him out. I had to get out first, then haul him out. I did mouth-to-mouth, CPR. We're all required to know how to do that. I don't know how long, but he wasn't breathing. I hit the intercom, called Carin – Nurse Brennan. I told her to call nine-one-one and to come to the pool.'

'Which she did.'

'Yes. She came right away. She tried, when she got here, she tried. Then the MTs tried. But they said he was gone.'

'Where are your shoes?'

'Shoes?' He looked down at his bare feet. 'I forgot shoes. I had my work clothes on when I went into the pool. The police officer said it was all right for me to change. I forgot to put my skids on, I guess. Maybe if I'd gotten there sooner, just a minute or two sooner. If I hadn't looked in the lounge first.'

'I don't think so, Mr Dawson. I think you did all you could.'

'I hope I did. I nearly drowned once, when I was ten. My family always went to the Jersey shore in August. I went out too far, and I couldn't get back. The waves just kept pushing me farther out, and I couldn't stay up. My father pulled me back. He got to me and pulled me all the way back to shore. Blistered my ears for swimming out that far, then he cried. Just sat down and cried. I never forgot it, or how scared I was. It's a scary way to die.'

'Yeah, but mostly they all are.'

She questioned him further, but if he'd been responsible

for Williams's death instead of traumatized by it, she'd eat her badge.

She released him, then accessed Williams's locker for another search. One of his good suits, she noted, with shirt and tie, dress shoes. So he'd been planning to dude up for the day. Didn't sound like resignation time to her.

Could have had another appointment, she mused. She searched through his toiletry bag, found nothing out of line. Then hauled out his briefcase as she heard the sturdy strides of Peabody's winter boots.

'Williams is our DB,' Eve said without looking over. 'Found floating facedown in the pool, past reviving. Bruised and scraped on the jaw, could be he got clocked, but it looks to me as if he rapped himself on the edge of the pool. Some scrapes on the back consistent with being pulled out. No other visible trauma.'

'So it looks accidental.'

'Looks like. Isn't, or I'm a dancing monkey. We'll want to go through this disc, but by the looks of his briefcase, it appears he was set to resume his teacherly duties today.' Now she looked over at Peabody. 'Wit statement claims Williams was suspended, and termination proceedings were set to begin if he didn't resign within twenty-four.'

'But he comes in, uses the school facilities.' Peabody poked her head into the locker. 'And from all appearances was going to tough it out. Who'd he see this morning?'

'That's what we're going to find out, but my money's on Mosebly.'

They tracked the principal down in her office, easily cutting through the admin who sat bleary-eyed and sniffling. Mosebly paced the room as she spoke on an earpiece. She held up a hand, signalling Eve and Peabody to wait.

'Yes, of course. I will. The police are here now. I'll get back to you as soon as I've spoken with them.' Mosebly took off the earpiece, laid it on her desk. 'The chairman of our board,' she said, and rubbed her fingertips between her eyebrows. 'This is a very difficult time. If you'll give me a moment, I need to arrange for classes to be dismissed for the day.'

'Nobody leaves,' Eve said flatly.

'I beg your pardon? We've had a second death. You can't expect the students to—'

'Nobody leaves the building until I clear it. Nobody else comes in unless I clear it. What time did you speak with Mr Williams this morning?'

'I'm sorry, my head is splitting.' She moved to her desk, opened a drawer, and took out a small enameled case. She removed what Eve recognized as a standard blocker. After pouring herself a glass of water, she sat down, took the pill.

It would help the headache, Eve thought, and also gave Mosebly a few moments to gather her wits and decide what she'd say and how she'd say it.

'I signed in at seven, or shortly after. To be frank, Craig Foster's death has generated a great deal of concern among the parents, the board. I've held a number of conferences, and came in early today to catch up on other administrative duties.'

'Including preparing termination proceedings on Reed Williams.'

'Yes.' She pressed her lips together. 'It seems cold now, but there was no choice. He'd been charged with possessing illegal substances, and is − or it appears he was − under heavy suspicion for Craig's murder. He was obviously an unacceptable risk for our students. As I told him clearly yesterday when he returned to the school.'

'Yesterday? He came back here after his bail hearing?'

'Correct. I suggested, initially, he take some leave, but he was adamant about going on as if nothing had happened. Though most of the students had left by that time, I was worried about him causing a scene, so I asked him to speak with me in here. Privately.'

Mosebly brushed a hand over her hair, then tugged down the jacket of her suit. 'It was unpleasant, I'll be frank about that as well. I explained the need to avoid any more scandal. We've had three parents remove their children from the school and demand their tuition be returned. Once it became public that a teacher was arrested . . .'

She trailed off, shook her head.

'How'd he take it?' Eve asked.

'Poorly. It's within my rights to suspend a teacher for suspicion of illegal or immoral behavior, but termination is trickier. He knew it. He stalked out claiming that between his lawyer and his union rep, he'd squash any attempt I – or the BOD – might make to have him fired.'

'Wouldn't have gone down well with you.'

'No, it did not. It did not,' Mosebly repeated with some fire in her eyes. 'While I believe we could and would have succeeded in the termination, it would have been an ugly mess. And resulted, no doubt, in the loss of more students.'

'And more revenue.'

'Yes. Without revenue, we can't provide the education the students expect and deserve.'

'But he came in today regardless. Did you have words with him in the pool? You've been swimming this morning, Principal Mosebly.' She waited while Mosebly blinked. 'Your towel, still damp, was in the locker room hamper. Women's side. One towel.'

'As I've stated before, I often swim in the morning. I did see Reed, yes, as I was getting out of the pool. And yes, we had words. I told him I wanted him off the premises, and he informed me he was going to take a swim, then have some coffee and a muffin before he began his classes.'

'Defying your authority,' Eve prompted.

'He was very smug and arrogant about it. I don't deny we argued, or that I was very angry. And he was diving into the pool, very much alive, when I left. I showered, dressed, then came directly here to contact the chairman and relay the situation.'

'What time was that?'

246

'It would have been around eight when I got to my office and made the call. When I'd finished, I found Eric – Mr Dawson, and asked him to monitor Reed's fourth-period class today. I also spoke with Mirri and Dave, assigning each of them to one of Reed's classes.'

She stopped, sighed. 'A small scheduling nightmare. I had intended to wait for Reed to come out of the locker room, give him another chance to leave on his own. Then, as ordered by the board, I would call security and have him escorted out of the building. I didn't know Nurse Brennan had made the nine-one-one call until the medical technicians were rushing in. I didn't know . . . I had no idea what had happened.'

'You know the routine by now. I need the names of everyone who was in the building between seven and eight-thirty A.M. My partner and I will begin interviews.'

'But . . . but this was an accident.'

Eve smiled thinly. 'That's what you said about Foster.'

There was little variation as far as staff on premises, Eve noted. But it was very interesting to learn that Allika Straffo had signed in, with her daughter, at seven thirty-two, and hadn't signed out again until eight-twelve.

Her gauge had put Williams's TOD at seven-fifty.

She mulled it over as she set up to interview Mirri Hallywell.

'I don't know how much more we can take,' Mirri began. 'This place, it's like a tomb. Like it's cursed. That sounds dramatic, but that's how it feels to me.'

'Why were you here so early? I show you signing in at seven-fifteen.'

'Oh. Drama Club. We're meeting before classes. In the theater. Discussion, a vid of some scenes from *Our Town*.'

'I'll need a list of the students and staff present. Parents and guardians.'

'Of course, no problem. I was the only staff there.'

'Did you leave the theater at any time during the meeting?'

'No. I was there from seven-thirty to eight-fifteen. Actually, a little before seven-thirty as I set up the vid, and probably a few minutes after eight-fifteen as I broke them down. I didn't hear about Reed until I was back in my classroom.'

'You knew Williams had been arrested yesterday.'

'Everyone knew.' She lifted a shoulder. 'I can't say I was surprised, and maybe – I probably shouldn't say this, but maybe a little pleased. Comeuppance, you know? But this? Drowning the way he did, that's horrible. I just don't know how it could've happened.'

'We're going to chat with the fragile and lovely Mrs Straffo.' Eve got behind the wheel. 'I wonder how she handled the irony of having her husband defending the guy she dicked around on him with. And what she was doing in the building for forty-five minutes.'

'Straffo wasn't on Hallywell's memory list of parents in the theater during the meeting.' Peabody shifted a little, kept looking straight out the windshield. 'So, how are things?'

'What things?'

'I, ah, happened to have the screen on this morning when I was grabbing a bagel. Caught that stupid bit about that blonde and Roarke. Anybody could see it was bullcrap.'

'Then why do you bring it up?'

'Sorry.'

'No,' Eve said after a minute. 'No, no point in slapping at you for it. It's outside the box right now, that's all. And it's staying outside the box because it's not part of the job. Clear?'

'Sure.'

'I can't let it in right now,' Eve said after another moment of screaming silence. 'I can't think about it right now.'

'Okay. I'm just going to say this one thing, then lock the lid. Bullcrap.'

'Thanks. Okay, why did Mrs Straffo take the kid to school today. Why not the babysitter?'

'That would be the au pair on their level. Good question.'

Eve pulled up in front of the apartment building. 'Then let's ask it.'

She had to cut through the doorman who tried to block them. 'Mrs Straffo has her penthouse on privacy mode. Door and 'links. She doesn't want to be disturbed.'

'Pal, I don't know what kind of Christmas bonus you get from the Straffos, but now's the time to ask yourself if it's worth you getting hauled into Central and held for obstruction of justice. This is a badge. Read it and weep. Now step back, or you're going to be sitting in holding for the next several hours.'

'I'm just doing my job.'

'Aren't we all.' Eve moved by him, then paused. 'Have you seen the au pair this morning?'

'Cora? She went out about nine. Errands. She said Mrs Straffo wasn't feeling very well, and activated the privacy mode. She hasn't come back yet.'

'What about Mrs Straffo? What time did she get back this morning?'

'About eight-thirty, maybe a little later. Didn't look well either.'

'On foot, or by car?'

'Walking. Walked the kid to school. It's about ten minutes away. They were scooting some. The kid said she'd be late for her meeting if they didn't hurry.'

'Doesn't the au pair usually take the kid in, pick her up?' Peabody wondered.

'Most of the time, sure,' the doorman confirmed. 'One of the Straffos takes her now and then.'

Riding up to the penthouse, Eve worked on the timing. Leaves the school, walks home. Takes a good fifteen minutes to do it. Not hurrying then. Goes upstairs, gives the au pair errands to run. Shuts down.

Wants privacy.

At the penthouse, Eve pressed the buzzer. The security blinked, and the computer clicked on.

We're sorry. The Straffo family has activated
full privacy. If you care to leave your name
and contact information, one of the family will
return your call when available.

Eve held her badge to the scanner. 'This is police business. You're ordered to override privacy mode and inform
Mrs Straffo to open the door.'

One moment, please, while your identification
is verified . . . ID verified. Please wait . . .

Eve was just toying with the idea of pounding a fist on
the door when it opened. The doorman had it right. Allika
Straffo didn't look well.

She may have been dressed in silk lounging pajamas, but
they were wasted on her as she stood pale and
hollow-eyed.

'Please, can't this wait? I'm sick.'

'You were well enough to walk your daughter to school
this morning. Something happen there that made you sick?
Or maybe you've been feeling a little off since your husband
agreed to defend your lover.'

'He isn't my lover. He was a mistake. Please, leave me
alone.'

'Not going to happen.' Eve laid a hand on the door
before Allika could close it. 'You fix that mistake this
morning?'

'I'm tired.' Tears began to gather and fall. 'I'm just sick and I'm tired. I just want all of this to go away.'

'So you helped Williams go under for the third time?'

'What are you talking about? Oh, God, come in then. Just come in. I'm too tired to stand here arguing with you.' She turned away from the door, went to the living area to sit on one of the sofas, dropped her head in her hand.

'I was such a fool, such a stupid fool ever to let him touch me. Now, how much am I going to have to pay for that?'

'Did he put the squeeze on you for money?'

'Money?' She lifted her head. 'No, no. That he would call Oliver, convince Oliver to defend him. What kind of a man is that? And he had those vials in his bedroom? Now, how can I be sure he didn't use them on me? I feel sick.'

'So you confronted him this morning?'

'No. I intended to. I tried to talk Oliver out of representing him, but Oliver's determined. I had to know what Reed said to him, had to convince Reed to find another lawyer.'

Eve sat. 'Let's get this on record, just so everyone's protected. I'm going to read you your rights.'

'But—'

'You're married to a lawyer. You know how this works. Record on.' Eve recited the Revised Miranda, watching Allika's face as she did. 'Do you understand your rights and obligations in this matter.'

'Of course, I do.'

'You took your daughter to school this morning, arrived about seven-thirty.'

'Yes, I thought if I took her in, and Reed was there . . . I saw that he was, on the sign-in screen. So I walked Rayleen to the theater and I went back. I thought, at that time of the morning, he'd be in the fitness center. But I didn't see him there. I decided to check the pool. I heard them as I stepped through the doorway of the locker room.'

'Heard who?'

'Reed and Principal Mosebly. Arguing, shouting at each other. She told him he was done, that he would no longer be attached to the school. If he didn't resign, she'd see he was terminated.'

'Why would that upset you?' Eve asked.

'It didn't — I mean, it wasn't pleasant, but that wasn't what upset me. I started to leave. I didn't want her to find me there. But then . . . he said, "Try it, Arnette." He said it like he was so amused. I think he even laughed.'

She shuddered. 'I'd never heard him speak like that, so hard, so ugly. He was always so gentle and charming with me, even when I told him I'd made a mistake. He was very understanding. But this . . .'

'What else did you hear?'

Allika moistened her lips. 'He told her he wouldn't be the only one out on his ass. Push him, he'd push back. How did she think the board would feel if they found out she'd fucked him – that's exactly how he said it. She'd fucked him, one of her faculty members in that very pool. On sacred school grounds. And in her office. It made me sick to hear it, to hear him start to describe what they'd done together.'

'And Mosebly?' Eve began. 'How did she react to the threat of exposure?'

'I don't know. I ran out, because I was sick. I went to one of the bathrooms and threw up.'

She pressed her fingers to her lips, squeezed her eyes shut. 'I was so ashamed. Ashamed and disgusted with myself, with what I did. This was the kind of man I've betrayed my husband with. And now he was using that, using Oliver because he knows I'm too big a coward to tell Oliver what I've done. He knows I'll keep quiet, and I suppose Principal Mosebly will, too. So he'll just go on to the next.'

'No, he won't. He's dead.'

Allika stared at Eve. Then her eyes rolled up and she slid bonelessly to the polished floor.

13

When Allika revived, she careened directly into hysteria. The sobbing, the shaking, the wild eyes could have been guilt, a good act or shock. Eve decided to reserve judgment when the au pair rushed in, carting market bags.

'What is it? What's happened. Oh, God, is it Rayleen?'

'Kid's fine.' Eve waited while Cora dumped the bags on the floor and hurried to Allika's side. 'Calm her down. Tranq her if you have to. We'll finish the interview later.'

'Mr Straffo?'

'He's fine, too, as far as I know. Calm her down, then come back. I've got a couple of questions for you.'

'All right then, shh, shh, darling.' In the way of women who are natural caregivers, Cora tuned a voice to a soft song. 'Come on with Cora now, won't you? Everything's going to be all right.'

'It's all falling apart,' Allika sobbed as Cora drew her up. 'He's dead. My God, he's dead.'

Cora's gaze zipped to Eve's. 'Another teacher,' Eve told her.

'Oh, sweet Jesus. Yes, sweetheart, come and lie down awhile.'

Cora led her toward the elevator rather than the staircase. She had her arm around Allika when the doors closed, bearing the other woman's weight as though she weighed no more than a child.

'Contact Mosebly, Peabody,' Eve said with her eyes trained on the second floor. 'I want her to come down to Central. Make it pleasant, apologetic. You know how to play it.'

'Just a few more questions, better for everyone if we talk away from the school. Got it.'

As Peabody got out her pocket 'link, Eve walked casually up the stairs. Just checking on a possible wit, possible suspect, she thought. Perfectly understandable, perfectly acceptable. Perfectly legal.

And if she took her time, looking into the other rooms from their doorways, it wasn't a violation.

She scanned what she assumed was Straffo's home office. Spacious, slick, touches of pricey chocolate brown leather. Good view, with privacy screens engaged. Small sofa, not what a guy would stretch out on for a nap. All business then.

Across from it was what she supposed would be called Allika's sitting room. There was a small desk with dramatically curved legs, a matching chair. Pastels, she noted. Pinks and greens and a pretty little fireplace. On the mantel were framed photos. She could see several of the kid, the family, one of husband and wife – younger, softer – beaming out. But there was no photo of a little boy.

The doomed son.

Privacy screens again, but with soft green drapes flanking them. A little footstool, a fancy tea set, flowers.

In the room beyond that was what looked like a playroom. Kiddie domain, Eve thought. Toys, a scaled-down desk, lots of bright colors, so heavy on the candy pink it made Eve's teeth ache.

The kid rated her own comp, Eve noted, her own screen and entertainment center, her own tea set, with table and chairs. The desk area had been fashioned like an office – for the school generation. Disk files, art supplies, which had likely been used to create some of the pictures on the wall.

The room adjoined, Eve saw through an open door, a large cushy bedroom. Very, very girlie, very, very frothy with its pink and white theme, its collection of dolls, doll furniture.

Which struck Eve as a bit creepy. What did dolls need with chairs, beds, tables? Unless they came to life in the dead, dead of night. And used them.

Yeah, definitely creepy.

She moved on, past the door Cora had shut. Eve could hear the woman murmuring to Allika, crooning to her.

She found a guest room that would have passed muster at a five-star hotel.

That made three bedrooms, three baths – no doubt the master bedroom claimed its own – playroom, sitting room, office on the second floor.

She glanced up, wishing she had an excuse to wander up to the top level.

Instead, she waited until Cora slipped out of the master bedroom. Cora put a finger to her lips as she eased the door shut.

'No soundproofing,' she whispered and gestured for Eve to follow her to the steps leading down.

'Why no soundproofing in a place like this?'

'Missus wouldn't have it, I'm told. She wants to be able to hear Rayleen in the night. They had a son, you know, and he died.'

'Yeah, I know about that.'

'I gave her a tranquilizer as you said. She should sleep a couple of hours. I told her I'd call her husband, but she said I mustn't, and cried all the harder. I don't know what I should do.'

'How's it been between the Straffos the last day or two?'

'Ah, well,' Cora pushed at her bright hair. 'She's been nervy. I guess since you're the police it's not talking out of school to say she didn't like him lawyering for that teacher who'd been arrested. They had some words about it yesterday. She was upset, no doubt, and demanded what he'd do if this man was to be charged with Mr Foster's murder. Mister, he said it wasn't her place to interfere with his profession.

'No soundproofing,' Cora added with a wry smile. 'It's the first I've heard them argue in that way since I came here. I went up to distract Rayleen from it, but she was in her playroom at her desk doing her school work as she does before family dinner each day. Had her music on.'

Cora tapped her ears. 'The headset. So she'd have been spared hearing them fight.'

'And this morning?'

'Tense. As it was during dinner last night as well. But there was no talk of it while Rayleen and I were about.' Cora glanced at the bags she'd dropped when she'd come in. 'Would you mind if I took these back to the kitchen, put things away?'

'No. Fine.' Eve signalled Peabody with a glance, and picked up one of the bags herself. 'I'll take this one.'

Dining room through archway, she noted – lots of silver and black, with a wide terrace beyond. The kitchen – same color scheme with splashes of electric blue – through the door to the right.

'Mrs Straffo took Rayleen to school today,' Eve began, and set the bag on a wide, stainless work counter.

'Thanks for that. She did, yes.' Cora began to put supplies away in glossy black cupboards or the huge silver fridge. 'One of them will, now and then. Though it's always planned out before. They're considerate that way, letting me know if I'll have a bit of time to myself. But the missus told me this morning, just after the mister left.'

She closed the last cupboard door. 'Can I get you or your partner something, Lieutenant? Some tea perhaps.'

'No, thanks.'

'If you wouldn't mind, I'm going to get myself a cup. I'm that upset. Another teacher dead, you said. And things come in threes, such things do.' As she programmed the tea, she sent Eve a sheepish smile. 'Superstition, I know. But still. Oh, God, Rayleen. Should I go get her from school? But I shouldn't leave the missus.'

'Her father was going to be contacted.'

'All right then, sure that's best.' She took out the tea, sighed. 'What a state of affairs.'

'How was Mrs Straffo when she came back from walking Rayleen to school?'

'She looked poorly, and said she felt that way as well.' Cora slid onto a stool at a short eating bar to drink her tea. 'She gave me some errands to run, and said she wanted the flat on privacy so she could sleep undisturbed. I made her some tea, then went out for the errands.'

'You run a lot of errands for her?'

'Oh, indeed. It's part of my position. I don't mean it to sound she works me half to death, for she doesn't.'

Eve thought of the elaborate playroom/bedroom upstairs. 'And you spend a lot of time with Rayleen.'

'I do, yes, and she's a pleasure. Most of the time,' Cora said with a laugh. 'But the missus doesn't leave the rearing to me, if you understand me. And some do. They spend considerable time together, this family – work and play. She's a lovely woman, the missus, and very kind, as is the mister. Still, I have to say, it seems to me the mister shouldn't have been defending that man if it upset the missus so. And now he's dead. She told me he was dead when I tucked her in bed. Poor lamb. Her nerves are just shattered by all this.'

When they left the penthouse and Peabody informed Eve Mosebly had agreed to a followup interview at Central, Eve thought she'd see who else's nerves she could shatter that day.

Her own stretched and threatened to fray when she walked into her bull pen. Several conversations took a hitch – that telling best of silence – before they continued. Gazes flicked her way, then aside.

Not one smart remark was made about her appearance with Nadine the evening before.

Because that wasn't the top story, Eve thought as she strode straight into her office, forced herself not to slam the door. The top story was now the lieutenant's spouse and a stunning blonde.

She programmed coffee, noted she had messages from Nadine, from Mavis, from Mira – from the on-air reporter who'd relayed the gossip piece that morning. And she could fry in everlasting hell, Eve thought.

She ignored the guilt when she ignored Mavis and Nadine, brought up Mira's.

'Eve, I have your more detailed profile, which I've sent to you. I hope, if there's a personal matter you'd like to speak with me about, you'll get in touch. I'll be available.'

'No, I don't want to speak about it,' Eve mumbled and shut down the message.

Instead she contacted her commander's office for permission to give an oral. She'd deal with the written later. Check with Morris, she added as she headed out again. Take another pass through Williams's apartment. Put Feeney on the electronics.

She knew what to do, how to run the case. How to close it.

It was the rest of her life she didn't know how to run.

She took the glides up. She may have felt looks aimed her way, but it was better than having them drilled into the back of her head in the confines of the elevators.

Whitney's admin avoided her eyes altogether. 'You can go right in, Lieutenant. He's expecting you.'

Whitney sat behind his desk of command, big shoulders, big hands. His face was somber, his dark eyes direct. 'Lieutenant.'

'Sir. I believe there may be a break in the Foster homicide that connects it to the drowning death of Reed Williams.'

He sat back as she gave her report, let her complete it uninterrupted. 'You opted not to bring Allika Straffo in for questioning.'

'Not at this time. We wouldn't get anything out of her, Commander. I think pressuring Mosebly will give us more juice. While they both have motive and opportunity, it's easier to see Mosebly helping the vic into the water – or under it. They both had something to lose, but the tone of Straffo's statement prior to being informed of Williams's death gives it credence. She could have used the time between the murder—'

'If it was murder.'

'Yes, sir, if it was, she could have used the time to prepare, to plan how she would deal with questioning. I'm still looking at her, but Mosebly fits more cleanly.'

'And Foster?'

'It's possible Williams poisoned him. Williams doesn't like being pushed, and we know Foster pushed, at least on one occasion, on the sexual activities. With this new information, that Williams had been sexual with Mosebly, and if we can verify that Foster was aware of that, it turns it. Mosebly had more to lose. Foster's knowledge compromised her position, and her sense of authority. Nobody likes their private issues made public, particularly by those under their command.'

'True enough.' His eyes remained level with hers. 'Use it, and squeeze that juice.'

'Yes, sir.'

'My wife and I watched you on Nadine Furst's new program last night.' He smiled a little. 'You did very well. Your demeanor and your answers were a credit to the department. Chief Tribble has already contacted me this morning to say the same.'

'Thank you, Commander.'

'It's good public relations, Dallas, and you handled yourself. It can be . . . difficult to become a public figure, to maintain and handle the inevitable invasions of privacy that go hand-in-hand with any sort of notoriety. If you feel, at any point, that pull and tug is affecting your work, I hope you'll speak to me about it.'

263

'It won't affect my work.'

He nodded. 'I'll observe the interview with Mosebly, if possible. Otherwise, I'll review it at the first opportunity. Dismissed.'

She started out.

'Dallas? Gossip is an ugly and insidious form of entertainment. Maybe that's why people can't resist it. A good cop knows it has its uses, just as a good cop knows it's often twisted and pummelled into a different shape for the purpose of the purveyor. You're a good cop.'

'Yes, sir. Thank you.'

Though she knew he'd meant it kindly, the sting of embarrassment plagued her all the way down the glides.

Her pocket 'link signalled a message straight to voicemail before she stepped into the bull pen. She drew it out, saw from the display it was from Roarke.

The urge to simply delete without checking made her feel small and cowardly. She cursed, and played the message.

His face filled her 'link screen, and those lethal blue eyes burned into hers. 'Lieutenant. I didn't want to disturb you. If you can carve out some time today, I'd like some of it. If it's not possible – or you're just too bloody stubborn to make it possible – I expect to have your time and attention tonight. At home. I'll end by saying this much. You piss me off, and still I love you with everything I am. I'd best hear from you, Eve, or I swear I'm going to kick your ass.'

She stuffed the 'link back in her pocket. 'We'll see whose ass gets kicked, pal.'

But her heart had twisted again — in pleasure or in pain, she just didn't know.

'Hey, Dallas.' Baxter pushed away from his desk, strode after her. 'Ah, nice job with Nadine last night.'

'You got something to say to me that applies to a case, Detective?'

'Not really. I just . . . Listen, Dallas, you don't want to pay attention to—'

She closed her office door in his face, but not before she saw the look of concerned sympathy on it.

She put another lock on the lid of her emotional box, sat and focused on writing her report until she got the signal Arnette Mosebly had arrived.

When she walked in, Mosebly scowled. 'Really, Lieutenant, I assumed we'd do this in your office.'

'You haven't seen my office. There's barely enough room for me in there, much less the three of us. Appreciate you coming in.'

'I want to cooperate, both as a private citizen and as principal of Sarah Child. The sooner all of this is cleared up, closed away, the better for the school.'

'Yeah, the school's important to you.'

'Of course.'

'Just let me set up. Record on. Interview with Mosebly, Arnette, conducted by Dallas, Lieutenant Eve, and Peabody, Detective Delia, all present, in the matter of the death of Williams, Reed, on this date.' Eve took her seat. 'Ms Mosebly, are you here of your own volition?'

'I am. As I said, I want to cooperate.'

'And we appreciate it. To insure your protection, I'm going to read you your rights.'

'My rights? I don't—'

'It's routine,' Eve said casually, and ran through them. 'Do you understand your rights and obligations in this matter?'

'Of course I do.'

'Okay then. Again, we appreciate your cooperation.'

'Reed's death is a shock to all of us, a loss for all of us,' she added. 'Particularly coming so close on the heels of Craig's.'

'You refer to Craig Foster, who was murdered in the school you head.'

'Yes. It was, and is, a tragedy.'

'Oh, sorry. You want coffee or anything?'

'I'm fine, but thank you.'

'Both these men,' Eve continued, 'Foster and Williams, were known to you.'

'Yes.' Mosebly folded her hands neatly on the table. Her nails were perfectly manicured and painted a pale coral. 'They served on the faculty of Sarah Child, where I stand as principal.'

'Are you aware that Reed Williams was questioned in the matter of Foster's death?'

Her jaw tightened into a stern expression Eve imagined laid little licks of fear in any student's belly. 'We all were, yes. I was aware you'd spoken to him, and that he'd been arrested on other charges.'

'The possession of illegals, specifically two banned substances that are most commonly used in sexual activities.'

'They're rape drugs.' Mosebly's mouth went razor thin. 'It's appalling. I respected Reed as a teacher, but this information about his personal life . . . It's shocking.'

'You confronted Mr Williams on this matter.'

'I did.' And here was the pride and authority in the lift of her chin, the chilly hauteur in her eyes. 'When he was arrested and charged, I contacted our board of directors to inform them of same. It was agreed that Reed be immediately suspended, that his resignation be called for. If he refused to tender it, I was to begin termination proceedings.'

'Those are complicated and often difficult. And given the circumstances would generate considerable undesirable publicity for the school.'

'Yes. But under the circumstances, there was no choice. The students are our first priority, in every matter.'

Understanding the rhythm, Peabody poured a cup of water and offered it to Mosebly. 'Some parents had already pulled a couple of your students,' Peabody commented. 'You've probably had to reassure plenty of others. It's happened under your watch. You must have gotten some heat from the board, too.'

'The board's concerned, of course. But has been very supportive.'

'It would've murked it up even more, though, if Williams made a stink. You know how it is, Lieutenant, somebody

267

gets out of line then tries to take the whole ship down with him.'

'People like that,' Eve agreed, 'they don't want to go down alone, and don't care what they break on the way. You stated earlier that you'd seen and spoken to Williams this morning, in the pool area.'

'Yes. I was leaving as he came in, and I reminded him – firmly – of his suspension, again asked for his resignation, and explained the consequences should he refuse.'

'How did he respond?'

'That he was confident his lawyer and his union rep would block any termination.' She shook her head in obvious disgust. 'I left him there to contact the chairman of our board, and had decided to have Mr Williams removed by security.'

'You just left him there to paddle around in the pool?' Eve said. 'After he'd defied your authority?'

'I could hardly remove him bodily myself.'

'Guess not.' Frowning, Eve flipped through her file. 'You don't mention a shouting match with him.'

'I may have raised my voice, but I'd hardly call our conversation a shouting match.'

'Really? I like to get good and loud when I argue. Especially when I'm being threatened. You didn't mention that either. That he'd threatened you.'

There was a quick flicker as Mosebly's gaze slid away from Eve's. 'I don't recall that he did.'

'You were overheard. He threatened you all right, Arnette.

Threatened to make it known you and he had used that pool for more than swimming laps, had used your office for more than lesson planning. How do you figure the BOD would take that information? How long would you stand as principal when Williams told them you'd had sex with him?'

'This is absurd.' Her throat worked on a swallow, and her neatly folded hands unlinked to press palms against the table. 'This is insulting.'

'You know, I had to ask myself how it was that a woman so staunch – so proud of her reputation and the school she served – would allow a scumbag like Williams to stay on staff. I wondered about that. You had to know he'd been dipping.'

'There was never a complaint filed—'

'Oh, let's can that, Arnette. You knew damn well he was engaging in extracurricular activities. Your watch.' Eve pointed at Mosebly across the table. 'Your ship. But you let it go. How could you bring the hammer down on him for it, when he'd already nailed you?'

'Rock and a hard place,' Peabody agreed. 'Go to the board on it, and you leave yourself wide open. Say nothing and have to tolerate his behavior. Still, the second option preserves reputations.'

'Yours,' Eve continued, and shifted to sit on the side of the table, crowding Mosebly a little. 'The school's. Did Foster come to you, off record, unofficially, to tell you Williams was harassing Laina Sanchez? Did he ask your advice on how to handle it?'

269

'I think . . . I think I should have an attorney present before I answer any more questions.'

'Sure, you can pull that chain. Of course, once you do, things are going to get stickier. How do you think that vaunted BOD is going to react, Peabody, when they find out Principal Mosebly needs a lawyer?'

'Not good.' Peabody pursed her lips, shook her head. 'They probably wouldn't react well.'

'There's no reason for this.' Mosebly held up a hand. 'We'll straighten this out here and now. There's no reason to involve a lawyer or the board.'

'No lawyer, Arnette?'

'No. Let's just . . . I'll tell you what I know. Yes, Craig came to me last year. He was upset and concerned. He said Reed had been pressuring Laina for sex, had been making her uncomfortable, and had touched her inappropriately. He said he'd spoken to Reed himself, and warned him, but as he knew Reed had made other inappropriate remarks and approached other staff members, he wanted me to make the warning official.'

'Did you?'

'I called Reed in. Yes. He was unrepentant, but he did stay away from Laina. He was annoyed with Craig. And amused by me as shortly after I came on as principal, he . . . we had a sexual encounter. It was a terrible mistake, a moment of weakness. It should never have happened, and I swore it wouldn't happen again.'

'But it did.'

'Last month, during my morning swim. He came in, got into the pool. It just – we were – things simply happened.' She lifted her water, took a long drink. Then she lowered her lashes. 'I blamed myself. I was sick at my lack of judgment and control. Now I realize that it happened because he drugged me.'

She looked up again, and Eve saw the lie in her eyes, and the calculation with it. 'He gave me the rape drug, and I'm sure he did the first time. I held myself responsible, but I wasn't. No one is under those conditions.'

'How'd he slip it to you?'

'He . . . offered me a bottle of water, as I recall.'

'While you were doing laps, you stopped, and while treading water, drank water?'

'I wasn't in the pool. Obviously I haven't been clear. I got out when he came in. Though we worked together well enough, I wasn't comfortable being with him alone in that situation.'

'But comfortable enough to take a bottle of water from him.'

'I was thirsty. Then I felt hot and strange. I can barely remember.' She lowered her head, braced it with her hand. 'We were in the water again, and he was . . . I was . . .'

Now, like choreography, Mosebly covered her face with both hands and began to weep. 'I've been so ashamed.'

'Yeah, I bet. Say you play that tune and we dance to it. What happened when you were done being taken advantage of?'

'How can you be so callous?'

'Years of practice and enjoyment. Craig Foster told his wife shortly before his death that he'd seen Williams with someone he shouldn't have been with. I vote he saw him with you. Foster used the pool routinely.'

Mosebly closed her eyes. Eve wondered what was going on behind those closed lids. 'He did see us. After . . . after Reed laughed and said that Craig really got an eyeful this time. It was horrid.'

'What did you do about it?'

'Nothing. *Nothing*. I'd hoped Reed was lying. Saying it to make me more afraid, more guilty.'

'Then, pretty damn conveniently from your stand, Craig ends up chugging bad hot chocolate.'

'Convenient!' Mosebly's shoulders reared back, her eyes went hot. 'Craig's death was a tragedy on a personal level and a potential disaster for the school.'

'Spared your ass, though. With him out of the way, nobody knew about your . . . indiscretion but Williams. He's mum on it because he likes his job, the security of it, and the field of play.'

She swung around the back of Mosebly's chair, leaned in, leaned hard. 'But once that job's threatened, he'd drag you down into the muck with him. You and the school. You're a strong, healthy woman, Arnette. A strong, healthy swimmer. I bet you could, especially pissed, find the muscle to drown a man.'

'He was alive when I left the pool. He was alive.' She

grabbed at her water with a hand that trembled. 'Yes, I was angry, but I walked away. He could threaten to tell the board that we'd had sexual intercourse, but how could he prove it? It would be his word against mine. The word of an illegals user who had seduced or attempted to seduce members of the staff. Or the principal whose reputation is unblemished? I had every intention of securing his termination.'

'I believe you. And he's well and truly terminated, isn't he?'

'I didn't kill anyone. I was raped. As a rape victim, I'm entitled to privacy, and to counseling. I'm requesting both at this time. If you make my rape a matter of record, using my name, I can and will sue this department. Unless I'm charged with a crime connected to my rape, you're required to preserve my anonymity. I want to see a rape counselor. I can't answer any more questions now. I'm too upset.'

'As per subject's request, interview end. Peabody.'

'I'll set up the counselor.' Peabody curled her lip as she started for the door. Then she stopped. 'Off record, I can say what I want. You're a disgrace,' she said to Mosebly. 'You're an insult to every woman who's ever been forced. One way or the other, we're going to nail your sorry ass.'

Mosebly lifted her chin as Peabody stomped out. 'It's horrifying how the victim is still forced to bear the guilt of sexual abuse.'

Eve thought of the child she'd been, of the nightmares that had dogged her all of her life. 'You're nobody's victim.'

*   *   *

'Bitch. Lying bitch.' Peabody steamed her way down the corridor. 'I want to fry her ass.' When Peabody paused in front of a vending machine, Eve waited for her to kick it. Really hoped she would.

But in the end Peabody dug out credits for a tube of Pepsi, and one of the no-cal variety.

'Why is she a lying bitch?'

'Come *on*!'

'No, I'm asking you.'

Peabody sucked on the tube, then leaned back against the machine. 'You jolted her when you pinned her on having sex with Williams. She figured she was in the clear there. Then the wheels start turning. Jeez, you could see them. Clack, clack, clack.

'Bitch,' she repeated and took another gulp. 'She used the fact that Williams got busted for having illegals at his residence. Her reactions were all off, Dallas. There's no rape victim in her. No misplaced shame or guilt, no anger, no fear, no sign whatsoever of personal violation. Body language, tone of voice, facial expressions. It may pass with her famed board of directors, but it's crap.'

Peabody paused for breath, then blew a long one out before she chugged Diet Pepsi. 'Williams was slime, but she's just another form of slime. A user, a manipulator, a coward, and a hypocrite. She's bitch slime.'

'What a proud day this is for me.' Eve laid a hand on Peabody's shoulder. 'Yeah, she's bitch slime. She went into the synchronized swimming round with Williams of her own volition. Tough to prove otherwise seeing as he's been eliminated from the competition, but we know what we know. But is the bitch slime a murderer?'

'Probably. She had motive and opportunity on both vics.'

'We'd like her to be the killer,' Eve acknowledged, 'as righteous bitches to bitch slime, we'd love to take her down for a couple of murders in the first. But we don't have enough to lock either one. The next thing we have to do is verify our own infallible instincts and prove Williams was murdered.'

'Oh, yeah.' Peabody hunched her shoulders. 'I sort of forgot that little step.'

'It's the little ones that trip you and send your face into the concrete. Let's go to the morgue.'

14

She swung through the bull pen, then into her office for her coat. Stopped, kicked the desk lightly. She wasn't answering those messages. She wasn't a frigging saint. But she could do something about something else.

Pulling on her coat she walked back into the bull pen and straight to Baxter's desk where he was slugging back cop coffee and reading a sweeper's report.

'I saw you closed the underground case. Got a Murder Two. Trueheart handle the interview?'

'Yeah. He did good.'

She glanced over to the cube where the undeniably adorable Officer Trueheart was pecking away at paperwork. 'Trueheart.'

He swiveled around immediately, blinked at her. 'Sir.'

'Nice work on the Sykes interview.'

He flushed. 'Thanks, Lieutenant.'

'Taught him all he knows,' Baxter claimed with a grin.

'Hopefully, he'll overcome that. As for earlier, I appreciate the sentiment. Let's leave it there.'

'Got that.'

Satisfied, she left to study the dead.

★　　★　　★

'Welcome back. Can I offer you some refreshments?' Morris was in pewter today, with a purple shirt and braided pewter tie. His hair was in a long tail that made Eve think of glossy thoroughbreds.

'Rather have a ruling.' Eve glanced down at Williams's body. 'Homicide.'

'I have fudge brownies. Home-baked by the lovely hands of a Southern goddess.'

Eve's eyes narrowed on the mention of brownies. She swore she heard saliva pool in Peabody's mouth. Then the Southern goddess mention struck. 'Detective Coltraine?'

Morris laid a hand on his heart, thumped it to mime a beating heart. And Eve thought, 'What *was* it with men and blondes with big tits?'

Morris wiggled his dark, sharp eyebrows. 'Our transplanted magnolia bakes for relaxation, it seems.'

'Huh.' Eve cocked her head. 'What, you smitten, Morris?'

'Who wouldn't be?'

'I could eat, like, a half a brownie.'

Morris smiled at Peabody. 'In the personal friggie over there. Help yourself.' Then he turned to Eve. 'Accident or murder? You be the judge.'

'It's murder.'

'Well, well.' He stepped back from the body, gestured. 'What do we see? A superficial wound under the chin.'

'Cracked it on the pool edging. Sweepers found some of his skin on the tile. It would've smarted, but I'm damned if it knocked him unconscious and caused him to drown.'

'Hmm. More superficial wounds on the back.'

'Consistent with injury sustained when he was dragged out of the pool. More skin found. That's postmortem.'

'It is, it is, my canny student. We have a very fit individual, other than his being dead, of course. Excellent muscle tone. Your on-scene notes indicated he was a swimmer, that there was no sign of struggle. Yet you cry murder.'

'I say it, straight out.'

'And knowing you, knowing you wouldn't send me a body unless you had strong cause, we've proceeded accordingly. His tox screen isn't back yet. Shortly, as I flagged it.'

'What do you think's in him, and how did it get there?'

'For the what, we'll wait. For the how. Have a look.'

He handed her goggles, then gave her a finger curl. When she walked to Williams's head, she noted Morris had shaved a circle of hair away on the crown.

'Man, would he hate that. Bald spot. And lookie, lookie.' She bent closer, and with the goggles could just make out the faint mark. 'Pressure syringe,' she said. 'Barely shows, and on the scalp, with a headful of hair, the naked eye isn't going to see it.'

'Speak for yourself.'

Now she glanced over at Morris, grinned. 'Yours excepted. I missed it. I looked over his body, between his fingers and his toes, even checked his tongue, the inside of his cheeks, but I missed this. Nice catch.'

'I ate a whole brownie,' Peabody confessed.

'Who could blame you?' Morris patted her arm when she joined them.

'We got our homicide, Peabody. Vic's doing laps, maybe finishes up, or just stops when he sees someone. Grips the edging. Maybe says something . . . "Hey, what's up?" But there's no time for conversation. Have to get it down, get out. It's a risk, but like with Foster, calculated. All you do is bend down, pump the syringe.'

Drawing off the goggles, she pictured it. 'Had to be quick. No poison this time. He didn't show any symptoms of any poison I know. Maybe the shock of the buzz on the scalp had him lose his grip, rap his chin. But . . . not a sedative. Too slow. He might have been able to make it out, or try. If he'd clawed at the edging, we'd have seen signs of that on his hands, his fingers. Numbed him, that's what it did. Like the stuff MTs and doctors use to block pain and movements for some treatments. You're awake, even aware on some levels, but you don't feel anything, you can't move anything.'

'And we are, once more, in accord.' Morris nodded. 'I believe the tox results will come back with a standard surgical paralytic substance, injected through the scalp. Strong, fast-acting, and quite temporary.'

'Not temporary enough for him. He would've struggled. Strong guy, he'd have been able to keep his head up for a while, maybe try to float. There's a set of stairs about five feet from where the sweepers found the skin. If he'd thought of it, tried to get there, prop his head . . . The killer might have had to help him out a little, hurry the process before someone wandered in. There are some long poles in there. Nets, brushes. Wouldn't have taken much to nudge him under, keep him under until it was done.

'Then you just walk out, slide right back into the mainstream.'

'Slime bitch,' Peabody said, with relish. But Eve frowned.

'Morris, do you figure they keep paralytics in the nurse's station at a private school?'

'They would probably have low doses of a basic number. For pain relief, but I can't imagine they'd be authorized to have anything like this.'

'More likely the killer brought it in rather than took it from the school. So, impulse, passion is again unlikely. Prepared and calculated and controlled, while able to take risks.'

She'd run probabilities, she'd go back over every point, re-evaluate time lines and wit statements. But for now, she looked back down at Williams.

'You were a sleazy son of a bitch, but you weren't a killer after all. Whoever did Foster did you both.'

At Eve's order, Peabody put in a request for a warrant to search Arnette Mosebly's residence. Eve tapped her fingers on the wheel as she drove back to the school.

'Tag Reo back,' she decided. 'I want a warrant for the Straffo residence.'

'You really think Allika Straffo might've done them?'

'I figure beautiful women know how to play, how to act the victim. I also figure Oliver Straffo's a tough nut. Maybe he finds out his wife's diddling with the teacher. And he finds out Foster knows and is considering blowing the horn. Protect the home front, protect the reputation and your own personal pride.'

'Stretching.'

'Is it?' She sighed. 'If I'd known about that vid they aired this morning, I'd have been tempted to hunt down the operator, the reporter, the producer, whoever I needed to find, and do them some bodily harm. I'd have rather kicked ass than feel humiliated publicly, then have to walk into that bull pen and feel it all over again.'

'Sorry. Um, can I just ask why that Magdelana whore-slut wasn't in line for bodily harm?'

'I'd have saved her for last.' Eve's fingers tightened and released on the wheel. 'Which means I'd have probably blown my wad before I got to her, and still feel the way I do now. What's the point?'

'Don't say that, Dallas. You can't—'

'It's going back in the box.' Where it should have stayed, Eve reminded herself. 'I only brought it out to illustrate a possibility we have to consider. Straffo's a lawyer, and to give him his due, he's a damn good one. He plans, he calculates, he strategizes. And as a defense lawyer he often knows going in that he's doing all this to set the guilty free.'

'Lack of conscience.'

'We're cops, we like to think that of defense lawyers. But it's the job. That's what it is. It's their job, and it's the law. But you have to have some stones to work at getting a killer, a rapist, an illegals dealer a walk – or a deal, for that matter. So he fits the profile, and we take a closer look.'

Just to be certain, Peabody checked her notes. 'He wasn't signed in this morning at the school.'

'No matter how good the security, there's a way around it.' She'd learned that from Roarke. 'And the security at the school is no more than decent. Something else that needs to be checked out more carefully.'

She'd have asked Roarke to help out in that area. That was a habit she'd fallen into, another kind of rhythm, she supposed. But she'd just do it without the aid of her expert consultant, civilian, this time around.

At the school, she uncoded the locks with her master, then stood inside, hands in her pockets, studying the security scanner.

The student or visitor was obliged to use the thumb plate – all prints of authorized students, guardians, staff, and faculty were on file. Guests were required to be cleared before entry. Bags were scanned for weapons and illegals.

In a facility like this, Eve imagined the scans probably worked ninety percent of the time. In the state schools of her education, they *hadn't* worked ninety percent of the time.

So money, as money could, brought a certain edge of safety.

At the same time, she imagined the system could be caused to jam or hiccup by a five-year-old with reasonable e-skills.

'Let's have EDD go over this security. Dig down in it to see if it blipped at any time.'

Her bootsteps echoed as she walked the halls. Empty schools were like haunted houses, she thought. If you listened you could hear the sound of voices, the rush of bodies. Generations of kids, she imagined, trooping along in whatever footwear met the current fashion criteria.

She stopped at the nurse's station, unlocked the door. Inside was a short counter, a stool behind it, a comp unit. There were four chairs and two cots covered with crisp white linens.

Under the counter were standard first-aid supplies. Packs of Nu Skin, cold packs, heat packs, temperature gauges, a home version of the suture wand the MTs carried. Gauze, swabs.

In a drawer, neatly stowed, were diagnostic aids for checking pulses, pupils, ears, throats. As innocuous as they were, she had to block a shudder.

Medicine in any form wigged her.

All drugs – kid- and adult-dose blockers, nausea remedies, fever reducers, cold tabs – were under lock in a cabinet that required a master like hers or a thumb print and code.

Nothing inside fit her requirements. Though she did study the individually wrapped pressure syringes.

As far as she could see, Nurse Brennan ran a tight ship. Tight, safe, and secured.

Since the comp was passcoded, Eve tagged it for EDD.

'Kind of creepy in here, isn't it?' Peabody said from behind her.

'Schools are always creepy. Anything fun in Mosebly's office?'

'Nothing jumped, but I tagged the electronics, and boxed up her disc files. She had the blockers – case we saw her use earlier – and a couple of soothers in stock. Tagged her admin's stuff, too. Just in case.'

'Good. Let's go back through the lockers in the fitness area. And just for jollies, we'll go through the kids' lockers.'

'All of them? It'll take hours.'

'Then we'd better get started.'

She could have called a team in, probably should have. They found a mountain of discs, a good chunk of them graphic novels rather than textbooks. Enough candy and salty treats to stock the shelves of a 24/7, memo cubes, comp games, moldy apples.

Flashlights, hairbrushes, lip dye, art supplies, an ancient sandwich of indeterminate origin. Doodles, sketches, empty wrappers, a number of mittens and gloves, neck scarves and caps.

Photographs, music vids, smelly socks, fashionable sunshades, broken sunshades, loose credits, and a forest of chewed-on pencils.

They also found a bag of poppers and three joints of zoner.

'Jesus.' Peabody shook her head. 'Oldest kid in this place is barely thirteen.'

Eve noted down the locker numbers, confiscated the illegals. 'Top dealer when I was in fifth, or maybe it was sixth grade was an eight-year-old named Zipper. You wanted it, he'd score it.'

'I never even saw a popper until I was sixteen.' Then Peabody waited while Eve answered her 'link.

'Dallas.'

'Reo. Warrant's in on Mosebly. Took a little time as she tried to block. Still working on Straffo. He's having a lot more luck bogging the works. You're not going to get that one through tonight.'

'We'll start with Mosebly. Thanks.' She clicked off. 'Match the locker numbers with the students on those illegals, Peabody. Don't file anything yet. We'll talk to them first.'

'Parental notification?'

Eve shook her head. 'We'll talk to them first. Better, I'll pass them to Detective Sherry in Illegals.'

'Ooooh, Scary Sherry.'

'Yeah, she'll have them crying for their mommies and taking the pledge.' Eve checked her wrist unit, calculated the time. 'Let's call in a team to help with Mosebly's.'

'Coming up to end of shift.' Peabody rubbed her hands together in gleeful anticipation. 'Whose evening plans would you care to screw with?'

'Baxter and Truehcart just closed one. Tap them. And

go ahead and tap McNab on the e-work there, if he's clear.'

It infuriated Mosebly to have a small platoon of cops in her space. A very nice uptown space, Eve noted. Private school brass did just fine, particularly when they were divorced with no kids of their own to pay to educate.

She had a female lawyer at her side who squinted at every word in the warrant, then made noises about police insensitivity and harassment.

It was interesting that under the conservative suits Mosebly – from the contents of her drawers – preferred sexy to slutty lingerie. Interesting that among the literature disc and collection of paper novels, she had a supply of popular romances.

And it was too damn bad they found no illegals, no poisons, no paralytics.

They trooped out with boxes of discs, electronics, and paper files. Eve handed the receipt to the lawyer, then heard, with some surprise, Mosebly burst into what sounded like genuine tears just before Eve closed the door behind her.

'Everything in my vehicle,' Eve ordered. 'I'll take it back to Central, log it in. Baxter, you and Trueheart are off the clock.'

'Let's chow, my young apprentice.' Baxter slung an arm around Trueheart's shoulders. 'I know a place not far away where the food is questionable, but the waitresses are delicious.'

'Well . . . I could give you a hand with the carting and logging, Lieutenant.'

Eve shook her head. 'Go eat and ogle, Trueheart. I've got this. I'll dump you and McNab at Central, Peabody.'

'Excellent.' She didn't say it would make more sense for them to snag a radio car and haul the boxes downtown since her lieutenant lived only a few blocks away.

Eve tuned them out on the drive. Obviously her partner and the e-geek were off the clock, too. Their conversation was primarily about a vid they both wanted to see, and if they should go for pizza or Chinese.

'We'll give you a hand with this, Dallas.' Peabody climbed out in Central's garage. 'We're thinking of going for pot stickers, moo goo, and Chinese beer after. Our treat.'

God, was all Eve could think. She must look pathetic. 'I got it, go on. I want to put a couple hours in while I'm here. I'll see you tomorrow.'

'It'll take you three trips, at least.' McNab pulled out his communicator. 'I'll tag a couple of uniforms for the hauling.'

Eve started to object, then shrugged. It would take her three trips, and that was a waste of time and energy.

'Sure you don't want to grab a bite?' Peabody asked. 'You didn't even snag a brownie today.'

'I'll grab something here.'

Peabody's hesitation told Eve she wanted to push, but she backed off. 'If you change your mind, the place we're going's only a couple blocks down. Beijing South.'

She wasn't going to change her mind, but Eve found,

after the evidence was logged, she wasn't going to put in a couple hours either. She was done, finished, out of steam.

But neither could she face going home.

So she went where she supposed she'd known she'd end up. She went to Mavis.

It had been her apartment building once, and one Roarke owned. Just one more of the links between them, she supposed. Not long after she'd moved in with Roarke, Mavis and Leonardo had set up house in Eve's old apartment. They'd worked a deal with Roarke months before, and had expanded their unit by renting the one next to it, and taking out walls, building more.

With Mavis a hot-ticket music star, and Leonardo a major fashion designer, they could have lived in any exclusive building, bought any trendy house. But this was where they wanted to be, with Peabody and McNab as their neighbors.

She'd never been attached to the apartment, Eve thought as she headed up to it. She'd never been attached to any place she'd lived. Just a place to dress and sleep between shifts.

She'd tried not to become attached to the warm and magnificent glamour of Roarke's home, but she'd lost the battle. She loved it, every room, probably even those she hadn't been in yet. She loved the sweep of the lawn, the trees, the way he used the space.

Now, here she was, back at the start, dragging her heels about going back to the house she loved. And the man.

Leonardo answered. She saw it in his eyes, those big, liquid eyes of his, the sympathy. Then he simply enfolded her. The gesture had tears rushing to her throat that had to be brutally swallowed down.

'I'm so glad to see you.' Those enormous hands rubbed, gently as bird wings, up and down Eve's back. 'Mavis is just changing Belle. Come in.' He laid his wide hands on her cheeks and kissed her. 'How about some wine?'

She started to refuse. Wine, empty stomach, stress. Then she shrugged. Fuck it. 'That'd be good.'

He took her coat, and bless him, didn't ask how she was or where Roarke might be. 'Why don't you go back and see Mavis and Belle? I'll bring you the wine.'

'Back? Back to . . .'

'The nursery.' He beamed a smile. His face was big, like the rest of him, the color of burnished copper. His at-home wear was a pair of brilliantly blue pants with legs as wide as Utah and a silky sweater in snow-blind white.

When she hesitated, he gave her a little nudge. 'Go on. To the right through the archway, then left. Mavis will be thrilled.'

The apartment looked nothing like it had under her style. There was so much color it was dizzying, and yet it was cheerful. So much clutter it was impossible to see it all, and yet it was happy.

She passed under an archway that struck her as probably Moroccan in style, then turned into the nursery.

She thought of Rayleen Straffo's pink and white and

frothy bedroom. There was pink here, too, and some white. And there was blue and yellow and green and purple in flashes and streaks, rivers and pools. There was everything.

It was Mavis's rainbow.

The crib was swirled with color, as was the rocker system chair Eve had given Mavis for her baby shower. There were dolls and stuffed animals and pretty lights. On the walls fairies danced under more rainbows or around fanciful trees bursting with glossy fruit or flowers.

And Eve saw stars sparkling on the ceiling.

Under them Mavis stood, bent over a kind of high, padded table, singing in the squeaky voice millions loved to a wriggling baby.

'No more poopie for Bella Eve. You have the prettiest poopie in the history of poopies, but my beautiful Belle's butt is all clean, all shiny. My beautiful, beautiful Belle. Mommy loves her beautiful Bellarina.'

She lifted the baby now, who wore some sort of dress in pale pink that fell in soft folds and flounces. There were bows in the shape of flowers in the baby's soft crop of dark hair.

Mavis nestled and swayed, then did a little dancing turn.

And saw Eve.

Her face, soft with mother love, went bright and happy, and told Eve everyone had been exactly right. She should have come here before.

'Poopie?' Eve commented. 'You say poopie now?'

'Dallas!' Mavis rushed over in green slippers that were made to look like grinning frogs. With the baby cradled in one arm, she hugged Eve hard with the other. She smelled of powder and lotion. 'I didn't hear you come in.'

'Just got here.' Eve made the effort, and found it wasn't as hard as she imagined. She took a good look at the baby. 'She's bigger,' she observed. 'Looks more . . .'

Mavis lifted a glossy black brow. 'You were going to say human.'

'Okay, yeah, because she does. She also looks like some of you, some of Leonardo. How do you feel?'

'Tired, happy, weepy, thrilled. Want to hold her?'

'No.'

'For one minute,' Mavis insisted. 'You can time it.'

'I could break her.'

'You won't break her. Sit down first, if you're nervous about it.'

Trapped, Eve avoided the rainbow chair and took the traditional rocker in neon pink. She braced herself when Mavis leaned over and laid the baby in her arms.

No poopie, at least, Eve reminded herself, and stared down as Belle stared up. 'I don't like the way she's looking at me. Like she's planning something.'

'She's figuring you out, that's all.' Mavis turned and beamed as Leonardo came in with drinks.

Where he was big, redwood big, Mavis was a pixie. A little ball of energy with an explosion of hair currently the color of ripe apricots. She wore a lounge suit with more frogs hopping over her legs and a crowned one in the middle of her chest.

'You can rock her,' Mavis suggested.

'I'm not moving. Something may happen.' And at that moment, Belle poked out her bottom lip, then scrunched up her pretty face. Then let out a pitiful wail.

'Okay, time's up,' Eve decided, absolutely. 'Come and get her, Mavis.'

'She's just hungry. I was going to feed her before, but she needed changing first.'

To Eve's relief, Mavis took the baby and sat in the rainbow chair. Then to Eve's astonishment, Mavis tugged at the frog prince. Her breast popped out, and Belle's mouth latched on like a hungry leech.

'Wow.'

'There you are, my baby. There you go. Mommy's milk train is in the station.'

'You both really got the hang of that.'

'We're a mag team. Leonardo, would you mind if we had a little all-girl time?'

'Absolutely not.' But he bent first to kiss his wife, then his daughter. 'My beauties. My angels. I'll be right out in my studio if you need me.'

He set something frothy in the holder of the system chair, then gave Eve her wine.

In the ensuing silence all Eve could hear was an active sucking sound.

'So . . .' Mavis nursed and rocked, nursed and rocked. 'Why haven't I heard any media dirt about a blonde fuck-head found floating in the East River?'

Eve lifted her wine, set it down. And did what she'd needed to do all day. She cried like a baby.

'Sorry. Sorry.' When she had herself under some control, she scrubbed her face. 'That was bottled up, I guess.' She saw Mavis had tears of sympathy on her cheeks, and had shifted Belle to the other breast. 'I shouldn't be here like this. It probably screws up the milk or something.'

'My milk's completely uptown. Tell me what's going on.'

'I don't know. I just don't know. He's . . . she's . . . Fuck, Mavis. Fuck.'

'You're not going to tell me Roarkc's doing her, because NPW – no possible way. He wouldn't. All guys have the small jerk gene, it makes them guys. But only some have the big jerk gene. He doesn't.'

'No, he's not doing her. But he used to.'

'I used to pick pockets. You used to arrest me.'

'It's different.'

'Yeah.'

Eve told her some of it. The red dress, the look she'd caught in Roarke's eyes, the meeting in her office, and so on.

'Uber bitch came there to flip you.'

'Yeah, she did.' Knowing it, Eve thought, didn't make it better. 'Mission accomplished.'

'Give me, like, a rundown on her. What kind are we dealing with?'

'She's kick-your-dick-up gorgeous, smart, sexy, sophisti-cated. Multilingual, rich, slick, and polished.' Eve pushed out of the chair to pace. 'She's a custom fit for him.'

293

'Bullpoopie.'

'You know what I mean, Mavis. The image. She's everything I'm not.' Eve threw up her hands. 'She's the
anti-me.'

'That's good. That's completely mag.'

'Good? Mag? How?'

'Because if you two had solid common, it could be said
– I wouldn't, but it *could* be said – that Roarke hooked on
you because you reminded him of her. That you were the
type he went for. But, see, you're not. He went for *you,*
not for a type. I bet that burns her surgically shaped ass.'

'It . . . oh.' Eve dragged a hand through her hair. 'I don't
get this female business. Or it takes me awhile. It would
burn her ass that I'm the anti-her? That he didn't keep
looking for her, so to speak.'

'We have a winner.' Mavis slid the baby up over her
shoulder and began to rub and pat Belle's back. 'Bet the
bitch goes frothy at the mouth every time she thinks about
it. Right, Belle-issimo?'

In answer, Belle burped firmly. 'There's my girl. That's
why she set up that vid.'

'Set up the vid?'

Mavis's frog green eyes popped. 'Jesus, Dallas, you must
be knotted up like last week's hairdo if you missed that. I
may have been out of the game a few years, but I know a
con when it smacks my adorable, post-pregnancy ass. Did
you *look* at it?'

'I got – I guess I got knotted up.'

'Hold on. I'm going to put Belle down. Get your wine. We're going to view the evidence.'

She didn't want to watch it again, but there was too much curiosity in her to refuse. In the living area, Mavis turned on the screen, hit the replay for previous programming, and cued up the piece from that morning.

'Now, watch like a cop instead of the injured wife.' Even as she said it, Mavis slid a comforting arm around Eve's waist. 'He's looking down at her, yeah, because she's talking to him, angling up at him. Making sure he's looking at her while the camera rolls. Now catch it? The way she shifts so they're both turned just enough for the camera to zoom onto both their faces. Then she even cheats hers out.'

'She what?'

'Cheats her face – turns it a little more, so the camera can catch that soulful expression she's plastered on for it. Slick, but obvious if you pay attention. She's playing you. Both of you.'

Mavis drew back. 'Go kick her ass.'

'There's a problem with that. If I kick her ass, it gives her weight.'

'Shit.' Mavis puffed out a breath. 'It does.'

'Another problem is, he feels something for her. That already gives her weight. She knows it.'

'You're on the other side of the scale, Dallas. Head to head, she doesn't have a ice-fizzy's chance in hell.'

'Maybe not. But she's drawn all the blood so far. I'm bleeding, Mavis, and he doesn't see it.'

'Go make him.' Even as Eve shook her head, Mavis walked over to get Eve's coat. 'Time to stop letting her run the game, Dallas. And FYI?' She shoved the coat into Eve's hands. 'Roarke called here about a half an hour before you showed up.'

'He did?'

'Real casual like. Asked about the baby, like that. I may not have seen it if I hadn't been looking, because he's just that good. But you're not the only one bleeding tonight.'

15

Roarke reached for the 'link again, cursed himself for a fool, then turned away from it. He wasn't going to keep calling her, her friends, her haunts, hoping for a scrap.

Bugger that.

She'd be home when she came home. Or she wouldn't.

Christ Jesus, where was she?

Why the hell was she putting him through this? He'd done nothing to earn it. God knew he'd done plenty along the way to earn her wrath, but not this time. Not this way.

Still that look on her face that morning had etched itself in his head, on his heart, into his guts. He couldn't burn it out.

He'd seen that look once or twice before, but not on his account.

He'd seen it when they'd gone to that fucking room in Dallas where she'd once suffered beyond reason. He'd seen it when she tore out of a nightmare.

Didn't she know he'd cut off his own hand before he'd put that look on her face?

She bloody well should know it. Should know him.

This was her own doing, and she'd best get her stubborn

ass home right quick so they could have this out as they were supposed to have things out. She could kick something. Punch something. Punch him if that would put an end to it. A good rage, that's what was needed here, he told himself, then they'd be done with this nonsense once and for all.

Where the fucking hell was she?

He considered his own rage righteous, deserved – and struggled not to acknowledge it hid a sick panic that she didn't mean to come back to him.

She'd damn well come back, he thought furiously. If she thought she could do otherwise, he had a bulletin for her. He'd hunt her down, by Christ, he would, and he'd drag her back where she belonged.

Goddamn it all, he needed her back where she belonged.

He paced the parlor like a cat in a cage, praying as he rarely prayed, for the remote in his pocket to beep, signalling the gates had opened. And she was coming home.

'Shall I bring you something to eat?' Summerset asked from the doorway.

'No.'

'No word from her then?'

'No. And don't you saddle your high horse and think to ride it here. I did nothing to cause this.'

The hurled ball of fury merely bounced off Summerset's composure. 'And nothing to prevent it.'

'Prevent what?' Roarke whirled. Here, at least, was a target for the rage. 'My wife's sudden turn into an unreasonable, jealous mass of moods?'

'Your wife's astute reaction to the manipulations of a clever woman. Which you'd recognize if you weren't so hellbent on being right.'

'Bollocks. There's nothing astute about thinking I'd prefer Maggie over her. And manipulation be damned.'

'The video was well timed.'

'What the fuck does that mean?'

'Perfectly timed, perfectly executed,' Summerset said coolly. 'She was always good.'

'Staged it, did she? For what possible purpose?'

'You're here, alone, angry, worried about your wife, your marriage.' Summerset ignored the cat who skulked in to wind through his legs like a bloated ribbon. 'I imagine the lieutenant is somewhere in exactly the same position. That, Roarke, is pinpoint accuracy.'

'That's bloody nonsense.' But it pushed a very small seed into his mind. 'There's no profit in it for her, no point.'

'Retribution and entertainment.'

'Retribution for *what*?' At that moment, Roarke felt he might very well be going mad. 'You may have forgotten, but she left me. She betrayed me and left me hanging by the balls.'

'No, I haven't forgotten. I'm glad to know you haven't either.'

'There's been enough talk of Magdelana in this house, and I'm not the one who keeps bringing her in.' He strode out, and riding on temper went down to pummel a sparring droid to broken bits.

He wore himself out, but it didn't help, it didn't reach the rawness in his gut.

He showered off the sweat, and the blood on his knuckles. He changed and ordered himself up to his office. He'd work, he told himself. He'd just work, and if she wasn't home in another hour, he'd . . .

He hadn't a clue.

And when he saw the light was on in her office, the relief made him so weak it seemed the world tipped and shuddered for a moment before going solid again.

And the weakness refired his temper on all circuits. He stalked in, his mind already flexing its fists for battle.

She was at her desk, comp humming, data scrolling on screen. Her eyes were closed, and the shadows under them etched fatigue against pallor.

It nearly stopped him, perhaps that unhappy weariness would have. But then her eyes flashed open.

'Lieutenant.'

'I'm working.'

'It'll have to wait. Computer off.'

'Hey.'

'Is this how you handle things? How you punish me for crimes you've decided I've committed? I'm not even granted an interview?'

'Look, I'm tired. I need—'

'So the bloody hell am I.'

He looked it, she realized, as he so rarely did. 'Then go to bed. I'm going to—'

'If you think about walking out on me again,' he said, voice dangerously soft as she started to push out of the chair, 'think again. Think carefully.'

She knew the heat – and the more deadly ice – of his wrath when it was fully formed. She felt the blast of it now, and it chilled her to the bone. 'I'm going to make coffee.'

'You can wait for it, as I've waited half the goddamn night for you.' He stepped toward her, those eyes piercing like sabers. 'How am I supposed to know you're not dead in some alley, and the next time I open the door there'll be a cop and a grief counselor on the doorstep.'

She hadn't thought, not for an instant, he'd worry she'd gone down in the line. She hadn't meant to punish, just to get through the day. So now she only shook her head. 'You should trust me to handle myself.'

'Oh, now I should trust you when you've shown such undiluted trust for me. You've no right and no cause to put me through this.'

'Same goes.'

'Through what?' He braced his hands on her desk, leaned down. 'What am I putting you through, what the bleeding hell have I done? Be specific.'

'You looked at her.'

He stared, and for a moment those molten blue eyes were simply astonished. 'Well, as I haven't been struck blind in the last day or two I've looked at any number of women. Castrate me.'

'Don't diminish my feelings, my instincts or what I *know*.

Don't you make a joke of this or of me. You *looked* at her, and for a second, the first time you saw her again, you gave her what's supposed to be mine.'

'You're wrong.'

'I'm *not*!' She shoved up now so they were eye to eye. 'I'm a fucking trained observer, and I know your face, I know your eyes. I know what I saw.'

'And your police training tells you that this look I gave her, for a second you say, is cause for this irrational bout of jealousy?'

'It's not jealousy. I wish it were. I wish it were that stupid, that shallow, that definitive. But it's not jealousy. It's fear.' She dropped down in her chair again as her voice began to crumble. 'It's fear.'

That stopped him, had him straightening again. 'Can you really believe this? Believe that I'd regret what we are, what we have? That I'd regret it was you and not her? Haven't I told you enough, shown you enough, that you're every-thing to me?'

She struggled for calm, fought for the words. 'She's not like the others. The connection, it matters. You know it, and I know it. And maybe worse, she knows it. The connec-tion, this history, they show. Show enough that people looked at me with pity today. That I was humiliated walking through my own bull pen to my own office.'

'And what of our connection, Eve, our history?'

Her eyes were swimming. She would never use tears as some did, he knew, and was battling them back even now. Her struggle not to give into them made it all the worse.

He walked over to her window, stared out at nothing. So they wouldn't rage at each other until it was burned away, he realized. They would pick their way through it, uncover it. Then they'd see.

'You need to know, is it, what it was, how it was, and how and what it is now?'

'I know—'

'You think you do,' he corrected. 'And maybe you're not altogether wrong, or altogether right. Do you want it?'

'No.' God, no, she thought. 'But I need it.'

'Well, then, I'll tell you. I was, what, three and twenty or thereabouts, doing business as it were in Barcelona. I'd had considerable success in the game, and in business by that time. Always, I'd enjoyed keeping a foot on either side of the line. Light and shadow, you could say. Such an interesting mix.'

He said nothing for a moment, then went on. 'And it was there, in Barcelona, she and I crossed paths, with the same job in mind.'

He could see it now, as he looked through the dark window. The noisy club, the colored lights. It had been sultry in September, and the music had been a pulse in the blood.

'She came in where I was watching the mark for a time. Walked in, a red dress, an attitude. She flipped me a look, then moved straight in on my mark. Within minutes he was buying her a drink. She was good. I barely saw her pinch his passkey.'

He turned from the window. 'It was rubies — bloody red rubies, you see. The star display of a gallery. Three passkeys required, and I had two of them already. What she did, she pinched his, then slid off to the loo, made a copy, and slipped it right back to him with him none the wiser. Neither of us could get to the damn jewels now, and it pissed me off.'

'Sure.'

'I waited for her to come to me, which she did the next day. We did the job together in the end, and stayed together for a time. She was young and fearless, passionate. We liked living fast, traveling, riding the wave, you could say.'

'Did you love her?'

He crossed over to get them both a glass of wine. 'I fancied I did. She was capricious, unpredictable. She kept me on my toes. The legitimate bits I was involved in bored her.' He set a glass of wine on Eve's desk. 'She could never understand why I bothered, why I wanted what I wanted. What she understood was the game, and the thirst for money, for the shine. She didn't understand what it was to come from nothing as she'd come from a decent family, a decent home. What she wanted was more, then to move on and pick up more somewhere else.'

'What did you want?'

'Her, of course. I don't mean that to hurt you.'

'It doesn't.'

'I wanted the more, for different reasons, I suppose, but I wanted the more.' He studied the wine before he drank. 'I wanted respect and power and the shields and walls and weapons that insured I'd never be nothing again. You know.'

'Yeah.'

'She didn't. Couldn't. That was the crack in the jewel, I imagine.' The flaw, he thought, he'd seen even then. 'And still, it was shiny enough that we worked together, played together, stayed together. Until Nice. The mark had an exceptional art collection, with two Renoirs, among others. It was the Renoirs we wanted, had a buyer set for them. We spent weeks on it, with Maggie moving to the inside by seducing the mark.'

To stop him, Eve held up a hand. 'She slept with him? That didn't bother you? Knowing she was with another guy.'

'It was work, and he was more than twice her age. And the Renoirs? They were worth a great deal.'

'She wasn't yours,' Eve murmured, and something inside her unknotted. 'You never thought of her as yours.'

'Did you think otherwise?'

'Yes.'

'Not altogether right,' he repeated and eased down to sit on the edge of her desk. 'I had complicated feelings for her, and I believed she had them for me. I thought because of those feelings, and that wave we rode, I could trust her. And there I was altogether wrong.'

As he drank, Eve could see he was looking back. 'The night before we were to make the score, she didn't come back to the villa where we were staying. Nor did she come in the morning. I was afraid something had gone wrong, she'd done something foolish and been caught. Then I got word she'd run off with the mark. Left me for him. Not only that, but if I'd gone through with the job that night, as planned, there would have been a number of gendarmes waiting to scoop me up.'

'She ratted you out.'

'As I said, she was capricious. I was angry, I was hurt. My pride was battered. She'd played me, as we'd played so many others.'

'Why didn't you go after her?'

He studied his wife – those tired brown eyes – sipped his wine. 'I never considered it. She'd done to me, and that was that. I wouldn't give her the satisfaction of it. I should add here, leaping forward a number of years, that I'd planned to hunt you down if you didn't come home within another hour. Hunt you down, drag you back. I never considered not going after you.'

She took a breath to steady her voice. 'Did you ever get the Renoirs?'

'I did.' His lips curved. 'Of course I did. Three years later. And in those years and the ones after, I had a lot of women as well. I enjoyed them, and I never, not purposely, hurt one of them. I gave them what I had to give, and took what they were willing to give back. But there was nothing there.'

'But you didn't forget her.'

'Not altogether wrong,' he acknowledged. 'No, I didn't forget her. She left a hole in me, Eve, one I didn't want filled. Why risk that?'

'She . . .' Once again she hunted for the words, the right ones. 'She had a major influence on you. That's, maybe, that's part of what I feel. Part of what I see.'

'I can't, won't, deny that what she did, what I gave her the power to do, had some influence on the way I approached relationships. I said I didn't forget her, but neither did I actively think of her after the first weeks had gone by. Do you understand that?'

'Yeah. I get it.'

'I had work. I like work. I had money, then more of it. And the power, the respect. I built this place, and a great deal more. I cared for the women I was with, but they were never more than momentary pleasure.'

'She hurt you a lot.'

'She did, and seeing her again, I remember it, and in fact, those complicated feelings that made her able to hurt me.'

'It helps,' Eve managed, 'for you to tell me that. For you to lay it out instead of brushing it off.'

'Difficult to admit – to myself, to you. But I didn't lie when I told you it was done. And still . . . I'll lay this out as well. I remember, too, the beautiful young woman in the red dress gliding into a crowded club. The moment of it, the vibrancy of it. It may be that's what I saw, for that second, the memory of that might be what I was looking at. I can't erase what was from mind and memory, Eve.'

'No. Okay. Okay. Let's just—'

'We're not done here. You'll hear me out.' As if to hold her in place, he laid a hand over hers. 'I had that hole in

307

me, that empty space. I could have lived my life with it, content enough. I wasn't an unhappy man.'

He kept his eyes on hers as his thumb brushed lightly over the back of her hand. 'Then, one day I felt something – a prickle at the back of my neck, a heat at the base of my spine. And standing at a memorial for the dead, I turned, and there you were.'

He turned her hand over, interlocking fingers. 'There you were, and it all shifted under my feet. You were everything I shouldn't have, shouldn't want or need. A cop for Jesus' sake, with eyes that looked right into me.'

He reached out, just a whisper of fingers on her face. And the quiet touch was somehow wildly passionate, desperately intimate.

'A cop wearing a bad gray suit and a coat that didn't even fit. From that moment, the hole inside me began to fill. I couldn't stop it. I couldn't stop what rooted there, or what grew.

'She put it in me, you filled it. Can you understand that's part of this – the connection you worry about? Can you understand that whatever it was I felt for her it's nothing. It's so pale, so thin and weak compared to what I feel for you.'

The tears came now. He watched them drip down her cheeks, wondered if she were even aware they leaked out of her. 'She was part of my life. You are my life. If I have a regret, it's that even for an instant you could think otherwise. Or that I allowed you to.'

'When I saw you with her on screen—'

'I was saying good-bye to the girl I'd once fancied, and I think, to the man I'd been who'd fancied her. Only that. Don't cry. Here now.' He brushed her tears away with his thumbs. 'Don't cry.'

'I feel stupid.'

'Good. So do I.'

'I love you. Scary.' She pushed up again, and this time into his arms. 'So fucking scary.'

'I know.' She felt him tremble when he pressed his face to her neck. 'Don't leave me again. God. God. Don't leave me again.'

'I didn't.'

'Part of you did.' He moved her back, and his eyes swarmed with emotion. 'Part of you left me, and I couldn't stand it.'

'I'm not going anywhere. We're not going anywhere.' Needing to soothe, she worked up a smile. 'Besides, you'd just drag me back again.'

'Damn right.'

'Or try.' She closed her hands over his, and felt the abraded skin on his knuckles. Lowering them, she studied. 'Wow. Beat the hell out of someone?'

'Just a droid. It seems to work so well for you when you're pissed at me.'

'You should get your R and D department to come up with one that regenerates or something.' She touched her lips to them. 'You should put something on them.'

'You just did. Look how tired you are,' he said, stroking

309

her cheek. 'My Eve. Worn to the bone. And I wager you didn't eat at all today.'

'I couldn't. Morris even had homemade brownies. Fudge brownies.'

'We'll have some soup.'

'I'm too tired to eat.'

'All right then. No soup, no work. Just sleep.' He slid his arm around her waist, and she slid hers around his as they started out of the room. 'Will you let me back in there? Into the work.'

She'd shut him out there, she realized. They'd shut each other out here and there. Little doors closing. 'Yeah. I could use some help. Questions about a security system to start.'

'I'm your man.'

She looked over at him, smiled. 'Yeah, you are.'

She slid into sleep, then before dawn lightened the sky, slid into love. His mouth woke her, warm on hers. Sweet and warm and welcoming. And steeped in his taste, hers answered. His hands stirred her, so her heart seemed to sigh. Feeling the beat of his against her, she opened.

In the utter quiet, in the soft, soothing dark, they moved together.

Comfort was sought, and found. Pledges were remade without words. And everything needed was given.

She lay, tucked in the curve of his arm. Drifting.

'I should've let you sleep.'

'The way I feel right now, you did just fine. Pretty damn

310

'perfect.' So perfect, she thought, she could curl there for the next millennium. 'What time is it anyway?'

'Nearly six.'

'You probably have to get up.'

'I'm liking where I am at the moment.'

She smiled in the dark. 'I'm starving.'

'Are you now?'

'Seriously starving. I wish I had a damn fudge brownie.'

'It isn't fudge your system needs.'

'You want to bang again, ace, I need coffee first.'

And, he thought, *We're back.* 'The cat got the best part of two full Irish breakfasts yesterday. Why don't we try that again, and eat them ourselves.'

'You didn't eat either?'

'I didn't, no.'

She smiled again. It was nice to know he'd suffered along with her. But she rolled, bracing on her elbows to look down at him. 'Let's eat. A lot.'

They ate in bed, sitting crosslegged, the plates between them. She shoveled in eggs as if they were going to be banned within the hour.

There was color back in her face, he noted. And those shadows, those hints of wounds behind her eyes were gone. Then she aimed them at him, and he saw there was something else in them.

'What?'

'I don't want to screw things up, but I want to mention something that's bugging me.'

'All right then.'

'Red dress.'

'Fuck.'

'No, no.' She waggled her fork, determined to get through this part without a fight or an emotional crisis. 'Just hear me out, okay? You said when you first saw her she was wearing a red dress. Are you going to buy the coincidence that she was wearing a red dress when you saw her again out of the blue?'

'Well, I doubt she's worn red all these years, in case we crossed paths again.'

'You're not thinking. You've still got blinders on when it comes to her. Don't get pissed.'

'It's hard work not to.' Somewhat irritably, he stabbed a fried potato. 'What's your point?'

'My point is, she set it up. She didn't just happen to be in that restaurant, at that time, in a red fucking dress, Roarke. She knew you'd be there, and wanted to give you the jolt. Remember, lover? Remember me?'

'Well, how would she know where . . .' He trailed off, and she saw the blinders fall away.

It took considerable strength of will – and she congratulated herself on it – not to leap up and do a dance of joy and victory on the bed.

'You said she was good, and you probably taught her more. You knew the guy she was with that night, you do business with him. Not that hard, if you want to take some time, to pin down where Roarke has a dinner reservation.'

'No, she could work that.'

'Tags you at home, early morning, then it's lunch – give me some advice, some help for old times' sake. I bet she was full of apologies and shame for what she did to you all those years ago.'

She paused a moment, then decided it would fester if she just didn't say it. 'And you're not going to tell me she didn't make a move on you. At least test the waters.'

'The waters,' he said, 'were not receptive.'

'If they had been, I'd have drowned her in them already.'

'Darling, that's so . . . you.'

'Keep that in mind,' she warned, and since she'd finished her bacon, stole a slice of his. 'That had to chap her thighs. Then there's the fact she's the anti-me.'

'Sorry? The what again?'

Shaking her head, Eve ate the bacon. 'That's too complicated to explain. Forget that. But after you turned down the offer to see her tits—'

'She has very nice ones, as I recall.'

'You'd better shut up.' And when he grinned, Eve felt warm all over. 'So, when you turned down her generous offer, what did she do?'

'Stanched her bitter disappointment with a vodka martini.'

'No. Jesus. She bounced to me, gave me a couple of good jabs. Ended with the vid. Mavis said—'

'Mavis?'

Eve toyed with what was left of her eggs. 'I went by there last night. I forgot the teddy bear deal.'

313

'Forgot me as well.'

'No, I didn't. I needed to see Mavis. I needed to talk to her.'

'All right.' He reached over to touch a hand to Eve's knee. 'That's fair enough.'

'Mavis ran grifts for a long time. She wasn't half-bad either. She spotted what Magdelana was doing, where I missed it. But when Mavis pushed it in my face, I saw it, too. She set up that vid, Roarke. If you look at it again, you'll see it. She angled toward the camera, she – Mavis called it cheating – she cheated her face so it caught her just right. It wasn't just some wild coincidence that some schmuck caught the two of you on camera and got it on screen. She produced it.'

'Summerset said the same, and I blew him off. Even though a part of me thought well and sure she did. I blew him off.'

'She wants you back.' Eve took a vicious stab at her eggs because even knowing what she knew, having what she had, *that* was a pisser. 'She's been through a couple of rich guys, got herself a nice cushion. But you. You're the grand prize, and she miscalculated before. Ditched you for the bird in the hand. Now you're . . . What's a really big bird?'

'An ostrich?'

'Yeah, but that doesn't sound right. Anyway, you're the bird in the big-ass shiny gold nest, and she wants to cozy in with you. Just got to get me out of the way. Maybe see if you can pick up where you left off first . . .'

'As I said, she may have intimated that possibility, which

I, being a faithful husband, nipped even before the bud. And yes,' he added with a nod, 'after which, she went to see you, test the ground, make you wonder. It was well played all in all, and caused considerable trouble and grief. Still, I'd made it very clear, I promise you, that you and I were a unit. And committed to being one.'

'She might have figured she could, eventually, convince you otherwise. And in the meantime, she gets to cause trouble and grief. It's pretty much no lose for her.'

'Yes,' he replied, 'that would amuse her. She's bored by the ordinary, or what she perceives as the ordinary.'

Outlasted the terms of the prenups in both cases, she'd said.

'Marriage would be a means to an end, even a toy.'

'How can I make this work for me?' Eve suggested. 'Or failing that, just break it.'

'I'm sorry. Sorry I didn't see through it.'

'She miscalculated,' Eve said and took his hand.

He linked his fingers with hers. 'That she did.'

'I still want to kick her ass.'

'Would it be unseemly if I wanted to watch?'

'Men always want to watch. The problem is, if we make anything of all this, it's just slop for the gossip pigs. It's going to have to be enough to know ignoring it pisses her off. Let's just be done with her.'

'Agreed.'

'Meanwhile, I've got to . . . get that,' she said as her 'link signalled. 'Block video. Dallas.'

'Reo, one more time. Got your warrant for Straffo's

315

residence. Pain in the ass. As a courtesy, the judge agreed no one would enforce it until after eight A.M. this morning.'

'I can live with that. Thanks, Reo.'

'Get something, Dallas. Straffo's going to cream up in the media otherwise.'

'I'll get something.'

'Oliver Straffo?' Roarke said when she'd clicked off. 'You suspect him in this teacher's murder?'

'Teachers, as of yesterday. The suspect who was heading our list was killed.'

'Ah.' He was behind, he realized, and it was past time to catch up. 'Well, why don't we start off the day as we so often end it.'

'I thought we just did. That was you who rolled off me awhile ago, wasn't it?'

'As memory serves. Not with sex, Lieutenant, though it is a lovely way to end and begin almost anything. Tell me about the case.'

She told him while they showered, while they dressed, while they wound their way to her office.

And as they walked into it, his pocket 'link beeped. He glanced at the readout, put it back in his pocket.

'Is that how you want to handle her?' Eve asked.

'At the moment. So your theory is Straffo killed Foster because Foster knew about the affair.'

'I wouldn't call it a theory. It's one of the possibilities. The other being Straffo's wife did it, same motive. Or Mosebly did it, because Foster knew about *her* affair.'

'For a school, it's certainly a hotbed of illicit sex.'

'It's still possible Williams killed Foster to preserve his career and reputation. Then either of the Straffos or Mosebly tied it off by eliminating Williams. I was going to run probabilities last night, but one thing and another.'

'You'd like me to verify that Straffo could have evaded the security for each murder.'

'If the arrow starts pointing at him, it'd help if I had that in my pocket.'

'Quiver,' Roarke said absently. 'You keep arrows in a quiver. I'll check out the security for you, but it seems to me that killing Foster was putting the cart before the horse. Williams was the primary threat, in your three possibilities.'

'I know that, but I've got no evidence or indication that Williams threatened exposure, until he used it on Mosebly on the morning of his death. It's possible Foster pushed it. Then Williams says, "Screw the bastard," and kills him. Or . . .'

'One of the Straffos panics and does so. Or Mosebly.' Roarke worked to line up all the players in his head. 'Too many Indians, not enough chiefs.'

'Replay?'

'A lot of suspects, but none of them standing out as the one doing the real work.'

'Yeah. There's a core problem with all of it. Foster. I can't find a strong, clear motive. Not really. So I'm going with the murky ones. He was a straight shooter, but he wasn't a troublemaker. I've got a wit who saw him and Williams the morning of Foster's death, chatting amiably in the teachers' lounge. Foster couldn't have pulled that off, not to my way of thinking, if he and Williams were having serious trouble.'

'You said Foster had reported Williams's harassment of Sanchez,' Roarke reminded her.

'Yeah, but it was a knuckle tap. Foster told him, some time before, to lay off the nutritionist. He laid off. Problem solved. Now I know Foster saw Mosebly and Williams playing dunk and dick in the school pool, and he tells his wife that he's seen Williams with someone he shouldn't have been with. But he *doesn't* say who, or talk about confronting anyone about it.'

Circling the murder board, Roarke studied Mosebly's picture. 'A formidable-looking woman. And being the principal, an authority figure. The nutritionist was support staff. She was upset by the advances, Mosebly obviously wasn't.'

'Yeah, because her rape claim is bogus. So why kill Foster if he's decided to mind his own? Why dump public scandal on your own doorstep?'

Eve shook her head. It just didn't fit, just didn't work. 'So, I'm back to revenge or protection or just plain pissiness. I don't much like any of those pictures.'

'Then you'll get a clearer one. You've been off your stride.'

'And then some. Yeah, we'll see what a look through Straffo's penthouse brings into focus.'

16

It was more than being off her stride, Eve decided as she worked and waited for Peabody and McNab. The case itself had no solid point, no focus.

It was the motives that were murky.

The probability scans ran dead even between her primary suspects, with Allika Straffo dropping to the base according to profile.

There was something just slightly off about the woman, something more than a stumble on the fidelity path. What did she know? Eve wondered. What did she think? What made her so vulnerable and skittish?

The death of a child. Could that, did that damage run so deep it left the foundation forever cracked and shaky? Maybe it did, how would she know? But Oliver Straffo appeared to have learned to live with the loss.

Maybe it was different for a mother.

But there was another child in the house, alive and well.

Not enough, apparently, to keep Allika steady. The kid, the successful husband, the penthouse, the au pair, none of it was quite enough. So she slipped, and Williams had been right there to catch her.

Maybe it wasn't the first slip.

'Maybe it wasn't,' she muttered. 'And . . . so what? So what?'

She turned and saw Roarke in the doorway between their offices. 'So what?' she repeated. 'If it wasn't the first time Allika had grabbed for a little strange, wouldn't a man as astute as Straffo know the signs?'

'People stray from marriages every day, and not all their spouses, however astute, know. Or admit to knowing. Or for that matter,' Roarke added, 'particularly care if they do know.'

'He's got pride. He's *involved*. He'd know, he'd care. And if it was the first time, is his reaction going to be to kill an innocent bystander? And where his daughter's going to be touched by it?' Two big hitches. Eve decided as she shook her head.

'It doesn't play straight for me,' she continued. 'But if he knew, why would he agree to defend the man his wife strayed with? *And*, since he did agree, why would he turn around a day later and kill the son of a bitch?'

'Maybe to have the primary on the case ask herself that very question.'

'Huh. Well, it's working.' Rolling the possibility around in her head, she tipped back in the chair. 'He's a slick one in court, always has the angles figured, knows how to twist the – wait a minute. Wait. Here's an angle. What if he agreed to rep Williams because he wanted to make sure he lost? He doesn't even have to drop the ball, he just has to make sure he doesn't kick it through the goalposts.'

'Ah. He takes the case to insure his client's found guilty. Clever, and all but impossible to prove.'

'Like I said, slick guy. He tried an order to overturn the warrant, suppress the evidence. And he had to know Reo would mow that down. Starts off weak.'

Roarke picked up her coffee from the desk, helped himself to a sip. 'A nice, tidy line of revenge.'

'So why kill the guy if you were going to help put him in a cage anyway?'

After setting the coffee down, he reached out, tapped his finger on the dent in her chin. 'You're circling, Lieutenant.'

'Yeah, I'm circling, because there's something there, but I can't see it. There's something there.' She shoved to her feet. 'I need my murder board.'

'I wondered if you'd update the one up here.' He walked to her then, slipped his arms around her. 'It cost you time.' He pressed his lips to her brow, quietly pleased when her body leaned into his. 'What pushed between us cost you time.'

'I'll make it up.' *They'd* make it up, she corrected. That was part of the benefits of being a team. She linked her arms around his waist, watched him smile. 'What do you think about the security?'

'The system's very basic. You were right there. Easily slipped through.' Wrapped around each other, they both turned their heads to study her board. 'A weapon would be more difficult, but hardly impossible. A person would cause barely a blip if they knew anything about the system.'

'That's something anyway.'

'I'll look at the discs for you, see if anyone jammed one of them for the second or two it would take.'

'McNab was going to look at that. You've got work of your own.'

'I owe you time.'

'Awww.' Peabody stopped in the doorway. 'Sorry. Hi. Nice to see you.' And she was grinning from ear to ear.

'Don't take off the coat, we're going. I'll see you later,' she said to Roarke, then found her mouth caught by his.

'Awww,' Peabody repeated.

'Later, Lieutenant. Good morning, Peabody, McNab.'

'Hey! How's it going!'

'Don't talk to them,' Eve ordered as she started out. 'They'll start begging for danishes. With me, both of you. And stop smiling like that,' she demanded as she strode ahead of them. 'What if it sticks on your faces and I have to look at it all day? It's scary.'

'We're just happy. Things are good, right?'

'Keep going,' she told McNab, then slowed just a little. 'Let's just close this up with me saying I appreciate the ear, and the faith and the support.'

'That's what friends do, and partners.'

'Yeah, but thanks.' She hesitated as they started down the stairs. 'You go on out with McNab. I'm right behind you.' But she paused, taking her coat off the newel where Summerset would have replaced it for her.

She looked at him as she put it on. 'He's okay. We're okay. She's not going to be a problem for him anymore.'

'Or for you?'

'Or for me.'

'I'm very glad to hear it.'

'I know you are. Appreciate it.'

'I've brought that unfortunate vehicle you've yet to wreck around in anticipation of your departure. I hope you won't leave it soiling the front of the house much longer.'

'Kiss my ass, scarecrow.'

'There.' He smiled at her. 'We're back to normal.'

She let out a snorting laugh, then strode out.

Straffo met them at the door. He didn't elect to have his own lawyer present, as was his right. Pride, Eve decided. He was too proud to have someone else handle the legalities.

It surprised her a little to note he hadn't sent his wife and kid, and the au pair, away. Went back to pride, she assumed. He was showing them he'd handle this nonsense, that he was still in charge of the household.

He read the warrant thoroughly, taking his time about it, his face expressionless. Oh, but he was pissed, Eve thought. He was steaming under that smooth exterior.

'It's in order,' he stated, then met her eyes. 'I expect you and your team to proceed with this in an expeditious and respectful manner. You'll be accountable for any damage.'

'So noted. The record is on, and will remain on throughout. Detective McNab will handle the electronics. If any of your possessions require confiscation, you'll be given receipts. Do you wish to remain on the premises during the execution of the warrant?'

'I certainly do.'

'That'll be handy.' She nodded to McNab, then to Baxter and Trueheart as they arrived. 'Baxter, you and Trueheart take the main level. Peabody, with me.'

She started toward the stairs, passed Allika who stood gripping Rayleen's hand.

'Excuse me, Lieutenant?'

Eve paused, looked at the child. 'Yeah?'

'Are you really going to search my room?'

'We're going to search all the rooms, including yours.'

'Wow. Could I—'

'Rayleen.' Straffo's voice was quick and sharp. 'Let the police get on with what they came to do.'

Still looking more excited than abashed, Rayleen lowered her eyes. 'Yes, sir.'

Eve started with the third floor. There was what she supposed was termed a family room. A couple of long, cushy sofas, double-sized chairs, oversized entertainment screen.

A fireplace, currently cold, was topped by a wide white mantel that held copper urns and a grouping of family pictures in matching copper frames. The family at the shore, Rayleen in school uniform, another of the kid in a pink tutu, the couple in black tie, looking polished and happy.

Sectioned off from the lounge area was a home gym. Nicely equipped, Eve noted, and with a view of the city from a long ribbon of windows.

There was a small second kitchen – minifriggie, mini-AutoChef, short counter with a couple of stools.

A full bath complete with jet tub and steam shower.

There was no work space.

Still, she searched cabinets, drawers, cushions, took art from the walls to check backings and frames.

'Looks clear,' she said to Peabody. 'McNab will check the electronics.'

'Family sanctuary. Pretty juicy one.' Peabody took one more scan. 'They use this place more than the living area downstairs when they're going to hang. Watch some screen, play games on the table over by the window. Downstairs is more for entertaining. This is where they get together as a fam.'

'Yeah, I'd say.' She glanced toward the fireplace again, studied the pictures on the mantel. 'Let's take the second floor.'

They separated, with Peabody taking Straffo's home office and Eve taking Allika's sitting room. She studied the fireplace again, the mantel, the family pictures and portraits.

Interesting, she thought. Then dug into the room.

It was all very female, Eve decided. Mags and discs on fashion and decorating and child rearing. Memo cubes were reminders to send thank-you notes for parties or gifts, to send invites for dinner or cocktails or lunch. Reminders to buy a hostess gift for so and so or an anniversary gift for him and her whoever. The sort of thing the wife of a high-powered and successful man did, she supposed.

The sort of thing she never did.

Who did? she wondered. Did Roarke handle that himself, or Summerset, or Caro?

Allika kept separate date books for herself, for her husband, for her kid.

Straffo's golf dates, dinner meetings (whether she was needed to attend or not), his salon appointments, doctors' appointments, meetings with his tailor, scheduled out-of-town trips. A family trip scheduled for March, which coincided with the kid's spring break from school.

She compared it with Allika's. Shopping dates, lunch dates, salon dates, dinner with her husband, some with clients or friends, some without.

She noted that neither of them had scheduled appointments during the time frame of either murder.

The kid's appointment book was a shocker. Dance class, twice weekly, socialization dates (what the hell?) three times a week with various other kids. Melodie Branch was down for every Thursday afternoon from three-thirty until four-thirty. Swapping houses, Eve saw. One week at the Branch place, one week here at the Straffos's.

There was soccer practice once a week beginning in March, and something called Brain Teasers the kid attended every Saturday morning. Followed, two Saturdays a month, with a volunteer stint with an organization called From the Kids.

In addition to the monthly schedule, there were additions of birthday parties, field trips, school projects, Drama Club meetings, doctors' appointments, museum and library trips, art projects, family outings.

As far as Eve could see, the kid had more going on than both of her parents.

No wonder they needed the au pair, Eve mused. Though it was a little odd that Allika had carried professional mother status from the time Rayleen was born until the death of the son. Though she wasn't pursuing a career, or even a paying hobby outside the home, Allika had let that status lapse.

Eve bagged the notebooks. She wanted more time to study them, and to verify all the names and groups and locations.

She went through the little desk. Monogrammed stationery – so Allika handwrote some of those thank-yous and invites, Eve mused. Huh. An organized-by-occasion selection of cards – birthdays (humorous, flowery, formal, youth), sympathy, congratulations, and so on.

Spare discs and memo cubes, address book, a file of clippings on decorating.

It made Eve think of the clippings Peabody had found in Lissette Foster's cube. Common ground, Eve mused. Something there? Maybe the women had crossed paths in their interest in decorating.

She made a note to check it out, though she doubted Allika and Lissette shopped for doodads or draperies at the same level.

Correspondence Allika had saved ran to cute little cards

or notes from girlfriends, printed out emails from same, or from the kid.

There were birthday cards and feel-better cards from Rayleen, all of them handmade. And with more style and skill, Eve admitted, than she herself could claim. Pretty paper and colors, some comp generated, some hand-drawn.

DON'T BE SAD, MOMMY!

One of the cards announced in big, careful printing on heavy pink paper. There was a drawing of a woman's face with shiny tears on the cheeks.

Inside the woman was smiling, with her cheek pressed to the cheek of a girl's face. Flowers bloomed all around the edges and a wide rainbow curved at the top. The sentiment read:

I'LL ALWAYS BE HERE TO MAKE YOU SMILE!
LOVE,
YOUR OWN RAYLEEN

Eve noted Allika had written the date on the back of the card. January 10, 2057.

In the closet she found some art supplies, a paint smock, clear boxes filled with things like glass marbles, stones, beads, ribbons, silk flowers. Hobby stuff, Eve supposed, all as organized as the rest of the place.

And on the top shelf, behind boxes of supplies, a large and lovely fabric-covered box with a jeweled latch.

Eve took it down, opened it. Found the dead son.

Here were the photographs, from infant to toddler. A beaming and pregnant Allika, a dreamy-eyed Allika holding an infant wrapped in a blue blanket. Pictures of the baby boy with his big sister, with his father, and so on.

She found a swatch of the blanket, a lock of downy hair, a small stuffed dog, a single plastic block.

Eve thought of the memory box Mavis and Leonardo had given her and Roarke one Christmas. This was Allika's memory box, dedicated to her son.

How often did she take it out, Eve wondered. Look through all the pictures, rub that blue fabric between her fingers or stroke that lock of hair against her cheek?

Yet she kept it all on a high shelf at the back of a closet. Tucked away. And not one memento of the boy, that Eve had seen, touched the rest of the house.

Why?

She went through it all, every piece. Then replaced it and put the box back.

When she finished with the room, she stepped over to where Peabody was just winding up with Straffo's home office.

'Nearly done here. McNab started on the master bedroom up here so we wouldn't get in each other's way. Boxed a lot of discs and files. Nothing's popped out though.'

'You find anything on the kid? Their dead kid?'

'Who? Oh, oh, right. Forgot. No, nothing here on their son.' Peabody stopped, frowned. 'Nothing,' she repeated. 'That's kind of odd, really.'

'One more thing. There's a stash of decorating clippings in Allika's sitting room. Lissette had some in her cube.'

'Yeah, she did. So maybe they crossed there?' Peabody frowned, shrugged. 'Maybe. But I've got a stash of my own, and a bunch of decorating sites bookmarked on my home comp. Don't you ever . . . Forget I nearly asked,' Peabody said when Eve stared at her.

'It's worth checking out. Running the name by Lissette, showing her Allika's picture.'

'Okay. Do you want me to tag her now, ask her?'

'Yeah, let's cross that off the list, then take the master bedroom next.' She walked over. McNab turned. 'Anything shaking?' she asked him.

'Steady as they go. A lot of incomings and outgoings, but nothing that pops. Mostly personal data – banking, marketing, schedules, and like that on the main-level units. Nanny's unit more of the same. Talks to family and pals back in Ireland a couple times a week, emails regular. All chatty, little bits on the Straffos and the kid, but nothing that'd make you jump.'

'Keep looking.'

It didn't take long for Eve to discern that both Straffos preferred good fabrics in classic cuts – and plenty of it. The his and hers closets were spacious and pristine, and loaded.

Shoes were organized according to type and tone and all in clear protective boxes. Wardrobe was color-coordinated into groupings. Causal, work, cocktail, black-tie. The more formal wear hung with ID tags that described the outfit, when and where it had been worn.

If they liked sex toys, those playthings had been smuggled out before the warrant was executed. The nightstand drawers held book discs, memo cubes, minilights.

But there was some very provocative lingerie in Allika's dresser, and a varied selection of body creams and oils. Since there'd been a reminder in Allika's date book to renew her semiannual birth control, sex was likely part of the regularly scheduled events.

She found anti-anxiety and antidepression medication, and sleeping pills in Allika's underwear drawer.

Eve took a sample of each medication, bagged it.

'Lissette didn't recognize Allika's name or image,' Peabody reported.

'Long shot.'

'Yeah. Dallas, I know we're not supposed to get wound up in the personal areas of an investigation, but that woman, Lissette, just breaks my heart. She asked, the way they do, if we had anything new, anything we could tell her. I had to give her the standard line. She took it.' Sympathy, all those personal feelings an investigator is supposed to block out, resonated in her voice, on her face. 'Held onto it like it was the only thing keeping her head above water right now.'

'Then we'd better follow through on the line, Peabody, and give her the answers she needs.'

Leaving Peabody, Eve headed down to find either one of the Straffos. He was pacing, talking on a headset, while she pretended to be absorbed in a magazine. The minute he spotted Eve, Straffo ended the transmission.

'Finished?'

'No. You've got a big place. Takes time. There's a safe in the master bedroom closet. I need it opened.'

His lips tightened, just a little, and before Allika could rise, he waved her down. 'I'll see to it,' he told her. Then looked at Eve again. 'Have you completed your business on the third floor?'

'It's clear.'

'Allika, why don't you have Cora take Rayleen up to the family room when they get back?'

'All right.'

He stopped, and Eve saw something in him soften as he touched a hand to her shoulder. She thought, Okay, he loves his wife. What does that mean?

He didn't speak until they were far enough up the steps to be out of his wife's hearing. 'How would you feel, I wonder, to have your home turned inside out this way, your personal things pawed over?'

'We try not to paw. We've got two bodies, Straffo, both of whom you knew, one of whom was your client.' She sent him a look, let a little sarcasm leak into it. 'Tough way to lose a client, by the way.'

'A foolish way to dismiss one,' he countered. 'And yes, I knew them both – casually. Maybe you're theorizing that I'm annoyed with Rayleen's academic program, and I'm working my way one by one through her instructors.'

'Maybe I'm wondering why you took a lowlife like Williams as a client. If I knew that, we might have avoided this.'

'I'm a defense attorney.' His tone was as cool and flat as hers. 'My client list isn't always the bright lights of the city.'

'You got that. We all do what we do, Straffo.'

'Yes, we all do what we do.' He went into the bedroom, ignored Peabody, and went straight to the closet safe. 'I opened the one in the study downstairs for your associates,' he said as he plugged in the combination, finished with his thumbprint.

'Appreciate it.'

It was jewelry – his and hers. Pricey wrist units, some antique wrist watches, glittering stones, gleaming pearls. While he stood watch, Eve went through it, checked for false bottoms, compartments.

When she was satisfied, she stepped back. 'You can lock her up.'

He did so. 'How much longer?'

'Couple hours, at a guess. I want to ask one question. Lot of family photographs around the house. I haven't seen one out of your son. Why is that?'

There was a look in his eye, for only a moment, and the look was bleak. 'It's painful. And it's private.' He turned and left.

Questions and possibilities circled in Eve's mind as she watched him go. 'Have Baxter and Trueheart take the guest room up here, Peabody. You handle the bathrooms to start, I'm taking the kid's room.'

What was interesting, Eve thought, was that with the kid's schedule, Rayleen had time to use the elaborate space. But it was obvious she did from the art projects in progress, the school work discs filed in her pink, monogrammed case. A paper desk calendar with a pair of insanely adorable puppies was turned to the correct date.

She had photos as well. One which had to be her classmates at Sarah Child all lined up by height, facing the camera in their spiffy uniforms. Another of a vacation shot with Rayleen flanked by her parents, all looking sun-kissed and windblown. Her own solo school picture, and another solo of her in a pink party dress.

There were a couple of thriving live green plants on her windowsill in pink and white pots. Obviously Rayleen didn't tire of the color scheme. Or had no choice in it.

Eve was voting for the former.

The kid had more clothes than Eve could have claimed for all the years of her own childhood put together. All as neat and organized as her parents' had been. There were dance clothes, dance shoes, a soccer uniform, soccer shoes. Three identical school uniforms, dressy clothes, casual clothes, and play clothes, all with appropriate shoes.

There was a forest of hair ties, bands, clips, pins, and ribbons, all meticulously kept in a designated drawer.

At least nothing was tagged to indicate where and when she'd worn anything. But a lot of items – notebooks, bags, stickers, writing tools, art cases, and so on were labeled with her name.

A big decorative pillow on her bed had PRINCESS RAYLEEN splashed across it, as did a fluffy pink bathrobe and the matching slippers.

She had her own date book, with all of her activities and appointments plugged in, her own address book with the names of schoolmates, relatives, her father's various 'link numbers.

Eve bagged them.

'How come you're allowed to take that?'

Eve turned, though she'd known Rayleen was there. 'Aren't you supposed to be someplace else?'

'Yes.' A smile curved, charming, conspiratorial. 'Don't tell. Please? I just wanted to watch how you searched. I think maybe I'll work in crime investigation one day.'

'Is that so?'

'Daddy thinks I'd make a good lawyer, and Mom hopes I'll go into art, or dance. I like to dance. But I like to figure things out more. I think maybe I'll study to be a criminalist. That's the right word, because I looked it up. It's somebody who studies evidence. You gather it, but then other people study it. Is that right?'

'More or less.'

'I think anyone can gather it, but studying it and analyzing it would be *important*. But I don't understand how come my address book and stuff could be evidence.'

'That's why I'm the cop, and you're not.'

The smile turned right down into a pout. 'That's not a very nice thing to say.'

'I'm not very nice. I take things because I need to look at them when I have more time. Your father will get receipts for anything that leaves the premises.'

'I don't care. It's just a stupid book.' Rayleen shrugged. 'I remember everyone's numbers and codes anyway. I have an excellent head for numbers.'

'Good for you.'

'I looked you up and you've solved lots of cases.'

'It's "closed." If you're going to work with cops, you have to use the right term. We close cases.'

'Closed,' Rayleen repeated. 'I'll remember. You closed the one where those men broke into a house and killed everyone in it but a girl, younger than me. Her name was Nixie.'

'Still is.'

'Did she give you clues? To help you close the case?'

'As a matter of fact. Shouldn't you go find your mother or something?'

'I've been trying to think of clues for this one.' She wandered to a mirror, studied her own reflection, fluffed her curls. 'Because I was right there and everything. I saw, and I'm very, very observant. So I could help close the case.'

'If you think of anything, be sure to let me know. Now scram.'

Her eyes met Eve's in the mirror, a quick flash, then Rayleen turned. 'It's *my* room.'

'It's my warrant. Beat it.'

Rayleen narrowed her eyes, folded her arms. 'Will not.'

The kid's face was a study of defiance, arrogance, confidence, temper. And Eve noted, challenge. *Make me.*

Eve took her time absorbing it all as she crossed over. Then she took Rayleen by the arm, pulled her out of the room.

'Taking me on's a mistake.' Eve said it quietly, then closed the door. Locked it.

In case Rayleen got ideas, Eve strode down to the bedroom door, closed and locked that as well.

Then she went back to work.

She was undisturbed until Peabody knocked. 'Why'd you lock the door?'

'Kid got under my feet.'

'Oh. Well. I had the guys haul some of the boxes we're taking out. They're labeled, receipts done. Unfortunately, we didn't come across any poison in the spice cabinet or blackmail notes in the library. But we've got some shit to cull over once we log it in at Central. You get anything in here?'

'This and that. Here's what I haven't got. Her diary.'

'Maybe she doesn't keep one.'

'She mentioned she did when Foster was killed. I'm not finding it.'

'They can hide them good.'

'I can find them good, when they're here.'

'Yeah.' Peabody pursed her lips, looked around. 'Maybe she doesn't keep one after all. Ten's a pretty much between-age for boys, and boys are the big topic of diaries.'

'She's got an active, busy brain for any age. So where's

the "Mom and Dad won't let me have a tattoo. It's so bogus!" Or "Johnnie Dreamboat looked at me in the hall today!"'

'Can't say, and can't think what that would tell us if she had a journal going and we found it.'

'Daily stuff – what Mommy said to Daddy, what this teacher did, and so on. The kid notices things. Got a snotty streak, too.'

Peabody grinned. 'You think all kids are snots.'

'Goes without saying. But this one's got something in there.' Eve glanced back at the mirror, saw again the way Rayleen had looked at herself, then the flash in her eyes. 'If something pissed her off or hurt her tender feelings, you bet your ass she'd document. Where's her documentation?'

'Well . . . Maybe McNab will find something buried on her comp. She's smart enough, she'd want to keep her observations and bitches where Mommy and Daddy and the au pair wouldn't find them if they poked around.'

'Put a flag on that.'

'Sure. Seems a little out there, Dallas.'

'Maybe.' She turned, studied the vacation shot again. 'Maybe not.'

17

When the items from the Straffo residence were logged, Eve commandeered a conference room. There, she and Peabody spread everything out, grouping according to area, subgrouping by person or persons who owned or used the item.

She dragged in her murder board, clipping up pictures of various items or groupings.

She studied, she circled, she paced.

'Please, sir, I must have food.'

Distracted, Eve glanced over. 'What?'

'Food, Dallas. I gotta eat something or I'm going to start gnawing on my own tongue. I can order something in or run down to the Eatery.'

'Go ahead.'

'Mag-o. What do you want?'

'To nail this bastard down.'

'To eat, Dallas. Food.'

'Doesn't matter, as long as it comes with caffeine. She had a box full of pictures.'

'Sorry?'

'Allika, in her sitting room. A big pretty box, up in her

closet, not quite hidden, but not out in the open. It was full of pictures of the dead kid, had a lock of his hair, some of his toys, a piece of his blanket.'

'Jeez.' Peabody's tender heart ached a little. 'Poor woman. It must be awful.'

'Not one picture of the kid anywhere in the open, but bunches of them in her box. Hers.' Eve moved around the groupings again, stopped by the section taken or copied from Oliver Straffo's office. 'Nothing like that in Straffo's office or in the bedroom or any of the family areas.'

Peabody moved over to stand by Eve, tried to see what her lieutenant might be seeing. 'I had a second cousin who drowned when he was a kid. His mother got rid of all his things. All of them except this one shirt. She kept it in her sewing basket. I guess you can't predict how anyone's going to handle the death of their kid. I'll bring food and caffeine.'

She zipped out before Eve could delay her.

Alone, Eve circled the table, the board. And thought about the dead.

The boy had been good-looking, fun-looking, she added. Big, goofy grin on his face in most of the pictures that weren't taken in infancy. Happy, healthy family, she mused, studying the picture she'd copied of one in Allika's box – the four Straffos grinning at the camera. Kids in the middle, parents flanking them.

Everyone touching some part of someone else. An attractive unit. Somehow complete.

She compared it to the one she'd copied from Rayleen's

room. One kid now framed by mom and dad. And yeah, even though Allika grinned into the camera there was a hollowness around her eyes, a hint of strain around her mouth.

Something missing.

Did she try to fill that void with social functions, routines, appointments, structure? Medications and men?

Don't be sad, Mommy!

Bright kid, that Rayleen. Smart, perceptive, pissy. Eve couldn't hold the pissy against her. So Rayleen had looked up her data, her service record, her cases. Easy enough to do, Eve mused, but interesting work for a ten-year-old.

Nixie, she remembered. Nixie had been another bright, perceptive kid. Courageous kid. One who'd lost a brother, too – and her entire family, her entire world, in one horrible night.

Nixie'd been full of questions, as Rayleen seemed to be. Maybe they just popped out smarter and more full of curiosity now.

At their age, Eve had barely started real school. Had she been curious? she wondered. Maybe, maybe, but she hadn't been one to ask questions. Not then, not for quite a while. For the first eight years of her life asking too many questions meant a fist in the face. Maybe worse.

Better to stay quiet, watch, figure it out than to ask and end up bloody.

Something was going on in that house, Eve thought. Something was just a little tilted in that perfect space. She wasn't afraid to ask questions any more. But she needed to figure out the right ones to ask.

She ate something that might have once wished to be chicken inside of cardboard pretending to be bread. And ran a series of probabilities.

She was fishing and knew it, following various lines of logic – and one knotted string of pure instinct.

The computer told her that her instinct was crap, but that didn't surprise her. Then she ran a hypothetical, omitting certain details, and the computer called her a genius.

'Yeah, wouldn't that be a kick in the ass?'

She sat back. It was, of course, bullshit to run a hypothetical or probability without including known details or evidence. But she'd satisfied her curiosity.

Intrigued, she copied it all to Mira and asked for an opinion. She sent copies to her home unit, then gathered what she wanted to take home before she headed out to the bull pen and Peabody's desk.

'I'm going to work from home.'

'It's nearly end of shift.'

'And your point is?'

'Nothing. Nothing at all.'

'I'm swinging by the school on the way. Just want another feel of the place. Tell McNab I want individual d and c's from the Straffos's dug deep. Any shadow, any smudges, I want to know.'

'Um, day off tomorrow. Yours, mine, and ours. Valentine's Day, too.'

'Jesus. Consider yourself on call, Detective. So be prepared to throw something over whatever embarrassing outfit you're going to put yourself into for McNab's perverted delight if and when I tag you.'

Peabody gave a sober nod. 'I have a trench coat reserved for that purpose, sir.'

Eve considered it. 'I'm forced to say: Ick. You don't head out until you get your report written and copied to my unit here and at home. I want your notes, too. Impressions, opinions.'

'You've got something.'

'Dunno. Between bouts of physical expression I can't bear thinking about, take another look at both vic's student files — grades, discussions, parental meetings, the works.'

'And I'd be looking for?'

'Let me know when you find it,' Eve said as she strode out.

She took the glides down to the main level, cast a couple of wistful glances at the vending machine. She wanted a Pepsi, but didn't want to interact with the damn machines.

They hated her.

Rather than squeeze onto the elevator, she jogged down the steps to the garage, pulling out her 'link as she went.

She hit Caro first, and Roarke's ever-efficient admin sent out a warm smile. 'Lieutenant, how are you?'

'Good enough. Can—' She stopped herself from shooting

right to the point. How-are-yous required a how-are-you-doing back. She kept forgetting those sort of details. 'How're you doing?'

'Just fine. I want to thank you for the use of your house in Mexico. Reva and I had a lovely mother and daughter weekend there. It's just beautiful, and the weather couldn't have been better. It was a perfect break from the winter for both of us.'

'Ah.' She didn't know Roarke had given Caro and her daughter a couple of days in Mexico. 'That's good.' Now she had to ask about Reva, didn't she? 'So, how's Reva doing?'

'Really well, thank you. She's dating again – casually. It's nice to see her enjoying herself again. I'm sure you'd like to speak to Roarke.'

Whew, she thought, navigated the chatty session of the program with no casualties. 'If he's tied up, you could just pass him a message whenever.'

'I'll check.'

Just a little worn out by the 'link socializing, Eve got into her vehicle as Caro switched her to blue screen hold. Moments later, it was Roarke's blue eyes that blazed on screen.

'Lieutenant.'

God, he was pretty. 'Sorry to interrupt any world domination meeting.'

'That was this morning. We're finishing up satellite and planetoid dominations just now.'

'Okay, then. I'm just heading out, going to swing by the school.'

'For?'

'Not sure. I just want another run through on scene.'

His smile was easy and still made her insides curl. 'Would you like some company?'

'What about satellite and planetoid domination?'

'I believe we have that under control. I'll meet you there.'

'Good. Great.' In fact, it was perfect. 'See you.'

'Lieutenant?'

'Damn stupid traffic,' she muttered as she fought her way into it. 'What?'

'I love you.'

Okay, *that* was perfect. 'I heard that somewhere. There's a rumor going around I love you, too. God*damn* maxibus. Gotta go.'

She stuffed her 'link back in her pocket and enjoyed the armed combat of driving uptown. Once there, she scouted out then fought for a parking spot, another type of warfare, then walked the block and a half to the school.

He was getting out of a car when she was half a block away. Tall and rangy, long black coat billowing in the wind. As the car cruised off – he'd have arranged that so they could drive home together – he turned. Just as he'd done the very first time. Turned as if he sensed her, knew she was there, and latched those wild blue eyes on her face.

Just like the first time, the very first time, something inside her leaped.

It wasn't her style, it wasn't her way, but there were times, she thought, you just went with the moment. She strode right up to him, gripped the front of his coat in her fists and took his mouth with hers. Strong and hot and real.

He drew her in. He always drew her in. So they stood, drenched in the heat of the kiss while the cold blew around them, and New York's irritable traffic bitched and complained.

'There she is,' he murmured.

'Yeah, here I am.' She drew back. 'You've got a great mouth, ace. I happen to know your hands are pretty damn good, too. Get us in.'

He lifted his brow. 'Are you suggesting I break into the school, Lieutenant?'

'I'm ordering it, if you're standing as expert consultant, civilian.'

'I love when you pull rank. Stirs me up.'

'A wink and a smile stirs you up, pal. Give it a shot.'

He strolled up to the door, removing a small palm device from his inside coat pocket. After keying in a code, he aimed it at the security plate, engaged.

The locks gave up without a whimper of protest.

'Showoff.'

'Well, I did have a minute or so to look over the system last night. And in anticipation of orders, programmed a little bypass.' He opened the door, gestured smoothly. 'After you.'

'Security?'

'Please.'

She shrugged, stepped in. 'Interior security? Log-in scan?'

He glanced up at the scanner, keyed another code into his palm unit. 'There you go. As you could have done the same with your master, I assume you wanted to test how simple it might be to slide into the place without authorization or detection.'

'Something like that. Say someone didn't have your sort of education. How much trouble would it be to do what you just did?'

'More, certainly, as I was top of my class, so to speak. But it's not a complicated system. Your average going-out-of-business-endlessly sale shop on Fifth would have better.'

He tapped her side and her sidearm under the coat. 'However, the fact that you're carrying is a bit more problematic. I'll need a minute to shut down the weapon scan.'

'Go ahead.' That was just for convenience, she thought. It wasn't smuggling in a stunner or blaster that concerned her.

'Scanner wouldn't detect poison. Why should it?' she mused. 'Pressure syringe, same thing. Killer or killers could have walked right in, at any time, with both.'

'You're clear.' He stood a moment, scanning the area. 'So what are we doing here?'

'Not sure.'

'Not, I imagine – unfortunately – to play teacher-keeps-the-naughty-student-after-school.'

'No,' she agreed. 'Empty schools are even creepier than when they're otherwise.' She slid her hands into her pockets as she walked.

347

'The ghosts of students past. Bloody prisons, really.'

She laughed, gave him a friendly elbow bump. 'Yes!'

'Not that I spent a great deal of time inside places like this. At least not until Summerset took charge of me. He was rather insistent about attendance.'

'The state-run schools I was stuck in weren't like this. None of this air of privilege, and the security was a hell of a lot tighter. I hated them.'

She stopped by an open classroom door. One of the cells – or so it had seemed to her – of the prison. 'First few years I just felt scared and stupid, then later it was "Okay I get all this. When can I get out?"'

'And once you did, you jumped right into the police academy.'

'That was different.'

'Because it was a choice.' He touched her arm, just a brush of understanding. 'And a need.'

'Yeah. And nobody in the academy gave a shit if you recognized a dangling participle or could write a brilliant essay on the sociopolitical ramifications of the Urban Wars. Then there was geometry. That's sort of the thing, though.'

'Geometry's the thing?'

'Lines and spaces and crap. Area, radius, blah, blah. It gave me a headache. But I'm thinking geometry. The distance, the angles, the shortest route between two points.' She started up the stairs.

'First vic's classroom. That's the – shit, what's the middle of the thing.'

348

'Which thing?'

'The middle of the space.' She lifted her hand, fashioned a space in the air.

'Well, that would depend, wouldn't it? If you're meaning a circle, it might be simply the center. Or, staying with a circle as the space, you may mean the central angle, and that's the angle whose vertex is at the center.'

She stopped walking at *vertex* to stare at him.

'Then, as every central angle cuts the circle in two arcs, there'd be the minor arc – the smaller, which would be less than one hundred and eighty degrees, and the major, the larger, which is always more.'

'Jesus.'

He grinned, shrugged. 'I always liked geometry.'

'Geek.' She scowled down the hallway. 'Now I forgot what I was doing.'

'Or you may be after the tangent,' he said, unconcerned. 'The point of tangency would be the point where a line intersects the circle at precisely one point, and one only.'

'Shut up.'

'You asked. Of course, your shape might be a triangle, say, and in that case—'

'I'm going to draw down on you in five flat seconds and stun you senseless.'

'You know what I liked even more than geometry? Finding the blind spots on the security cams,' he said. 'Which, in fact, geometry helped me with. Then snagging some sweet young thing, and—'

He snagged her, whipped her around, back to the wall, and grinning, kissed her lavishly.

His mouth managed just what geometry did. It fuzzed her mind.

'Work now, tonsil hockey later.'

'You romantic fool. Now then, I think I understand what you're trying to figure out, and it's more to do with intersections and betweenness.'

She actually had to press her fingers under her eye to still a twitch. 'Betweenness can't possibly be an actual word.'

'It is, in fact, in math language. And I think would be your first victim's classroom. That's the point between the others. And also, I'd think, where your lines intersect, in the first theorem.'

'Let's just leave the higher math out of it because it's going to separate my mind from my body, and I'd rather save that for sex. Foster's classroom.' She gestured. 'Which was empty for at least fifty minutes, twice that day – before class and during his fourth period, giving the killer ample opportunity to doctor the go-cup, or simply replace it. I'm going to push on the replacement angle tonight. Maybe get lucky there. It was inscribed with his name. Anyway . . .'

She walked over, uncoded the seal, opened the door. 'Other classes are in session, including the second vic's. Here.' She walked over, opened the door on Williams's classroom. 'During the second fifty-minute segment when Foster's classroom was unoccupied, Williams leaves his classroom for about ten minutes. Used the bathroom, he claimed.'

'Which gives you a segment line, from point to point. Opportunity and motive.'

'Yeah. Means is yet to be proven. I can't tie the poison to Williams. How'd he get it, why would he choose it? Meanwhile, there's some foot traffic. There's a janitor in the students' bathroom – male. He's clean and clear. No record, no motive, excellent work record, married, father of three, and two grandkids who attend this school.'

'But he's another intersection.'

'Yeah, yeah. He sees, and is seen by Mosebly, Hallywell, Williams, and Dawson. Then by Rayleen Straffo and Melodie Branch. Each pass by at some point, with Dawson, um, intersecting again with the two students. On the lower level, Hallywell intersects with two other students.'

'There's also your unknown.' Following her equation, Roarke added to the data. 'The possibility someone not identified ran a parallel line. A segment that didn't intersect with another segment, but arrived at your center.'

'The outsider. Allika or Oliver Straffo, for instance, both of whom could – with forethought and planning – have bypassed the security check, arrived at the center when Foster was out – known information – doctored or replaced, and left. Under six minutes to come in, walk up, go in, do it, walk out. I've timed it.'

She stopped again, turned a circle. Puffed out a breath. 'It's possible it could have been done by one of them without being seen. Low risk, as if they had been seen, their kid goes here. Any handy excuse or reason to be on site would have passed without a blink.'

'But they weren't seen.'

'No, they weren't. Straffo was in his office off and on that morning, door closed. Did he slip out, get over here, and do it? Possibly – very tight, but possibly. Allika was shopping. Same deal. However, Allika *was* seen on the day Williams was killed. Signed in, hung around.'

Again, he followed her reasoning. 'If she decided to eliminate teachers, why run the parallel line with one and intersect on the other?'

'Exactly. I've got other reasons for and against, but that one sticks on me. Nobody'd have thought anything about it if she'd come into the school the day Foster was killed. Any excuse would've worked.'

She crossed to Foster's classroom. Saw him again, lying on the floor in pools of his own waste. 'These killings aren't passionate and impulsive, and they're pretty damn smart. Smarter for her – Allika – to have come in clean. I don't like her for it, and she's too emotional to have pulled this off. Straffo, now, he's got the control and the focus, but not his wife. And still . . .'

'Something bothers you about her.'

'A few things. But I need to turn it around in my head some before I lay it out. Meanwhile, Foster comes back, goes in, closes his door for his daily lunch/lesson-planning deal. Drinks really bad hot chocolate. If he'd got medical attention in the first few minutes, he might have made it. But the killer's banking on it going as it did.'

She stepped in for a moment, and again saw Foster. Alive now, going through his habitual routine. 'He sits. Shoots off a cheerful little email to his wife, gets working on the pop quiz he has planned. He drinks, he dies.'

'Painfully,' Roarke murmured, knowing what she was seeing.

'Painfully. Then the two kids, sprung from their study session on the main level, come up, see the janitor, speak with Dawson, show their passes, go to the classroom.'

'Question? Why is it Dawson doesn't seem to blip on your radar?'

'No motive, no sense, no buzz. Teacher for twenty-odd years, fifteen right here. No current around him. He's the . . . What is it? He's the tortoise type.'

'Slow and steady.'

'Yeah.'

'Followup. You're veering well away from Principal Mosebly, though you've shown she had motive.'

'Yeah.' Raking her fingers through her hair, Eve walked out of the classroom again. 'I could be way off on her, but I can't see her for it either. Murders on her sanctified ground, under her watch? It's a nightmare for her, worse than having her sexual indiscretion revealed. She's hemorrhaging students out of here, getting slammed with unpleasant media. Maybe she did it, maybe she thought she could spin it all and weather the damage. But it doesn't ring. Still like to fry her for crying rape. Bitch.'

She frowned. 'Where was I?'

'The two girls go to the classroom.'

'Right. If they'd come up fifteen minutes earlier, Foster's got a chance. Instead, he's gone and they run out screaming. Dawson runs over, sees what's happened, calls the principal.'

'A fairly predictable series of events.'

'It is, isn't it? Now we'll take Williams.'

She led the way downstairs, through the fitness center, into the pool area.

'Not bad,' Roarke commented.

'Yeah, a pretty sweet setup for a kid or a teacher. In here, Williams intersects with Mosebly. Allika Straffo is on premises – no intersections reported – then, according to her statement, she went looking for Williams, and – using your terms – ran a parallel line with him and Mosebly, overhearing their argument.'

From where she stood, Eve could see the exits, entrances into the pool area. Staff. Students.

'She leaves, Mosebly leaves, more intersections with her and Hallywell, Dawson. Dawson comes in to see Williams, and for the second time in a week finds himself a dead body.'

'Quite the coincidence.'

'Yeah, yeah. But he and the nurse, who was also called to both scenes, they're peripheral. Someone else reached the center of both these circles, undetected.' Eve stared down at the surface of the water. 'Both times.'

'You're sure it was the same killer?'

'Yeah. Yeah, I am. Pretty sure I know who the killer is, but I don't have the why. I have to have the why on this one.'

'Well now, share.'

She nearly did, then shook her head. 'Not yet, okay? I'd like to see what a geek like you comes up with without prejudicing the, ah, theorem. Want to talk it over with Mira, too. But that's all gut right now. I'm going to look at the solid first, and track the go-cup angle.'

'Are we going shopping?'

'Just going to check a few of the places that sell that make and model, in a ten-block radius.'

'You said radius. Does that make you a geek?'

'Smart-ass.'

He took her hand. 'That's more like it.'

It didn't blow the investigation open for her. Like the majority of cop work it was routine – repetitious and tedious.

She spoke to clerks, to managers, to the clueless and the chirpy. The item in question was a popular model, not the cheapest or the priciest. A good value, she was told endlessly. Practical, attractive, and hard-wearing.

'We had to order in another shipment two weeks before Christmas,' Eve was told by an eager-to-help assistant manager. 'Great stocking stuffer or emergency gift, and we had them on sale. Couldn't keep them on the shelf. We're still selling them briskly. Valentine's Day. Free inscription inside a heart, or with heart motif.'

'Adorable. You've got records. I'm interested in one of these models inscribed to "Craig".' She spelled it out.

'Sure, I'll look it up. If they went credit or debit, we'd have a record. Cash, we wouldn't. Most people don't do cash because once they come in, they end up buying multiple items.'

'Uh-huh.' Eve glanced around, noticed that Roarke was roaming, browsing, examining. All the things that people who actually liked to shop ended up doing.

'I'm really sorry.' And the guy actually looked it. 'We don't have a sale of that model – or any other – with an inscription added that says "Craig" – any spelling – during the last thirty days.'

'Go back another thirty.'

'Oh. Um.' He looked distressed now. 'That'll take me a few minutes, and on the main unit in the back, since I'd have to go back into last year. You'll have to excuse me.'

'Done. I'll wait.' She turned now and saw that Roarke wasn't just shopping, he was buying. She crossed the store, winding around displays. 'What are you doing?'

'I'm making a purchase.'

'How? Why?' It must be a kind of sickness, she decided. 'You already own six of everything.'

He only smiled, and took the bag from the clerk. 'Thank

you. And now,' he said to Eve, 'it appears I have more of everything. Any luck?'

'No. Still checking. It was always going to come down to cash. Killer thinks clearly. Not going to leave a paper trail. It's easy to breeze into one of these places, buy something, add the fee for inscription, pass some paper money, and walk out. Nobody's going to remember you.'

The clerk came back, dripping apology. 'I'm so sorry, I couldn't find what you're looking for. I can ask around, see if any of the clerks remember.'

'Yeah, great. Thanks. You can contact me if you find out anything.' She dug out a card, passed it over.

'That's one to cross off,' she said when they were outside. 'Had to be done though.'

'Here.' He took out a pair of gloves from the shopping bag. 'To replace the ones you've lost since Christmas.'

'I haven't lost them.' Why was she always losing them? 'They're just somewhere else.'

'Of course. These can go on your hands. And these' – he tapped the bag – 'will go in your vehicle to replace the ones on your hands once you lose those.'

'And when I lose those?'

'Back to square one. Now, should we go out to dinner, or go back to work?'

'We could eat dinner while we work.'

'How strangely that sort of thing suits us.' He draped an arm around her shoulders. 'I'll drive.'

★　★　★

Since she'd picked the place for takeout, she let him pick the meal. She should've known it would be fish. Maybe it came from being born on an island, though she knew it was more likely he picked it because it was good for her.

Still, it was tasty, as was the bed of spicy rice that almost disguised the vegetables mixed in it. Besides, it washed down just fine with a crisp glass of white.

She told him about the search at the Straffos's penthouse. This was what she wanted from him now, impressions, comments, insights. Telling him what she knew, what she'd seen, heard, observed. And for now, leaving out the seed of certainty planted dead center of her gut.

'Sad,' he said.

'What is?'

'Who. Straffo's wife. That's how she strikes me. Keeping everyone's records and schedules with her own – needs to know, doesn't she, where everyone is, what they're doing. Wouldn't want to have her own schedule, interests, impulses conflict with theirs. Then there's her memorial box.'

'Memorial. I thought memory.'

'It's both, isn't it? To keep his memory fresh for her, and to memorialize him. For herself. Just for her. That's sad. It must be a terrible thing for a mother. Then you said she hid some of her meds. Doesn't want her husband to know she's taking them. Doesn't want to – what, upset, disappoint, worry him? So she keeps her little secrets.'

'Yeah, she does,' Eve agreed. 'She's got secrets.'

'And you think they apply to these murders? How?'

'Keeping the status quo is vital to her.' Because visuals helped, Eve brought Allika's photo ID onto the wall screen. 'She broke it off with Williams. Betrayed her husband, sure.' Split-screened Allika's image with Oliver Straffo's. 'But in addition she rocked her own boat. That spooked her. She needs those waters calm again. Still, I don't think they ever are. Not inside her anyway. It's pretense. So she needs her chemical boosts.'

'I don't see how that connects to your investigation.'

'Everything connects. She loses a kid.' Now, Eve added a third image, the innocent and doomed little boy.

'He's charming, isn't he?' Roarke commented.

'Yeah. He's got a look. So does Allika. Hers is like before and after, and that's how it strikes me in that house. You can see it in the pictures. In their eyes. They're wounded, walking wounded, but they get through it. His way, her way. Now she stumbles, has this affair. He knows it, or close enough. I think he knew she ended it, and he doesn't confront her. Keep up the pretense, the status quo. Already lost a kid, can't put themselves or their surviving children through a divorce.'

She added Rayleen's photo so the screen held four images. 'Now there are two murders, slapped back to back and right in their faces. She's shaking and scared. He's closed up and angry.'

'And the girl?'

Eve looked at the screen. 'She's fascinated.'

'Ah. Children can be cold-blooded. Death's other for

359

them. They're so far from it. Innocent enough to believe it can't touch them, so it's compelling.'

'Is it innocence?'

'It's childhood, I suppose.' He topped off her wine, then his own. 'So very different from yours or mine.'

'Yeah. Different by a long shot. Roarke?'

'Hmm.'

She started to speak, then changed her mind. 'I wonder if either of us can really be objective about a family unit like that.' She gestured toward the screen. 'But I know there are answers in that house. I'm going to find them. Each one of them, each segment of that square that became a triangle. Mother, father, daughter.' She drew a triangle in the air. 'Each knows something. Something that connects them and keeps them separate at the same time. I'm going to have to take each segment separately to figure it out.'

18

After dinner, Eve began to search and cross-reference every name in the address books she'd taken during the search of the Straffo penthouse. While it ran, she started a chart of schedules.

Intersections, she thought again. Parallel lines. But a triangle here, not a circle.

Idly, she doodled a triangle on a pad, drew a horizontal line through its center. 'What would you call this?'

Roarke glanced over her shoulder. 'What you have there is a midpoint proportionality, a segment whose endpoints are the midpoints of two sides of a triangle. A segment that is parallel to the third side – its length half the length of that third side.'

'Jeez, uber-geek. I see a kind of box inside a triangle. A connect from another source.'

'That as well.'

'Huh.' While he wandered off to the kitchen, she rose and updated her murder board. Her computer signaled the assigned task was completed before she was finished.

'Display results.' She started to turn just as Roarke came out of the kitchen with a tray. 'We already ate.'

'We did indeed.' He crossed, set the tray on the table, then took off a small plate. And turning, offered it. 'And this is a homemade fudge brownie.'

Her heart, she was embarrassed to realize, just melted. 'Man, you never miss a trick.'

'You can thank Summerset later.'

'Uh-uh.'

'I asked if he'd bake a batch. So you can thank me as well.' Roarke held the plate just out of reach, tapped his lips with the index finger of his free hand.

She rolled her eyes, but it was only for form. Then leaned in, pecked a kiss on his lips, and snatched the brownie. 'Damn me if I'm kissing those bird lips of Summerset.' She bit in, then just groaned. 'Oh, God, this is really . . . Are there more?'

'Maybe.'

'I'd better space it out. I think this is the chocolate equivalent of Zeus.' On another bite she turned to read the data. 'Son of a bitch! I fucking knew I was right.'

'About . . .' He scanned the data. 'One Harmon, Quella, female, age fifty-eight of Taos, New Mexico. Two marriages, two divorces, no offspring. Occupation, artist.'

'What kind of artist?'

Cocking his head, he continued to read the data. 'Specializes in fashion and jewelry, stone and leatherwork. Leatherwork. Ah.'

'Ah, my ass. Bull's-fucking-eye. If that's not the ricin source, I *will* kiss the hideous lips of Summerset. The castor beans, they still grow wild in arid areas. I bet New Mexico has some arid areas. And I bet a leather artist living out there uses the oil in leather preparation.'

'Certainly that may be, and how does Quella Harmon connect, or are we still using intersect, with your victims?'

'By being the maternal aunt of Allika Straffo. Means,' Eve stated. 'Closing right in on means. Computer, search date books on each Straffo individual in evidence for any travel to New Mexico over the past six months. No, amend. A full year. And/or any mention during that time period in same of Harmon, Quella, to New York.'

Acknowledged. Working . . .

'You think Straffo took a sample of ricin from this woman, with or without her knowledge, carried it back to New York, then used it to poison Foster.'

'I damn well do.'

'All right, means I'll give you, Eve, but you've lost motive again, haven't you? Unless the computer reports that there was contact with this Harmon in the last couple of months, it would have been prior to Allika's affair with Williams, prior to Foster having knowledge of it.'

'Uh-huh. Parallel lines.'

Task complete. Straffo, Oliver, Allika, and Rayleen traveled by commercial shuttle from New York to Taos, New Mexico, on November

twenty-six. Returned to New York by commercial
shuttle on November thirty . . .

'That's before Allika took up with Williams, according
to their statements. Isn't it?'

'Yeah.' But Eve was smiling grimly.

'Then unless Straffo is a sensitive with psychic tendencies,
why would he transport a poisonous substance on a
commercial carrier *before* his wife strayed?'

'Maybe it wasn't a poisonous substance at that time,
maybe it was just a bag of beans. But it's all about planning
and possibilities. Opportunities. Curiosity.'

As she spoke, she walked back, circling the board again.
Then she continued to pin photos, lists, notes, data.
'Computer, print out displayed data. Hard copy.'

Acknowledged . . .

And now Roarke circled, studied, scanned while she went
to retrieve the printout.

He could see she was building something. It was the way
she'd arranged the pieces on the board, how she continued
to arrange them. Into some sort of pattern she, obviously,
saw in her head. Or felt in her gut.

Her mind, he knew, was labyrinthine and linear, fluid,
flexible and stubbornly rigid. He could and did admire it
without ever fully understanding its workings. Her gut, he
believed absolutely, was close to infallible.

He stepped back, and let his own mind clear, refocus, in an attempt to see what she was moving toward.

When he did, his shock was instant. His denial automatic. 'You can't be serious.'

'You see it?'

'I see what you're stitching together, what pattern you've made out of it. But I can't put my head around why you'd aim in that direction.'

'What? You don't think a ten-year-old girl can be a stone-cold killer?'

She said it casually as she pinned Harmon's photo and data to the side of the triangle she'd made out of the Straffos. 'I murdered at eight,' she reminded him.

'Not murder, not close to it. You saved your own life, and destroyed a monster. You're talking about a child deliberately and coldly planning and carrying out the murder of two adults.'

'Maybe more than that.' Eve reached into her file, took out the ID photo of the Straffos's son she'd already printed. And pinned it in the center of the triangle.

'Christ Jesus, Eve.'

'Maybe he fell down the steps. Maybe he did. Maybe he had help. Maybe it was a tragic accident, which involved his sister.'

Her gaze was pinned now, to Rayleen Straffo's violet eyes. 'Excited, running, a couple of kids, one trips over the other, over his own feet. Whatever. But you know what?'

She turned, and those flat cop's eyes met Roarke's now.

'I don't think so. I think she pushed him. I think she got him up when her parents were sleeping, lured him out of bed. Don't make any noise. Santa's downstairs! Let's peek.'

'Well, my God,' Roarke muttered.

'Then when he gets to the steps, a good hard shove. No more little brother edging in on your territory. Squeezing into the center of your circle.'

'How can you think this? She'd have been all but a baby herself when that happened.'

'Seven. She'd have been seven. She'd had all the spotlight for five of those years, and now she has to share it. Maybe it's a novelty at first, let's play with the baby. But it got old, and they're not paying nearly enough attention to Rayleen. Princess Rayleen. Just have to fix that, won't we?'

'What you're saying, it's obscene.'

'Murder always is. The mother knows,' Eve said quietly. 'She knows. She's terrified and she's sick and she tries different ways to escape the horror of it. But she can't.'

'You're so sure of it.'

'I saw it in her. I know it. But knowing it and proving it, especially something like this, are way different.'

He had to struggle to overcome an innate and instinctive denial. 'All right, even considering you may be right about the boy, why Foster? Why Williams? Because of her mother's affair?'

'I don't think she'd give a flat shit about her mother's affair. Sex isn't on her radar, not really. And it doesn't really apply to her directly. I don't know why, that's the bitch of it. I've got Peabody searching through Foster's student records to start. Maybe he caught her cheating, or stealing.'

Didn't fit, she thought, annoyed with herself. Didn't really jibe. 'There were a few illegals in student lockers. Maybe she's selling or using. If she was threatened by him in some way, or felt he could or would do something to screw up her perfect world, she could kill him to prevent it.'

She began to pace. 'I need Mira's take. For me, this kid fits the profile down the line. But I need Mira to back that up. I need that, and I need to catch Allika alone tomorrow. Wear her down, break through the protective shield. I need more than what I've got because unless I'm completely crazy, this kid's killed three people in her first decade. And she hasn't even come close to hitting her stride.'

'How would she know what ricin is, much less how to use it?'

'Kid's smart. Smart enough to listen, observe, and check the web.'

'And the paralytic used on Williams. How'd she get her hands on it?'

'She volunteers, some organization called From the Kids. You know what they do?' She tapped the copy of Rayleen's busy schedule. 'They visit pediatric wards, geriatric wards, spend time with the sick and infirm to brighten their day. I bet she could get whatever the hell she wanted. Who's going to look at some sweet, socially conscious little girl? I need to find her diary.'

'You're sure she has one?'

'That was a little mistake she made right off, mentioning her diary to me when she was pulling the spotlight on herself. Cued in to that from the get,' Eve told him. 'All those I's. *I* saw, *I* found, *I* think, *I* know. But I didn't see, not clearly enough.'

Her mouth firmed. 'Well, neither did she. How could she know I'd go poking around in her personal space? It'll be in her diary – all of it. Who can pat her on the back but herself? The only way to do that is to write it down. She got it out of the house before we searched it.'

She circled the board again, picking out details, separating them, mixing them together again. 'Plenty of time to get it out of the house while her daddy flexed his lawyer muscles. Hell, maybe she destroyed it. She's smart enough to have done that, cover herself. Maybe I just have to prove, for now, she *had* a diary.'

'You're cool about this,' Roarke commented.

'I have to be. I let it slip by, again and again. I didn't want to look there. Jesus, who would? I didn't want to look at that kid with her pretty curls and see a murderer. But I did. I do. If I'm going to get justice for the dead, I have to have every detail and tie them up with a bow. Nobody's going to want to hang multiple premeditated murders on a sweet-faced school girl.'

'If you're right . . . what if there are more?'

Letting out a breath, Eve switched displays on screen manually, brought up Rayleen's ID photo. 'Yeah, that's gone through my head, and stuck in my gut. What if there are more? Sick kids, sick elderly. Did she put one down? She's got activities scheduled all over hell and back. How many people does she *intersect* with every day, every week, month, and so on? Was there another accident, another death, another unsolved murder? Going to find out eventually.'

'She must be very, very sick.'

'I don't know what she is, but I know I'm going to do everything I know how to do so she pays for what she's done.' She saw his face, felt her muscles tighten. 'You think I should feel sorry for her?'

'I can't say, that's God's truth. I'm not sure what to think, but the fact is you believe, and you've crafted a very convincing argument that this *child* has committed cold-blooded murder.'

He stepped up to her triangle again, her family gallery. 'Let me argue back. Have you considered that one or both of her parents killed, that somehow *she* knows. That this is what you sense in her.'

'We'll keep it on the table.'

'Eve.' He turned to her, his intense eyes in contrast to his gentle hand as he touched her hair. 'I need to ask. Is there something in you that wants it to be her?'

'No. No. There's something in me that doesn't want it to be her. So I let it slip by, I didn't look close enough. Then today, standing with her in that perfect little girl's room, I couldn't not look. I couldn't not see. I'm not going to feel sorry for her, Roarke. But I can feel sick about it.'

'All right then.' He rested his brow on hers. 'All right. What can I do?'

'Can you think like a homicidal ten-year-old girl?'

'It's not in my usual repertoire, but I can give it a try.'

'If you kept a diary, and didn't destroy it, *and* were smart enough to know you had to get it out of the house, where would you put it?'

She turned away, paced around the board once more. 'She's got dance class, probably has a locker of some kind there, or she could have a hidey-hole at one of the wards she visits. The school's too risky, she wouldn't be that careless. Maybe—'

'Who's her closest mate?'

'Her what? I figure her for a killer, but I don't think she's already having sex.'

'Friend, Eve. Her best friend.'

'Oh.' Eve narrowed her eyes. 'I'd vote for Melodie Branch. That's the kid who was with her when they found Foster. She has regularly scheduled socialization dates with her. That's a strong maybe. I'm going to tag Peabody for some OT. We'll pay a visit to Melodie tomorrow, and to Allika. I need to talk to Mira.'

'Eve, it's nearly eleven at night.'

'So? Shit,' she muttered when he only sent her a mild stare. 'Okay, I'll save that for the morning. Better, probably. It'll give me time to write this all up, set it up, lay it out. I'm going to need a lot of muscle – mine, hers, Whitney's – to pull the kid in for formal interview.'

She went back to her desk, sat, and prepared to get started. 'So . . . I figure I should ask so it's not hanging anywhere. Did Magdelana contact you after she tried your 'link before?'

'No.'

'Have you thought about how you're going to handle it – her – whatever, when she does?'

'If and when, I'll take care of it. She won't cause us more trouble, Eve. My word on that.'

'Good. Well, this is going to take me a few hours.'

'I've some work I can catch up on.'

'Are we still on for that date tomorrow? Schmaltzy hearts and flowers followed by crazed sex?'

'I believe I have it as "inventive sex" on my schedule. I'll just amend that to "crazed."'

'Why can't it be both?'

He beamed those blue eyes at her. 'There's my Valentine.'

She expected the nightmare, and still wasn't prepared for it. She wasn't prepared to see herself as she'd once been – small and thin – standing in Rayleen's pink and white room.

She didn't like the dolls, she didn't like the way they stared and stared like dead people, but still seemed to watch her. But it was so warm, and the air smelled so nice.

The bed looked like something out of the fairy tale she'd once watched on screen when no one was around to stop her. A princess bed. Nothing bad would ever happen in a bed like that.

No one would come in, in the dark, lay on top of her, hurt her, hurt her. Not in that beautiful, beautiful bed.

She walked to it, but was afraid to touch. She reached out, then jerked her hand back. He'd probably beat her if she touched it. Probably pound his fists on her if she touched something so beautiful.

'Go ahead. You can touch it. You can even lie down on it.'

She whirled around. It wasn't him. It was a little girl, like her. But not like her. Her hair was shiny, her face was pretty and soft-looking. There were no bruises on it. She smiled.

'This is my room.'

'You're the princess,' Eve murmured.

The little girl's smile widened. 'That's right. I'm the princess. Everything here is mine. If I say you can touch something, you can. If I don't, and you do, I can have you thrown in the dungeon. Where it's dark all the time.'

Eve whipped her hands behind her back. 'I didn't touch anything.'

'You have to ask first, then I'll give my permission. Or I won't.' The pretty little girl walked over to a table where a pink and white tea set was laid out. 'I think we should have some hot chocolate. I have my servants make it whenever I want it. Do you like hot chocolate?'

'I don't know. I've never had any. Is it good?'

Rayleen poured it from pot to cup. 'It's a killer.' Then she laughed, and laughed. 'You have to drink it if I say you do. You're in my room, and I'm the princess. I say it's time for you to drink your hot chocolate.'

Obediently – she'd learned to be obedient – Eve stepped over and picked up one of the pink cups. She sipped. 'It's . . . it's so good. I never had anything like it.' She drank it fast, greedily, then held out the cup. 'Could I have more?'

'All right.' Rayleen's smile was sharp now, like her eyes. In the look Eve saw something that made her stomach fist. And when Rayleen poured from pot to cup, what streamed out was red, red blood.

Biting back a scream, Eve dropped the cup. The red spread and pooled on the white carpet.

'Now look what you've done! You'll have to pay for that.' Setting down the pot, Rayleen clapped her hands twice.

And he came in, smiling that sharp smile, looking with those sharp eyes.

'No. Please. I didn't mean it. I'll clean it up. Please, don't. Please.'

'I've been looking for you, little girl,' her father said.

He struck her first, one quick, hard blow that sent her sprawling to the floor. Then he fell on her.

She fought, she begged, she screamed when the bone in her arm snapped like a pencil. While Rayleen stood, idly sipping from her cup.

'Only one way to stop it,' Rayleen said as he began to push and shove himself inside Eve, to tear her. 'Killing takes care of everything. So kill him. Kill him. Kill him.'

Rayleen chanted it, her voice rising with excitement.

'Kill him!'

Finding the knife in her hand, Eve did.

'Ssh, ssh. Stop now, Eve. Just a dream. Nothing but a dream. You need to wake up for me. Come back to me now. I have you.'

'It was blood. Pink and white and red. All the blood.'

'It's done now. You're awake now, with me now.' They tore at him, these nightmares, even as they tore at her. He held her, and rocked her, pressing his lips to her hair, her temples even when she'd stopped shaking.

When she turned her face against his throat, he felt the tears.

'I'm sorry.'

'No, baby. Don't.'

'Am I projecting, Roarke? Is that all it is? Do I look at that kid and see all I never had, never felt, never knew? Is it some sort of jealousy? Is it all just some sort of twisted envy? With Magdelana, too?'

Now he drew her back, ordered the lights on at ten percent so she could see his face, see his eyes. 'It's not, no. It could never be. You don't have it in you for that. If I planted that there with Magdelana, the flaw was mine. You look straight, darling Eve. You see what is, even when you'd rather not. And you look at things others turn from.'

'They'd have locked me away for what I did to him.'

'You're wrong. And if they had, even for an hour, for the smallest part of an hour, even God would have had no pity on them for it.' He stroked the tears away with his thumbs. 'The cop in you knows that perfectly well.'

'Maybe. Yes. Most of the time.' Sighing, she let her head rest on his shoulder. 'Thanks.'

'Part of the service. Can you sleep now?'

'Yeah.'

He lay down with her, kept his arms wrapped around her, and dimmed the lights again.

It left her draggy in the morning, as nightmares often did. But she put it away. By eight she was dressed, fueled, and ready to deal with what needed to be done.

'How are you going to approach this?' Roarke asked her.

'I expect both Mira and Whitney to contact me after they've read the report I sent them last night. Meanwhile, I'm hitting the best pal first. If I get lucky, there's a diary and best pal has it for safe-keeping.'

She sat on the arm of the sofa in the bedroom sitting area and drank her second cup of coffee. 'Then I try for Allika. Straffo has a golf date this morning – nine-thirty tee time, then lunch at his club. The kid has a nine o'clock deal at something called Brain Teasers, followed by a museum trip. Allika's supposed to meet the kid and au pair at one, take over as the au pair has the rest of the day off. There's lunch at a place called Zoology, followed by mother-daughter salon treatments this afternoon.'

'Full day.'

'Yeah, they fill 'em. I'm banking on catching Allika alone

at the penthouse this morning. Depending on the results, I'll either pick up the kid, or have a sit-down with Mira and/or Whitney first. Interviewing the kid's the tough part. Her father's going to block me, Child Protection's going to weigh in. I need more than theory and more than circumstantial to break it down.'

'Full day for you, too.'

'I can still manage sex and dinner.'

He laughed. 'I like the order of this evening's menu. Here, have this first.'

He walked to his closet, brought back a box wrapped in Valentine red, topped with a white silk bow.

'Oh, man.'

'I know, yes. A gift.' His lips twitched in amusement. 'So annoying. Open it anyway.'

She lifted the lid, found another box inside of dull gold. Nestled in it on red velvet was a long, slim bottle.

She'd expected jewelry, it was his habit to buy her glitters. And she supposed he had as – knowing him – the stones encrusted on the bottle wouldn't be glass. Who would buy a bottle decorated with diamonds and rubies except Roarke?

She lifted it, studied the pale gold liquid inside. 'Magic potion?'

'It may be. Scent. Yours. Made it for you – your skin, your style, your preferences. Here.' He took it, lifted the ruby stopper, then dabbed some on her wrist himself. 'See what you think.'

She sniffed, frowned, sniffed again. It was subtle, and it wasn't frilly. Wasn't what she thought of as flower juice or come-nail-me-against-the-nearest-wall musk.

'And?'

'It's nice. More — I guess, it's one more thing that proves you know me.' To please him, she stroked a little on her throat. 'You know the bottle's over the top, right?'

'Naturally. The diamonds are from the Forty-seventh Street heist.'

'Yeah?' The idea of it amused and delighted her. 'That's fairly frosty.' She took the bottle to her dresser, high enough that Galahad couldn't leap with the pudge he carried. Then she came back and offered her neck for a sniff. 'And?'

'Perfectly you.' He tugged on her hair to lower her face for a kiss. 'My one and only Valentine.'

'Save that sloppy talk for later. I have to get moving. Peabody will be here any minute, or risks having her ass kicked.'

'Should we say dinner at eight, unless work intervenes?'

'Eight. I'll try to make sure to wrap up whatever I can wrap up by seven-thirty.'

Though she'd read Eve's report as ordered before she arrived, Peabody was still resistant to the idea of, as she put it, a kiddie killer.

'Okay, I know, at some of the rougher schools, teachers and other students have been threatened or attacked. Stickers, fists, hell, kitchen utensils. But those are hard-line situations and most often involve hard-line kids.'

'So because this one wears a nice uniform and lives in a penthouse, she's immune.'

'No, but it's a different foundation. And we're talking about revenge crimes, impulse violence or innate violent tendencies. In this case, they're premeditated and coolly executed without any clear-cut motive.'

'Motive will come.'

'Dallas, I went through Foster's records. I went through Williams's records. There were a handful of disciplinary actions and/or parental conferences due to behavior, slipping grades, chronic lateness on assignments and that sort of thing. But not one of them involved Rayleen Straffo. Her grades are stellar, her deportment evaluations the same. She's top of the class.'

'Maybe she doctored them.'

'Man, you've got it in for her.' Immediately, Peabody winced. 'I didn't mean it the way it sounded. I just can't get there with you. I just don't see it. I sure don't feel it.'

'Let's follow through on these interviews today. Maybe one of us will change her mind.'

The in-dash 'link signalled as Eve pulled to the curb in front of the building where Melodie Branch lived.

'Dallas.'

'Eve, I've read your report.' Mira's face was knitted with concern. 'We need to discuss this. At length.'

'Figured that. This isn't a good time. I'm about to do a followup with a wit.'

'Not Rayleen Straffo.'

'Not at this time, no. I can meet with you, and with the commander — as I'm sure he'll feel this requires a discussion as well — this afternoon.'

'All right. I'll contact the commander now and set it up. I'd prefer you didn't speak with Rayleen Straffo until we've had this discussion.'

'She's pretty booked up today anyway. It can wait. From what I'm hearing, you're not on board with me on this.'

'We'll discuss it this afternoon. I do have some concerns, yes. Tread carefully here, Eve.'

'I'll do my best.' Eve clicked off. 'Sounds like Mira's on your side of the line with this one.'

'It's not sides, Dallas.'

'No. You're right.'

But it felt like sides, Eve thought, as she got out of the car and started into the building with the full intention of intimidating a young girl into betraying her best friend.

19

Angela Miles-Branch opened the door herself. She was dressed uptown casual in tweed pants and a cream angora turtleneck. On her feet were soft, low-heeled leather boots in the same tone as the sweater.

She led them both into a stylishly streamlined living room. 'I assume this is about the situation at Sarah Child. Melodie's in her room, currently not speaking to me.'

'Oh?' was all Eve said.

'I've taken her out of the academy. I'm not sending my daughter to a school where there have been two murders. She's upset that I won't factor in her side of things, as in, her best friends in the entire universe go there, she doesn't want to go to another school where she doesn't know anyone and where they have to wear uniforms that are minus-zero, and so on.'

Like a woman suffering battle fatigue, Angela dropped into a chair. 'We're head-to-head on this issue, and since I'm in charge of her life for the next several years, I win. Still.' She sighed, pushed at her bright hair. 'It's awful to be ten and think your entire world just broke to pieces on you. I'm giving her the time and space to sulk and be mad at me.'

'It sounds like you're doing exactly what you feel is best for your kid,' Peabody commented. 'Kids don't always get it. That's why they're not in charge.'

'Thanks for that. I'm not the only parent who's taken this step, or is seriously considering taking it. Melodie doesn't get that either. So, I'm hoping that at least a couple of the kids she knows and likes end up at West Side Academy, where I enrolled her yesterday. Meanwhile . . .' She trailed off, let her hands lift and fall.

'Has Melodie had contact with any of her friends from Sarah Child?' Eve asked.

'Yes, of course. We're all trying to keep things as normal as we can. It isn't easy.'

'How about Rayleen Straffo?'

'Her in particular. They're tight, and tighter yet since they had that awful experience together. We had Rayleen over Thursday, that's a usual date for them. Allika and I felt it would be good for them to see each other as they normally do. Then Melodie had dinner over at the Straffos's last night.'

'Two days in a row? Is that usual?'

'It's not a usual situation. Frankly, I was relieved to have Melodie out of my hair for a few hours after we clashed about her starting a new school on Monday.'

'We'd like to talk with her.'

'Lieutenant, I know you have a job to do, and believe me, I want you to do it. I just don't want Melodie upset again. I don't want her to have to go through the details of what happened to Craig Foster again. She has nightmares.'

'We'll try to stay away from that. It's another avenue we need to explore.'

'All right. But in her current mood you may not get anything but the silent treatment, too. I'll get her.'

Angela rose and walked out of the room. Eve could hear muted voices – the impatience in the mother's, the sulky defiance in the child's.

Shortly, a grim-faced little girl was marched into the living area by her equally grim-faced parent. 'Melodie, sit. And if you're as impolite to Lieutenant Dallas and Detective Peabody as you have been to me, you can expect to be on house arrest for the next two weeks.'

Melodie shrugged, a pissy little gesture, and kept her gaze on the floor as she plopped into a chair.

'It's not my fault Mr Foster and Mr Williams are dead. But I get punished.'

'I'm not going to start this round again,' Angela said wearily.

Eve decided to do a straight push. 'Melodie, I need Rayleen's diary.'

The girl's chin jerked up, quick shock, then just as quickly lowered. 'I'm sorry. I don't understand.'

'Sure you do. Rayleen gave you her diary. I need to have it.'

'I don't have Rayleen's diary.'

'But she has a diary.'

'She . . . I don't know. Diaries are private.'

'Do you have one?'

'Yes, ma'am. It's private.' And she looked imploringly at her mother.

'Yes, it is.' Angela sat on the arm of Melodie's chair, laid a hand on her daughter's shoulder. Whatever their battle lines, Eve noted, this was a united front. 'Melodie knows she can write whatever she needs or wants to write in her diary, and no one will read it. I don't understand what this is about.'

'Privacy's important,' Eve agreed. 'So's friendship. I guess a lot of friends don't mind sharing what's in their diary. Did you read Rayleen's?'

'No, she wouldn't . . . Um. Maybe she doesn't have one.'

Eve took the logical leap. 'She gave it to you Thursday, when she came over. What did she tell you to do with it?'

'She just came over to play, that's all. And to hang. We can't go to school because Mr Williams drowned in the pool.' Tears began to swim in Melodie's eyes. 'And everything's totally base, and now Ray and I won't even go to the same school anymore. She's my best friend. Best friends stick together.'

'Melodie, do you know what a warrant is? I can get one,' Eve continued as Melodie just hunched up. 'It'll give me permission to search your room. I don't want to do that.'

'Lieutenant,' Angela said, shocked. 'My God, what *is* this?'

'I need to see the diary, Melodie. I'll search your room if I have to.'

'You won't find it. You won't! Because Ray—' She broke off, gripped her mother's hand. 'I promised. I promised. Mom. You're not supposed to break a promise.'

'No, you're not. It's all right, baby.' She gathered Melodie up. 'Is Rayleen in trouble?' she asked Eve.

'I'll know more when I have the diary. This is in Melodie's best interest.'

'Wait. Just wait.' Angela closed her eyes a moment, the struggle on her face obvious. Then she tipped Melodie's face up to hers and spoke quietly. 'Sweetie, you have to tell the police the truth. That's important.'

'I promised!'

'The truth is as important as a promise. Tell me, sweetie, do you have Rayleen's diary?'

'I don't! I don't! I took it back to her last night. I only had it for a little while, and I didn't read it. It's locked up, but I wouldn't have read it even if it wasn't. I swore an *oath*.'

'Okay, baby, that's okay. She doesn't have it,' Angela said to Eve. 'I won't insist you get a warrant if you feel compelled to look for it. But I'm telling you, if she says she doesn't have it, she doesn't have it.'

'That won't be necessary. Melodie, what did Rayleen tell you when she gave you the diary?'

'She said the police were going to come and go through all her things.'

'Oh, my God,' Angela murmured. 'You searched the Straffos's apartment? I didn't know. I let Melodie go over there. I—'

'Nothing happened to Melodie, and nothing will,' Eve interrupted. 'Go on, Melodie.'

'She just asked me to keep it, not to tell about what was going on, not to tell *anyone* that she gave it to me. It's private, it's a diary. It wouldn't be right for strangers to read her private thoughts. She could trust me because we're best friends. And I took it back to her last night, just like she asked. Now she'll be mad at me because I told.'

'No, she won't.' Angela said it absently, staring at Eve's face. 'It's going to be all right, don't worry.' She rose, standing Melodie on her feet. 'I'm proud that you told the truth, because that was the right thing to do, and the hard thing to do. You go on, get yourself a cherry fizzy. I'll be right there.'

'I'm sorry I've been mean to you.'

'I'm sorry, too, sweetie. Go get us both a big fizzy.'

Sniffling, Melodie nodded, and left the room, dragging her heels.

'I don't know why you'd need a child's diary. I don't understand how that could possibly pertain to your investigation.'

'It's an element that requires attention.'

'You're not going to tell me what I need or want to know about this, and my daughter needs *my* attention. But I want you to tell me if I should keep Melodie away from the Straffos. I want you to tell me if her being with Rayleen and the family is dangerous to her.'

'I don't believe she's in any danger, but you may feel more comfortable, for the time being, restricting that contact.' Better, all around, Eve thought, and made sure

Angela understood it. 'It's important that neither you nor Melodie speak of this conversation or the diary to the Straffos, or to anyone else.'

'I think Melodie and I are going away for the rest of the weekend, maybe take a long weekend trip.' Angela let out an unsteady breath. 'She can start school on Tuesday.'

'That sounds like a nice idea,' Eve said. 'I'm no authority on kids, Ms Miles-Branch, but my impression is you've got a good one there.'

'I've got a very good one there. Thank you.'

Eve gave Peabody a chance to speak as they rode down from the Miles-Branch apartment. When she remained silent, Eve waited until they were in the car.

'Thoughts? Comments? Questions?'

'I guess I'm compiling them.' Peabody puffed out her cheeks. 'I have to say, on the surface, it seems pretty inno-cent, and fairly typical, for a kid to hide her diary, or ask a trusted friend to hold it for her if she's afraid somebody – an adult, an authority figure – is going to put eyes on it. Girls, especially girls, are hypersensitive about that kind of thing.'

'And under the surface?'

'Which is where you're looking, and I get that. From that point of view, the fact there is a diary, that Rayleen went to some trouble to get it out of the house before we searched, adds a certain weight to your theory.'

And Eve heard the doubt. 'But from where you're sitting, it's still typical girl stuff.'

'It's pretty hard for me to see it differently. Sorry, Dallas, she *is* a girl.'

'What if she were sixteen, or twenty-six?'

'Dallas, you know there's a world of difference.'

'That's what I'm trying to decide,' Eve said, and swung toward the curb in front of the Straffos's building.

It was Allika who opened the door. She looked pinched and heavy-eyed, like someone who'd slept poorly several nights running. She wasn't yet dressed for the day, and wore a long gray robe.

'Please,' she said, 'can't you leave us alone?'

'We need to speak with you, Mrs Straffo. We'd prefer to do it inside, where it's private and you can be comfortable.'

'Why do the police feel being interrogated in your own home is comfortable?'

'I said speak with you, not interrogate you. Is there a reason you're hesitant to hold a conversation with us?'

Allika closed her eyes a moment. 'I'll need to contact my husband.'

'Do you feel you need a lawyer?'

'He's not just a lawyer.' She snapped it, then pressed the heel of her hand to her forehead. 'I have a headache. I'm trying to rest before I need to pick up my daughter.'

'I'm sorry to disturb you, but we have questions that

require answers.' Eve took aim and pushed the weak spot. 'If you feel the need to contact your husband, why don't you suggest he meet the three of us down at Central? We'll make this formal.'

'That sounds almost threatening.'

'The three of us here, the four of us there. Take it anyway you like.'

'Oh, come in then. Get it over with. You police have a way of making victims feel like criminals.'

She stalked into the living area, and in a gesture very similar to the sulky Melodie's dropped into a chair. 'What do you want?'

'We have reason to believe there was an item taken off the premises prior to the execution of the search that may be germane to the investigation.'

'That's ridiculous. Nothing was taken out of the house, and nothing that was ever in it is *germane* to your investigation.'

'Your daughter removed her diary.'

'I beg your pardon?' Allika sat up now, and there was a ripple, just the faintest ripple of fear in her voice. 'What does Rayleen's diary have to do with anything?'

'She removed it prior to the search, and has since taken possession of it again. Do you know where it is?'

'No, I don't.'

'Have you read it?'

'No, I haven't. We respect each other's privacy in this house.'

'We need to see the diary, Mrs Straffo.'

'What's wrong with you? How can you accuse a child of something so horrible?'

'I haven't accused Rayleen of anything. What do you think she did? What do you think she's capable of doing, Allika?' Eve leaned forward. 'What has you sick, and sleepless, and scared?'

'I don't know what you're talking about. I don't know what you mean.' Her fingers began to pleat the skirt of her robe. 'You have to stop this. You have to stop it.'

'I'm going to stop it. I'm going to stop her. You know this can't go on.'

'You need to go. I want you to leave now.'

Eve pressed down hard on the next weak spot. 'Why do you keep all your son's pictures hidden away? Why do you hide a piece of his blanket, his little toy dog, all of those parts of him? Why is that, Allika?'

'He was my baby. He was my boy.' Tears gushed now.

'But you don't have pictures of your baby, you don't have memories of your boy sitting out, in the open. Why is that?'

'It's painful. It's upsetting to . . .'

'To Rayleen. She doesn't like it, does she? Doesn't like you or Oliver looking at pictures of another child. It needs to be about her, only her. She never liked sharing the attention, did she?'

'It's natural, it's perfectly natural for a first child to be jealous of a new baby. To have a period of adjustment. Sibling – sibling rivalry.'

389

'It was more than that, wasn't it? Then she finally did something about it, on that Christmas Eve. Why should she have to share those toys? Why should he get your time, when *she* was first. So she got him out of bed, she led him to the top of the stairs. Didn't she?'

'It was an accident.' Allika covered her face with her hands, rocked. 'It was an accident. She was asleep. We were all asleep. Oh, God, please, don't do this.'

'No, she wasn't asleep. You know she wasn't.'

'She didn't mean . . . she couldn't have meant . . . Please, God.'

'Tell me what happened that morning, Allika.'

'It was just as I told you. We were all asleep, all asleep.' She dropped her hands now, and her face was ghost white, her eyes dull.

'How much longer can you keep it inside without breaking?' Eve demanded. 'How much longer can you mask it with pills and busy work? With pretense? Until the next Reed Williams?'

'No. No. That was one time, that was a mistake.'

'You know you can't live with it, Allika. You need to tell me. Tell me what she did to your little boy. To your baby.'

'She was only seven.'

Seeing the fissure in Allika, Peabody did her job. She moved over, sat beside Allika. 'You're her mother, and you want to protect her. You want to do what's right for her.'

'Yes, of course. Yes.'

'You wanted to protect Trevor, too. You want to do what's

right for him. Telling the truth now, you have to know that's what's right for both of them.'

'My babies.'

'What happened Christmas morning, Allika?' Eve demanded. 'What happened to Trevor?'

'Children wake up early on Christmas morning,' Allika murmured as tears streamed down her cheeks. 'It's natural. So much excitement, so much anticipation. She came in, Rayleen came into our room just before dawn, jumped on the bed. So excited, so happy. We got up, Oliver and I. We got up, and Oliver said he would go get Trev.'

She pressed a hand to her mouth. 'The year before, his first Christmas, Trev was so young, not even a year old. He didn't understand any of it. But this year, he was nearly two, and he was . . . It would be his first real Christmas. Oliver said he'd go get Trev, and we'd all go down together and see if Santa had come.'

'Where was Rayleen?' Eve prompted.

'Rayleen stayed with me while I got my robe. She was jumping up and down, clapping her hands. So happy, her face just shining as a little girl's would on Christmas morning.

'And I saw . . . I saw she was wearing the little pink slippers I'd tucked in her stocking the night before. The ones she'd seen and wanted so much when we'd gone shopping one day.'

Allika's face went blank, as if everything inside her had gone away. 'Rayleen was wearing the slippers,' Eve said.

'They had sparkles on them, pretty sparkles all over them,

spelling out her name. She loved things to have her name on them. I started to say something, to tell her she shouldn't have gone down there by herself – how Daddy and I, we'd promised we'd get up whenever she woke. But then I heard Oliver cry out. He cried out as if his heart had been ripped away, and I heard him running down the steps. And I ran, I ran, and I saw . . . My baby. Oliver was holding our baby at the bottom of the stairs, and I ran down. And he was cold. My sweet little boy. There was blood on his face, and he was cold.'

'What did Rayleen do?'

'I don't know. I – it all blurred. Oliver was crying, and I think, I think I tried to take Trev from him, but Oliver was holding Trev so tight. So tight. I . . . yes, I ran to the 'link to call for help, and Ray . . .'

'What did she do?'

Allika closed her eyes, and she shuddered. 'She was already playing with the dollhouse Oliver and I had set up under the tree. She was just sitting there in her pajamas, wearing her sparkly pink slippers, playing with her dolls. Like nothing had happened.'

'And you knew.'

'No. No. She was just a little girl. She didn't understand. She couldn't have understood. It was an accident.'

No, Eve thought, no, it wasn't. And some part of this woman was being eaten away, day after day, because she knew it.

'Allika, you don't have soundproofing in your home, not

because you're afraid something might happen to Rayleen and you wouldn't hear. You don't have it because you're afraid of Rayleen, and what you might not hear.'

'She's my child. She's my child, too.'

'You went to see your aunt in New Mexico a few months ago. She works in leather. She uses castor beans, the oil from them, to work the leather.'

'Oh, God, stop. You have to stop.'

'Did Rayleen spend time with her? Watching her, asking questions? She likes to know things, doesn't she? Rayleen likes to know.'

'She liked Craig Foster. He was her favorite teacher.'

'But you wonder. And Williams. Rayleen volunteers in hospital wards. She's a clever girl. She could get her hands on a syringe, on drugs if she put her mind to it.'

'Then she'd be a monster. Do you want me to say that?' Hysteria bubbled up in her voice, and her streaming eyes went wild. 'Do you want me to say my daughter's a monster? She came from me.' She fisted a hand on her belly. 'From me and Oliver. We loved her from the first beat of her heart.'

'The way you loved Trevor. If I'm wrong,' Eve said when Allika's face crumbled, 'then reading her diary isn't going to hurt anything or anyone. If I'm right, she'll get help before anyone else is hurt.'

'Get it then. Take it away. Take it away and leave me alone.'

★   ★   ★

They searched. They went over every inch of the bedroom, the playroom. They turned out drawers, emptied the closet, searched among the toys, the art supplies.

'Maybe she hid it in another part of the house,' Peabody suggested.

'Or has it with her. Either way, we'll get it. The fact that it exists has some weight. We need to interview the aunt, and get some eyes on the kid right away. If she's got it, I don't want her mother shifting her feet, and getting word to the kid we're looking for it. Let's – hell.'

She broke off to pull out her communicator. 'Dallas.'

'Lieutenant, report to my office. Immediately.'

'Sir, I'm at this moment in the process of gathering evidence I believe will lead to an arrest on the Foster and Williams investigations.'

'I want you in my office, Lieutenant Dallas, before you take any further steps. Is that clear?'

'Sir, it's clear. I'm on my way. Fuck,' she added after she'd ended the transmission. She glanced at her wrist unit, calculated. 'Museum tour. Met. Get there, shadow the suspect.'

'But, Dallas, the commander ordered—'

'Me. He didn't say anything about you. I want you to locate the suspect and keep her under surveillance. Keep me apprised. Don't let her make you, Peabody.'

'Well, Jesus, she's ten. I think I can shadow a tweener without being made.'

'This *tweener* is the prime suspect in two homicides, and

very possibly guilty of fratricide as well. You're not shadowing a kid, Peabody, and don't forget it.'

She dumped Peabody at the elegant entrance of the Metropolitan Museum, then headed downtown. As she drove, she contacted one Quella Harmon in Taos, New Mexico.

Even as Peabody climbed the long sweep of steps, she wondered how the hell she was supposed to find one kid and her Irish au pair in the vast cathedral to art.

And as she wondered, Cora bundled Rayleen into a cab on Eighty-first Street.

'But Mom's supposed to meet us, and take me to lunch.'

'Well, she's rung me up, hasn't she, and said she needs you home straight away. So home we go, Ray darling.'

Rayleen gave a windy sigh, and clutched her pretty pink fur purse.

Both Mira and Whitney were waiting for her, and both looked grim.

'Sit down, Lieutenant.'

With no choice, Eve sat.

'Your partner?'

'She's in the field, sir.'

Whitney's lips tightened. 'I considered it understood I wanted both of you here, and neither of you in the field at this time.'

'I apologize for the misunderstanding, Commander.'

'Don't bullshit me, Dallas, I'm not in the mood. I've read

your report, and it's my opinion that you're putting this investigation, and this department in a very tenuous position.'

'I disagree, respectfully. Sir.'

'You're pursuing an avenue that is fraught with land mines, and pursuing it without any solid physical evidence, any solid facts.'

'Again, sir, I disagree. The suspect—'

'The child,' he corrected.

'The suspect is a minor. That doesn't preclude her from being capable of murder. Children have been known to kill, and to kill with malice. With intent, even with glee.'

Whitney laid the palms of his hands on his desk. 'This girl is the daughter of one of the city's most prominent defense attorneys. She is well-educated, she is the product of a privileged home, and even according to your own report, has never been involved in any crime, much less one of violence. Has never been treated for any emotional or mental instability. Dr Mira?'

'Children do commit violent acts,' Mira began. 'And while there are certainly cases where a child of this age, even younger, has killed, such cases usually involve other children. Such cases are most generally preceded by smaller acts of violence. On pets, for instance. Rayleen Straffo's profile doesn't indicate any predilection for violence.'

Eve had expected barriers to be erected, but it didn't stop the frustration. 'So because her father's rich and she aces it in school and doesn't kick little puppies, I should step back from what I know.'

'What do you know?' Whitney interrupted. 'You know that this girl attended a school where two teachers were murdered. So did over a hundred other children. You know that her mother had admitted to having a brief affair with the second victim.'

Eve got to her feet; she couldn't handle this sitting down. 'I know that the suspect found the first victim, that she had opportunity in both cases, I know that she had the means. I've spoken with her aunt, and have learned that the suspect had access to castor beans, and was showed how the oil was made from them. I know that she did, in fact, have a diary that she removed from the penthouse before the search, giving same to a friend to hold until yesterday.'

Whitney inclined his head. 'You have this diary?'

'I don't. I believe the suspect has hidden or destroyed it, or is currently keeping it on her person. She removed it because it would incriminate her.'

'Eve, a great many young girls keep diaries, and consider them sacred and private,' Mira began.

'She's not a young girl in anything other than years. I've looked at her. I know what she is. You don't want to look,' she said, whipping back to Whitney. 'People don't want to look at a child, at the innocence of the face and form, and see evil. But that's what's in her.'

'Your opinion, however passionate, isn't evidence.'

'If she were ten years older, five years older, you wouldn't question my opinion. If you can't trust my instincts and intellect and my skill, let me factor in more data. I killed at eight.'

'We're aware of that, Eve,' Mira said gently.

'And you think I look at her and see myself? That this is some sort of transference?'

'I know when we spoke at the early stages of this investigation you were troubled. You were upset and very stressed over a personal matter.'

'Which has nothing to do with this. It may have distracted me, and that's on me. But it doesn't apply to my conclusions in this case. You're not letting me do the job because of this bull.'

'Careful, Lieutenant,' Whitney warned.

She was done being careful. 'That's what she's counting on. That we'll all be so fucking careful. That we won't look at her because she's a nice little girl from a nice family. She killed two people inside of a week. And she's got me beat, because she killed at seven. Not her father, but her two-year-old brother.'

Whitney's eyes narrowed. 'You included the information on Trevor Straffo in your earlier reports, and the investigator's report, the ME's report, which both concluded accidental death.'

'They were both wrong. I've spoken with Allika Straffo.'

While Eve fought to make her case and Peabody sat in the Met's security office scanning the screens for Rayleen, Allika sent Cora away again.

'It's your half-day off.'

'But you don't look well, missus. I'm happy to stay. I'll make you some tea.'

'No. No. It's just a headache. Rayleen and I will be fine. We'll be fine. We'll . . . we'll just have some lunch here, then go ahead to the salon.'

'I'll put lunch together for you then, and—'

'We'll manage, Cora. Go meet your friends.'

'If you're sure then. You can ring me back anytime. I'm not doing anything special.'

'Enjoy yourself. Don't worry about us.' Allika nearly cracked before she could get Cora out the door. Then she leaned back against it. 'Rayleen,' she murmured. 'Rayleen.'

'What's the matter, Mommy?' Rayleen's eyes were sharp as lasers. 'Why can't we go to lunch at Zoology? I love seeing the animals.'

'We can't. We have to leave. We're going to take a trip. A trip.'

'Really.' Now Rayleen brightened. 'Where? Where are we going? Will there be a pool?'

'I don't know. I can't think.' How could she *think*? 'We have to go.'

'You're not even dressed.'

'I'm not dressed?' Allika looked down, studying her robe as if she'd never seen it before.

'Are you sick again? I hate when you're sick. When's Daddy coming home?' she asked, already losing interest in her mother. 'When are we leaving?'

'He's not coming. Just you and me. It's best. That's best. We have to pack. They didn't find it, but they'll come back again.'

'Find what?' Now Rayleen's attention swung back, and zeroed in. 'Who'll come back?'

'They looked.' Allika's gaze shifted up. 'But they didn't find it. What should I do? What's best for you?'

Without a word, Rayleen turned away to walk upstairs. She stood at the doorway of her room, saw that her things were moved. And she understood perfectly.

She'd imagined something like this. In fact, she'd written what she could do, might need to do, in her diary the night before. Even as she walked down the hall to her parents' room, her only genuine emotion was a quiet fury that her things had been gone through again, moved around, left untidy.

She liked her things *exact*. She expected her personal space to be *respected*.

She went into her mother's drawers where the medications were hidden. As if anyone could actually hide something from her. They were so stupid, really. She slipped the bottle of sleeping pills into her purse along with her diary, then moved to the sitting area and programmed herbal tea.

Her mother favored ginseng. She programmed it sweet, though her mother rarely took much sweetener.

Then she dissolved a killing dose of sleeping pills into the sweet, fragrant tea.

It was all simple, really, and she'd thought about doing this before. Considered it. They would think her mother had self-terminated, out of guilt and despair. They'd think her mother had killed Mr Foster, Mr Williams, then hadn't been able to live with it.

She knew her mother had had sex with Mr Williams. She'd confessed it the night before the police had come to search. Rayleen was good at hearing things adults didn't want her to hear. Her mother and father had talked and talked, and her mother had cried like a baby. Disgusting.

And her father had forgiven her mother. It had been a mistake, he said. They'd start fresh.

That had been disgusting, too – just like the sounds they'd made when they had sex after. If anyone lied to her the way her mother had to her father, she'd have made them pay. And pay and pay.

Actually, that's what she was doing now, she decided as she set the oversized teacup on a tray. Mommy had to be punished for being bad. And by punishing her, it would all be tidied up again.

Then it would just be her and Daddy. She'd really be his one and only with Mommy gone.

She'd have to put her diary in the recycler now, and that made her mad. All because of that mean, nosy Lieutenant Dallas. One day she'd find a way to make *her* pay for that.

But for now, it was better to get rid of it.

Daddy would buy her a brand-new one.

'Rayleen.' Allika came to the doorway. 'What are you doing?'

'I think you should rest, Mommy. Look, I made you tea. Ginseng because you like it best. I'm going to take good care of you.'

Allika looked at the cup on the tray, on the bed. Everything inside her went weak. 'Rayleen.'

'You're tired and you have a headache.' Rayleen folded down the duvet, the sheets, plumped the pillows. 'I'm going to make it all better. I'm going to sit with you while you rest. We girls have to take care of each other, don't we?'

Rayleen turned with a bright, bright smile.

And maybe it was best, Allika thought as she moved like a sleepwalker to the bed. Maybe it was the only way. She let Rayleen smooth out the sheets, let her place the tray, even lift the cup.

'I love you,' Allika said.

'I love *you*, Mommy. Now drink your tea, and everything will be better.'

With her eyes on her daughter's, Allika drank.

20

Whitney listened, and he absorbed. His hands, which had been very still throughout his questioning of his lieutenant began to tap fingers on the edge of his desk.

'The mother suspects her daughter caused the boy to fall.'

'The mother knows her daughter caused the boy to fall,' Eve insisted. 'She may have convinced herself, or tried to convince herself, it was an accident. Tried to patch her life back together, suffering from periodic bouts of depression and anxiety. In her gut she knows exactly what I know. It was no accident.'

'No one witnessed the fall.' But Whitney's face was stony, his eyes dark and deep.

'Dr Mira, in your opinion, given the scenario, is it natural for a girl to step over or around her younger brother's dead body, while her parents are hysterical, to play with a toy?'

'That's a broad question. The child may have been in shock or denial.'

'She was wearing the slippers. Ones she had to go down-stairs to get, before she woke her parents.'

'Yes.'

'According to the investigator's report on the death of Straffo, he died just after four A.M. on the morning of December twenty-fifth,' Eve continued. 'Statements given by both parents claim they were up, setting up the gifts, filling the stockings until about two-thirty. At which time, they had a glass of wine, then went upstairs, checking on both children before they retired, at around three. Rayleen woke them at five.'

For a moment Mira thought of the times she and Dennis had been up until the early hours of Christmas morning, putting everything together while their children slept. And how they'd snatched a few hours of exhausted sleep before the kids woke and rushed into the bedroom.

'It would be possible that the girl snuck down between the times her parents went to bed and her brother got up. But the slippers are an oddity,' Mira agreed. 'I agree, it seems strange for a child of that age to sneak down, put on slippers, then go back to bed for nearly two hours.'

'Because she didn't,' Eve said flatly. 'She got up – and I'll guarantee she had an alarm set for it because she's a planner – fitting your profile – she likes her schedules. She got up, went into her brother's room. She got him up, told him to be very quiet. When they got to the top of the stairs – which according to the investigators' reports was at the opposite end of the second floor from the master bedroom – she pushed him.'

That little body flying out, tumbling, tumbling. Breaking.

'Then she walked down, checked to make sure she'd

done a good job of it, before she went in to see what goodies she was getting from Santa. And what sort of things she would enjoy that would have been for her brother.'

She saw the horror of the picture she was painting play across Mira's face. 'She put the slippers on. She likes things with her name on them. That was a little mistake,' Eve added. 'Like mentioning the diary to me. But she couldn't resist. She probably played awhile. Her parents weren't going to notice if she'd moved something a little, and she wouldn't have resisted. It was all hers now.

'Then she went back up. I wonder if she even noticed her brother's body at that point. He was no longer an issue.'

She shifted her gaze to Whitney, noted that his hands had gone still again, and that his face showed nothing. Nothing at all. 'She might have tried to go back to sleep for a little while, but it was too hard. All those toys downstairs, and nobody to share them with anymore. So she woke up her parents so she could get back to what she wanted to do.'

'What you're describing . . .' Mira began.

'Is a sociopath. And that's exactly what she is. A sociopath with homicidal tendencies, a very keen intellect, and a big-ass chunk of narcissism. That's why she kept the diary. It's her only way of bragging about what she can do, and get away with doing.'

'We need the diary.'

'Yes, sir.' She nodded at Whitney.

'Why Foster and Williams?'

'Foster, I don't know, unless it was for the hell of it. I don't know,' she said again, 'because she doesn't strike me as a for-the-hell-of-it type. Williams was a very handy and unexpected goat. That's on me, too. I pushed at him, and she saw the opportunity not only to kill again – because I think this time she got a taste for it – but to hand me a suspect. Either in him or in Mosebly. I wouldn't doubt she knew something had gone on between them.'

'Even with the diary, even if it gives chapter and verse, it may be difficult to prove she did this on her own, or at all. Her father will, no doubt, block every step you take from here.'

'I'll handle Straffo, sir, and I'll get Rayleen to confess.'

'How?' Mira wondered.

'I'll make her want to tell me.' Her communicator signalled. 'With permission, Commander?' At his nod, she pulled it out of her pocket. 'Dallas.'

'Sir, she left the museum minutes before I got here. I've been going over the place with the security cameras, and just now asked them to do a playback of the hour before I arrived. I tagged her. The nanny got a 'link call, then they exited the building on the Eight-first Street side almost as I was coming in on Fifth.'

'Her mother. Damn it. Head back to the Straffo apartment. I'm on my way.'

'I'll come with you. I may be useful,' Mira insisted.

'Yes, you may.' Whitney got to his feet. 'Lieutenant, I

want to know the minute you locate . . . the suspect. I want to know if and when you find this diary.'

'Yes, sir. You're going to have to keep up,' she said to Mira, then moved fast.

Cora's conscience pricked her until she got off the subway heading downtown, crossed over, and took the uptown train. It was too early to meet her friends for the vid matinee they'd planned on. And she didn't really need to browse the shops where she'd just spend money she'd be better off keeping.

Most of all, she couldn't get Mrs Straffo's poor, pale face out of her head. Maybe it was just a headache, maybe it was. But she knew very well the woman went into the blue place every now and then. It wasn't right to leave her there, to leave Rayleen alone with her if the mum was feeling sad and sick.

She'd just check another time, she told herself. Fix that nice cuppa for the missus, and a bite to eat. If the missus needed to rest, why, she'd just cancel her date with her friends and take the girl out herself. No point in having the mite's day spoiled because her mum was doing poorly.

Fact was, she'd never be easy, wouldn't have a good time at all worrying about the missus and the mite.

Such a rough patch they were all going through, with those horrible murders right at the school, and the police swarming all over the house like ants.

Hardly a wonder poor Mrs Straffo was feeling blue.

Some tea, maybe a little soup, a nice nap. Those were the tickets.

Cora got off the subway, climbed up the steps to street level and began to walk through the blustery air. She was so lucky to have a position like this, with such a lovely family in such a beautiful home in such an exciting city.

The girl was fun and bright – a bit testy now and then, sure, but neat as a pin. And so interested in every little thing. And never did you hear a raised voice or dodge a thrown dish, as you would as a matter of course in her own house back in Ireland.

Truth be told, she missed the yelling and carryings-on from time to time. But she couldn't ask for a better position with a nicer family.

She smiled at the doorman, gave him a bit of a flirt. Now if that one had asked her to a vid matinee, she might have ignored those pricks in her conscience.

She took out her key as she rode up to the top. When she let herself in, it was so quiet, she wondered if she'd overreacted and Mrs Straffo and Rayleen had gone out to lunch and the salon after all.

Wouldn't she just *kick* herself if she'd wasted the subway fare!

She called out, got no answer. Rolled her eyes. 'Aren't you an arse, Cora?'

She nearly turned right around and went back out, but decided to glance in the coat closet first. Surely if the missus had gone out, she'd have worn a coat, and there were none missing that she could see.

She called out again as she started upstairs.

And there was Rayleen, sitting at her desk in her room with her headset on while she worked on her art. No point in bothering her, Cora thought, though she did raise her eyebrows at the snack of chocolate cake and a fizzy on the desk.

They'd have a bit of a word about that one later.

For now, she was worried about the missus. Probably gone to bed with that headache, she thought. And without a bite to eat.

Since the bedroom door was closed, she knocked softly, then opened it to peek in.

There was Mrs Straffo in bed, a tray across her lap, and a cup overturned on it. Fell asleep sitting up, poor lamb, spilled the tea, Cora thought, and moved forward quietly to take it away.

She saw the pill bottle then, the empty bottle lying on the duvet.

'Oh, Mother of God. Sweet Jesus. Missus!' She grabbed Allika's shoulders, shook. When there was no response, she slapped her once, twice.

Terrified, she grabbed for the bedside 'link.

'Are you troubled by this situation on a personal level?' Mira asked.

'I haven't decided.' Eve was running hot, sirens screaming.

409

'I don't know if I didn't look at her hard enough, straight enough, right from the get because I didn't want to, because I was fucked up about Roarke or because it just didn't click. Probably won't ever know.'

'Do you want to know what I think?'

'Yeah, sure. You stupid son of a bitch, don't you *hear* the sirens?'

'I think . . .' And Mira decided she'd just close her eyes so the image of oncoming death by traffic wouldn't distract her. 'No one would have looked at her hard enough or straight enough initially. We're wired to protect the young, not to believe them capable of premeditated murder. You may be right about her, about all of it. I believe you're right about what happened to her brother. However, my opinion on this veers more heavily toward Arnette Mosebly.'

'Fifty.'

'Fifty what?'

'I got fifty that says I'm right, you're wrong.'

'You want to bet on a murderer?'

'It's just money.'

'All right,' Mira said after a moment. 'Fifty it is.'

'Done. Now I'll tell you why she didn't do it. The school's her core, her pride, her vanity. Maybe she could kill, but she'd do it off school grounds. She wouldn't bring that kind of publicity, that kind of smear to her beloved Sarah Child. This is costing her students. And it's probably going to cost her her job.'

'A good argument, but self-preservation supersedes even

a treasured job. If Foster knew about her relationship with Williams, he was a direct threat – and may have told her he intended to report her. Williams, by her own statement, did just that, in an attempt to blackmail her into keeping him on.'

'Want to make it a hundred?'

Before Mira could answer, Eve's communicator signalled again. 'Okay, what now? Dallas.'

'Dallas, Allika Straffo's on her way to the hospital. OD'd. Her condition is critical.'

'Where's the kid?'

'The au pair took her. They left right after the ambulance, took a cab to Parkside, it's the closest. I missed this by minutes, again. First on scene said the kid was hysterical.'

'I bet she was. You in the penthouse?'

'I came up to talk to the cops who responded to the nine-one-one. MT's were called in by the au pair. Reported overdose, which sent out the uniforms.'

'I want the diary. Find it. I'm headed to the hospital.'

'This isn't your fault.' Mira shifted in her seat when Eve whipped the wheel. 'If this woman couldn't face the idea that her daughter killed and tried – or succeeded – in self-terminating, it isn't on you.'

'The fact that I didn't figure the kid would kill her own mother is on me. If Allika Straffo swallowed a fistful of pills, it's because that little bitch gave them to her. Goddamn it.'

She punched the gas. 'If she was going to do herself, she'd have left a note. Going to protect the kid, she'd have

411

left a note confessing. If she was just going to give it up, can't face it anymore, why did she call the kid home?'

'Rayleen realized her mother knew, and might be a threat.' Mira shook her head. 'Induce her to take an overdose, and the threat's removed. Her own mother.'

'She shoved her little brother, who was wearing footie pj's, down the steps on Christmas morning. Pumping Mom full of pills isn't much of a stretch.'

'If Allika Straffo dies, you'll never prove it. Even if she lives, she may not implicate her own child.'

'She'll be counting on that. She's going to be wrong.'

Eve strode into the chaotic misery of the ER, scanned the bruised, the bleeding, the broken. She snagged a hustling nurse, then flipped out her badge to cut through any bull. 'Straffo, Allika, OD. Where?'

'Trauma Room Three. Badge or no badge, you can't go in. Dr Dimatto's a little busy trying to save her life.'

Louise Dimatto. Eve smiled. Sometimes it actually paid to have friends.

'You can get in there. So go in, tell Louise that Dallas needs a status report on her patient. Where's the kid? The Straffo kid?'

'In the A chairs, with her nanny, father's on the way. You know Doctor D?'

'Yeah, we go back. A chairs?'

'Follow me.'

Apparently claiming Louise had grease, and slid Eve and

Mira straight through the general area to the trauma section. In an alcove across from a set of double swinging doors sat Rayleen, huddled against Cora.

The kid's face was splotchy from weeping, eyes red and swollen. Eve thought: *Good job. Drama Club paid off.*

Cora spotted Eve first, and her eyes went weepy. 'Lieutenant Dallas. It's . . . it's the missus.'

But Eve's eyes were all for Rayleen. The girl's body stiffened. *Didn't expect me to drop in, did you?* Eve thought. Then Rayleen pressed closer to Cora.

'I don't want to talk to her. I don't want to talk to anybody. I just want my mommy.'

'There, there now, darling. Don't you fret. The lieutenant's only here to try to help. Everyone's here to help.'

Eve glanced at Mira, jerked her head. Understanding, Mira stepped forward.

'Rayleen, I'm Dr Mira. I know you're very frightened and very upset.'

Rayleen sniffled, raised her head to study Mira's face. 'You're a doctor? Are you going to fix my mother?'

'Yes, I'm a doctor, and I know the doctor who's helping your mother now. She's a very, very good doctor.' Mira crouched down, all compassion and concern.

Good, Eve decided. Good and smart. Don't align yourself with me. Just an attractive, female doctor. A motherly one. Eve turned, looking through the glass porthole on the trauma room door as Mira talked to Rayleen.

Inside, it looked to her as if they'd pumped stuff out of

Allika, and were pumping stuff in. Louise wore a protective cape, her delicate blonde hair clipped back, her smoky eyes intense.

If Allika had a shot, Eve knew Louise would give it to her.

Behind her, Mira spoke in a voice that exuded sympathy and authority. 'I know you're going to be brave now, Rayleen.'

'I'll try, but—'

'I know it's very hard. Can you tell me what happened?'

'I don't know. My mom . . . We were supposed to have lunch at Zoology, then go to the salon. It's our girl time.'

'Isn't that nice?'

'We have lots and lots of fun together. But she called when we were in the museum and said we had to come home instead of her coming to meet us. She didn't say why. She looked really tired, and she was acting funny.'

'Funny?'

'She said Cora should go, because it's her half-day off. When she did, my mom cried.'

'I shouldn't have gone out. I should have stayed.'

'It's not your fault, Cora. My mom said she was sorry, and not to be mad at her. But I wasn't mad at her. She couldn't help it if she was sick. She gets sick sometimes, and needs to rest.'

'I see.'

'She hugged me, really, really tight. Like she does when she and Daddy go on a trip, and I don't. A good-bye hug.

She told me I was her princess, and the best part of her whole life, and how she loved me.'

Rayleen's mouth quivered as she took a handkerchief with her name embroidered on the corner from her purse. She wiped at her eyes. 'How she knew I'd be brave and strong, no matter what.' Her gaze ticked up to Eve's back, held for an instant. 'She said to remember, no matter what, she loved me best of all. Then she said I could get a snack and go play in my room, to be good. She was going to sleep. I was really quiet.' Fresh tears gushed. 'So I wouldn't wake her up.'

The nurse swung out, took a look at the weeping little girl. Her face radiated compassion, then she drew Eve out of earshot. 'Condition's still critical. If Dr D manages to stabilize her, they're sending her up to CCU. Her chances aren't very good, but Dr D's fighting the fight.'

'Okay. Appreciate it.' Eve stared over the nurse's shoulder. 'That's the husband coming down.'

Straffo bolted down the corridor, and Eve could all but feel the fear radiating from him. Rayleen jumped up, and into his arms. Cora rose, weeping and babbling.

Eve left them to it, while Straffo clutched his daughter, murmured to her. Then he set her down, brushed the hair from her face. She nodded, then sat with Cora again. Straffo went to the porthole, staring in as Eve had done.

Eve went to stand beside him.

'What do you know?'

'I know the doctor who's working on her,' Eve told him. 'She's good, and she doesn't give up easy.'

She heard him draw in a breath, let it out, and the sound was raw. 'Thank you.'

'She's critical, once she's stable enough they'll move her to CCU. She was overdosed with sleeping pills.'

'Oh, God, oh, God.' He laid his forehead on the glass.

'What was her mood when you left this morning?'

'She was stressed. We've both been stressed, for Christ's sake. But . . . this has to wait. For God's sake, Dallas, that's my wife in there.'

'All right. I need to talk with Cora.'

'Yes, yes, fine.'

'Straffo?' She waited until he tore his gaze from the trauma room, met her eyes. 'I'm pulling for her. For both of you. Believe me.'

Tears swam as he nodded. 'Thank you.'

'Dr Mira happened to be with me when we were informed. You know her, you know she's good. She can stay with your daughter, talk to Rayleen while I interview Cora, and you're focused on Allika.'

'Mira.' Distracted, he glanced around, saw Mira standing to the side. 'Yes, yes. I'd appreciate that. I don't want Rayleen left alone, and I need . . .'

'You need to be with Allika. Got it.'

Eve turned, walked over to the chairs. 'Cora, I need to talk to you. Dr Mira will sit with Rayleen.'

'I want my daddy.'

Two could play, Eve decided, and sent Rayleen a sympathetic look. 'Yeah, I know, and he's not going anywhere.

Try not to worry. I just need Cora to talk to me about your mother.'

'Will it help my mommy?'

'I hope so.'

Rayleen straightened her shoulders. Brave little soldier. 'I'll be okay.'

'I know you will. How about if Cora and I get you something to drink?'

'May I have some juice, please?'

'You got it. Cora, let's take a walk.' Eve could feel Rayleen's smug delight as she turned away.

'Run it through for me, Cora.'

'I shouldn't have left her, I'm telling you that straight off. I could see how poorly the missus was feeling, but off I went.'

'How long were you out of the apartment?'

'Too long, that's the truth of it. Less than an hour. I don't know exactly.'

Eve listened, let Cora select juice from a machine.

'Then I saw the pills,' Cora continued. 'And I knew. I couldn't wake her up. I shook her, I slapped her, but I couldn't wake her. I called nine-one-one, and I told them to come, and why. I couldn't tell if she was breathing, so I did CPR until I heard them at the door. Then I ran down, let them in.'

'What about Rayleen?'

'Oh, merciful Mary, the poor child.' Cora paused, pressed both hands to her face, scrubbed hard. 'She came out of her room just as I was running down for the door. I knew I had to hurry, and didn't even stop.'

'Did she say anything?'

'Well, she did. I imagine she was puzzled as I must've looked to frighten the devil himself, and wasn't supposed to be there at all. That's what she said, come to that. "What are you doing here? You're not supposed to be here."'

'Annoyed?'

'Aye, I'd say. She likes things to run as they're planned, and there I was on her day with her mum. Oh, Lieutenant, what an awful thing for a child. She just went into hysterics when the MT's charged in.'

'I bet.'

'If I hadn't left—'

'You came back,' Eve interrupted. 'If you hadn't, she'd be dead. If she pulls through this, it's not just the doctors who'll have saved her life. You did.'

'Thanks. Thanks for that. I can't stop leaking.' Cora wiped at tears. 'She's good as gold to me, the missus. Good as gold.' They headed back, then Cora clamped her free hand on Eve's arm. 'They're bringing her out.'

'Yeah.' Eve watched the trauma team move the gurney out of the room toward the elevators. 'That means they've stabilized her.' For now. 'Listen to me, Cora. Look at me.'

'What?'

'You have friends in the city?'

'I do, yes.'

'I want you to stay with them tonight.'

'Oh, but . . . I'll be with little Ray. She'll need me, poor mite.'

'No.' Eve wasn't going to risk another innocent. With her latest plans thwarted, Rayleen might take out her frustration on Cora. 'When you leave here, you're going straight to your friends', and you're going to stay there tonight. I'll make arrangements for Mr Straffo and Rayleen.'

'I don't understand.'

'You don't have to, yet. But if you don't give me your word you'll do what I'm telling you, I'm having you taken down to Central and held as a material witness. Your choice.'

'Well, that's harsh.'

'It's going to get harsher. Straffo and the kid are heading up. You can go up and take Rayleen her juice, talk to them, reassure yourself as best as you can. Then I want you to leave, and do what I've told you.'

'All right, all right then, I will. I suppose she'll only want her da now anyway.'

Satisfied, Eve headed for Louise.

'Dallas. Small world.'

'And why are you in it?'

Louise smiled. 'I'm a rotating Attending here, and took the big Valentine's Day Saturday shift. Charles is busy, and we're having our romantic rendezvous tomorrow.'

As Louise's main man was a high-class licensed companion, Eve imagined he was fully booked on heart day.

'You look beat.'

'Rough one. And if you're going to ask me her chances,

I can tell you they're very shaky. We've got her on life support. She's not breathing on her own yet, and may not respond. But if she'd gotten here ten minutes later, she wouldn't have had any chance at all. So we take what we can get.'

'My lab's going to need a sample of what you pumped out of her.'

'No problem. The au pair has a steady head on her shoulders. Gave the nine-one-one the name of the med, gave the MT's the bottle. We knew what we were dealing with straight off, and that made a difference, too. She'd started CPR, gave the patient another fighting chance. Beautiful woman, the patient. Husband, sweet little girl. You never know.'

'Nope, you never know.'

21

As Louise needed to get up to CCU, Eve turned to Mira. 'Well?'

'She's an excellent actor.'

'She's in Drama Club.'

'I'm not surprised. I'd need a longer session with her, probably more than one to be definitive, but I tend to agree with your analysis. She enjoyed having me focused on her, even though she was very aware of you. She wanted to be sure you were listening to her.'

'And I was. She was pretty damn detailed in the conversation she claims to have had with her mother. "I love you best. I know you'll be brave." Made sure she got in there, too, how her mother sometimes gets sick. She's planned it all, rehearsed it all. Had to ad lib since Cora ruined it for her.'

'Or postponed it. Allika Straffo may never wake up. Eve, she's enjoying this now. The hospital, the crisis, the way the medical staff treats her so gently. Her father's fear and grief, her nanny's attention.'

'Yeah, she'll milk it. But it's going to run dry real soon. I need you and Louise to use some muscle, get Straffo and the kid in one of the family rooms here tonight. I don't want the girl in with her mother.'

'In a situation like this, with the mother critical, the CCU staff will encourage family to spend time with the patient.' Like Eve, Mira considered the options. 'If you alert the staff, it'll show,' Mira said. 'She may pick up on it.'

'Yeah, yeah, she would.' Eve paced a few strides down the corridor, then back. 'Okay. I want a twenty-four/seven guard on her. I'll get one who has some medical training, but it's going to be my man on her.'

'Because you think Rayleen may try to finish what she started.'

'Probably not, not at this point, but I'm not taking any chances. I'll couch Louise, so she makes sure it trickles down to the kid that her mother's going to be watched every minute, for medical reasons. I'm going to have to slip the knife into Straffo, and tell him Allika's under suspicion of two murders, and I'm putting a guard on the door.'

'The man's barely holding on.'

'I'm counting on that,' Eve countered. 'And I have to count on him letting go. Rayleen doesn't do things out of desperation or impulse, so I think Allika's secure for now. This is just precaution.'

'How are you going to handle her?'

'I'm going to let her think she's sliding through it. Let her relax, and make sure she believes she's snowed me. Poor kid, her mother kills a couple of people, then tries to do herself. I need to lay it out for Straffo, and that's not going to be easy.'

'He won't believe you.'

'I don't know, maybe not. I'm working on that part.'

Daddy was furious. Rayleen couldn't hear everything he said, or that Lieutenant Dallas said to him, but she could tell it made Daddy mad. Still, the snippets she caught when her father's voice rose were enough to please her.

Stupid police, she thought as she lay curled up on the sofa of the waiting area, pretending to sleep. They thought they were so smart, but she was *so* much smarter.

If nosy-posy Cora hadn't interfered, her mother would already be dead. But Rayleen wasn't sure that would be better. She could tell by the tight faces around her that everybody knew her mother was going to die anyway. This was so much more interesting.

It was like Ms Hallywell said about being on stage. If someone forgets a line or says the wrong one, you have to be able to think, *in character,* and keep going.

She kept her eyes closed and smiled inside when she heard her father.

'My wife is fighting for her life.'

'Your wife tried to take her life. I'm sorry.' The lieutenant's voice was calm. 'I hope she makes it. Sincerely.'

'So you can charge her with two murders? Allika could never hurt anyone.'

'But herself? Look, again, I'm sorry. I'm not saying we're going to charge her, I'm telling you now, as a favor, that we have to weigh this act in. If and when she's able to talk, I'm going to have to question her. It's hard on you, and God knows it's hard on your kid. I'm trying to give you some time to prepare.'

'Just go. Just go and leave me alone with my family.'

'I'm leaving. I'll be back if she comes out of it. Oliver . . . take care of yourself and your daughter. The kid's been through more than any kid should have to handle.'

Rayleen kept her eyes closed as she felt her father sit down beside her. As he gently, gently stroked her hair. And she kept them closed when she heard him begin to quietly weep.

She wondered how long she'd have to wait to get pizza and a fizzy.

Eve pulled her communicator out as she headed down. It signalled in her hand before she could use it to tag Peabody.

'Dallas.'

'You clear?' Peabody asked.

'Yeah, heading out. Allika's critical, on life support. Chances slim. I got a guard on her door and another with med training inside her room. Louise was on.'

'Handy.'

'Yeah. I heard her tell Straffo he should spend as much time as possible in her room with her, talking to her, telling her to fight. Might help. Who the hell knows? The kid's playing it out perfectly, but she didn't stump Mira, not this time. So we're getting some weight.'

'We've got more. I found the diary.'

Eve had to stop herself from doing a victory dance as she pushed out the hospital doors. 'I knew there was a reason I kept you around.'

'You're damn straight. Took freaking hours.'

'Where?'

'In the kitchen recycler. I went over every damn inch of this place, kept the uniforms on to help. Why the hell didn't I think of the recycler first?'

'How much is left?'

'All, I'd say, as it's inside a fancy metal box embossed with her name. I can tell there's a book inside it – the weight, and it thumps around when I shake it. Only went through one cycle, I think. Banged up. Locked tight, too. Lock's too small for a master, and it's caved in. Probably have to cut through it.'

'I'm swinging by to get it. Roarke will beat the lock.'

'Mag. I'll touch on McNab, tell him to put Valentine's on hold.'

'No.' Eve climbed into her vehicle. 'It's going to take time to put all this together. Fucking tricky business. I'll take the diary, log it in and out of evidence.'

'Already logged it in by remote.'

'Even better. For now, you go home, have a drink, have sex with McNab if you must.'

'I must,' Peabody concurred. 'I must.'

'Be sure to block video if I tag you later. I don't wish to be struck blind. We're going to put this together, and we're going to lock it down.'

She clicked off. 'Rayleen, you little shitbag,' she mumbled. 'I got you.'

While Eve drove, contacting both Whitney and Mira to update, Roarke selected the champagne he wanted for dinner.

He'd worked most of the day, and very soon, he hoped, both he and Eve would put their responsibilities aside. And just enjoy each other.

He knew she'd be pleased, and get a good laugh out of his choice for the meal. For their intimate, at-home dinner for two, he'd chosen pepperoni pizza. A personal favorite of hers.

He'd also selected what could loosely be called lingerie for her dinner attire. She'd laugh at that, too. And he would certainly enjoy seeing his wife in the red silk chemise trimmed with white ermine.

As she hadn't contacted him to tell him she'd gotten hung up, he thought the chances were good they'd make that dinner at eight. He'd decided they'd dine in Prague, courtesy of the holo-room. The romantic architecture, a thickly falling snow outside the windows, gypsy violins singing in the air.

A bit over the top, he supposed, but why the hell not?

'Roarke.'

'Hmm.' He acknowledged Summerset as he completed his selections, set the programming.

'Magdelana is at the gate.'

'She's what?'

'At the gate,' Summerset repeated. 'Asking to come in, a bit tearfully. She claims she must speak with you, even for just a moment. Should I tell her you're unavailable?'

That would be the easy way, Roarke supposed, and damned if he wasn't tempted to take it easy. But if he didn't deal with this now, he'd just have to deal with it later. And he could admit to a certain curiosity. Just how would Maggie explain herself this time?

'No, let her in. Show her into the parlor. I'll deal with her.'

'The lieutenant should, I believe, be home within the hour.'

'Yes, so make it quick. Let's move this business along and be done with it.'

Troublemaker, Roarke thought as Summerset went to give Magdelana access. He'd always known she was one, and had, in fact, found that attractive. But he hadn't seen, not clearly, just how deep the penchant for stirring up the pot went in her.

He knew how to handle troublemakers. Once he had, she'd go off, understanding him perfectly. And that would most definitely be that.

He took his time going down. Do her good to cool her heels, he thought. And Summerset would make certain she didn't palm any of the silver.

As he expected, Summerset remained in the parlor, and had given Magdelana, who looked pale and delicate in ivory satin, a glass of wine.

She stood by the fire, at the optimum distance, the perfect angle for the flames to sprinkle light over her skin, to glow light through the satin.

Setting the stage had always been a skill of hers. Only this time he'd been the mark. And as far as she was concerned, he still was.

'Roarke.' She lowered her head, as if in shame. But not before the thinnest sheen of tears sparkled over her eyes. 'Oh, Roarke, can you ever forgive me?'

'You'll excuse me?' he said to Summerset.

As Summerset left the room, she set down the wine with the slightest tremor in her hand. 'I feel absolutely dreadful about this. I just . . . Roarke, I've been out of town for the last two days, only just got back. But I heard – and saw. I tried to contact you before I left, as soon as I . . . But—'

'I've been busy.'

'Avoiding me,' she said with those tears in her voice. 'I wasn't sure you'd see me at all. Damn paparazzi. They should all be hanged.'

'Even they have to make a living.'

'But to imply something so completely innocent was . . . was something illicit. We should sue them. But, of course, that only makes it worse. I know, I know.' She lifted a hand, waved it distractedly. 'I can't imagine how upset you are. And your wife. Is she very angry?'

He angled his head. 'What do you suppose?'

'In her place, I'd be furious! They made it look as if we were . . . We were only saying good-bye. You and I know, Roarke, we were only saying good-bye.'

'We do yes, and we were.'

'Perhaps if I tried to explain to her. Is she here? I could try—'

'You'd already know she isn't here.'

Magdelana closed her swimming eyes. Regroup, he thought. Reconfigure.

'All right, yes. I admit it. I wanted to speak to you alone first, so I called downtown. They said she was in the field, so I came right over. God, I'm such a coward.' She touched her fingers to her lips. 'But if it would help, even a little, I'd try to explain to her.'

'I think not. She's perfectly aware of the circumstances.'

'Oh. Good. Good. What a relief.'

'Perfectly aware that you set it up, that you staged it, and paid the camera to get the vid out.'

'What? That's ridiculous. That's . . . Roarke.' She said his name with a soupçon of injured feeling, just the right addition to shock. 'How could you possibly think I'd do something like that? I understand you're angry and upset – so am I – but to accuse me of deliberately trying to hurt you and your wife. For what purpose?'

It was hardly a wonder they'd done so well, professionally speaking, in the months they'd worked together. She was brilliant. 'I'd say the amusement would be quite enough for you.'

'That's a despicable thing to say to me.' She picked up the wine again. 'Absolutely despicable.'

'Do you think I can't track down the camera, that I can't bribe well enough to learn all the details? You underestimate me, Maggie.'

She carried her wine to the window, stood with her back to him. 'No. No,' she said quietly. 'I could never underestimate you. Maybe I wanted you to know. Knew you would, in the end. It's you who underestimate me, Roarke, my feelings for you. My regret.' And looked over her shoulder. 'My desire. I admit it. I'm not proud of what I did, but I won't be ashamed either. I did what I thought I needed to do. I'd have done anything to get you back. Nothing else matters to me. Only being with you again.'

He waited a beat. 'Bollocks.'

'How can you mock my feelings?' She threw the wine down, shattering the glass. 'How dare you when I stand here, stripped bare?'

'I'm not mocking them, I'm clearly saying you haven't any feelings. You never did, for me or for anyone but yourself.' He let out a half-laugh. 'Took me longer to get to that than it should have.'

Then even that half-laugh was gone, and he was ice. 'You came here, to New York, to test the waters. I have a great deal more than I once had, and you hoped for a piece of it. She saw through you, you know. The first look.'

Magdelana tossed her head, strode toward him. 'And

from the first look at you again, I saw she had you under her thumb. How that made me laugh! The rich and powerful Roarke, tamed and trained by a skinny cop with no style or beauty.'

'Odd. From where I'm standing, she has more style, more beauty, and – Christ knows – more class than you can ever claim.'

He didn't so much as flinch when she slapped him. 'You won't want to do that again,' he said, softly enough to have her lower her hand.

'Roarke—'

'It's you who wanted to put a leash on me, Maggie, who thought she could just by snapping fingers. And when I didn't go to heel you did what you could to cause trouble for me and my marriage, to hurt my wife.'

'So what if I did? It's just a game. You used to have a sense of humor, but apparently she's whipped that out of you, too.'

'You'll never understand her, or me. You'll never understand what we have. More pity for you, you'll never have it. You're not capable. So here's how this plays now. Listen carefully: You'll never step foot in my home again, or in any of my other properties or businesses – which includes every hotel, transportation system, shop, restaurant, and so forth that I own or have majority interest in. There are quite a number of them.'

'Oh, for Christ's sake. You can't block me from—'

'I can,' he corrected, so coolly her color ebbed. 'I will.

You're going to leave New York, and in fact, the country, within three hours.'

'You can't control the whole damn country,' she shot back.

'Actually, I'd give that a good try, if only to watch you sweat. But, I don't need to. If you're not gone, well gone, within those three hours beginning . . .' he checked his wrist unit, '. . . now, Interpol and Global will receive some very interesting and very detailed information on you.'

This time, she went dead white. 'You'd betray me that way?'

'Again, listen carefully. I'd crush you like a bug for causing my wife one single moment of pain. Believe it. Fear it.'

'If you tried anything like that, I'd take you down with me.'

This time he smiled. 'You could try. I'm so much more than you, you'd never pull it off. And, Maggie, you'd find the accommodations in prison very limiting, and not at all to your taste.'

He saw her lips tremble before she managed to firm them. He saw her absorb the shock of the truth. Then she shrugged, carelessly. 'I don't need you. I never did.' She strolled away, circling the room. 'I only thought we might have some fun together, but obviously you don't know how to play anymore.'

'The clock's ticking,' he warned her.

She whirled around. 'I prefer Europe anyway. New York bores me. You bore me.'

She saw the flash of headlights strike the window glass, and changed tack instantly. 'Oh, what the hell.' She let out a robust laugh. 'You found me out, shut me down. No point in whining about it. Time to cut my losses and move on. Plenty of fish to fry.'

She looked at him, smiled. 'I'll never understand how you could possibly want her and not me.'

'No, you'll never understand it.'

She stepped forward as if to pick up the fur she'd tossed over a chair. Smoothly, she turned to hand it to him. And with perfect timing, flung herself into his arms.

The sable fell as he took her shoulders to shove her back.

Eve stepped to the doorway to see Magdelana with her arms locked around Roarke's neck, his hands on her bare shoulders – one of the ivory straps sliding to her elbow.

'Son of a bitch,' she said.

On cue, Magdelana spun around, her face full of passion and shock. 'Oh, God. Oh . . . it's not what it looks like.'

'Bet.' Eve strode in.

Actually, Roarke thought, it was more of a swagger. He had a moment to admire it, before Eve rammed her fist in his face.

'Fuck.' His head snapped back, and he tasted blood.

Magdelana cried out, but even the deaf would have caught the suppressed laughter in the sound. 'Roarke! Oh, my God, you're *bleeding*. Please, let me just—'

'Don't look now,' Eve said cheerfully. 'But he's not the only one.' She decked Magdelana with a straight-armed jab. 'Bitch,' Eve added as Magdelana's eyes rolled back and she fell, unconscious, to the floor.

Roarke looked down. 'Well, now, fuck us all!'

'You're going to want to get that mess out of my house.' With this, Eve strode out again.

She passed Summerset in the foyer. She assumed the expression on his face was a grin, but couldn't be absolutely sure. 'You're going to want to be careful – spreading your mouth like that could split your whole face in half.'

'I thought applauding would be a bit inappropriate.'

She snorted, and kept right on going upstairs.

Face throbbing, sensibilities insulted, Roarke stepped over Magdelana. In the foyer, he sent Summerset an icy look. 'Take care of that.'

'With absolute pleasure.' Still, Summerset stood another moment, watching Roarke head upstairs after his wife.

He caught up with her in the bedroom. 'Damn it all to hell and back again, you know very well that was a setup. You bloody well know I couldn't put my hands on her.'

'Yeah, yeah, sure, sure.' Eve shrugged off her coat, tossed it aside. 'I know a setup when I see it, and I know your face, ace. I didn't see desire on it, I saw annoyance.'

'Is that so? Is that bloody well so? Well, if you knew it was just what it was, why did you sucker punch me?'

'Mostly?' She turned, cocked a hip. 'Because you're a man.'

Eyes narrowed on her face, he tried to staunch the blood with the back of his hand. 'And do you have any sort of idea just how often I might expect your fist in my goddamn face because of my bleeding DNA?'

'No, really don't.' He looked so furious, so incredibly

insulted. She wanted to rip off his clothes and bite his ass. 'In fact, I think you've earned a good whooping.'

'Bugger that. I've had about enough of women altogether.' The absurdity of the entire thing began to wind through his temper. 'You're fearsome and irrational creatures.'

She rolled up on the balls of her feet and back again, flexed her knees. 'Afraid to take me on? Come on, hotshot, you got punched for being a man. Act like one.'

'It's a man you want, is it?' He began to circle as she did. 'I'm going to take you down.'

'Look how scared I am. I'm shaking.' She feinted with her left, spun, and back-kicked. 'Oh, no, that's suppressed laughter.'

He blocked the kick, then the next with his forearm, forced her to jump over the sweep of his foot. He worked her back toward the bed, and when he'd judged the distance, spun, then flipped her.

She landed on her back on the bed, but when he dived after, she'd rolled off the other side. Crouched into fighting stance.

'Not going to be that easy, ace.'

'Who said I wanted it easy?'

He rolled as well, and she had to give him credit for both speed and agility. She danced back, aimed a jab – blocked – then an elbow jab that connected. She pulled it. After all, she didn't want him on the disabled list, not with what she had in mind.

But she didn't mind if he limped a little. Serve him right.

She started to bring her heel down on his instep, but he turned into her, knocked her off balance.

Together they rolled down the short steps of the platform and hit the floor with her on top.

'Ready to throw in the towel?' she asked, breathlessly.

'No.' He scissored his legs, trapping hers, and reversed their positions. 'You?'

'My ass.' And she ripped his shirt open.

'You'll have to pay for that.'

'Try to make me.'

He hooked a hand in the collar of her shirt, tore it down the front. On a chain under it, she wore the diamond and the saint's medal he'd given her. The arms of the shirt hung on her weapon harness.

'Bloody cop,' he muttered, hitting the release.

'Bloody criminal.'

'Former, and no convictions.' He pressed his mouth to hers, swore at the burn in his wounded lip. 'You pack a punch, Lieutenant.' He reared up enough to look down at her face – brown eyes full of challenge, wide mouth curved in a smug smile. 'You're my goddamn Valentine.'

She laughed, grabbed two fistfuls of his hair. 'You'd better believe it, buster.'

She wanted to devour him, one greedy bite at a time, and let her nails dig a little into his back once she'd torn the tattered shirt away. She'd seen more than annoyance on his face when Magdelana had clung to him.

Eve had seen what she might have missed if she and

Roarke had been stupid enough, crazy enough, blind enough to pass each other by.

'I love you.' She closed her teeth over his shoulder, gasped when his scraped down her throat. She hooked her legs around his waist, shoved so that he was under her again. With her mouth like a fever on his, on his flesh.

So it wouldn't be romantic and dreamy, a snowfall outside the window and gypsy violins singing in the air. It would be desperate, and a little rough. And as real and urgent as their heartbeats.

He felt his survival depended on the taste and texture of her skin. He pulled and dragged at her clothes like a man possessed by demons.

'You'll give me all of you. All.'

'Take it,' she told him, and was under him again. His mouth ravaged her breast, and his hands . . . his hands, his hands.

She cried out, rocketing up as the orgasm gathered and flashed through her like a ball of lightning. She heard him murmuring to her, the sound thick and Irish. Felt him quiver as he held himself back.

And that she wouldn't allow. 'You'll give me all of you,' she said. 'All.'

She shattered his will, undid his control, her hands and lips taking him as he'd taken her. Beyond what was reason. Near to delirium, he dragged her mouth back to his, and devoured.

Lips and teeth and tongues, fingers that demanded and

took, bruises be damned. Her breath was burning even as she took from him, gave to him. His blood burned under his own skin.

'Now, now, now.' She chanted it, arching up.

When he drove into her, she cried out again, the sound close to a scream. And still her hips pumped fast and strong, whipping him into the glorious dark.

Her hands lost their grip on his hips, slid away to thump against the floor. Inside her body, everything had been pummeled, twisted, wrung out, then smoothed soft again. Her toes wanted to curl in pleasure, but there wasn't enough energy left for the movement.

'Jesus,' she managed. 'Holy dancing Jesus.'

'When I can actually stand up again, some time in the distant future, I'm going to let you punch me in the face again, so we can see if all that finishes up the same way as this.'

'Okay.'

'Or maybe we'll try that romantic dinner. Then you can punch me.' He actually felt her wince. 'Problem?' He lifted his head, saw by her face there was. 'What?'

'I'm really sorry.'

'I think, considering our current positions, and state of being, apologies are unnecessary.' But he read the look. 'Not sorry for the punch, I see. It's work?'

'I didn't contact you to tell you to hold dinner, because I wanted to tell you face to face. Which we now are, in addition to other body parts. It's a lot to explain, but I will. I've got something I need to deal with, and I could use your help with it.'

'All right.'

'Maybe we could fit in the candlelight and so on before midnight, but—'

'It doesn't matter, Eve. I promise you.'

Yeah, we got lucky, she thought. God, didn't they just. 'I got you a present.'

'Did you?'

'It's a book of poetry – romancy stuff. I thought, "How schmaltzy is that," so it seemed like the thing. Then I screwed up and left it in my desk at work.'

He smiled, leaned down to kiss her softly. 'Thank you.'

She touched his cheek. 'I've got to grab a shower and get to this. I planned to dig straight in, so we could maybe have a really late dinner, but then I had to punch you and your blonde tart, and one thing led to another.'

'Of course. Well, we'll have a shower and you can fill me in.'

He listened, saying little as she ran it through for him. 'So,' he said, as she pulled on loose flannel pants and a sweatshirt. 'You were right about the girl.'

'That's no girl, but yeah, I was right. The diary's going to be one of the nails. I could have it cut open – the box, it's in—'

'I can promise that's not necessary.'

'Let's take it in my office.' She hauled up a field bag. 'I

439

want it all on record. So maybe you could fumble just a little with the lock.'

'I certainly will not.'

'Okay, okay.'

'I'd like to explain what Magdelana was doing here.'

She slanted him a look. 'Other than trying to lock lips with you?'

'More specifically,' he said carefully as they started out of the bedroom, 'why I allowed her in our home.'

'I already got that. You needed to deal with it, with her. Needed to spell it out for her, give her the get lost, and put some of the fear of Roarke in her.'

'How fortunate I am, under the circumstances, to have a woman who understands me. Fear of Roarke?' he repeated.

'You can do the fear of God thing, but see, you can't see Him, and most people feel He's not going to really – what is it – smite them. You, however, are flesh and blood, and would do a lot worse than a smite. You're a lot scarier than God.'

'I don't know quite how to take that,' he said after a moment. 'But meanwhile, do you want to know how this was handled?'

'Yeah, actually, I would.'

He told her while they made their way to her office, while she set down her bag, took out her diary. While she simply stood, staring at him.

'See? See? Holy crap. God wouldn't have made her insides quiver like that, and you can bet your fine Irish ass they quivered like jelly. Can you really ban her from all your stuff? That's like eighty percent of the known universe.'

'You exaggerate, it wouldn't be more than fifty, and, oh, aye.' His grin was fast and fierce. 'I bloody well can.'

'And you've got data on her that would interest the international authorities?'

'What do you take me for? Of course I do.' He waited a moment, reading her face perfectly. 'I'm not giving it to you, Eve. Two reasons.'

'They'd better be good ones.'

'First, it's not your concern, and don't even think about raising that fist to me. This is my doing, her coming here, her causing trouble. Second, it'll keep her up at night, for some time to come, wondering what I have, and what I might do with it. She'll be looking over her shoulder a long time.'

'I think your first reason's crap, but the second is really mean, really insidious. I like it a lot, so we'll call it a wash.'

'Good. Well, I'll open that for you, shall I, and we'll have our Valentine's dinner while we see what's inside.'

'Um . . .'

'It's pizza. It was to be pizza and champagne actually.'

'Seriously?'

'I know my wife as she knows me.' He tapped a finger on her nose. 'So it'll be pepperoni pizza and coffee – with the champagne for another time.'

'You know, you really are my Valentine.'

22

Before breaking the seal on the evidence bag containing Rayleen's diary, Eve turned on her recorder, logged in the necessary data. She took the metal box – embossed with some sort of wide-petaled flowers – out of the evidence bag, set it on her desk.

'Peabody found it in the kitchen recycler.'

'Clever Peabody,' Roarke replied as he chose a tool.

'If things hadn't moved as fast as they did – au pair coming back and so on – if Peabody hadn't been basically on the scene with the direct purpose of finding this, it might've been garbage by morning. Takes more than one cycle for something of this size, material, and density to break down. All she managed was to bang the box up.'

'A pity, too. It's a lovely box. Sturdy, well-made, which is why it held up as well as it did. The girl should have taken the book out of it. That might have broken down before it was found.'

'Some, but she doesn't know everything. There's a lot we can put back together in the lab. And . . . okay, nice work,' she added as he had the crushed and passcoded lock open in under ten seconds.

'Well, it's not a titanium vault, after all.'

Hands already sealed, Eve lifted out the bright pink book inside. It was leather-bound, and again had Rayleen's name across it in glittery silver letters. It also had a lock, and this one appeared to use an old-fashioned key.

'Comp would be faster than handwritten pages,' she commented.

'And I'll wager, however indulgent her parents, they wouldn't allow her to passcode anything on a comp. This . . .' He tapped a finger on the book. 'This seems harmless, very traditional, something a young girl might enjoy.'

She stepped back and let Roarke finesse the lock.

'I'm going to want copies of everything inside there,' she told him.

'Before you read it?'

'No. I want to put the last few pages on record first, then make the copies. But even more, I want to know.'

She flipped through the pink-tipped pages, found the last entry. With her recorder trained on the tidy handwriting on pale pink pages with shiny gold edges, she read out loud.

'This morning I wore my pink and black plaid skirt and pink knee boots, and my white sweater with flowers on the hem and cuffs. I looked very pretty. I had fruit and yogurt and seven-grain toast for breakfast, and asked Cora to make real orange juice. That's what she gets paid for. I had Brain Teasers. It's getting a little boring, so I might find a way to quit

But still, I like knowing I'm smarter than any of the other students. Just like I'm better than anyone in my dance class. I could, if I wanted, be a prima ballerina one day.

'After BT, Cora and I took a cab to the Met. I don't see why we couldn't use a car service. I'm going to ask Daddy about that. I like the art, but mostly everyone who painted anything is dead anyway. I could be a famous artist if I wanted, and have my paintings in the Met. People would pay a lot of money just to look at my paintings. But I think I'd sell mine to collectors. I don't want people who don't know anything and don't deserve it to just stand there and stare at my work.'

'Interesting ego,' Roarke remarked.

Eve glanced up. 'She had to have written this after her mother called them back home. And still, it's full of I, I, I. Mira's going to have a field day with this one.'

She looked back at the book, continued to read.

'I was supposed to meet my mother for lunch at Zoology. It's my favorite place for lunch, and we had to book three weeks in advance for the reservation. One day, when I'm famous, I won't need a stupid reservation to go anywhere. People will be grateful if I bother to eat in their restaurant.

'After, I was going to the salon for a hair styling

and a pedicure. I'd already decided on the Carnival polish, with glitter. Then Cora's 'link beeped and it was my mother calling us home. We had plans! We had reservations, but I had to come home, and the whole day was spoiled. My mother wasn't even dressed when we got there. She's so selfish.

'But it's really all that nosy Lieutenant Dallas's fault. I thought, at first, she was interesting, but she's not. She's just mean and pushy and stupid. Now I've had to fix everything. Again. It's just as well, really. My mother's so weak and silly, and my daddy's been paying more attention to her lately than to me. So, I've taken care of it. It was easy. The easiest one so far.

'She hid pills in her lingerie drawer. As if I wouldn't find them! All I had to do was make her some tea, and put the pills in it. Like I did with smelly old Mrs Versy at the Kinley House last year. I had to use more with Mommy because Mrs Versy was old and half-dead anyway.'

'Well, Christ,' Roarke murmured.

'Yeah. I wondered if there were others along the way.' Eve read on.

'She got into bed just like a baby for me. I watched her drink the tea. That was the best part. She drank it just like I told her, then I waited until she fell asleep. I left the empty bottle right there, so when Daddy gets

445

home in a few hours he'll find her that way. I'll cry and cry. I've been practicing in the mirror, and I'm so good at it! Everyone will feel so sorry for me, and give me whatever I want. Everyone will think my mother killed that idiot Mr Foster and that nasty Mr Williams. It's such a tragedy! I have to laugh.

'I'm going to do some art now, and listen to some music. I'll just be in my room when Daddy gets home. His best girl being quiet as a mouse so her mother can sleep. And sleep and sleep.

'I have to go put this book in the recycler now. That's annoying, and that's Lieutenant Dallas's fault, too! But, it's okay. Daddy will buy me another diary, a better one. He'll buy me anything I want now, and take me anywhere I want to go.

'I think we should go somewhere warm and pretty, with a really nice beach.'

Roarke said nothing for a moment. 'She wrote that while her mother was, as far as she knew, dead or dying in the other room.'

'Oh, yeah.'

'She shouldn't waste her time with art and ballet. She should consider becoming a professional assassin. She has the constitution for it.'

'I'm going to make sure she has plenty of time to consider her options – inside maximum security.' She looked down at the book again, at the tidy yet still childish penmanship.

'Let's get this copied. I want Mira and Whitney to see it ASAP. Then I want to read the rest.'

It was all there, meticulously documented: motives, means, opportunities, plans, execution. Rayleen didn't stint on details.

If it had been the journal of an adult killer, Eve would have wrapped the investigation and the perpetrator in a heavy chain and locked the door.

But the sticking point was how to handle a killer of such a young age, whose father was a top defense counsel.

By seven A.M., Eve had Mira and Peabody in her home office, and her commander on hologram.

'I'm not going to buy she's legally insane,' Eve began.

'Did she and does she know right from wrong? Most certainly,' Mira agreed. 'Her crimes are planned and executed, and her motives in each case are self-serving. The motives are the very reason a psychiatrist hired by the defense will argue insanity.'

'Will you argue against it for the prosecution?'

'Yes. I'll need to examine her, of course, but at this point, most certainly I can argue against. Eve, either way, she must be put away, and I believe she will be. She won't stop.'

Mira drew a deep breath as she studied the pretty face on Eve's murder board. 'Unless she's stopped by the system, there's no reason for her to stop. This process works for her. It's satisfying to her, and proves her superiority. In a childish way, this gets her what she wants, and getting what she wants is her primary goal.'

'Her own mother,' Peabody added. 'She writes about killing her own mother without a moment's regret or hesitation. She didn't feel a thing about it.'

'I want to get her for the brother. He's not mentioned in the diary. He's not part of her scope any longer.' Eve glanced at Mira, got a nod of agreement. 'It's not just that he's not worth her time, or the space, she doesn't think about him or what she did to him now. Everything is *now* with her.'

'You said before you'd get a confession, see that she wanted to tell you,' Mira continued. 'But—'

'I'll get a confession. The hitch will be Straffo. If he decides to protect her, she'll clam. If she believes I can use what she tells me, she'll clam. I have to get to him, through him first.'

'He's a father, who'll instinctively want to protect his child.'

'He's a father whose son was carelessly disposed of, and he's a husband whose wife may very well be Rayleen's next victim.' And those, Eve knew, were her weapons. 'Hard place for him. He's going to have to choose who he stands up for.'

'If you give him this information,' Whitney cut in, 'you're giving a potential defense a heads up, a running start. He could, potentially, erect a shield around his daughter that will take months to hack through.'

'Yes, sir, he could. And if I don't slap this in his face, knock his feet out from under him while he's still shaky over his wife, he could do that anyway. He needs to see her for what she is. And for that, I could use the expert consultant, civilian.' She glanced at Roarke.

'Lay it out, Lieutenant,' Whitney told her.

It took time, and Eve struggled against impatience. It took care and caution, and she fought not to push. So it was nearing ten before she, Peabody, and Mira headed out to the hospital, well after Roarke, Feeny, and McNab were already in play.

When her 'link beeped, she snapped it up. 'Dallas.'

'Lieutenant? I don't know if you remember me. This is Billy Kimball, the assistant manager from Kline's? You were in the other day making inquiries about a go-cup we carry.'

'I remember you. You got something?'

'One of our seasonal clerks happened to stop in last night, near closing? I mentioned the go-cup to her, just on the off chance that she knew anything about it. She did.'

'What did she know?'

'She remembers the sale very well. It was after the holiday. She worked through our January clearance sales? She said a young girl came in, with a nanny, she thought it was a nanny. As the girl wanted to purchase something as a surprise, she asked the nanny to go to another part of the store for a while. And this was a bit of a struggle of willpower as the nanny didn't want to—'

'Wind this up for me, Billy.'

'Sorry. Well, the clerk promised the nanny she'd keep a

close eye on the girl, so the nanny went to another department. The girl wanted the go-cup you asked about, and
had it engraved. The clerk remembers the girl because she
was so bright and charming, and very polite. Now, the
clerk isn't a hundred percent sure of the name, but she did
recall that the girl told her it was a going-away present for
her favorite teacher. She paid cash. Since it was after the
first of the year, it was easy for me to pull up the store
copy of the receipt, for cash. It was a go-cup of the make
and model you asked about, in black, with the additional
fee for silver engraving in the Roman script font. Does
that help at all?'

'It does.' Sometimes, Eve thought, the stars just freaking
aligned. 'Good job, Billy. I'm going to pass you to my
partner. I need you to give her the name and contact info
on your clerk. I want her to look at some pictures, see if
she can identify the little girl.'

'I'm sure she'd be glad to help. She mentioned the girl
was a pretty little blonde, curly hair? With very unique eyes.
Nearly purple.'

'And the walls keep tumbling down,' Eve mumbled as
Peabody took the data. 'Outsmarted herself on this one.
Should've made it quick, not engaged the clerk. But she's
just got to show off.'

'She'd have disposed of his original cup,' Mira commented.

'Yeah, probably carried it right out of the school, right
under our noses. Goddamn it.'

'You're trained,' Mira said. 'So am I. I'm trained in

450

abnormal psychiatry, and I believe she would have carried it out under my nose, too.'

'That ends today.'

Eve found Straffo in his wife's room, sitting vigil beside her bed. He looked over at Eve with dull, heavy eyes. 'If you've come to file charges, you can—'

'How is she?' Eve interrupted.

He dragged a hand through his hair, then reached down to take Allika's again. 'She's still critical. They're going to run more tests soon.' He stroked his wife's hand as he spoke. 'I don't know. I just don't know. But you won't push those murders on her.'

Eve walked over to stand at the opposite side of the bed. 'How much do you love your wife?'

'That's a stupid question.' Some of the steel came back into his eyes, his voice. 'However much I love her, I don't have to cover for her, or use any legal magic to protect her. She's incapable of hurting anyone. And I'm damned if she tried to kill herself, especially with Rayleen alone in the house. She'd never put our daughter through this. Never.'

'I agree with you.'

He looked up. 'Then what is this?'

'How much did you love your son?'

'How can you come in here, at a time like this, and bring that kind of pain back to me?'

'A great deal, I'm betting. Even though you don't have

pictures of him in your home. Even though your wife keeps them locked away.'

'It hurts beyond the telling. You can't possibly understand. Do you think I've forgotten him? It's not how much *did* I love him, but how much I do.' He lurched up, pulled out a small leather folder from his pocket. 'Is this one of your essential details to tie up, Lieutenant? Here then. Here. I keep him in here. Look at that face.'

He held out the photo case, with a snapshot of the little boy smiling out of it. 'He was the sweetest boy. So happy all the time. You couldn't be around Trev and not smile. No matter how crappy the day had been, five minutes with him, and everything was good again. The day he . . . the day we lost him was the worst day of my life, up until now. Is that what you need to hear?'

'Yeah, it is. I've got something hard for you, Oliver. Something no one should ever have laid on them. I want you to remember how you feel about your wife and your son. I need you to read this.'

'What is it?'

She held out the printout from the last pages of the diary. 'I think you'll recognize the handwriting. I think you'll know what it is. I'm showing these to you now because of her.' She gestured toward Allika. 'And because I saw the pictures of your son. His face is in my head.'

That made Trevor Straffo hers, Eve acknowledged. As much as Craig Foster. Even the pathetic Reed Williams was hers.

Straffo took the pages, scanned the first line. 'This is Rayleen's handwriting. From her diary? What possible—'

'The last entry was written before she tossed it, inside its lockbox, in your kitchen recycler. Date's right there. You're going to want to read the whole thing.'

As he did, he went gray. As he did, his hands began to shake. 'This isn't possible.'

'Somewhere in you, you know it is. Your wife knew it was, and even in her horror and grief, she tried to protect Rayleen. So Rayleen did this to her, to protect herself, to throw suspicion on Allika, to focus you, your time, your attention on her.'

'No.'

'There were other entries, Oliver. Details of how she killed both Foster and Williams. And a mention of a woman named Versey at the Kinley House.'

'No. No. You're out of your mind.' He swayed like a man would when the world tipped sharply on its axis. 'I'm going out of mine.'

Push, Eve ordered herself. No choice but to push. 'What isn't in there, as the diary only goes back seven months, is how she killed your son.'

Even the gray leached out of his face. 'That's insane.'

'You both knew Rayleen had been up some time before she came in to wake you.'

'She—'

'You decided it was an accident, what parent wouldn't? That he'd tripped and she'd gone into shock and denial. You put all the pieces of him out of sight because she got upset if she saw them. More, if she saw either you or her mother looking at them.'

'For God's sake, for God's sake. She was seven. You can't believe—'

'I can. Look at your wife, Oliver. Does she deserve what was done to her? Take out the picture of your son again. Did he? She took these lives without a quibble. I have a rock-solid case, which includes her buying a go-cup with Craig's name engraved on it.'

'What? What?' He fisted both hands in his hair, all but tore at it.

'I have a wit,' Eve continued, relentlessly. 'The clerk who waited on Rayleen, and who's already identified her photo. Cora verifies they stopped in to that particular store on that particular day at Rayleen's request.

'I have a statement from her great-aunt, Quella Harmon, verifying she had interest in and knowledge of how ricin was made. Don't even think saying circumstantial to me,' she snapped.

Kick him and keep kicking him while he's done, she thought. It's the only way.

'In her own words, Oliver.' She leaned over to pick up the pages he'd dropped. 'In her own words she writes how she decided to kill her mother, how she left Allika to die while she herself went to make a snack, to listen to music. She did this without a single twinge of regret.'

'I can't . . . You can't expect me to believe.'

'You already believe, in that place inside you. That's what's making you sick. But you're going to have to suck it in, because I'm going to tell you what's going to be done. And . . . look at me, Oliver. Look at me.'

His eyes were glazed over with shock and unspeakable pain when they met hers. 'She wrote it down,' he said dully. 'She wrote it down while Allika was . . .'

'That's right. Allika was a barrier, like Trevor was.' Use their names, Eve thought. 'Allika and Trev stood in the way of something she wanted, so she *removed* them.'

'She's my daughter, she's my child. She's . . .'

'I'm going to make you a deal right here. You and me. If I don't prove to you that everything I've told you is true, I won't fight any attempt to try her as a minor instead of an adult.'

'She's ten years old. She's only ten.'

'Multiple premeditated murders. She gets legal adult status, unless I pull it out of the mix. That's the deal. I prove to you that she put your wife, that she put Allika in that hospital bed, with a machine breathing for her, I prove she pushed Trevor down the stairs on fucking Christmas morning, that she did Foster and Williams, and some sick old lady in a nursing home. All of it. Without a shadow of a doubt. If I don't, you'll have ammo to break down my case. That's the deal. Take it, or I take her down now.'

Rayleen was in the CCU family room, drawing. When Eve stepped in, she stopped, let her eyes swim with shining tears. 'My mommy—'

Eve closed the doors behind her. 'I know the doctor who's been working on her. She thinks your mother's going to pull through this.'

She wandered over to the counter. Hospital coffee was nearly as lethal as cop coffee. But it would make a nice prop. Eve poured a cup, turned. 'Not such good news for you, Ray.'

'What?'

'Just you and me, Ray. Door's shut.' Eve pulled off her jacket, turned. I'm not wearing a wire. Here's my recorder.' She unpinned it, set it down. 'Turned off. Haven't read you your rights. Your father's a lawyer, and you're smart, so you know I can't use anything you say to me.'

Eve sat down, stretched out her legs, sipped at the coffee. Maybe hospital coffee was, actually, worse than cop coffee. 'I've come across some tricky ones, but I have to say, you're the trickiest. Even if your mother comes out of it, she's not going to point the finger at you. Still, it must've pissed you off when Cora came back and found her before it was finished.'

'I don't want to talk to you.' The tears spilled out now. 'You're so mean.'

'Oh, come on. I don't scare you. You know I've got zip. I'll give you better.' Eve shrugged, chanced another sip. 'My commander and the house shrink think I'm full of it. Maybe tipping over the edge myself because I tried to sell them on you. I value my career, kid. I'm not going to toss it away on this. I'm done. The investigation will remain open for a while, then we'll move it to inactive. Then to cold.'

She leaned forward. 'I'm not having the brass and the

456

shrinks looking over my shoulder because of you, screwing up my very excellent chances for promotion over you. I'm riding a wave right now. Icove, the black-market baby bust. Big, juicy cases I closed. I can afford to let this one slide.'

Rayleen tilted her head. 'You can lie in an interview with a suspect.'

'Yeah. But I can't even hold an interview with a minor suspect without parental permission. So, officially, I'm not even here.'

Rayleen went back to drawing. 'Why are you here? I can go to my daddy right now, and you'll be in trouble.'

'Shit. I just came in to see how you were doing, no reason for him to think otherwise. If you make a stink about it, he's going to wonder why I'd hassle you. Yeah.' Eve smiled, set the hideous coffee aside. 'Why don't you do that, Ray? He might start thinking how your mother wouldn't have done herself with you alone with her in the apartment. Go ahead and get him. Last I saw him he was sitting beside your mother's bed.'

'He shouldn't have left me alone. He should be with me. When she dies—'

'If. It's still *if*.' Playfully, Eve wagged a finger. 'Don't count your chickens, kid. I could hang the two murders on her, and maybe make it stick. But I'm not quite as practical as you are. I like to close cases, but doing that would stick in my craw. So . . . it goes cold.'

'You're just giving up?'

'It's what we call "knowing when to fold." A couple

of teachers aren't going to get much more screen play anyway.' Casually, Eve crossed her ankles. 'I can figure out how you did your mother. Can't prove it, but I can get how you played it. You made the tea, you put in the pills. Did she know?'

Rayleen shrugged. 'My mother tried to kill herself, and it's terrible. I could be scarred for life. Daddy and I are going to need to go on a long trip, just the two of us, so I can adjust.'

'Then why'd she call you home first? Why did your mother call you back instead of just taking the pills while she was alone?'

'I guess she wanted to say good-bye.' Rayleen lifted her gaze, fluttered her lashes. And was smiling just a little as she worked up a tear. 'She loved me more than anything.'

Already using past tense, Eve noted. Allika was gone in Rayleen's mind. 'That could work,' Eve agreed. 'Come on, Ray, it must be infuriating for a smart girl like you not to be able to share what you can do with anyone else. I know about taking a life from both sides of it. You've got me cold, tied my hands. You win; I lose. But goddamn it, I'm curious.'

'You use very bad language. In my house, we don't approve of bad language.'

'Screw that,' Eve said, and made Rayleen giggle. 'Why'd you do Foster? I can, again, work out the how. You got the ricin from somewhere. Can't track that, either, but you got it, dumped it in his thermos.'

'It's called a go-cup,' Rayleen said primly.

'Right. You walked in when he had the outside class upstairs, doctored the drink. Then you got your friend to go down to class a few minutes early, so you could find him. Slick.'

'If you were right, you still wouldn't be *all* right. You don't know everything.'

'No, you got me. Why would you kill him? Did he try to hurt you? Did he try some sort of abuse. Touch you?'

'Please. That's disgusting.'

'I'm not going to buy it was just a whim. You went to too much trouble, planned it out too well.'

Rayleen's lips twitched. 'If you were really smart, you'd know everything.'

'Got me there.'

'Maybe, and this is just like pretending I'm talking to you about it. Maybe, he was stupid and mean and made a really dumb mistake and wouldn't listen even when I gave him a chance to fix it.'

'What kind of mistake? Since we're pretending.'

'He gave me an A minus on my oral report. A *minus*. I always get an A or an A plus. He had no business giving me a minus, just because he thought my presentation needed more work. I practiced and practiced. I was the *best* in the whole class, and getting less than a solid A means I could drop to second instead of first.'

'You poisoned him because he gave you an A minus on a presentation?' Eve repeated.

'I *told* him I needed him to change it to an A, at least. That I didn't want to drop to second in the class, and how hard I'd worked. Do you know what he said?'

'I'm riveted.'

'He said the grade wasn't as important as the *learning* and the experience. Can you believe anything that base? That stupid.'

'Boggling.'

'*And* he gave Melodie an A, and now we're almost *tied* for first in the class. I fixed her, too.'

It was all in the diary, Eve thought, all these details. But it was fascinating, and horrible, to hear them out of the girl's mouth. 'By making sure she saw what happened to Mr Foster?'

'She has nightmares.' Rayleen laughed. 'And her attendance record's blown! She's such a big baby.'

'What about Williams?'

Now Rayleen rolled her eyes. 'If you're not totally stupid, you know why.'

'So I'd think he killed Mr Foster? But—'

'That's so lame-o.'

Rayleen got up to go to the little pay AutoChef, digging credits from the pocket of her pink jeans. She plugged them in and ordered herself a lemon fizzy.

'Why's it lame-o?'

Rayleen got a straw from the counter, and her lips curved around it as she sucked up the drink. 'You were supposed to think Principal Mosebly killed them both. Because of having sex. That's disgusting, too, and she should pay fo~~Anyway, she's too strict, and I was getting tired of it.'

'I looked at her,' Eve agreed, and spoke conversationally. 'I thought, initially, Williams did Foster to cover the fact that he was a pervert, then Mosebly killed Williams because he tried to blackmail her. But the timing kept hanging me up, and every time I ran it through, it pulled out to the same killer for both. I couldn't pin Foster on Mosebly. Didn't fit.'

'You could if you wanted. He had the dumb cup in his ugly old briefcase in the class all the time, so she could've. Now, I guess you won't ever arrest anyone.'

'It's looking that way.' Eve picked up the dreadful coffee again. Just a couple of girls, she thought, having a drink and talking shop. 'Where'd you get the drug you used on Williams? It was damn good thinking to get him in the pool. We nearly missed the drug since you used such a small amount. Timing worked against you that time.'

'Stupid Mr Williams. The stuff is supposed to be absorbed and be pretty much undetectable after a couple hours. I got it from the old, ugly people's home where I have to go volunteer and pretend not to want to puke. I sing for them, and dance and read and listen to their *booor*-ing stories. And I can go anywhere I want because everyone knows me. They keep it locked up, but it's easy to distract the nurse or the orderly for a few minutes.'

She studied Eve's weapon. 'Did you ever kill anyone with that?'

'Yes.'

'How did it feel?'

'Powerful.'

'Uh-huh. But it doesn't last very long. It's like eating ice cream, and then the bowl's empty.' Rayleen set the fizzy aside, did a series of pirouettes. 'You can tell everybody in the whole galaxy what I said to you, and not one single person will believe you.'

'That's pretty much it. Who'd believe me if I said you'd killed two people, and tried – maybe succeeded – in killing a third. And her own mother. At ten years old.'

Rayleen executed a graceful plié. 'That's not all.' She sang it.

'What else?'

'Maybe I'll tell, maybe I won't. People would lock you up in a loony box if you said I did it.'

'You don't want to tell, fine. It's getting late anyway, and it's my day off.' Eve got to her feet. 'I've spent enough of my time on all this.'

On tiptoe, arms curved overhead, Rayleen danced a circle around Eve. 'You'll never, never, never guess.'

'I'm too old for games, kid. And as things stand, the sooner I forget about you, the better it is for me.'

With a little thump, Rayleen dropped down to the flats of her feet. 'You don't just walk away from me! I'm not finished. I'm the one who beat you. I won! You're being a poor sport.'

'Sue me.' Eve reached for the door.

'I killed the first time when I was only seven.'

Eve stopped, turned, leaned back on the door. 'Bullshit.'

'If you curse at me, I won't tell you how I killed my baby brother.'

'He fell down the steps. I read the investigator reports, the notes. All the files.'

'They were stupid, too.'

'You expect me to believe you pulled that off, and nobody knows?'

'I can do anything I want. I got him up early, early. I had to put my hand over his mouth when he giggled. But he listened to me, he always listened to me. He loved me.'

'I bet he did,' Eve said, and almost lost her ability to sound mildly interested.

'And he was quiet, just like I told him to be. I said we were going to go down and see the toys, and maybe even Santa. He believed in Santa. He was a *joke*. It was their fault anyway.'

'Whose?'

'My parents, for God's sake. They should never have had him in the first place. He was always in the way, and they were always spending time with him when they should have spent it with me. I was the first.'

'You pushed him down the steps?'

'It was easy.' She executed a small leap, then picked up her drink again. 'Just one shove and he went tumble, tumble, tumble. Snap! And that was that.' On a giggle, she drank – and Eve's stomach churned.

'Things were the way they were supposed to be. I got *all* the toys that Christmas. All I had to do was cry when Daddy started to put the ones for Trev away. I got them all, and now I always get them all.'

She did another pirouette, followed it with a grand plié, then a long deep bow. 'I bet you've never been beaten by a kid before. I'm better than any of the rest. Than anyone. Say it. Say that Rayleen is better and smarter than anyone you've ever met.'

'Hold that thought,' Eve suggested at the knock on the door. She opened it to Peabody, who handed Eve Rayleen's diary. 'Well, well, what have we here?'

'Where did you get that! That's *mine!*' The smirking child was gone, and it was an enraged killer who charged at Eve. 'Give that to me. Now!'

Eve took the vicious shove, even the clawing hands as she held the diary out of reach. 'Well, now, that's what we call assaulting an officer. Rayleen Straffo, you're under arrest for—'

'You shut up. You'd better shut up right now, or you're going to be sorry. That's my diary and I want it back! My father's going to make you pay.'

Eve tossed the diary to Peabody, then gripped Rayleen's arms, spun her around. She clamped on restraints while Rayleen screamed and cried and kicked. 'You're the one who's going to pay, for all of it. You were right, Ray. I can lie during interviews. I wasn't wired, but the room was.'

'You didn't read me my rights.'

'True. But I don't need anything you told me in there.

464

I've already got it. From the diary we pulled out of the recycler yesterday, from the clerk who sold you the engraved go-cup you used to replace Craig Foster's, from your mother, who told us – before you tried to kill her – that she knew you'd been up earlier on Christmas.'

'No one's going to believe you.' Rayleen's face was wildly red with rage, and not a hint of fear. 'My daddy will fix it all.'

'Wrong again.' Eve took a firm hold of Rayleen's arm while Peabody took the other.

A few feet away, Straffo stood staring at his daughter like a man still gripped in a nightmare. 'Rayleen.'

'Daddy! Daddy! They're hurting me! Stop them.'

He took two lurching steps toward her. 'He was just a baby. He was just a little boy. He loved you so much. How could you do that, Rayleen, to people who loved you so much?'

'It's lies, Daddy. She's lying to you. I'm your best girl. I'm . . . Mommy did it! I saw her do it, Daddy. She pushed Trev, and then she killed Mr Foster and Mr Williams. I didn't want to tell on her, Daddy. I didn't want them to take her away from us. I—'

'Stop. Oh, God.' He covered his face with his hands. 'Oh, God.'

'Take her, Peabody. Take her, Mira, and the CP agent to Central. I'll follow as soon as I can.'

'You'll pay,' Rayleen said to Eve under her breath as Peabody signaled a uniform to help her. 'You'll pay, just like the others. I'll enjoy you the most.'

'Spoiled brats don't scare me. Read her her rights, Peabody, and book her, three counts murder one, one attempted murder. We'll add on Adele Versy when we have that locked in.'

'Daddy! Don't let them take me away from you. Daddy!'

Eve turned away and walked toward Straffo without looking back. 'Let's go sit down, Oliver.'

'I have nothing left. I have nothing. That's my child. She . . . I made her.'

'You didn't. Sometimes the unspeakable can come from the decent. And sometimes, it's possible to make yourself decent out of the unspeakable. I know about this.'

Eve put her hand on his arm, then stood where she was as she saw Louise coming toward them.

'Mr Straffo.'

He looked at Louise. 'She's dead. Allika.'

'No, she's conscious. She isn't lucid, not yet, and I can't make you any promises. But she needs you with her now. She's confused and disoriented, and she needs you. Let me take you to her now.'

'Allika.' He turned desperate, streaming eyes to Eve. 'Rayleen.'

'How much do you love your wife, Oliver? How much do you love your son?'

Weeping, nodding, he let Louise lead him away.

EPILOGUE

After the long, miserable process, Eve walked back to her office.

And there was Roarke, sitting at her desk, working on her comp.

'Police property, pal.'

'Mmm-hmm. Just passing the time with a little work, which is now on its way to my home unit.' He swiveled around. 'You've had a rough one, Lieutenant.'

'I've had rougher, that's what I keep telling myself. You should've gone home.'

'And I told myself you might need me.' He rose, wrapped his arms around her. 'Do you?'

'Oh, yeah.' She let out a long sigh. 'I thought, hoped I'd feel better after this part was done. When I got the answers, tied it up, got her booked, and started the process, I'd feel better. Satisfied. I can't figure out, not exactly, how I do feel.'

'Sorry for Oliver and Allika Straffo, sick to think of some poor, innocent little boy, some old woman, or a good man, a good teacher who died because of a selfish child's ego. And sorry for the wife who will grieve for him.'

'I got in touch with her, Foster's wife, told her we'd closed the case and I was coming by to explain it to her. Jesus.' She shut her eyes. 'You should go home.'

'No, what I'll do is go with you.'

'Yeah.' Now she sighed. 'That would help. She used tears on the CP agent. They're working. They're not working on Mira. The arraignment's set for tomorrow. Meanwhile, due to the heinous nature of the crimes, and with no parental dissent, she's being held in adult lockup – separated from the general population. You heard it, didn't you? All of it.'

'I did, yes. And in my life I don't believe I've heard anything quite so chilling.'

Roarke pressed his lips to Eve's hair because he thought they both needed it. 'No one spoke in the control area. There was none of the asides or bad jokes you often hear during the e-part of any op. No one said a bloody thing while you worked her, while she bragged to you about what she'd done. Straffo sat like a ghost through it, like a man who'd already had the guts and heart ripped out of him.'

'She's got a PD now. Her father may decide he's obliged to secure her other counsel. It won't matter. I can't use her confession, but I have everything else. And you know what? I'll get it out of her again, on record.'

'How?'

'The ego. Think of it: Ray, you're the best. Not only the best, but you're unique. You're going to be famous, the only one of your kind.'

'And you say I'm scary.' He kissed her brow. 'It's you who are one of a kind. And you're all mine.'

'I'm not going to let myself stay sick about this one. I'm not going to keep asking myself how this could all be. There are some questions that don't have answers. You've got to let them be.'

'Allika Straffo's been moved up to guarded condition. I spoke with Louise.'

'Well, that's something anyway, and I'll interview her as soon as she's able to talk to me. Once I've done what I have to do today, let's just go home. Let's open the champagne. In fact, let's open one bottle for each of us, get a little drunk – maybe very – and do whatever comes next.'

'An excellent plan.' He retrieved her coat, brought it to her. 'I've a number of ideas on whatever comes next.'

'Yeah, you're always full of ideas.' She took his hand. 'And you're all mine.'

There would be sanity again, Eve thought, and a little peace, and the unity she'd come to depend on. It would all be there, with him, with whatever happened next.

Read an extract from

DELUSION
IN DEATH

The J.D. Robb thriller, out now

After a killer day at the office, nothing smoothed those raw edges like Happy Hour. On The Rocks, on Manhattan's Lower West Side, catered to white collar working stiffs who wanted half-price drinks and some cheesy rice balls while they bitched about their bosses or hit on a co-worker.

Or the execs who wanted a couple of quick belts close to the office before their commute to the 'burbs.

From four-thirty to six, the long bar, the hightops and lowtops bulged with lower-rung execs, admins, assistants and secretaries who flooded out of the cubes, pools and tiny offices. Some washed up like shipwreck survivors. Others waded ashore ready to bask in the buzz. A few wanted nothing more than to huddle alone on their small square of claimed territory and drink the day away.

By five, the bar hummed like a hive while bartenders and wait staff rushed and scurried to serve those whose work day was behind them. The second of those half-price drinks tended to improve moods so the laughter, amiable chatter and pre-mating rituals punctuated the hum.

Files, accounts, slights, unanswered messages were forgotten in the warm gold light, the clink of glasses and complimentary beer nuts.

Now and again the door opened to welcome another survivor of New York's vicious business day. Cool fall air whisked in along with a blast of street noise. Then it was warm again, gold again, a humming hive again.

Midway through that happiest of hours (ninety minutes in bar time), some headed back out. Responsibilities, families, a hot date pulled them out the door to subways, airtrams, maxibuses, cabs. Those who remained settled back for one more, a little more time with friends and co-workers, a little more of that warm gold light before the bright or the dark.

Macie Snyder crowded at a plate-sized hightop with her boyfriend of three months and twelve days Travis, her best work pal CiCi, and Travis's friend Bren. Macie had wheedled and finagled for weeks to set CiCi up with Bren with the long view to double dates and shared boy talk. They made a happy, chattering group, with Macie perhaps the happiest of all.

CiCi and Bren had definitely *connected* – she could see it in the body language, the eye contact – and since CiCi texted her a couple times under the table, she had it verified.

By the time they ordered the second round, plans began to evolve to extend the evening with dinner.

After a quick signal to CiCi, Macie grabbed her purse. 'We'll be right back.'

She wound her way through tables, muttered when someone at the bar stood up and shoulder bumped her.

'Make a hole,' she called out cheerfully, and took CiCi
hand as they scurried down the narrow steps and queued
up for the thankfully short line in the rest room.

'Told ya!'

'I know, I know. You said he was adorable, and you
showed me his picture, but he's *so* much cuter in person.
And so funny! Blind dates are usually so lame, but this is
just mag.'

'Here's what we'll do. We'll talk them into going to
Nino's. That way, after dinner, we'll go one way, and you'll
have to go the other to get home. It'll give Bren a chance
to walk you home – and you can ask him up.'

'I don't know.' Always second-guessing with dates – which
was why she didn't have a boyfriend of three months and
twelve days – CiCi chewed at her bottom lip. 'I don't want
to rush it.'

'You don't have to sleep with him.' Macie rolled her
round blue eyes. 'Just offer him coffee, or, you know, a
nightcap. Maybe fool around a little.'

She dashed into the next open stall. She *really* had to
pee. 'Then text me after he leaves and tell me *everything*.
Full deets.'

Making a bee-line for the adjoining stall, CiCi peed in
solidarity. 'Maybe. Let's see how dinner goes. Maybe he
won't want to walk me home.'

'He will. He's a total sweetie. I wouldn't hook you up
with a jerkhead, CiCi.' She walked to the sink, sniffed at
the peachy-scented foam soap, then beamed a grin at her

end when CiCi joined her. 'If it works out, it'll be so much fun. We can double-date.'

'I really like him. I get a little nervous when I really like a guy.'

'He really likes you.'

'Are you sure?'

'Abso-poso,' Macie assured her, brushing her short curve of sunny blond hair while CiCi added some shine to her lip dye. Jesus, she thought, suddenly annoyed. Did she have to stroke and soothe all damn night?

'You're pretty and smart and fun.' I don't hang with jerkheads, Macie thought. 'Why wouldn't he like you? God, CiCi, loosen up and stop whining. Stop playing the nervous freaking virgin.'

'I'm not—'

'You want to get laid or not?' Macie snapped and had CiCi gaping. 'I went to a lot of trouble to set this up, now you're going to blow it.'

'I just—'

'Shit.' Macie rubbed at her temple. 'Now I'm getting a headache.'

A bad one, CiCi assumed. Macie never said mean things. And, well, maybe she was playing the nervous virgin. A little. 'Bren's got the nicest smile.' CiCi's eyes, a luminous green against her caramel skin, met Macie's in the narrow mirror. 'If he walks me home, I'll ask him up.'

'Now you're talking.'

They walked back. It seemed louder than it had, Macie

thought. All the voices, the clattering dishes, the chairs ground against her headache.

She told herself, with some bitterness, to ease off next drink.

Someone blocked her path, just for a moment, as they passed the bar. Annoyed, she rounded, shoved at him, but he was already murmuring an apology and moving toward the door.

'Asshole,' she muttered, and at least had the chance to snarl as he glanced back, smiled at her before he stepped outside.

'What's wrong?'

'Nothing – just a jerkhead.'

'Are you okay? I probably have a blocker if your head really hurts. I've got a little headache, too.'

'Always about you,' Macie muttered, then tried to take a calming breath. Good friends, she reminded herself. Good times.

As she sat again, Travis took her hand the way he did, gave her a wink.

'We want to go to Nino's,' she announced.

'We were just talking about going to Tortilla Flats. We'd need a reservation at Nino's,' Travis reminded her.

'We don't want Mexican crap. We want to go somewhere nice. Jesus, we'll split the bill if the tab's a BFD.'

Travis's eyebrows drew together, digging a thin line between them, the way they did when she said something stupid. She *hated* when he did that.

o's is twelve blocks away. The Mexican place is
.cally around the corner.'

.o angry her hands began to shake, she shoved her face
oward his. 'Are you in a fucking hurry? Why can't we do
something *I* want for a change?'

'We're doing something you wanted right now.'

Their voices rose to shouts, clanging with the sharp voices
all around them. As her head began to throb, CiCi glanced
toward Bren.

He sat, teeth bared in a snarl, staring into his glass,
muttering, muttering.

He wasn't adorable. He was horrible, just like Travis. Ugly,
ugly. He only wanted to fuck her. He'd rape her if she said
no. He'd beat her, rape her, first chance. Macie knew. She
knew and she'd laugh about it.

'Screw both of you,' CiCi said under her breath. 'Screw
all of you.'

'Stop looking at me like that,' Macie shouted. 'You
freak.'

Travis slammed his fist on the table. 'Shut your fucking
mouth.'

'I said stop!' Grabbing a fork from the table, Macie peeled
off a scream. And stabbed the prongs through Travis's
eye.

He howled, the sound tearing through CiCi's brain as
he leaped up, fell on her friend.

And the bloodbath began.

★　　★　　★

Lieutenant Eve Dallas stood in the carnage. Always something new, she thought. Always something just a little more terrible than even a cop could imagine.

Even for a veteran murder cop swimming in the bubbling stew of New York in the last quarter of the year 2060, there was always something worse.

Bodies floated on a sea of blood, booze and vomit. Some draped like rag dolls over the long bar or curled like grisly cats under broken tables. Jagged hunks of glass littered the floor, sparkled like deadly diamonds on what was left of tables and chairs – or jabbed, thick with gore, out of bodies.

The stench of blood, piss, vomit, emptied bowels clogged the air and made her think of old photos she'd seen of battlefields where no side could claim clear victory.

Gouged eyes, torn faces, slit throats, heads bashed in so violently she saw pieces of skull and gray matter only added to the impression of war waged and lost. A few victims were naked, or nearly, the exposed flesh painted with blood like ancient warriors.

She stood, waiting for the first wave of shock to pass. She'd forgotten she could be shocked. She turned, tall and lean, brown eyes flat, to the beat cop, and first on scene.

'What do you know?'

She heard him breathing between his teeth, gave him time.

'My partner and I were on our break, in the diner across the street. As I came out, I observed a female, late twenties,

way from the door of the location. She was
⸺g. She was still screaming when I reached her.'
⸺hat time was that?'

'We logged out for the break at seventeen-forty-
ive. I don't think we were in there over five minutes,
Lieutenant.'

'Okay. Continue.'

'The female was unable to speak coherently, but she
pointed to the door. While my partner attempted to calm
the female, I opened the door.'

He paused, cleared his throat. 'I've got twenty-two years
in, Lieutenant, and I've never seen anything like this.
Bodies, everywhere. Some were still alive. Crawling,
crying, moaning. I called it in, called for medicals. There
was no way to keep the scene undisturbed, sir. People
were dying.'

'Understood.'

'We got eight or ten out – the medicals, Lieutenant.
I'm sorry, I'm not clear on the number. They were in
pretty bad shape. They worked on some of them here,
transported all survivors to the Tribeca Health Center. At
that time we secured the scene. The medicals were all over
it, Lieutenant. We found more in the bathrooms, back in
the kitchen.'

'Were you able to question any of the survivors?'

'We got some names. The ones able to speak all said
basically the same thing. People were trying to kill them.'

'What people?'

'Sir? Everybody.'

'Okay. Let's keep everybody out of here for now.' walked with him to the door.

She spotted her partner. She'd parted ways with Peabody less than an hour before. Eve stayed back at Central to catch up on paperwork. She'd been on her way to the garage, thinking of home when she'd gotten the call.

At least, for once, she remembered to text her husband, letting Roarke know she'd be later than expected.

Again.

She moved forward to block the door and intercept her partner.

She knew Peabody was sturdy, solid – despite the pink cowgirl boots, rainbow-tinted sunshades and short, flippy ponytail. But what was beyond the door had shaken her, and a beat cop with over twenty on his hard, black shoes.

'Almost made it,' Peabody said. 'I'd stopped by the market on the way home. Thought I'd surprise McNab with a home-cooked.' She shook a small market bag. 'Good thing I hadn't started. What did we catch?'

'It's bad.'

Peabody easy expression slid away, leaving her face cold. 'How bad?'

'Pray to God you never see worse. Multiple bodies. Hacked, sliced, bashed, you name it. Seal up.' Eve tossed her a can of Seal-it from the field kit she carried. 'Put down that bag and grab your guts. If you need to puke, side. There's already plenty of puke in there, and I want yours mixed in. The crime scene's fucked. No around it. MTs and the responding officers had to get survivors, treat some of them right on scene.'

Have you read them all?

Eve and Roarke are back in September 2014 with
FESTIVE IN DEATH